With Blinders On

a Novel by
Richard J. Marco

PublishAmerica
Baltimore

Library of Congress - Copyright Office No. Txu-722-127

First printing

ISBN: 1-4137-0933-8
PUBLISHED BY PUBLISHAMERICA, LLLP
www.publishamerica.com
Baltimore

Printed in the United States of America

With Blinders On is a work of fiction.
Any similarity of characters to persons living or dead is a coincidence

For Shirley who has loved,
tolerated and understood me for many years.

One

Patrick Joseph gazed from the window of his office, looking at the town square and seeing the gray and red squirrels scampering without an apparent purpose up and down the hundred-year-old trees in the early morning sun. *Another glorious Ohio day*, he mused. A middle-aged lawyer born, raised, and educated in Cleveland before moving to Milltown where he now sat in his office admiring the rush-hour animal traffic through his front window. Milltown is a small rural community some thirty-five miles south of the City bordering Lake Erie. Even though he enjoyed his childhood in the inner city he wanted to raise his family in what he believed was a safer environ. Why these memories were playing around the edges of Joseph's mind on this August Monday morning, he had no idea, except they seemed to recur more frequently with advancing age.

Joseph slid down comfortably in the high-backed desk chair in front of the ancient library table he purchased for five dollars when the main branch of the Cleveland Public Library upgraded. The table was carefully located so he could see out the window and watch people walking by, or, of more importance, squirrels scampering in the park across the street. An ornate, eight-sided Gazebo occupied the center of the square where Friday night band concerts played during the summer. Years ago sheep grazed where the Gazebo now stands while an occasional miscreant was hanged from a gibbet constructed for the occasion. Joseph's clients were interviewed across that oak table for more than thirty years.

Joseph, feet propped on a wastebasket beneath the table since he could no longer reach the tabletop scarred from long service, laced his pudgy fingers comfortably across his expanding girth as he played tag with his memories and surveyed his domain. Each piece of furniture, mostly used and purchased as he could afford it, was carefully picked for comfort and indelibly marked by use, adding to earlier distressed marks. A leather couch sat beneath the window through which Joseph enjoyed watching the world. Matching Shaker chairs rested side by side in front of his table and an ancient iron safe occupied one corner of the room. Another corner held a set of shelves he had especially

7

made to house his collection of iron, porcelain, glass and ceramic pigs. Joseph gazed lovingly at his pigs. *Never saw a pig without a smile on its face,* he thought. Their content brought him pleasure. An unused fireplace faced Joseph's table, the mantle of which provides a handy resting place for photographs of grandchildren.

Joseph habitually arrived at the office before anyone else leaving him free to relax and prepare himself for the day. It seemed to take longer these days. Joseph pushed his round belly against the table on this hot, dry Monday morning, like so many mid-August days in Ohio, preparing to read the ***Milltown Reporter***, the local newspaper formerly published in the building now occupied by Joseph. As he spread the paper before him, his eyes scanned the front-page headline:

LOCAL MAN SHOT AT MT. CITY STREET FAIR

The headline caused Joseph's mind to drift back more than twenty years, to a time when he lived and worked in Cleveland. He had an active practice there that kept him from the things he believed important, his wife, his children, a plot of ground for vegetables and flowers. It was with little regret they moved from Cleveland to Milltown. They almost chose Mt. City, but since Milltown was the county seat, it would be easier to begin a new practice there.

Shortly after the move, and at his wife's urging, Joseph bought the building on the town square he occupied still encumbered by a mortgage that would ensure Joseph's continuing employment. It was an old redbrick and sandstone Victorian structure fronted by a large plate glass window and an ornate inset doorway five steps up from the sidewalk, built long before the government decided all public buildings required wheel chair access. The legend, ***PATRICK JOSEPH, ATTORNEY AT LAW***, curved gracefully across the window in fine gold leaf, leaving plenty of glass for Joseph's observations.

Still early morning, it was not surprising no one else had yet arrived at the office. Joseph's jacket hung from a hook on the hall tree placed conveniently next to the roll top desk at which he worked, his tie not yet tightened.

The elderly lawyer acknowledged, only to himself, that he sometimes missed his more colorful Cleveland practice, but was rarely sorry about the move as he perused the article in the paper that caught his interest.

By the time Joseph reached this point in his more frequently recurring introspection, he heard the back door of the office open. He assumed it was

8

his secretary, Della Raven. Della was truly her name. Although he often thought about it, he never knew whether or not she was named for the more famous fictitious legal secretary of the same name.

"Good morning, Della!" he barked without moving from his seat. "How come the coffee isn't on?"

His question elicited the same sort of "Humph!" received from his wife, Mary, when he asked a similarly dumb question at home. Della stuck her head in his office saying, "I'll put it on now ... " followed by, "Anything exciting, Pat?" gesturing toward the newspaper spread on his table. She only called him Pat when no one else was around, otherwise it was Mr. Joseph. She was as old-fashioned as he.

Joseph sighed as he lowered his feet to the floor, adjusted his tie and reached for his daybook.

"Nothing for us, but it looks like there was some commotion at the Mt. City Street Fair. Mary and I were going to go, but never got around to it. After Mass Saturday evening we went to dinner. By then, it was too late to go. Kind of glad we didn't make it."

Della walked into Pat's office and placed a cup of black coffee on the glass top of the table and sat across from him with a cup of her own. Looking through her book and several files, she told Joseph what was urgent for the day and what was not, finally asking, "Why are you glad you didn't make it?"

Joseph gestured toward the paper, but before he had a chance to respond, the phone rang. Reaching across the table, Della picked up Joseph's phone, pushed the correct button and said, "Good morning. Patrick Joseph's Law Office. Can I help you?"

Joseph looked at her expectantly as she shrugged an "I don't know," to the implied question.

"Mr. Joseph is in. May I tell him who is calling and what he can do for you?"

Waiting for Della to finish, Joseph continued reading the front-page article following the headline:

As the Mt. City Street Fair was ending this past Saturday with its usual brilliant fireworks display, fireworks of another kind were exploding in the small apartment of Robert Tucci, age 33, located over the garage at the rear of the family home on Garden Street. The noise of the Street Fair could be heard in the apartment over the sounds of a family argument. Tucci, his sister Emma Black, his common-law

9

wife Bliss Tucci, sister-in-law Arliss Conrad, mother-in-law Gabriella Bellow and two teen-age boys were in the apartment. The heated argument got out of hand, a gun was brandished and Tucci, shot once in the right temple, died immediately. The *Reporter* has learned through reliable sources that Bellow admitted ownership of the weapon that she brought to the apartment and confessed to the shooting. Tucci, a life long resident of Mt. City, lived in an apartment over the garage at the family property where his sister, her husband and children also reside...

The article continued with a personal history of the victim. But, since Joseph didn't recognize any of the names in the article as clients, he lost interest. Vague thoughts of an earlier attraction to criminal defense flitted through his mind. He washed them away by turning the page to see if the obituaries contained the names of any old friends or potential new business.

Two

Ohio has no significant mountain ranges, but does have some beautiful rolling terrain and fertile fields, and a hamlet inappropriately named Mt. City. It was founded long before the Civil War on one of the Freedom Railway routes. Its deceptive name is of importance to no one except its inhabitants most of whom don't remember, or probably never knew, why it came to be called Mt. City. The village fits on a pleasant spot on the banks of one of Rocky River's branches about thirty miles south-west of Cleveland.

Robert Tucci came to Mt. City as a child of nine. His father, a hardworking son of an immigrant, moved there as soon as he saved enough money for a down payment on a small house with a little land to provide for the interests dictated by his heritage. Odd how the same impetus precipitating Tucci's move led to Joseph's years later, as though somehow their lives one day might intertwine. Mr. Tucci's daily drive to work in Cleveland didn't matter. Backcountry roads weren't congested, and, besides, it was not too high a price to pay for the anticipated rewards.

Robert and his younger sister, four year old Emma, like most children had no trouble acclimating to the new life. But, it was different for Mrs. Tucci. Young and relatively good looking, she was particularly robust in her zest for life. She missed the family and friends left behind and, more particularly, the shops and the liquid, rich ethnic language that pervaded her former neighborhood in Little Italy. She loved walking on Murray Hill or Mayfield Road to shop and visit friends. Mrs. Tucci hadn't been consulted about the change.

The move accomplished, Mrs. Tucci was given the responsibility of setting up a new homestead. Afterwards she was left with time on her hands – time she could no longer fill as she had in the old neighborhood. Cleaning and cooking for a family of four, especially with the head of the household gone twelve to fourteen hours a day and, when home, sleeping or tending his garden, left a great deal of time for other activities. Papa rarely expressed appreciation for the things Mrs. Tucci did for the family. It was her job.

The house in Mt. City was on Garden Street two doors down and across a back yard from *The Bar*, a neighborhood-gathering place owned by a man known as "Hey' Smith. No one was exactly sure how he came to be called Hey, whether it was the diminutive of a name such as Heywood, or from customers frequent request, "Hey, how about another?"

With no place else to go and no new friends, Mrs. Tucci began spending time there. Hey Smith found her charming, felt sorry for her and enjoyed listening to her lightly accented English. She was one of the few people in the world he treated gently – something never available at home. Her loneliness increased as friends and family from the old life were unwilling to travel so far to visit. She had no car to visit them and couldn't drive anyway. Even if she could, Papa wouldn't have permitted it.

More and more she became a fixture at Hey's where she became friendly with the patrons, particularly those just traveling through. Her friendliness toward strangers was the talk of *The Bar*, especially when she began inviting the new acquaintances to her home. At first, she was afraid her husband might find out, but he showed little curiosity. He was always too busy or too tired to talk to her. She became bolder.

The visits customarily began in the kitchen with coffee or a glass of wine and friendly conversation. She never intended more, but somehow she and her new friends invariably found themselves in the bedroom she shared with her half-hearted husband. The time spent in the kitchen diminished. The bedroom became the focus of the visits.

There are few secrets in a town the size of Mt. City. But Mrs. Tucci had no friends close enough to counsel her, or care; and Mr. Tucci no friends close enough to inform him. The good neighbors could, and did, draw graphic word pictures of the dalliances among themselves. Hey wanted to warn Mrs. Tucci but didn't know how.

Robert Tucci discovered his mother's diversion in a distressing way. He had just turned ten – on one of those rare perfect summer days. The only chore he had was to keep an eye on his younger sister, Emma. The air was warm, the sky cloudless, the sun made jewels of the dust motes in the air. On this particular day the children decided to visit their special place down by the river – a bend where the moving water created a large flat area that accumulated and polished beautiful pebbles of all colors and sizes. It was to them a jewelry store. Not yet noon, they'd been playing for several hours, laughing and doing the silly, serious things kids do, when Robby slipped on a wet rock and cut his hand. It wasn't much of a cut and didn't really hurt, but Robert, had been warned of the dangers of infection. Frightened by the knowledge, he believed he must immediately clean, disinfect and bandage his finger.

It was just a short distance to the house, so he cautioned his sister to behave and left her by the river for the few minutes it would take. The house was quiet, the shades drawn against the summer heat. He entered quietly, through the kitchen, thinking, *Maybe Mamma's taking a nap.* He shrugged small shoulders. *It doesn't matter, I know where the peroxide and band-aids are.*

Tiptoeing past his parents' bedroom, he noticed the usually open door closed. He must be quiet and not disturb Mamma. She sometimes got angry if he woke her from a nap. As he crept past her door, he became aware of an unfamiliar rhythmic sound and little moaning cries. *Maybe Mamma's sick! Maybe she's having a bad dream! Maybe she needs help!*

Pausing to assess the risk, he opened the door quietly and peered in. Mamma was in bed, but she wasn't asleep – and she wasn't alone. He didn't know the man.

Robby first thought as he watched was, *he's hurting her. But she doesn't look scared.*

The squeak of the opening door caused Mrs. Tucci to raise her head. She stared at Robby, eyes wide and shocked. He had never seen them that big. Robby didn't know what to do. Gasping for breath, he held up his bleeding finger and, in a quavering voice, said, "I ... Uh ... I hurt my finger."

Both faced Robby. They hissed in unison, "Get out!" sounding like the two-headed animal they resembled. The dusty sunlight forcing its way though the shaded window made their naked flesh gleam wetly, reminding Robby of the frogs down by the river.

Robert whimpered, "Bu, but – I need a bandage ... " as he backed out the door. He needed more than a bandage.

Mrs. Tucci called after him, "I'll be right there ... hu … hu ... hon ... hone ... " her voice trailing off in a series of grunts. Her friend paid no further attention to Robby.

Robby closed the door softly. Without being aware of his actions, he stumbled to the bathroom, looked for and located the bandages, took them from the medicine cabinet and, clutching them to his skinny chest, sat slumped on the toilet seat. Hands shaking, he tried, without success, to separate one of the band-aids from its wrapper. He couldn't see through the tears he wasn't aware of shedding, or of the sobs wracking his body. He had no idea how long he sat there, shoulders shaking, fingers plucking unsuccessfully at the wrapped bandage, subconsciously aware of the murmurs, squeaks and grunts emanating from the next room. He didn't hear the silence when the body noises ceased followed by sounds of dressing, a whispered argument and slamming of the back door.

Mrs. Tucci, now covered with a house-dress, tentatively entered the bathroom, touched Robert's shoulder and whispered, "Robby, let me see your finger."

Robert recoiled from her touch, jumped up and backed away, eyes staring, wild and hurt. Saying nothing, he ran from the house turning toward the river – but couldn't go to the bend where he had left his sister – he didn't want to see his sister – he didn't want to see anyone. He knew what he didn't want. He had no idea what he did want.

After a time he slowed and finally stopped. He threw himself to the ground where he lay sobbing and hiccupping his heartbreak. Soon his tears dried, his labored breathing slowed. He looked around and, for the first time, became aware of his surroundings – at the bank of the river near a still pond. He had been here before but it didn't look the same – nothing would ever look the same. As he bent over the water to rinse his face, he was shocked that it looked as it always had. No one could tell from looking at him what his eyes had seen. How could that be? He knew the image would never fade.

It was near suppertime and Mr. Tucci would be home. Robby walked home as he had countless times before. Mr. Tucci and Emma were seated at the kitchen table – she had come home without him. Mrs. Tucci was standing by the stove. Everything looked normal. She turned as Robert entered and asked, a slight quaver in her voice, "How is your finger, Robby?" No one noticed.

Robert mumbled, "Okay," and sat in his usual place.

Later he couldn't remember supper, usually his favorite time of day. It was the only opportunity to talk to Mr. Tucci. Robby usually took full advantage of it, prattling about the day's adventures. If Papa noticed anything unusual, he didn't say so. He asked no questions.

In the days and weeks that followed, Mrs. Tucci had less and less to say and the closing of her bedroom door became more frequent. Even though Robert noticed, he said nothing. Emma was too young to notice.

In the summer of Robby's eleventh year, he awoke to a silent house. It didn't matter, he was used to fending for himself and caring for his sister. Mrs. Tucci was often about her business early in the day. He awakened his little sister and fixed their breakfast. "Come on, Emma, let's go down by the river," he suggested after they had eaten.

The house was quiet each time they returned that day so Robert prepared simple meals until Papa came home.

"Robby, where's your Mamma?" Mr. Tucci asked as he walked into the kitchen.

"I don' know. She hasn't been here all day."

Robby fixed a sandwich for his father and carried it to the table with a bottle of cheap whiskey and freshly made coffee. Mr. Tucci said, "She'll be back."

She never returned.

Mrs. Tucci's absence was the subject of talk in Mt. City for some time, but never at the Tucci home. On those occasions when her name was mentioned, Mr. Tucci would just say, "She'll be back." Shortly before Robert's twentieth birthday Mr. Tucci died as he lived – at the kitchen table, a bottle in front of him and a glass in his hand.

Robert and Emma remained close but were never friends. Though only five years older than she, he was the guardian of her morals – her protector, her instructor. He took care of her but expected obedience in return. Emma was a little afraid of him.

Eventually Robert got a job driving trucks cross-country. His absences from Mt. City became longer, but he kept close contact with his sister. Emma finished school, got a job and eventually married Jim Black, one of their childhood friends. Robert approved. Emma and Jim now occupied the bedroom that had created Robby's memories.

The house on Garden St. was big enough for Emma, her husband and the three daughters they eventually had. An old barn in the back had been made over into a three-car garage – its loft converted to a small but efficient apartment for Robby.

The arrangement was good. Tucci was home and felt like part of a family – something he hadn't felt for years. He was still away much of the time, but returned frequently to visit Emma, Jim and his nieces. He considered Mt. City his home. This gave Robert a sense of comfort. He had done his job. Emma hadn't turned out like their mother after all.

Emma wasn't particularly pleased with the arrangement, what with Robby popping in and out without warning, but couldn't say much since Robby owned a one-half interest in the property. She was still not comfortable with him.

Tucci had no wish to marry but enjoyed the company of ladies. He was unwilling to consider any kind of permanent commitment – something, he thought, women were incapable of anyway.

To Emma's surprise – and probably Tucci's as well – Robby arrived home after a lengthy absence accompanied by a young woman, Bliss Bellow. She had with her two suitcases containing "all her worldly belongings," she said and moved into the tiny garage apartment with Tucci. He seemed surprised and strangely uninvolved in it all.

Bliss was slightly older than Robert and attractive in a skinny sort of way. She exuded nervous energy, laughed a lot and liked to party. Her clothes were inexpensive and flashy and she wore rings on each finger. She wasn't the kind of woman Emma would have picked for a friend nor the kind she expected her brother to bring home. Emma found her fascinating.

Bliss didn't talk much about her past, but Emma soon learned she had grown up not far from Mt. City in the next county to the west. Emma also discovered Bliss had three children fathered by three different men, only one of whom she married. Emma envied the courage of a life style she would never dare.

Three

The house on Garden Street was well maintained by Emma and Jim Black. Robert Tucci did little to help. Robby's apartment – Emma still called Robert by his childhood nickname – over the three-car garage was just large enough to contain a living room, a miniature master bedroom, a second closet sized bedroom, and a kitchen.

Emma had tried to hold onto the good memories of her childhood from the time before her mother left, but Robby's exaggerated concerns for her behavior made it difficult for her to make or keep friends. Having a woman, even one like Bliss, close by to talk to helped. Yet her brother's overzealous policing of her morality during her teen years was a cloud on her memory. She was still a little afraid of Robby.

August meant it was time for the annual Mt. City Street Fair with its frog jumping contest, ox roast sandwiches, roasted ears of corn, sideshow barkers and fireworks. Bliss had never been to the Street Fair even though she lived close by as a child. Emma and Robbie reminisced about it on several occasions. Their excitement about the approaching Fair was contagious and Robbie's renewed interest helped allay Emma's fears. Robby seemed to have settled down – just like a regular family man.

Bliss appeared to enjoy belonging to this strange family and began to claim Robert as her husband, calling herself Bliss Tucci. Robert never referred to her as his wife, but neither did he deny the relationship. Emma knew they weren't married but liked to think it might happen. It added normalcy. Robby always said, "*If I get married, I want a woman who'll be true, and there ain't no such thing. No woman can stay with one man.*"

With Bliss seemingly a permanent part of the family, Emma made a real effort to befriend her. Although envious of Bliss' lifestyle, Emma was critical of her appearance. Robby, she believed, could have done a lot better.

Bliss' looks were deceptive. She seemed to be about the same height as Robby, but was some three inches shorter. Her posture was rigidly straight and she was the skinniest woman Emma had ever met, almost emaciated. Her hair, the least attractive feature, was mousy brown and stringy, occasionally managed by a home perm creating a shapeless mass of tightly spiraled curls. All of her features were pointed – nose, chin and even her ears. Her coloring wasn't pleasant – too pale. None of her features matched and, all together should have resulted in ugly, but didn't.

Bliss laughed a lot but had no sense of humor, understanding nothing but the crudest of jokes. Laughter never got past her high-pitched voice and pinched mouth. Intellectual endeavors were limited to pulp magazines and television soaps. She especially liked romance novels.

Her appearance was that of a hard, tough, well-used woman of the streets, yet she complained constantly about her health. *"My nerves are bad... I am coming down with something... I don't sleep so good... Damn doctors take my money but can't find what's wrong with me... I need my medicine!"*

Bliss and Emma' friendship meant little to Robert or Jim, but the four did things like a family and occasionally even shared confidences, but always a little was held in reserve.

Finally the long awaited Street Fair arrived. Although it was a new experience for Bliss, she had shared the others' anticipation. It brought back memories to Robby, some good, some not. It was everything Bliss expected; that is until the last Saturday of Fair Week.

Saturday arrived hot and dusty. The frog jumping contest and all of the other games would be held in the afternoon, the Ox Roast all day, with fireworks, the climax of the day and week, after dark. It would rival the Fourth of July Spectacle at Milltown.

An air of expectation infected everyone. Fair Week was about to end and even Bliss and Robert, sated by the week's activities, looked forward to the finale. Bliss wanted to have a little party and Robert, in uncharacteristic good humor, said "Okay."

Robert arose early to eat a large breakfast prepared by Bliss. She drank coffee and smoked. As he was leaving the house, he instructed, "Get a couple of cases of beer for this afternoon. I promised the guys those Italian Sausage sandwiches from the Fair. You won't have to fix no dinner."

"Can my kids come over too?" Bliss asked on a whim, not expecting his acquiescence.

Paying little attention to her, Robert responded, "I don't care – just don't make no big deal. Do what you want, but make sure you get the beer." With that he left.

The "kids' Bliss was talking about, was her daughter, Elaine Stone, by an early liaison and a son, Jake Bellow, by an actual marriage. Bliss' daughter, though yet unmarried, at age eighteen followed in her mother's footsteps, having a baby with a father of uncertain identity. It made Bliss a grandmother. She didn't like that much.

Jake – actually Jacob – was the product of a marriage between Bliss and a young man she met in her travels. At the time, both were heavily involved in drugs – using – selling – trading – whatever. When Jake was six weeks old, Bliss left him with her parents and took off with her husband. They got as far as Maryland before they were arrested and returned to New Castle, Pennsylvania where they were tried and convicted of armed robbery, extradited to Youngstown, Ohio, tried and convicted for trafficking in drugs and sentenced to jail terms in both states.

Jake's grandparents decided he would never return to his natural parents so they hired a lawyer, told their story to a Probate Judge and adopted Jake, changing his name to Bellow. They spent the next several years worrying needlessly about what would happen when Bliss and her husband got out of jail. Jake's father was stabbed to death in jail by an inmate-made knife trying to discourage the advances of an unwanted suitor. Bliss, when released, was too busy thinking about herself and her newfound freedom to want the burden of a child. It would interfere with her lifestyle.

* * * * *

Bliss cleaned the breakfast dishes and redded up the tiny apartment within minutes of the time Robert left for work. The morning stretched before her. She looked out the window to see if Emma was home. The back door of the front house was open and Jim's car gone. Emma's ugly pea-green Chevy station wagon with mismatched front fenders waiting for paint, was parked in its usual spot. "Why does she drive that ugly thing?" Bliss murmured, shaking her head in wonder.

Jim must be at work, Bliss thought. *If I'm gonna get the kids today, I got to call Ma. I'll go over and ask Emma to use her phone.* Bliss and Robby had no phone of their own.

Refilling her coffee cup from the always-hot pot and grabbing cigarettes, Bliss ran down the stairs, crossed the small back yard and stepped onto Emma's porch. It was already getting hot. Dressed in faded shorts and T-shirt, Bliss entered Emma's kitchen, without knocking, calling "Emma, you up?"

Bliss heard a muffled "Yeah, come on in. Want some coffee?"

Gesturing with the cup in her hand, she said, "Nah ... I brought my own. Just want to use the phone – call Ma. See if the kids can come up for the Fair

– maybe spend the night. Robby's ..." Bliss had picked up Emma's habit of calling Tucci by his childhood nickname, "having some guys over. I thought I might have a little party of my own. Do you mind?" Bliss chattered in her usual, nervous manner.

Bliss was obviously the older of the two – not only in looks, but manner. Emma was at least ten years younger – probably mid-twenties. Short and nicely rounded, she was the kind of a girl men find attractive and approachable.

"Sure, go ahead, use the phone. Isn't it a little early though? It's not even eight o'clock."

"It's okay. You know Ma. She's always up early. She lives at the wrong end of the clock." Bliss, prattling on, hadn't yet looked at Emma and was unaware of her distraught appearance. Bliss rarely noticed those around her.

Bliss lit a cigarette while dialing and, blowing smoke into the mouthpiece, said, "Hi, Ma? Bliss. Are the kids there? Can they come over today? It's the last day of the Fair. There's gonna be the frog jumpin' thing and fireworks, ya know. Can they spend the night? Robby's working today, but'll be home around lunchtime. I can get the kids by then. Do you think it'll be all right? Huh? Robby said so."

Her mother responded with a voice and style that duplicated Bliss', "I don't know. Con is staying here – visiting Jake for the weekend. He's going to spend the night. I got to ask Arliss if it's okay? You know how she is about her boy."

Con was the sixteen year son of Gabriella Bellow's youngest daughter, Arliss. Bliss didn't have much good to say to or about her sister, and Arliss couldn't stand Bliss.

Mrs. Bellow continued. "I would like to talk to your Father about this before I make up my mind, but he isn't around. I guess it's okay with me, but I should check."

Bliss's mother, Gay – short for Gabriella – was the pattern from which Bliss was drawn. They shared more than a similarity in voice and expression. Gay wasn't just an older version of Bliss. They were identical except in matters of taste. Gay was more sophisticated and not so self-centered. They didn't really care for each other. Gay constantly complained to her husband, or anyone else that would listen, "I just don't understand my first born daughter." She tried to settle their differences for the sake of the grandson she raised, but it was difficult.

"Ma," Bliss whined. "Let me pick up Jake and Elaine ... You know this is the last day of the Fair and I really want them to stay over. Robby won't be no trouble ... I promise ... He said it's okay ... "

"Are you sure? Con's planning to spend the night with Jake, and you know how your sister is."

Arliss Conrad, Bliss's younger sister, was everything Bliss was not. Although they looked enough alike to be twins, the resemblance ended there. Both bore such a strong physical likeness to each other, and their mother, it was as though Mr. Bellow's made no contribution to the genetic chain. Claude Bellow was pretty much ignored by life.

Both of the girls were anorectic, of medium height, hair mousy brown and shapeless – they probably both wore the same dress size, but would never know – their taste in clothing differed so. Both were filled with nervous energy that took completely different directions – Bliss needing fun, excitement, and rebellion – Arliss conformity and belonging. Bliss cared less what others thought, and, in fact, was pleased when her actions shocked. On the other hand, approval was as essential to Arliss as air. She would no more think of doing something that might hint of scandal, than wear dirty underwear.

"I know she's a fuss, but Jake can bring Con. He can spend the night."

Arliss' son was actually named Jason, but insisted on being called "Con," a diminutive of his surname. He was the same age as Jake and they were good friends, having been raised almost as brothers. It was amazing that sisters who hated each other so much chose names for their offspring as similar as Jason and Jacob.

"If you tell Arliss to do it, she'll let him come," Bliss said in her whiny voice.

Even though raised by his grandparents, Jake became close to his mother after he learned of her existence. He never said so, but was quietly proud that she spent eighteen months in prison. He wouldn't dare express this feeling in front of his grandparents.

Giving in, as usual, Gay said, "Okay, Bliss. You can pick Jake and Con up before noon. I'll clear it with Arliss. Elaine is here with her baby. You may as well get her too."

"Great! I want to see her and my granddaughter. God, that makes me sound old. You want to come out, too?"

"Maybe Arliss and I will this afternoon, but we can't stay long. Your dad's at work and he isn't supposed to be working so hard since his heart problem. I got to be home to fix his dinner," Gay answered.

Claude Bellow had suffered a minor heart attack some months earlier, nothing serious, but it gave him a rare opportunity to be fussed over. He had inherited a small business from his father in the Flats on the banks of the Cuyahoga River near the steel mills. The business, founded by Claude's great-grandfather who worked long hours driving himself, his sons and all others around him ruthlessly to gain a foothold in the auto and steel industry originating in Cleveland, never reached the stature hoped for, but did provide a comfortable living for the Bellow family as it passed from father to son. It took Claude most of his adult life to bring it to the verge of bankruptcy. His daughters had no interest in the business. In fact, they rarely thought of it, or him, except as a backdrop to their existence.

After a few more minutes of conversation, Bliss hung up and said to Emma, "It's already starting to get hot. Let's take our coffee outside where it's cooler."

Without waiting for a response, she walked into the back yard and sat at an empty cable spool used as a picnic table thinking, *I'll sweep out the garage later so we can sit there in case it rains or gets too hot. There's plenty of time for that. I'll just sit here and enjoy my coffee and cigarette.*

Bliss looked to see if Emma was following and noticed her carrying a fist full of tissues in one hand and coffee cup in the other. For the first time she became aware Emma had been crying. Bliss asked, "Hey, what's wrong?"

The sudden concern startled Emma, causing her to sob and blurt out, "Bliss, I ... I'm sorry ... I got a problem!"

"You don't look like you got just a problem. You look like you got major trouble. What's going on?"

"I really don't want to talk about it, Bliss, but I need help. Jim is really mad at me. I don't know what's going to happen."

Bliss said, "You got that far, you may as well tell me the rest – I can keep a secret – Lord knows, I've had trouble of my own."

Emma related a little of her history to Bliss. When she and Jim Black married, she was fairly inexperienced. Robby had seen to that. Even so, Jim hadn't been her first sexual encounter. Tom Roper, her next door neighbor, and she were in high school when hormones brought them together. They fell into an exploratory routine of occasionally sharing one another's bodies during her senior year. It wasn't a memorable liaison. She had almost forgotten about it.

To her surprise, shortly after her marriage to Jim, Roper, who had been out of her mind and bed for years, began to evidence renewed interest. He had never married and still lived next door.

* * * * *

Living in Mt. City for Roper was good. His mother did everything for him and he had little, if any, responsibilities. The dalliance with Emma when they were kids, though strictly experimental, was extremely satisfactory to Tom – he wanted nothing more from a woman. For Emma, it was a learning experience. She learned sex was fun, and Tom a poor lover.

Now, after all these years, Tom was beginning again to take an interest in Emma. Her marriage made her less dangerous to his life style and, in his mind, more approachable. At first she protested, but then Tom hinted, "Jim might like to know about your past."

Knowing her husband's jealous rages, Emma became frightened. Besides Tom's attention was flattering.

"Oh shit," she rationalized. "What could it hurt? Jim would never know." It didn't take long for Tom to persuade her into bed – not every night – but when he wanted her, and was able.

Emma tried to explain to Bliss why she allowed it to start up again. "I was so afraid Tom would say something to Jim. He is jealous, you know. Besides, Jim works long hours and is always tired when he comes home – I got needs too."

Once started, she couldn't quit, or maybe didn't want to.

She didn't even like Tom and he certainly wasn't much of a lover. In fact, he was completely selfish, concerned only for himself, caring little whether he pleased his partner. A lousy lay. "Now, the slimy bastard says he's going to tell Jim if I even think of cutting him off."

Tom was growing bolder. "The smug little bastard is always walking around with a smirk on his face and dropping little hints at *The Bar*. Jim's home a lot and sees Tom looking over here. I guess he's beginning to hear things. He's starting to get suspicious."

"Two nights ago," Emma sobbed, still clutching her tissues and coffee cup, "Jim got home from work before I expected. I was walking across the yard and Jim was on the porch. He asked why I was next door?"

"I couldn't think of anything quick enough, so told him Mrs. Roper wanted a recipe. Just then," she sighed, "Tom's mother walks up the drive. Jim says to me, '*How'd you give her a recipe if she wasn't home?*'"

Trying to regain her composure, Emma had stammered, "I...I...left it with Tom..."

"To make matters worse," she said, "Tom was standing at the back door with a grin on his face. He could hear us. The little bastard was enjoying himself."

"Jim saw him and didn't wait for me to say nothing," Emma explained to Bliss. "But went in the house. I ran after him, crying. The kids were watching television. Jim told me we'd talk later.... He went into the bedroom and slammed the door."

Catching her breath, hands clasped, Emma continued. "Jim comes out with his shotgun. It was an old one he used for hunting. In the coldest voice I ever heard, he said to me, *"Emma, if I ever find out you been fucking around..."* He didn't finish–but didn't have to. I ran outside. He followed me without saying nothing, just sat on the porch swing, holding his old gun. Tom saw him and must have gotten scared, too. He ran into his house. Mrs. Roper was just standing there in her yard looking like she didn't know what was going on. I don't think she did.

"After while," Emma said. "I was standing in the back yard for what seemed a lifetime. It started to get dark. Jim went in. I could hear him talking to the kids like nothing was wrong. He told them to go to bed. I watched from outside until the lights went out. I went in and crawled in bed. Jim wasn't there. I don't know where he was, but he was in the house somewhere. I didn't sleep all night. When I got up in the morning, Jim was gone. He's been acting like nothing's happened but it's awful quiet. He don't even talk to me. I've never been so scared in my life."

Emma told all of this to Bliss as their coffee cooled. Once started, she couldn't quit talking. Bliss's reaction was anything but what Emma expected.

"God, Emma!" Bliss exclaimed gleefully. "I didn't think you had it in you. Hee ... Hee ... It looks like you had it in you a hell of a lot more'n I thought. No one will believe this – with your sweet face – I can't wait to tell Robby – He'll never believe it – His innocent sister – Hell, he thought you only screwed Jim once for each kid – in fact he acts like maybe those was virgin births!" Bliss exploded into laughter.

"Bliss! For God's sake! This is serious." Emma was shocked. "I don't know what Jim will do if he finds out! You can't tell Robby. I know he'd kill me!"

"You're something alright! But what can Jim do? Leave you? He won't do that, he knows he's got it made. Shoot you? Naw ... he ain't the type. Nothing's gonna happen. I can't wait to see the expression on your brother's face when I tell him! Un-fuckin-believable!"

Desperate Emma begged, "God, Bliss, you can't tell Robby! He'll kill me! Promise you won't say anything. Please!!! Please!!! I'm scared of him–

when it comes to this kind of stuff! I really don't know what he'd do!! – but it won't be good. He warned me when I was a kid ... he threatened ... " Emma shuddered at her memories without finishing her sentence. Bliss could see Emma was terrified.

Shaking loose the recollections and catching her breath, Emma continued hopefully, "Do you really think it'll blow over, Bliss? Do you really think Jim will forget about it?"

"Shit, you know him better'n me – but the way I read him, he won't forget it, but won't do nothing. Just watch your step and everything'll get back to normal. One bit of sisterly advice, Emma, if you can't take the strain, don't fuck around.

"Now, quit worrying about it. I won't say nothing to Robby. My kids are coming for the Fair. I got to pick 'em up at Ma's. Some of Robby's buddies are coming for sausage sandwiches and beer. I got lots to do to get everything done. If you and Jim are talking, come on over, okay? Don't worry, I'll keep your secret, but I'd love to see Robby's face if he heard," Bliss babbled.

With a relieved look, Emma responded, "Thanks, Bliss. I'll try to make up with Jim. I'll think of something. He won't want to bust up the family." She added, wistfully, "Maybe everything will work out."

Four

Bliss, bemused by what she learned, cut short her visit with Emma so she could finish her chores and go shopping. She lugged everything she bought into the garage where she'd fixed a tub for the ice and beer. Everything was ready by noon in time for the trip to her mother's.

Robby's pickup was rounding the corner as she pulled out of the drive. She called to him when he came close enough to hear, "Robby, Everything's ready. The beer's cold and I fixed your lunch. It's in the fridge, with some pickles and stuff. You want me to get it for you?"

"Nah, I'll do it. Where you goin'? I told you the guys was comin'. I want you home when they get here."

"I'm going to get the kids like I told you," she said, adding, "You said it'd be okay..." uncertainly – then more brightly, "I'll be back in plenty of time."

Tucci shrugged indifferently. "Your daughter coming with her brat? Maybe she can take her fuckin' dog back. He's a real pain in the ass – just like her."

Elaine left her dog with them when she had her baby until she could find a place to keep it. Bliss agreed without asking Tucci. It was a sore point with him and he took every opportunity to remind her of her failing and his benevolence. His patience, as always, was wearing thin.

"Aw, come on Robby," Bliss wheedled. "Elaine ain't so bad and the baby's real cute. The dog's no bother. Elaine'll get him as soon as she can. She's at Ma's now, and's planning to come over with Jake and Con," adding, "Okay, honey?"

"Alright...alright. Just get back before my buddies show up."

Tucci pulled into the drive and parked next to his sister's station wagon. Bliss drove to her mother's, visited nervously through a lunch of coffee and cigarettes, picked up her guests and was home by two o'clock.

When she arrived with her charges, Robby was seated in front of the garage with several other people, beer in hand, empties beside his chair. "My frens are here," he complained. "Where the fuck you been? I told you I wanted you back before they got here. God damn women can't do nothing right... " Without pausing in his harangue, Tucci continued, "Jerry's old lady is upstairs

– go see her."

Bliss ran up the stairs and looked into the refrigerator where she saw Robby's untouched lunch – his day's nourishment drawn only from the iced beer Bliss had muscled into the garage.

Jake followed Bliss upstairs carrying a recently purchased electric guitar. He was still making payments on it. Con carried a shopping bag with their clothes, and Elaine her baby and diaper bag.

The dog, Bobo, who was tied in the garage, greeted Elaine with slobbering doggy fervor. Elaine hurried up the stairs, handed her baby to Bliss and ran back down to untie, pet and hug Bobo, taking him back upstairs with her. Bobo wasn't allowed in the apartment. Bliss hoped Robby hadn't noticed.

The baby was laid in an improvised crib and the boys things stowed. They all left – Elaine after releashing the dog – ran through the back yards to the Street Fair to see what was happening. Bliss stayed behind to join the men for a beer. Maybe two cases wasn't going to be enough.

The afternoon dragged on. The overpowering heat and dust cut with icy brew. The young people trotted back and forth between the house and Main St. A rock band blared and teenagers and older people alike danced in the street or on the boardwalk. Con and Jake engaged in their usual friendly rivalry over young ladies dressed in the day's fashion seemingly unaware of the tantalizing exposure of fresh, pubescent flesh.

Robby and his friends enjoying themselves were reminded of their appetite and the Fair's famous Italian sausage sandwiches. Cutting through the backyards towards Main St., Robby called to his brother-in-law as they passed through his yard, "Hey, Jim, were gonna get a sandwich. Come on."

Jim stuck his head out of the kitchen door and surveyed the group. Seeing it was just the men, he nodded. "Okay, I'll be right with you."

He turned back toward the house, said something too soft for Robby to hear and joined them. When the men were gone, Emma looked out the door and signaled Bliss. Bliss asked, walking towards the front house, "Are you coming out?"

Emma looked terrible – her eyes red, hair disheveled and a suspicious red mark on her cheek, "I better not. Things have been pretty bad. Jim won't talk to me – he don't want to hear nothing. I'm afraid. I don't know what to do ..." Her voice was pinched and frightened.

"Don't worry," Bliss assured her. "He'll have a few drinks with Robby and the guys and cool down. Come on out."

"I hope you're right, but I'd better not. Besides, I wouldn't be much fun.

I'll talk to you later." Emma re-entered her kitchen. Bliss, with a sigh, returned to her company. The day wasn't going exactly as planned.

* * * * *

The light was starting to fade as Bliss and Elaine fed and bathed the baby, getting her ready for bed. They had seen all they wanted of the Fair and enjoyed watching the baby play in the dust of the back yard until getting crankily tired. The visit had been good for Bliss and Elaine, unmarred by the men hanging around.

The fireworks would begin soon and Elaine didn't want the baby to be frightened or chance violating Tucci's rules. She took Bobo upstairs to keep her company while waiting for the baby to fall asleep. She didn't see Bobo often and really missed him.

Bliss sat in the back yard with Jerry's wife having another beer and talking quietly. She noted, "The men have been gone an awful long time." Jake and Con were still out, in their words, "Cruising." Bliss guessed. "Robby and his friends must of spent most of the afternoon at *The Bar.*" It was a good guess.

The men and boys returned at about the same time, just as the fireworks started. Despite the flashing colors, the chest-thumping whooshes and the "Oohs!" and "Ahhs!" coming from the crowds lining Main Street, a silence overlaid the small group gathered at the Tucci home. Jim was stonily quiet – Robby angry – the others embarrassed. They obviously would have preferred being elsewhere. Bliss knew enough to walk tender when Robby was in this mood.

Bliss and Jerry's wife opened beers and served the sausage sandwiches kept warm on the barbecue. Things were strained but they had no clue why. Maybe Bliss suspected. Con and Jake were the only ones with an appetite. Elaine, still upstairs with her dog, was unaware of the thickening tension.

Bliss said, "Come on everybody eat. These sandwiches don't taste so good if they ain't hot ..." Attempting to placate the men of the group, she thought, *Please, God, don't let him be real mad.* She feared Robby's rages – especially those fueled by beer. At such times he was capable of almost anything. He hurt her in the past and she didn't want anyone to know how bad it could be. She wasn't sure what he was mad about this time and hoped his anger wouldn't be directed at her.

"Where's that fuckin' dog? Bobo...! Bobo! Where the fuck are you? Get over here!" Tucci called. He walked over to the dog's chain almost falling as he bent to pick up the unhooked end.

Responding to his name and the hostility in Tucci's voice, the dog's whines could be heard from the open windows of the upstairs apartment. He had learned to fear Tucci. Elaine opened the door and Bobo slunk down the stairs, tail between his legs, crawling on his belly towards Tucci still holding the chain.

Robert kicked at the dog, catching it in his ribs with the toe of his boot. "For God's sake! What're you doin'? Leave him be!" Throwing herself over the dog, Elaine tried to cover him with her body, yelling, "Quit! Quit it! Leave him alone, asshole!!!" either unaware of his mood or not caring.

Tucci, in his anger, kept kicking at the dog and the girl, missing more often than not – coordination used up by beer and irrational behavior. His vocal powers were unimpaired.

"No good bitch!" he screamed. "If you hadn't got knocked up with your little bastard baby you wouldn't have to leave your dog here. You ain't no better than the dog anyway – spread your legs for anyone wanting a fuck! Get your dog – get the fuck out-a-here!!"

He babbled on, voice rising and falling – the finale of the fireworks providing a dramatic backdrop to his anger. The others stood staring, struck dumb by Tucci's uncontrolled outburst.

Tucci turned from the cowering pair with a glazed look and wandered toward the tub of beer mumbling so only an occasional word or phrase could be heard, "Fuckin' bitch ... she's whore ... no fuckin' good ...all 'like ...'"

Elaine lay on the cinder drive, dissolved in tears, hugging Bobo to her. Bobo forgot his pain in an effort to acquit hers – crawling to her, raising dust curls and licking the salty tears from her face leaving muddy tracks. She hugged him to her, rocking back and forth on the ground. She looked around, dazed. "I gotta get out of here – where's my baby?" she asked of nobody.

She stood, making no effort to straighten her disheveled clothing, and tottered towards the stairs in the garage. Bobo whined trying to follow, stopped by the chain. Elaine stumbled past Tucci, unseeing. He ignored her, completely engrossed in the effort required to open the beer. Elaine snatched up her sleeping baby and diaper bag and went down the stairs. No one had moved – no one had spoken – a bad painting.

As Elaine maneuvered uncertainly through the motionless group, the spell was broken. Bliss ran after her. "Elaine! – Elaine! Don't go! You can't leave like this! Wait for me, I'll get the car. I'll take you home. Please, Honey, he didn't mean it! He's drunk! Wait!"

Elaine didn't even look around.

Ron, one of the guests, turned to another. "Chick, what the fuck's wrong with Robby? Give me the keys to your car. I'm gonna take Elaine home – no one's got to put up with that shit."

Silently, Chick handed over his keys. Ron got into the car, started the motor and began backing out of the drive.

The sound of the motor aroused Tucci. He lurched towards the car. "Where the fuck you goin'? – Get back here! – Let the bitch walk." He kicked at the moving car, cracking the headlight, losing his balance and falling. No one laughed.

Ron caught up to Elaine before she reached the corner. She looked confused, unsure which way to turn or to go. The Fair crowd was thinning with the completion of the fireworks. It was over for another year.

Ron called from the car, "Elaine, come on, let me take you home." He reached over and opened the passenger door.

His sympathetic tones started her tears. Elaine hugged the baby to her breast, holding the open diaper bag by one strap, bottles and baby items spilling out thumping hollowly on the boardwalk as she sobbed.

Getting out of the car, Ron urged Elaine towards it and helped her enter, murmuring soothingly.

* * * * *

Tucci struggled from where he had fallen, drunkenly brushing cinders from the seat of his pants. He lurched toward his chair and sagged into it, clutching the bottle of beer that somehow hadn't spilled during his outburst. The remaining guests, embarrassed, mumbled goodbyes. Jerry offered to drive Chick home. Chick relieved, accepted.

Con and Jake were the least affected by Robby's behavior. They'd seen him and his tantrums before and knew it best to avoid him. Without goodnights, they went upstairs. Jake thought his mother should be able to handle herself anyway. He was disappointed the dog hadn't taken a piece out of the "asshole." The muted sounds of rock music soon floated from the open windows. Jim returned to the front house without a word – Emma had not made an appearance during the excitement.

Bliss began picking up, making small comforting sounds as she did, hoping to appease Robby. He ignored her, muttering under his breath, "Goddamn bitch ... No damn good ... No good ... Fuckin' women all alike ... Mamma ..." Bliss couldn't comprehend his words and wouldn't have understood even if she had.

Robby slouched in his chair, the beer bottle dangling from his hand unnoticed, studying a picture buried deep in his memory – one not seen for more than twenty years. It had lost none of its vivid color or detail.

Mamma in her room kneeling on her bed facing towards the door ten-year old Robby had opened, his bloody finger extended. Tucci saw his own child eyes open wide in shock and horror. He watched Mamma with no clothes on, sweat coursing down her nude body, her plump breasts clutched in the grasp of a man Robby didn't know, her erect brown nipples squeezed between pudgy fingers, one of which wore a plain gold ring.

The man was behind Mamma. He didn't have any clothes on either, and his fat belly was pressed up tight against Mamma, his male member stabbing into her from behind. Robby could see the bulge of it stretching Mamma's skin below her tummy. Robby was surprised she had hair there. He didn't – his sister didn't.

The man's sparse blond hair was plastered to his head with sweat. Robby could hear strange squishing noises as the man moved, staring at Robby, his porcine face flushed, washed out eyes wide, blank. His head was still, his lips drawn back showing little pointed, brown-stained teeth. Even though his head was unmoving, the man seemed unable to stop the hypnotic rhythm of his flabby body.

The memory hadn't come to Robby in years. He again felt the pain of the cut finger – the torn heart. His body shuddered.

Bliss couldn't see what was behind Robby's partially closed eyes. The screen of his memory, and expressionless face made him appear fairly peaceful to her, so she left him sitting there, beer bottle held loosely in his fingers, eyes slitted. She thought he was asleep, so she went upstairs.

Five

Ron, concerned about Elaine, didn't know where to take her but thought she shouldn't be alone. He asked, "Where do you wanna go? Your Grandma's?" He didn't know for sure where Mrs. Bellow lived, but had met her earlier and knew it was nearby.

"No! She can't see me like this. She'd get too upset. Pa's just getting over a heart attack. I can't wake them up."

The whole family called Claude Bellow, "Pa," a generic title identifying nothing specific – father, grandfather or just old man.

After a thoughtful pause, Elaine suggested, "Take me to Aunt Arliss'. I know she's home. Her husband's at work – she's by herself. She lives near Grandma – not too far – I can show you the way."

"No problem," Ron said, relieved that a destination had been chosen. Elaine was a responsibility he didn't want. It's just that he couldn't stand by and see anyone treated the way Tucci treated her. Elaine became more settled as she gave directions over the dark, country roads. Her eyes dried and the hiccupping sobs disappeared as she made cooing sounds to the baby sleeping in her arms.

Even though she felt better, she continued to fret about her dog and the others still at Tucci's place. There was no telling what he might do. Ron tried to reassure her.

"I ain't never seen Robby like this. My brother says he has a bad temper, but he never hurt noone. It must a' been the beer. I'm sure he's sober now. You know, sleeping it off. I'm sure everything's alright... " adding under his breath, "I hope!"

As they pulled into the drive Elaine pointed to, Ron noticed with relief, the lights were on. He thought it unusual until he realized it was still early, not yet midnight. The long hot day followed by the emotional explosion made it seem like the early morning hours.

Stopping the car, he jumped out and opened Elaine's door to help gather her things. He directed, "Get your stuff and go on in. I'll wait 'till you're inside. I got to get the car back."

Clutching the baby, Elaine leaned over to give Ron a light kiss on the cheek. "Thanks a million. I can't tell you how much I appreciate what you done. If you hadn't been there... I don't know what would a' happened. I really do appreciate it..." the thought trailing off.

Ron watched as she stepped out of the car and walked onto the front porch. She tapped lightly on the door, calling, "Aunt Arliss ... It's me."

Almost immediately, the curtains on the door were pulled aside and a woman's face peered out. Arliss lit the porch light as she unlocked and threw open the door, crying, "What's wrong? Why are you here? Is Con all right? Give me your baby! Get in here!" delivered in her usual rapid-fire speech pattern.

Pleased to be rid of the problem, Ron stepped into the car, backed into the street and drove away quickly.

Aunt Arliss' immediate panic rekindled Elaine's outrage. Before the door closed behind her, she began to describe Tucci's behavior and what he had done to her and Bobo. She showed her aunt the marks on her wrists, the bruise on her face and torn garment. She became indignant, describing in exaggerated terms, Tucci's drunken and vicious conduct.

Arliss, always bordering on the verge of hysteria and expecting trouble, became more agitated. "We have to tell Ma! ... She'll know what to do! ... We have to get the children away from there! They may all be dead by now! No telling what that monster's done...!"

As she spoke, she ran aimlessly around the cluttered room waving her arms, looking for and finally locating a sweater to wear in preparation for leaving. "Come on ... ! We're going to Ma's ... We have to get Con and Jake right now ... !" The words tumbled from her as she scurried about.

The obvious overreaction made Elaine fear she'd gone too far in her description of the events. She suggested, "Aunt Arliss, I can't go back there. The baby's asleep. Everything is gonna be alright," in a belated effort to placate her Aunt. "I'm sure Robby's already sleeping it off. Let me put the baby down while you fix some coffee. We can talk about it and maybe call over to the front house – make sure everything's okay."

By way of answer, Arliss struggled into her sweater, grabbed her purse and rummaged in it looking for car keys. "You stay here. I'm going to get Ma and get those kids back here where they belong! Shouldn't have let them go in the first place...! That son-of-a-bitch ain't gonna get away with this!"

Elaine began, "Bu ... But ... Aunt ..." Before the words were formed, Arliss fled the house, started her big Lincoln sedan and backed it from the garage. She would not be deterred.

* * * * *

Even though not yet midnight on a Saturday night, Claude and Gay Bellow had been asleep for several hours. The house was dark, save for a night light in the hall and a lamp on a timer in the living room. Claude, nearly recovered from his recent bout with an over-strained heart, was sleeping soundly. Gay's constant pain from a fairly recent injury and natural agitation kept her on the verge of wakefulness. She heard the racing car long before it tore into her dark driveway, and was sitting up in bed putting her feet to the floor before it skidded to a stop next to the house.

Gay heard the car door slam open, motor still running, and someone leap from the car. Rapid footsteps crunching on the gravel approached the side-door. Whoever it was hadn't taken the time to close the car door.

The steps reached the kitchen entry to the old-fashioned farmhouse. A rapping sound on the door was quickly followed by a shaking of the knob. Arliss' hysterical voice called, "Ma! Ma! It's me! Are you up? Let me in!"

Gay ran to the door, not bothering to cover her flannel nightgown with a robe. "I'm coming, Arliss! Shhh ... For God's sake, keep it down. No need to wake your father!" No matter the crisis, Gay would not have Claude disturbed. He was a sound sleeper, not easily awakened, but Gay had spent more than forty years worrying about him. It was a habit.

She wrestled the door open to allow Arliss entry. Pushing past her mother, Arliss began, words spilling out in a jumble. "We got to go to Bliss' house...! Robby's... He's acting crazy... He beat up Elaine... her baby... Bobo... Elaine's afraid he's gonna kill someone!"

Arliss grabbed her mother and began pulling her toward the open door wailing, "Come on... We got t' go ... The boys aren't safe ...! Oh, my God ...! Why did you let them go ...? What's gonna happen to Con ...? Maybe he's already dead! Maaaa ... !!"

Gay tried to calm Arliss. At least enough to make sense of what she was saying. Planting her feet firmly and resisting the pull, she demanded, "Arliss, for God's sake! Calm down! Slow down! Take a breath."

Arliss tried, taking deep shuddering breaths.

"There, that's better," Gay said. "Now, tell me, what in the world is going on?"

Taking several more breaths, ending with a catch, a sob and a quaver, Arliss told her mother in short, quick sentences the story Elaine had related, adding a few embellishments of her own and ending with, "so Ron drove her to my house."

Gay interrupted, leading Arliss into the kitchen and lighting the overhead light, "Who's Ron?"

"I don't know... a friend of Robert's. He was at his house today when Robert... " She continued. "Ma, for God sake, it don't matter. We got to go. We got to get those kids home. Please!"

As Gay listened to her daughter, she gathered some articles of clothing from her bedroom – the same clothing she had worn earlier – and quickly slipped into them. She shooed Arliss out the door, saying, "Wait in the car for me. I'll drive. You're in no state. I have to check Pa. I'll be right out."

Gay left the kitchen light on and entered the darkened bedroom she shared with Claude. She made no effort to be quiet, striding purposefully toward the closet. Grabbing an old sweater of her husband's, she shrugged into it. Standing on tip toes, she reached to the back of the shelf and felt around until she found what she was looking for – an old .38 caliber Smith and Wesson revolver that had been in the family for at least two generations. Claude taught her to use it years ago. It was in a tan leather flap holster cracked and dried with age.

She didn't know whether it would shoot or not – it hadn't been fired in years – but it didn't matter. She had no intention of using it.

The gun, holster and all, was slipped into the deep pocket of her husband's sweater, Gay thinking, *If Robert is really as bad as Arliss says, I may need to frighten him.*

She started to leave but, out of habit, stopped by the bed to check on Claude and make sure he was sleeping soundly and breathing evenly. She studied him for a moment, reached down to tuck the blanket around his shoulder, patted him once lightly on the cheek, and walked quickly from the room. At the doorway, she paused long enough to glance once more at Claude, blow him a kiss and leave. She closed the door firmly behind her.

She ran lightly through the kitchen, outside, and into the car where Arliss waited impatiently. Gay didn't like to drive Arliss' Lincoln, but it was easier than trying to switch the big car for her smaller model, especially with Arliss so distraught.

"Come on, Ma... Let's go!" Arliss urged.

Gay hadn't bothered turning off the house lights. She would be back long before Claude awoke.

It was still shy of midnight when they arrived at Mt. City. Several of the scattered houses on Garden Street showed lights and backyards occupied by those not yet ready to battle the heat in an effort to sleep. Gay pulled in the Tucci drive, parking directly behind Emma's grotesque green station wagon blocking the garage.

Arliss jumped from the car even before it came to a stop, running through the open door of the darkened garage.

Gay quickly followed, calling, "Arliss, wait!" not knowing what to expect.

The stairs against the sidewall were illuminated only by a light shining through the open apartment door. Arliss could see in the dim light six steps leading up to a landing and a sharp left turn – five more steps to the kitchen door. An elongated shadow darkened the stairs. Robert was standing in the doorway, hands on hips, head thrust belligerently forward.

His sister, Emma, was standing on the landing, practically invisible in the shadows. Arliss hardly noticed her as she brushed past. Robert's sister was looking at him, her pose rigid, a grimace of naked fury on her face replacing the usual expression of sisterly affection tinged with fear when in his presence.

Intent on her goal, Arliss ignored Emma as she pushed past, her concentration centered on Tucci.

Tucci, glaring at his sister, thought, *I never realized how much like Mamma she looks!* Then the unexpected presence of Arliss and Gay drew his attention unwillingly from his sister.

Robert was genuinely surprised to see Arliss and her mother – the surprise was followed quickly by renewed anger. "What the fuck you two doin' here?" he demanded a puzzled frown crowding his features.

Ignoring the question, Arliss demanded in a strident voice that he reveal the whereabouts of Con and Jake. "Where are the children? Where's my son? We've," gesturing toward her mother including her in the rescue mission, "come to take them home."

Without waiting for a response, she pushed imperiously past Tucci, walking uninvited into the kitchen. Bliss, standing behind Tucci, gaped, jaw sagging. She had seen her sister do outrageous things before, but this surpassed all. Arliss ignored her. Emma remained standing on the landing in shocked surprise. Arliss often had that effect on people.

Wasting no breath on them, she called, "Con! Jake! Get your things! We've come to get you!" Stamping her foot for emphasis, she added, "Right now...!"

Arliss marched across the kitchen to retrieve Jake's guitar leaning against the bedroom door. She picked it up and, holding it before her like a shield, reversed her direction back across the kitchen. She didn't look behind her, expecting the boys to follow and do her bidding without question. Bliss, reacted to the intrusion by looking from Arliss to her mother and back again, thinking, *My God, they don't know what they're doing. The shit is really going to hit the fan*! She hoped some explanation that might placate Robby would be made. She was too stunned to do more.

Gay tried to intercede, but had no chance. Arliss kept issuing orders – hurrying the boys along, "Come on...! Come on...! Let's go ... !!!"

Still dressed, they asked no questions, stuffing possessions into their shopping bags.

Robert still stood in the door, his hands on the jamb, looking over his shoulder into the room where Arliss had taken command, watching incredulously as she progressed across his kitchen. His mouth hung open – overwhelmed by her audacity. After a false start, he again found his voice. "Wh ... What the fuck you doing?" he hollered, body tense and poised. "Bustin' into my house, ordering everyone around? You are one crazy bitch! Get the fuck out'a here before I throw you down the fuckin' steps! You can't just bust into a man's house like this ... fuckin' crazy broad!"

His voice quavered with indignation as he turned toward the intruders. His anger grew to unbelievable proportions. His face reddened. His voice rose until he was almost screeching in rage. The cords on his neck protruded, a vein throbbed on his forehead. No sign of intoxication now in voice or manner.

Arliss, holding Jake's guitar before her, righteous in the face of Tucci's wrath, stormed toward Robert. Standing before him, she shook a finger in his face. "I have every right to take these children from an animal like you!" She looked over her shoulder to make sure they were following and began to push past Tucci.

The words had no effect on Tucci, but the pointing finger with its scarlet tip acted like a detonator. The color faded from his face – crimson to white. His eyes widened – nostrils flared – mouth worked spasmodically – no sound escaped from his tightened throat. Spittle sprayed from his snarling lips as his hands shot forward reaching past the guitar Arliss held and circled her neck with clutching fingers. He lifted her from the floor, flinging her about like a stuffed doll, legs flailing – hitting the wall, the door, the kitchen cupboard.

Arliss tried to yell, but no sound could pass the hands clamped around her neck. Desperately she clutched the guitar, trying to keep it between her and Tucci. She looked around wildly, her eyes imploring someone to help.

In his fury, Robert was oblivious to the damage he was doing to Arliss

37

and the room. Bliss screamed, "Robby! Robby! Let go! Let go ... !" Her pleas had no effect. Con and Jake stood staring, too stunned and frightened to intervene.

Robert had still uttered no intelligible sound, just deep animal-like growls.

Gay pushed back against the dishwasher to avoid being struck by her daughter's thrashing legs. Without thinking, she reached into her pocket and pulled out the revolver. Unexpectedly aware of the gun's presence in her hand, she pointed it at the ceiling screaming, "Robert...! Robert...! I have a gun...! L... le... let go of her! I'll kill you! I swear I'll kill you!"

She pulled the trigger with all her strength just as Tucci released Arliss throwing her into a glass-fronted cupboard near the door. Several antique Coca Cola bottles were displayed on the top of the cabinet into which Arliss was propelled with such force that the bottles shot forward as though from a catapult. One, on impact with Robert's head, exploded with a loud crack, and burst into fragments. Blood, glass and spittle flew in all directions, a gash appearing on Tucci's forehead.

Arliss slid to the floor, legs askew, in a sitting position her back to the cupboard, still clutching the guitar. She saw Tucci fall flat on his face with a satisfying thud, blood flowing freely from his head beginning to soak into the living room carpet and run across the kitchen linoleum. She had never seen so much blood.

Bliss dropped to her knees beside Tucci, trying to turn him over and pull his head into her lap – his eyes were wide, staring. "My God!" she shrieked. "Get help! Someone, get help! He's hurt!" Then she began crooning to him, "It's okay – you'll be okay...."

Arliss, afraid Tucci might get up and continue the attack, stood and brushed broken glass from her lap. She gagged and croaked, "Come on – get your things – let's get out of this place."

Gay looked at her hand. The gun wasn't there. She looked around and saw it on the floor amidst the broken glass and blood. She shuddered and stepped over Robert's still feet to usher Con and Jake from the apartment. She didn't notice where anyone else was, thinking only of the boys and her daughter.

In the yard, Gay held Arliss in an attempt to comfort her. Arliss, reacting to the aftermath of violence, tried to swallow her sobs while struggling to breathe, was overcome by a paroxysm of coughing.

Emma, now outside, ran toward a Mills County Deputy stationed at the corner of Main and Garden. He had been working Fair security. "Denny!

Denny!" Emma screamed. "I need help! My brother's been shot!"
The back yard began to fill.

Six

Gay trying to comfort Arliss, held her tightly in the circle of her arms. She was only subconsciously aware of the activity around her. Uniformed police officers were giving orders – someone touched her shoulder – people were talking to one another in hushed voices. An ambulance screamed into the yard spitting gravel from its wheels and pulling as close to the garage door as possible. Someone ran up the stairs to the apartment carrying something. Lights sprang to life up and down the street. The back yard where Arliss and Gay were standing was suddenly brightly illuminated. Gay looked at Arliss and could see the tears stream down her face – could hear the croaking sounds her daughter made as she tried to breathe. Someone joined the two women and asked, "What happened?" Gay would have none of it. This was her daughter and she would protect her from this stranger.

Gay noticed two men struggling nearby – one trying to hit the other with his fist – a policeman stepped between them. No words registered on her consciousness. She thought, *Something is terribly wrong. Robert is more than just hurt. Why are so many people here?*

A policeman took Gay's arm, saying, "Come with me, please."

Gay briefly resisted. She mustn't leave Arliss so she struggled to hold her until she recognized the uniformed man as a police officer. Police officers must be obeyed. She went with him, stumbling slightly, looking over her shoulder at her daughter. Another policeman took Arliss, placing her in the back of a marked car. Gay could see her sitting there sobbing. *She is so frightened.*

Gay sat quietly, hands folded in her lap. There was nothing to do except wait for instructions. She couldn't leave the car even if she wanted to – there were no inside handles for the doors or windows. She noted the ambulance leave, siren screaming. In the silence that followed, a man opened the car door and introduced himself.

"I'm Detective Mike Redding. I'm in charge of this investigation. Before we take your statement, I need to do a test. Okay?"

"What kind of test?" Gay asked in a subdued voice.

"Nothing important. It's called an atomic absorption test. Just routine," Redding explained.

"If it's to see whether I shot a gun, it isn't necessary," Gay began. "I already told your man that I brought a gun here and believe I may have fired it upstairs in Robert's apartment."

"We have to do it to everyone that was up there anyway," he said, repeating, "It's just routine."

"All right," Gay said, holding out her hands.

Redding opened a packet and removed what looked like a slightly damp cue-tip. He touched it to the back of Gay's right hand, repeating the process on the palm and back of each hand with additional swabs. Replacing everything in separate vials of the kit, he wrote on the outside of it and placed it in his pocket.

"All right, now Mrs. Bellow, we can go to the police station so you can give us a statement." Gay sat back and watched her daughter Arliss leave in the back seat of another police car. Bliss had gone earlier with the ambulance. Gay desperately hoped Arliss was all right. She suggested to Redding, "Maybe you should take Arliss to the hospital too, or have her seen by a doctor. Her throat is pretty badly bruised."

Redding replied perfunctorily, "If she needs a doctor, she'll get one."

Gay asked, "How will the boys get home?"

"Mrs. Bellow, everything will be taken care of. Don't worry. Once you've told us your story, you'll find out about everyone else. Right now, just worry about yourself."

Gay shivered as a cold breeze of premonition played along her spine.

* * * * *

Redding drove carefully without using the siren or flashing lights. He steered through Milltown's square, the amber streetlights casting a soft glow on the Gazebo and surrounding Victorian buildings. Gay had never seen the square at night and did not now appreciate its beauty. They passed the red brick courthouse with its stately clock tower, and pulled into the rear parking lot to gain entry to the jail's courtyard, guarded by an eight-foot fence topped with razor sharp coils. Gay gave no thought to the fact that this reality was hidden away from eyes that admired the preserved charm of the square.

Ushered from the car inside the fenced lot, Gay was led through a metal door into a small concrete block entry where she faced a second metal door that clicked open only when the door behind her slammed shut. She could see red-eyed cameras monitoring her progress through several more doors in

41

the same fashion – the one in front not opening until the one behind closed. She was aware of passing several rooms, some of which held people doing things she did not understand – talking quietly into a telephone or studying shimmering screens. No one seemed aware of her presence except Redding. But someone must have known they were there because the doors opened without their intervention. Her impression was of steel doors, iron bars and concrete walls painted a glossy green – easy to keep clean – but no one bothered.

After what seemed an eternity – Gay now completely confused by the maze of halls – they reached a room Redding opened with a key. It wasn't much of a room – not as big as her living room at home – yet it contained three desks, a long table and several folding chairs – all metal, all coldly governmental. *We must be in the basement,* she thought. The windows were small, made of glass block and high on the walls. She couldn't see out – no one could see in.

Redding conducted her inside, not bothering to seat her, and said, "Wait here." He then left, closing the door behind him. She heard the lock click.

Gay didn't look around the room, but perched on the very edge of the nearest metal chair, hands folded in her lap, not moving, withdrawn in thought.

How long she sat she didn't know, but was relieved to hear someone at the door. Redding came in carrying a small hand-held tape recorder. He plugged it into a wall outlet and explained, "I have to take a statement from you. We'll record it. But before we start the recorder, let's just talk about what happened tonight. After you have it straight in your mind, we'll put it on tape, okay?"

"Mr. Redding, please tell me if everyone is all right. I really have to get back home before my husband wakes up. He'll be upset if I'm not there when he does."

"Mrs. Bellow. I can't tell you anything. The quicker you cooperate with us and give us what we need, the quicker you can go home. Now tell me what happened," he ordered. Voice edging toward impatience, he added, "You understand you don't have to talk to me if you don't want to. You are not under arrest. If you need a lawyer, you can talk to one. If you can't afford one, the state will supply one for you." This last bit was mumbled to comply with the letter, if not the spirit, of the *Miranda* warnings dictated by the Supreme Court, obviously hoping Mrs. Bellow neither heard nor understood.

Gay began. "Just like I already said, several times. My daughter, Arliss, came to my house hysterical with worry ... " repeating the story exactly the way it happened. The questioning lasted for hours, Redding demanding that Gay repeat each detail over and over, picking at every possible discrepancy. He would, from time to time, leave the room without explanation. Occasionally another man would come in for whispered conversation, ignoring Gay. Sometime the other man would listen to the questions and insert one or two of his own. During the entire time, Gay perched delicately on the edge of her chair, neither asking for nor receiving refreshment or rest.

Finally, still not completely satisfied with the answers, Redding said, "Let's get this recorded. I'm getting sick and tired of your bullshit. You know goddamn well you killed Tucci. Give me some straight answers so I can go home and get some rest. This is your last chance if you want any help from us."

Stung by the words and without understanding the detective's growing belligerence, Gay said, "Mr. Redding, I have been very candid with you. If you're not satisfied, I'm sorry. Do what you have to, but if you use that tone with me again, you will get no further cooperation. I certainly don't understand why you are getting so angry. I will not be talked to that way. Please, do not swear again – such language – you should be ashamed!"

Curbing his impatience only slightly, the detective turned on the tape recorder sitting on the table between them. He had not dealt with many people like Gay Bellow. Talking into the microphone, Redding began. "It is 5:13 A.M. on August the 24th. Detective Michael Redding of the Mills County Sheriff Department is interviewing Gabriella Bellow. The interview is being recorded with the knowledge and permission of Mrs. Bellow. You understand, don't you that you are not under arrest and can end this interview at any time you want?" His voice trailed off as he recited the *Miranda* litany necessary to document the tape recording he intended to use against Gay in court.

* * * * *

The following Monday, just before noon, Claude Bellow stood on the south side of Milltown's square in front of the century old brick and stone structure studying the legend **PATRICK J. JOSEPH, ATTORNEY** etched in gold letters on the building's plate glass window. He looked at the five sandstone steps leading to the entry.

Disturbed by his wife's vague explanation of the Mt. City incident, he called his company lawyer. Though not completely aware of the details, he surmised his wife needed help. He turned to Tom Whale, a friend and senior partner in the prestigious Cleveland firm of **WHALE, SAUNDERS & JACK**.

Claude said, "Tom, I'm sorry to bother you on Sunday, but I don't know what else to do," explaining in as much detail as he could what little he had learned from his wife.

After a thoughtful silence, Whale said, "Claude, I read some of the story in this morning's *Plain Dealer*. Somebody was killed at the Mt. City Street Fair last night. It seems your wife and daughter were there when it happened. I don't know whether they are involved or not, but there isn't much advice I can give them. They need to talk to a criminal defense lawyer – preferably one who practices in Mills County. I don't do that kind of work and can't really be of much help. I do know a lawyer in Milltown. Went to school with him and hear he does criminal defense work. Being local, he should be able to help. At least he should know what's going on and be able to point you in the right direction."

"Would you please arrange an appointment for me for as soon as possible?" Bellow asked.

"Okay. Call me tomorrow before ten and I'll let you know what I can do."

The Bellow family had been clients for years providing lucrative fees to Whale's firm. Tom Whale got to his office early and dialed a number secured from a desk book. He hadn't talked to Pat Joseph in years, but remembered him fairly well from their law school days some thirty years earlier.

It was his call that Della had answered in Joseph's office early Monday morning. Placing her hand over the phone and handing it to Joseph, Della said, "Said his name is Tom Whale and went to school with you. Has to talk to you as soon as possible. Sounds important."

Pat Joseph took the phone, hearing, "Hi, Pat – Tom Whale."

After a thoughtful pause to allow his aged memory to report why the name was familiar, Joseph responded, "Well hello, Tom. Haven't talked to you in a long time." It wasn't apparent from his voice that Joseph was having a hard time putting a face to the name. "How have you been?"

"Fine, and you?"

"I'm fine, Tom. What can I do for you?"

Whale took a deep breath and said, "Pat, I have a client by the name of Claude Bellow. He has a business here in Cleveland that's been in the family for generations. They've had some financial problems the past couple of months – probably because of his health – not paying the kind of attention to his business he should – but sound people. They have some family problems..."

"Tom," Joseph interrupted trying to curb his impatience. He could only recall Whale vaguely. He wasn't anyone with whom he had a great deal in common. "I'm sure you know I don't handle business matters or domestic cases. My practice is mostly real estate and probate, some personal injury litigation and an occasional trial down here. I don't get to Cleveland much anymore. I'd like to help... but..."

"I know... I know... " Whale said. "I'm just giving you this for background. His wife and daughter were involved in a situation in Mt. City. Someone was killed and they need help. I gave your name to Mr. Bellow. Thought you might be able to help, or at least suggest something to him. It seems pretty urgent to me and I thought you might be willing to see him right away."

Joseph thought for a minute and said, "I was reading in this morning's *Reporter* about the killing at the Mt. City Street Fair last Saturday." While talking, Pat dropped his feet from their usual propped position to the floor and glanced at his calendar. "You know, I do some criminal stuff, but...a murder case...I don't know." Joseph's insecurity was creeping into his voice. "I'm pretty well booked and haven't done anything that heavy since I left Cleveland."

"Look, Pat. This is kind of an emergency. I gave him your name and don't know anyone else in Milltown. At least talk to him. If you can't help, steer him to someone who can. Will you do that?" Whale asked.

"I guess I can do that much," Joseph conceded, glancing at his desk top calendar. "He can come in at noon today."

"Noon today? He'll be there. His name is Claude Bellow, and thanks a million, Pat. I'm really indebted to you."

Joseph sank back into his chair and thought, *What the hell am I going to do now? I haven't defended a murder case since moving down here. Son-of-a-bitch. Why can't they leave me alone? I don't need this.* He had been looking forward to a quiet pleasant day, and was suddenly very uncomfortable.

* * * * *

Bellow hesitated before walking up the sandstone stairs to the carved wooden doors. A small brass plate declared that the building was first erected in 1837 to house *The Milltown Reporter*, the local newspaper still being published; then rebuilt following the great Milltown fire in 1895. Even though the newspaper had relocated to a modern brick building just outside of town, everyone still called the old stone structure *The Reporter Building*, no matter it now bore the name *The Joseph Building*.

Claude took a deep breath and drew himself up – more to gain the fortitude necessary to handle an unpleasant chore than to change his physical dimensions – and entered the Joseph offices. He was expected and asked to complete a new client information sheet.

Ushered into Joseph's presence, he heard, "How do you do Mr. Bellow. My name's Patrick Joseph, but everyone calls me Pat. Your attorney Tom Whale, an old friend, called and asked me to see you. He didn't give me much information except to say it was important."

Bellow stood just inside the doorway of the private office tense and uncertain. He seemed on the verge of fleeing. Joseph wasn't much more comfortable but tried to put the prospective client at ease, asking as he moved to shake hands, "Should I call you Claude? Please come in. Sit down."

Bellow obeyed, but did not relax. Holding onto Bellow's hand, Joseph guided him to a client chair in front of the scarred oak table. Instead of walking behind the desk, Joseph took a matching brown leather chair next to Claude and, in a conversational tone, began chatting. It was hard to say whether he was stalling for time or trying to make Bellow more comfortable.

To Joseph, Bellow appeared to be a bit shorter than average, slightly overweight in his late middle years – probably sixty-ish. The descriptive adjective that came to Joseph's mind was "round." Bellow's round head, garnished with sparse white hair, a thick unkempt fringe over the ears and long carelessly managed strands wildly loose on top, projected from round shoulders without benefit of a neck – his chest slight and sunken over a rounded paunch, arms too short, hands not knowing what to do, tried to clasp one another over the rounded belly.

His nondescript suit, shirt and tie were of questionable vintage, carelessly applied. The package slumped, rather than sat, as close to the door as possible, eyes cast down.

Bellow's obvious discomfort gave Joseph confidence to ask questions facing him, hoping to force eye contact. It didn't work. Bellow continued studying his absent lap. He answered readily enough, but sat silently for several minutes between inquiry and response to gather his thoughts or compose what he wanted to say.

Finally, after some urging, Bellow cleared his throat, washed a hand over his mouth and began. "I really don't know what to tell you. I don't know what happened. I had a heart attack a couple of months ago – not too serious – but my family, especially my wife, have insisted on babying me ever since. I'm not supposed to know what's going on. Nobody is telling me anything. Actually, they never have confided in me with anything of importance."

"Mr. Bellow – Claude," Joseph began. "You are here for a reason, what is it?" Pat Joseph was ordinarily patient, but seeing Bellow was a favor and he wanted him to say whatever he had to say as quickly as possible and be on his way. Joseph was set in his ways and liked to be disturbed as little as possible. His limited practice provided a pleasant and quiet living. Recently he found clients, more often than not, a distraction.

Bellow didn't respond immediately, but finally said, "I'm not sure ... I received a call early Sunday morning from your Sheriff's office. Some lady said they were holding my wife for questioning in the death of Robert Tucci, but I could come and get her. I asked if she was all right and what it was all about, but she wouldn't tell me anything except that my wife was not yet under arrest. Of course, I was shocked. When I went to sleep, my wife was in bed next to me. I didn't even know she had gotten up or left the house. I take pills to help me sleep since my attack ... " Bellow began to explain.

He continued in a voice so soft Joseph could hardly hear. "I got panicky, so I called my daughter Arliss to take me. She wasn't home either. Her husband answered the phone. He had worked all night and when he got home Arliss wasn't there. He was worried to death and then got the same kind of call I did and learned Arliss was with Gay. Gay – that's my wife – Gabriella Bellow. He got a call from the Sheriff's office too, and was on his way out of the house when I phoned. I asked him to pick me up. He didn't know any more about what was going on than I did.

"He picked me up and we came down here to the police station. Gay and Arliss were waiting for us. They looked awful. Arliss was crying and Mother – Gay – looked... " He couldn't find an adequate word.

"They told her she could go home, but wasn't to leave town. I asked what it was all about and the policeman said, "*Ask your wife.*" Then something about my daughter's boyfriend being killed."

"Are you talking about Robert Tucci?" Joseph inquired mildly.

"Yes, that's his name," acknowledged Bellow – then said, "We left the police station. Gay assured me she was all right. I asked what was going on. She said, "*Don't worry, everything will be fine.*" She said Tucci was dead but it had nothing to do with us – I shouldn't worry about it."

The entire story was delivered in a monotone. Bellow was holding himself together only by an extreme effort of will. "I got angry and insisted Gay talk to me – but she wouldn't. She can be very stubborn. The only thing I've learned is that Bliss' – that's my oldest daughter – the one living with Tucci – boyfriend is dead. He was shot with my gun, I think."

He paused to make sure he left out none of the facts, and then added, "I know my wife and daughter are involved, but I don't know how. They need help, but won't talk to me about it. Can you help them, please? Mr. Whale said you're a good lawyer and do criminal defense work. That's what we need ... " He had trouble uttering the words. "Nothing like this has ever happened to us. I don't know what to do. Can you help?"

Bellow delivered this, what was for him, lengthy speech without any inflection even though he appeared on the verge of tears – obviously distraught and out of his element. He looked like what he was – a man devoid of personality – a backdrop for his family. His role was to provide for them without becoming involved in their affairs. He cared deeply for his wife and children, even if he didn't know them.

Joseph thought, *Sure, I'm a criminal defense lawyer! I haven't handled a major case in ten years. I don't know what Whale told him, but I don't need this.* All of the criminal defense work done in recent years involved nothing more complicated than a drunk driving charge, yet Bellow evoked a surge of pity in Joseph that was almost palpable. The man epitomized the classic Mr. Milquetoast and was begging for help – not for himself – but his family.

Joseph surprised himself by saying, "I'm not sure I can, but I'll try to help. But someone will have to tell me what it's all about before I can do anything."

Bellow nodded, assuring Joseph his wife and daughter would cooperate. Joseph then talked about business arrangements, the costs involved in defending a criminal case if it became necessary to do so. Bellow said he understood and would make arrangements to retain the lawyer even though money was tight right now. Joseph wasn't convinced Bellow would remember.

Bellow went on to portray his wife as the strong one in the family; and that *She and you will hit if off.* Joseph paused to consider whether any explanation would register with Bellow, but felt compelled to inquire, "If there is a conflict between your wife's legal interest and your daughter's, I can only represent one of them – not both. In that event, which one do you want me to represent?"

"Mr. Whale says you are a fine criminal defense lawyer." Joseph thought, *Goddamn him!* but immodestly nodded his head. "If a choice has to be made, I want you to represent my wife." There was no question where Bellow's loyalties lie. He desperately loved his wife.

Joseph studied him for a moment thinking, *I wonder if she deserves such devotion?*

* * * * *

When Bellow left after arranging an appointment for his wife, Joseph asked Della to place a call. "Please call the Prosecutor's office for me so I can find out what is going on." Naturally, no one was saying anything.

Since the Sheriff's office was handling the investigation and Michael Redding was in charge, Pat would call him. They were social acquaintances. Redding, in his mid-forties, did all he could to deny his age. He worked at staying slender and in good physical condition. He hid his loss of hair with a god-awful toupee. A silly thing to do. He was blessed with a tall, slender and attractive appearance without artificial aids. A bachelor by choice, Redding was dedicated to his work. He was considered a likely target for the ladies. He liked them too, but not for marriage. Pat saw him frequently around town at the local social functions.

Picking up the phone, Joseph eventually got through to Redding saying easily, "Mike, Pat Joseph. I may get involved in the Tucci thing. Anything you can tell me about it?"

Redding had a reputation in the legal community for trying to cooperate with defense lawyers, believing shared information would make less work for both. For some reason, no one in the County Prosecutor's office had learned that lesson. Joseph hoped to take advantage of Redding's friendliness to learn something about the case.

Mike confirmed that he was in charge of the investigation, had interviewed all the witnesses and supervised the crime scene. "Tucci," he said, "was shot in the head and never regained consciousness. Milltown General life-flighted him to Cleveland. They tried to operate but he died on the table. An autopsy was done, but it's not typed up yet. The case is really pretty simple – family homicide."

"Very fast work, Mike," Joseph complimented. "He was just killed Saturday. How'd you wrap it up so quick?"

"Well, you know," he answered with a hint of brag. "One of our men was on the scene within a minute or two. He called in and, since I live out that way, I got there pretty quick. The only ones to beat me were life support and Denny, of course."

"Denny?" Joseph inquired.

"You know, Denny Baker, one of our Specials. He was working the Fair, and was our man on the scene within seconds," Redding explained.

"Anyway, we had the suspects separated and interrogated before they had a chance to talk to each other – get their stories straight. Hell, we had the gun before we knew he'd been shot," he laughed.

"Where'd you find the gun?" Joseph asked – just making conversation.

"Can't talk about that yet. Were going to the Grand Jury – probably tomorrow – no facts until the indictment is handed down. But, I will tell you that none of it matters anyway. We got a confession!" he said, a smug smile in his voice.

"You got a confession?" Joseph repeated surprised. "From whom?"

"Keep this to yourself," Redding lowered his voice as though afraid someone could overhear the conversation. "The old lady. She confessed. She brought the gun and shot the bastard. He probably deserved it from what I hear."

"Shit!" Joseph responded. "I think she's the one whose husband wants me to represent her."

"I wouldn't worry about it," Redding laughed. "She's a nice old lady. I'm sure you will be able to work out some kind of deal."

"Hell, I haven't even met her yet," Joseph explained.

"You'll like her. I made the mistake of swearing at her and she chewed me out royally. A real lady." Redding would add nothing more and Joseph didn't know what else to ask. The conversation ended and Joseph hung up. He sat at his desk, feet propped, clasped hands resting lightly on his girth. In the corner of his office was a shelf on which sat his collection of miniature pigs lovingly accumulated over the years. He studied them, inspecting their silent smiles. *Maybe this won't be so bad,* he thought. *All I need to do is plead Mrs. Bellow – make as good a deal as I can – collect my fee – be a hero. Don't need to be a genius to handle this one.*

Mike's parting shot had been, "If you do represent the old broad, get your money up front."

Seven

Gabriella Bellow and her daughter, Arliss Conrad, were waiting when the lawyer arrived at his office the next morning. It was not yet nine, but they were there a good fifteen minutes before he. Joseph was struck by the startling similarities between mother and daughter – the mother a softer version.

Mrs. Bellow appeared in her late fifty's, or maybe early sixty's. Her wrinkle-lined face bore witness to the fact that life hadn't treated her kindly. Her brow wore a meandering pattern of permanent creases and her lips, although mobile and ready to smile, were pursed as if pain were a frequent companion. As unpleasant as life may have treated her, she still looked like she expected gratifying surprises. Her eyes were a deep brown, lightly flecked with green. They looked sad. The pain with which she seemed so familiar may not always have been physical.

After Joseph introduced himself, he studied her for a few moments. She smiled, but it was tentative.

Mrs. Bellow's daughter, Arliss Conrad, was in her mid twenty's – the type to plow through life assured of being well treated, or at least well cared for. She shared the thin, bony physique, slender neck, high cheekbones, and pursed lips of her mother. On her, the appearance didn't carry the suggestion of poor health, rather her carriage, tall and straight, conveyed an athletic impression – a horsewoman or tennis player – both of which she had been.

Arliss' constant complaints of poor health did not evidence problems, rather a device for securing attention. Claude and Gay's youngest child, she expected and received pampering. Tantrums, tears, hysteria and fainting were tools she used frequently and well to gain her ends. She looked as though she had tried them all during this most recent tragedy and was confused at their inability to provide proper relief.

The lawyer, despite his trepidations, greeted them pleasantly and then, for the moment, ignored Arliss. "Good morning Mrs. Bellow. Your husband stopped to see me. He asked me to talk to both of you," he said, acknowledging Arliss with a nod. "Tom Whale, your husband's lawyer, suggested it."

Joseph noted a grimace of distaste pass across Mrs. Bellow's face. She apparently had no great love for Whale, which Joseph later learned had to do with Gay's belief that the lawyer took advantage of her husband because of his lack of business acumen. He hoped she was broad minded enough not to make similar judgments of him.

"Mr. Whale said you were both at Tucci's house when he was killed. Is that correct?" the lawyer asked diving right in.

They both nodded. Arliss saying nothing – Gay responding, "Yes, sir."

"Your husband said he only had a smattering of information, but seems to think one, or both of you, need a lawyer. He asked me to represent you." Joseph paused to allow them a response. When neither spoke, he continued, "Do you think you need representation?"

Again they nodded affirmatively in unison with Mrs. Bellow verbalizing, "I think so."

"Tucci, I've been told, died of a gunshot wound to the head. Both of you apparently made long and damaging admissions to the police. Those statements, along with everything else, are in the hands of the Prosecutor. She is going to the Grand Jury this week. The police expect an indictment to be handed down within a matter of hours," the lawyer said confidently, though not completely familiar with the local process.

Hesitating for a moment to assess how much the two women understood, Joseph continued. "Neither of you knows me and I, of course, don't know you. I do some criminal defense work and am pretty good at it," he added with no show of modesty but a little false bravado. "If there is a conflict between you – I can only represent one – not both. I don't care which one, but I've been told the statements made by you, Mrs. Bellow, are the most damaging."

Looking directly at her, he continued. "Besides, your husband made it very clear that we concern ourselves with your problems, first."

This brought a quick intake of breath from Arliss, accompanied by a sharp glance at her mother as if to say, *What is wrong with that man?*

During the silence that followed, Gabriella Bellow, who had been studying Joseph intently during the monologue, interjected, "Since my husband told me he met you and wanted me to talk to you, I've done some checking of my own." Joseph could feel his palms dampen. "They tell me you have a good reputation in Milltown and are considered a good lawyer."

He relaxed a little.

She smiled while talking in her tight self-contained way, careful to give no offense. "But, there is something you must know. My husband knows

52

nothing about what happened. I want it that way. He is recovering from a heart attack and I will not have his life endangered – I will not have it! If you are to work for us, you will not discuss this case with him! Is that understood?"

"Go on," the lawyer demurred.

"If my daughter, needs help, I will expect you to help her, and only her."

This brought a momentary look of relief to Arliss Conrad's face as her mother continued. "At the moment, it appears I am the one in the most trouble, so you will take my case until she needs you more. If that occurs, you will switch your allegiance to her." She uttered each word slowly and clearly, enunciating carefully to make sure the lawyer understood. He wondered if she'd ever been a teacher.

The lawyer reflected for a moment trying to pick his words carefully. He decided he couldn't allow her attempt to control the situation or to continue uninterrupted, so he said, "Excuse me."

He buzzed for his secretary, saying into the telephone, "Della, would you mind bringing in some coffee – cream and sugar for the ladies – black for me?" She appeared almost instantly, carrying a tray with the fixings. Joseph introduced her and offered the coffee. For some reason Joseph wasn't surprised when Mrs. Bellow said she drank it black while Arliss requested both cream and sugar. Della finished and left, pulling the door closed behind her.

After the ladies were settled, the lawyer sat up straighter in his chair, placing both feet flat on the floor and began, with a sigh, "Mrs. Bellow ... "

She interrupted. "Please call me Gay."

He nodded impatiently saying slowly and clearly, "Okay, Gay. If you choose to retain me, you will not dictate the terms. You will be permitted to make decisions – that is choose between alternatives I present. But you will not make legal, strategic or investigative decisions. Do you understand?"

Without waiting for her to acknowledge or respond to the question, he continued. "I am no longer a young man and can afford the luxury of deciding the cases I will accept and which I will not. I don't explain how I make those decisions to anyone. Most of the time, I'm not even sure myself." He didn't bother telling them that he rarely took criminal cases of this magnitude, especially since the opportunity hardly ever presented itself.

"What I am trying to say in my inarticulate way is, if we are to work together, we will do it my way. If you can accept that, we will get along just fine. If you cannot, enjoy your coffee and leave. Give my best to your husband. He impressed me as being a nice person, and a hell of a lot more astute than you seem to give him credit for."

He leaned back in his chair hands laced lightly over his paunch, smiled at the ladies, waiting for their reaction, much more nervous than he appeared. Gay sat unmoving on the edge of her chair, eyes bright as she studied Pat Joseph. What she saw was a man of uncertain years – probably in his late fifties – shorter than the theoretically average male with a gently sloping waistline that gave credence to his love for good cooking and obvious ethnic tastes. His head was large and housed intelligent hazel eyes – his most striking feature – topped by shaggy brows and a prominent nose set on a base of a shaggy grizzled moustache. His head was nude from the ears up with no effort made to rearrange the fringe to hide the baldness. He looked to be the kind of man willing to poke fun at his baldness as well as his other failings. He appeared comfortable – maybe complacent – with himself and his life. If the truth be known, he was. He had developed a comfortable legal practice in a community where there was seldom much excitement handling real estate transactions, probate, contracts and farm problems mostly – rarely handling a criminal matter more serious than a traffic offense. He enjoyed his routine and, especially did not like his evenings disrupted.

As Gay studied him, she thought, *He appears congenial at the moment, sort of like a clean-shaven Santa Claus in civvies. But I bet he could be a mean son-of-a-bitch – maybe even intimidating.*

He looked as though a kind smile or fearsome scowl would be equally at home on his face. She shivered at the thought, not so much out of fear, but out of a conviction that she preferred to have him on her side. As always, looks are deceiving. Pat Joseph did appear fierce, but was a kindly man. He didn't like to hurt anyone ever, but cultivated the expressive visage in order that he be left alone – allowed to live his life without interference – in peace.

Arliss looked angry – taken aback at the lawyer's effrontery. *How dare he talk to us in this manner?* She feared to say it aloud. Looking at her mother, coffee cup poised between the saucer and her mouth, she obviously expected her to put this man in his place. The lawyer wondered how long she could maintain that position, and whether the coffee would be warm enough to drink when it finally got to her lips.

Gay thoughtfully reached for her cup, tasted its content and studied Joseph intently. For the first time since walking into his office, she genuinely smiled. Expecting Arliss to interrupt, Gay shushed her and said to Joseph, "I think we can work together."

Joseph leaned toward her and thought, *Shit!* but smiled back, "I think so too."

He continued. "Now, we haven't talked about Saturday night yet and I don't want to talk to both of you at the same time in case a conflict should develop. Going over the details will take some time." He glanced at his watch and at his calendar. There was nothing scheduled for this morning and the estate he was working on could wait. "Which of you can spend, say, the next two hours with me?"

Gay suggested, "Could you talk to Arliss? I have to see to the boys. I can come back this afternoon, if that's all right?"

"Of course," he agreed. "I assume by the boys you mean your grandchildren? The ones that were at the Tucci residence with you? I want to talk to them, too. Before I do anything else though, there is an extremely important instruction I must give both of you. Do not talk about this case to anyone! That means anyone! If asked about the case, you will say that you'd like to talk about it but your lawyer will not permit it. I mean it! You will not discuss the case at all. If you receive a subpoena from the Grand Jury or if a police officer wants to talk to you – tell them to see me – nothing else. Can you do that?"

"Of course," Gay responded and rising said, "I'll see you after lunch."

* * * * *

As Gay Bellow left his office, Joseph rounded the desk and took a seat in the same brown leather chair next to Arliss he occupied when talking to her father. He made no effort to put her at ease. The lawyer reflected on how she could perch on the very edge of the chair. It didn't seem physically possible, and certainly couldn't have been comfortable. Her hands trembled and her glance darted around the room as though eager for escape. This was probably the first time she had ever been left alone, unprotected by at least one doting family member.

"What's going to happen to me?" she whimpered.

"Nothing for now," the lawyer responded in a calm voice. "But, there is no way I can predict the future. Before any decisions can be made, you have to tell me what happened," he said, thinking, *I need some facts before I can figure out what kind of deal I can make with the prosecutor.*

"You spent almost all Saturday night talking freely to the police, and they weren't trying to help you. They're investigating a crime or crimes for which you and your mother are the principal suspects. If they can get a quick conviction, their job is done. Now, I want to hear what you have to say," he explained. "At least for now I'm on your side. Just talk to me about Saturday."

"Where do I start?"

"Pick a place – just start talking."

She started hesitantly. "On Saturday, my son, Con, and my nephew, Jake wanted to spend the night at my sister's house so they could go to the Street Fair. My mother really had no business letting them go, but she's that way. Elaine – she's my niece – was there, and Robert was pushing her around and trying to take her baby. She told me he was drunk and we better get the boys. When my mother and I got there he grabbed me by the throat when I told the boys to get their stuff. He told me, *I was so fucking high and mighty coming into his house making demands and he had enough of my shit* – I grabbed Jake's guitar to try and push him off me and he had me by the throat and called me a whore – and was going to push me down the stairs. The boys were getting their things in the bedroom – my sister was yelling and hitting him to make him let go – so was my mother – we struggled and then Robby got hit by a bottle, fell and let me go. I couldn't breathe – no one helped me – we left – the police came!" her voice rising uncontrolled verging on hysteria.

Her story was disjointed, and although starting slowly, the words began to run together with the telling. The lawyer neither interrupted nor asked questions. He was fascinated by her style, memory and story. It never seemed to occur to her that she should feel bad someone was killed. Even though he wanted her to get used to talking about the night Tucci died – to desensitize her – it hardly seemed necessary.

When she appeared to be finished, he asked, "You told the police all this, didn't you?"

"Yes, a detective – I don't know his name – but he was with Detective Redding. Sometimes another detective came in. They talked to everybody that was there and had us in different rooms. Sometimes one of the policemen would come in and they would whisper to each other. Then the detective would tell me what one of the others said and try to help me remember what happened."

Joseph shook his head at her naiveté and didn't bother explaining the strategy used by the police – no need to frighten her more than she was. She was wired so tight he fully expected her to explode.

"Did the police record your conversation? Did you sign anything? Did you make a written statement?" In response to each question, she nodded affirmatively.

"Let's try to remember everything you told the police."

They talked – an hour went by – she was still perched on the edge of the chair. *How the hell does she do that?* Finally, her story began to be more cohesive and she filled in details. Joseph turned on his recorder.

"My sister Bliss came over and picked up Con and Jake around noon to go to the Street Fair. A couple of hours later Ma and I went there, too. The kids were going to stay at Bliss and Tucci's house for the night. Around midnight, Elaine came to my house with her baby to tell me that Robert was drunk and getting mean, pushing everyone around."

Adding particulars, she continued. "I was scared, so I went to Ma's house for help. We went to get the kids. It was a little past midnight when we got there. Robert was acting real crazy ... "

As she got to this part of the story, her voice broke – the memory increased her agitation and nervousness to the point that her recitation became disorganized. She was remembering faster than she could talk. Joseph wanted her to slow down but without breaking the cohesiveness of the story.

"Arliss, is it all right if I call you by your first name?"

She nodded. "Yes."

"Don't try to tell me everything that happened. Sometimes we remember better if we think about our senses separately instead of trying to remember everything at once. I suspect the psychologists have a name for it, but I don't know what it is. Anyway, let's try to do that."

"I'm not sure I know what you mean," she said with a frown, trying to understand what was wanted. Accustomed to receiving and following instructions, she wanted to please.

He explained. "Just talk to me. First tell me what you saw from the moment you arrived at Tucci's house. Not what you heard or felt – just what you saw – your visual memories. I don't want to know what you or anyone said, or what you felt or what you heard. We'll do that later. Okay?"

"Do you mean, just say what I saw with my eyes? Nothing else?" she asked.

"That's right. I want you to start when you entered the garage and approached the stairs. Try this for me – humor an old man. I'll ask questions as we go – to help out," he said, fascinated at her story and vivid memory of that night.

"Okay, I'll try," she began. "I looked in the garage and could see the stairs up to the landing where they turn. I could see Robert's sister on the landing looking up – I don't know her name."

"Emma Black?" the lawyer offered.

"Yeah, Emma. She looked mad – her face was all twisted, you know, like really angry. I pushed past her and could see Robert at the door looking down toward Emma. He said..."

"No," the lawyer interrupted. "Just what you saw. Later I'll ask you to tell me what you heard – what he said."

She nodded her understanding and continued to report her ocular recollections. She was good at it. Most witnesses have to be reminded constantly what is expected of them. Some are totally incapable of separating their sensory observations.

"When Robert grabbed me, I could see the fury in his face – his eyes were wide, but it was like he didn't see me – spit was flying out of his mouth – I could see the room swirling around me – My mother's face flashed past – my sister looked frightened – almost hysterical – I saw a Coke bottle fly from the top of the cupboard and hit Robert on the forehead. All of a sudden I was sitting on the floor. Robert was laying face down on the kitchen floor. I could see blood everywhere – on the carpet – on Robert – on Bliss's hands and jeans. I saw her turn Robert over – tears were running down her face – her mouth was moving."

"Who was near you?" Joseph prompted.

"My sister was kind of kneeling down, Robert's head in her lap. My mother was standing by the washer and Emma was leaning over her brother. Her husband – I think his name is Jim – pushed her aside and leaned down and felt around Robert's shirt – took something – stood up and left. The boys were coming out of the bedroom with their stuff – I saw the guitar still in my hands, stood up and walked down the stairs. My mother walked behind me. We stopped in the back yard. People were everywhere. There was enough light from the street lights and the light on the garage so I could see everyone plain."

After she completed these observations, Joseph had her run through the same events, reporting what she heard, and then what she felt. She talked for a long time, pausing only long enough for Joseph to change tapes or for an occasional prompt. Joseph was fascinated. He had tried this experiment before but no one had ever isolated their senses so well or was able to call them up so completely. He was so intrigued by her ability that much of what she said got past him – but it didn't matter, it was on tape.

Finally, they broke for lunch. Arliss, needing approval, even from this stranger who didn't seem to care, asked, "Did I do good? Will it help?"

The lawyer congratulated her on her performance and assured her it would be quite helpful. Gay returned and was brought into the office with sandwiches that Della had the foresight to order. Arliss and Gay stayed for lunch, but just pushed the food around, eating nothing. Joseph, as fond as he was of food, found it hard to believe anyone could sustain life with such sparse eating habits.

Finally Arliss left, saying, "Mother, I'll wait for you in the car."

* * * * *

The lawyer began to make the same explanations to Gay that he had to her daughter. She interrupted, saying, "First, I want you to protect my husband and daughter, in that order. When I say my daughter, I mean Arliss. Frankly, at the moment, I don't much care what happens to Bliss. She has never been anything but a source of sorrow to Claude and me. I know that Robert is dead and am sorry about that – especially since he died from a shot I fired. I killed him. What happens to me doesn't much matter ... "

Joseph held up his hand commanding, "Stop!" in a voice that would tolerate no foolishness. "Look, we have been through this. I was retained by your husband to represent you, and I will. If you killed Tucci ... " She was shaking her head from side to side trying to interrupt, but he wouldn't let her. " ... We will decide whether or not you have any legal defense to that act."

Undeterred by her efforts to speak, he continued. "And you will help me. Do you understand? At the moment, you are the most at risk – the most vulnerable. We will therefore concentrate on you. If we learn something different as we go along, we may change directions – but, again, we'll do it my way. Is that understood?"

He was almost hoping she would tell him to go to hell and relieve him of the task of representing her, even though it was probably going to be pretty easy money – especially if he could make a package deal. He didn't want it at all if it were going to involve too much work.

"If you are unwilling to proceed on that basis, find another lawyer," he said, adding *Please!* in his thoughts.

She nodded reluctantly, holding something back. She would go along with him for now but had reservations about the approach outlined. She would not give her wholehearted support if Arliss might be in danger.

Without pausing for Gay to verbalize her thoughts, Joseph instructed her to tell her story in the same way as had Arliss. Gay was almost as good, reporting the facts in nearly the identical way as her daughter, with the added fillip that, when she saw Tucci fall, she thought it may have been due to his drinking and that he might have passed out. She also had the impression that Robert followed them up the stairs when they first arrived – that he had been on the landing with Emma in the midst of a violent argument they interrupted.

59

Joseph noted another distinction – Gay seemed truly sorry Tucci was dead.

Having completed this phase of the interview, Joseph asked, "Tell me exactly what you told the police about the shooting."

"I'm not sure I can remember the exact words, but I said to them something about Robert choking Arliss and I had to save her – even Bliss was yelling for him to stop – and then I pulled out the gun and tried to stop him."

"Gay, just repeat for me, as close as you can, exactly what you told Detective Redding in the conversation he recorded," Joseph directed.

"After telling him about taking the gun out, I said *I guess I must have shot him.*" Gay added, "Then Mr. Redding asked me if, while I was in the kitchen, and the struggle was going on, did I remember reaching into my pocket and grabbing the gun?"

"Not remember *remember,* I told him," she said. "But I must have reached in and done it."

"Why do you say you must have reached in and done it?"

"Because it was done."

"What did you do with the gun?"

"I don't remember clearly. I thought I dropped it – or maybe I picked it up. I really don't know. Emma and Bliss were down on the floor with Robert. Arliss and I were staring in amazement. The boys did what I told them, getting their stuff, putting it in our car. I told them to wait there and that I had to stay and help. Arliss was crying, kind of gagging – choking – I was holding her trying to help her – she was hysterical, you know."

"What did you do with the gun afterwards?"

"I don't really remember doing anything with it. I thought I might have put it in the car – I told the officer to look there for it, but he said he couldn't find it. Maybe I dropped it outside. I don't remember... I just don't know..." she said with a look of concentration on her face.

She continued repeating, almost verbatim, the conversation she had with Redding. It had lasted for hours. Her reporting of it trance like – her memory encyclopedic.

"Did you tell anyone you actually shot Tucci?" Redding had asked.

"No," she responded. "Because I didn't really know I had at the time."

"Did you think that it was purely coincidental that, after you pulled the gun and shot it, he fell?" Redding had asked her sarcastically.

"No. He was drunk, there was a struggle, he fell, I didn't know he was hurt until I saw the blood. Even then I didn't know that I had shot him. I did not know that I had really done it."

"Did there come a time when you suspected that something had happened?"

"I think when I was kept sitting in the car that there must be something more wrong with Robert than falling or they wouldn't make us wait. Then when the officer did that thing on my hands – you know, rubbed cotton on them and then put the cotton in a plastic thing."

"Did you submit to the test voluntarily?"

"Yes."

"Was it explained to you?"

"No, they – they just said they were going to do a test. They didn't actually say why, but it didn't take any Einstein to figure out why."

Joseph sat listening to her recitation thoughtfully. He waved her silent for a moment, reflecting on what she had said. He then pointed out to her that, during the entire time she had talked to the police, she never actually said she shot Tucci.

"Did you shoot him?" he asked with no little trepidation. It is a question a defense lawyer should never ask. It shouldn't make any difference.

She sat quietly for almost a minute in deep thought as though reliving the night – examining her memory of the events. She began to speak slowly, carefully,

"I don't know... I must have... He was shot... I didn't intend to... The gun was in my pocket, I saw the struggle, I took it out and held it up like this..." she said, demonstrating by pointing her right hand straight up toward the ceiling. "I yelled for Robert to quit and pulled the trigger as hard as I could. That's all I know!"

She covered her face with her hands, crying softly.

A feeling of relief passed through the lawyer. He was satisfied that she shot and killed Tucci. He wasn't going to have to go through a complicated trial. He could just plead her and didn't have to worry about a long trial disrupting his life or office. His inadequacies wouldn't be revealed and he could maintain the fiction that he was a trial lawyer and make a quite good fee besides. He hoped he would be able to talk the prosecutor into allowing Gay to plead to something less than murder. She didn't intend to kill Tucci and had been through a great deal already.

When Gay demonstrated how she had pointed the gun toward the ceiling, the loose sleeve of her jacket fell away from her wrist revealing two black wires taped to her arm. Curious, and thinking to relax her, Joseph inquired,

"What are those wires?"

She explained that they were attached to a TENS unit – a Trans cutaneous Electrical Nerve Stimulation. "It is," she said, "some sort of electrical device used to relieve chronic muscle or nerve pain."

"Why are you wearing it?" he inquired quizzically.

She explained that she had been bitten by a dog. The muscles in her right arm were torn and damaged and she had to undergo numerous operations, none of which relieved the pain.

"Do you wear it all of the time?" he asked.

"Most of the time. It's the only thing that helps – short of some quite hefty doses of medicine. I don't like the feeling I get from drugs so I wear this."

"Were you wearing it Saturday night?"

"Yes, I usually wear it to bed. It allows me to sleep."

He considered her answer. Then he suggested, "I think we've covered enough today. I want to listen to the tapes. We'll go over them together later.

"In all probability," he added, "you will be indicted. We'll deal with it when it happens. I'll try to arrange some way for you to surrender yourself – turn yourself in – to avoid having the police come to your home and arrest you. But if they do, make sure someone calls me immediately."

She caught her breath and her eyes widened slightly. For the first time, she seemed to recognize the enormity of the situation. *She, who had never even been in a courtroom, was probably going to be indicted for murder.*

Before she could react, he took her hand. "Listen Gay, I know this seems like the end of the world – it's a nightmare – the average person sees court as some place where only bad people go – they can't visualize themselves involved in the criminal justice system. But it can, and does, happen. The courts are supposed to mete out justice. Often horrible injustices are done. We can only guarantee one thing – we will do our best for you. Try not to lose it. Call me if you want to talk. I can't promise anything but an ear, yet. Sooner or later we will find out what happened. In the meantime, we'll do what we can."

He remembered the instructions from an old trial manual he once read. The elderly lawyer wondered whether she derived any comfort from it, or even understood what he was talking about. The article had explained that, except for the professional criminal, defendants pass through stages – just like people dealing with the death of a loved one. Psychologists say it is necessary to work from denial to acceptance. One facing criminal charges suffers through the same phases – denial – anger –hopelessness – finally acceptance. It is only in the final stage that a defendant can be of any help to his lawyer. Some never get there.

Joseph thought, *I've tried to describe this theory to others. No one seems to understand it or believe it applies to them. Everyone assumes he is unique – fits no pattern – let alone one over which he has no control. Maybe I do too. No wonder it's impossible to speed the process.*

A fine line must be walked in creating a relationship with a client in the beginning – an aura of hope allowed to exist so the client will not be overcome by despair. After reality sets in, an understanding of the possible consequences is permitted. Getting over the hump, he realized, is going to be a bitch.

Gay left the lawyer's office promising to return within a few days, and to call immediately if anyone contacted or served papers on her.

Joseph sat back exhausted and propped his feet in his usual manner. The uncommon mixed feeling of exhilaration for a new and unexpected challenge and sorrow for the damaged people cavorted in his head. He sought solace in his pigs. They, at least, were still smiling.

Eight

Feeling exhausted by the interviews, but slightly rejuvenated by the contemplation of his pigs, Joseph dozed for a few minutes. The rotund lawyer sat at his desk accomplishing nothing – thinking of the years past. Every young lawyer dreams of the kind of client that had just left his office – the challenge – the opportunity to showcase his abilities – the fame – the reputation. He had waited through his youth for such opportunity, and had grown old. *Maybe all we do is wait for life to pass until it is gone*, he thought, looking at the vision of himself passing through the years, changing before his closed eyes. Startled for some reason, he noticed the quiet. He dragged his contemplative eyes from his pigs and glancing at his hands noticed a slight tremor, wondering whether to attribute it to his age or thoughts. The desk clock said it was past five. A lovely summer afternoon being wasted. Disdaining the intercom, he called,

"Della, where the hell is everyone?"

It constantly amused him that *Della* was really his secretary's name – Della Raven. Her first name the source of much humor in the legal community. Though never mentioned by Joseph to Della, a comedic attempt to link the names *Della* and *Perry* was usually accompanied by a smirk and comment about the criminal practice – or lack thereof by other lawyers in town familiar with Joseph's office. Actually Della, like the original, was attractive, competent and fiercely loyal. They had been together since the lawyer settled in Milltown. The only difference between their relationship and that of the fictional pair was the lack of romantic inclinations. Della and Joseph were both married and each had several children and grandchildren. Even more boring, their respective spouses liked each other and made a frequent foursome at social gatherings.

Della had her coat on ready to leave but, in response to the mild lawyer's bellow, stuck her head into his office clutching a handful of outgoing mail. "Gone. Its past five and I'm leaving too. Do you want me to lock up?"

"No, go ahead, leave if you insist on working only half days. No wonder you never amounted to much."

64

She shrugged her shoulders, pulled a face and left by way of the back door. Joseph gathered himself, sighed and went through his going home preparation, looking at the next day's calendar and muttered, *"Aw, the hell with everything,"* locked up and left.

He climbed into an old, but nicely kept, pickup truck parked by the back door. He liked the image that he was common. In a very few minutes, he was pulling into the tree lined driveway of his home – some of the trees were young long before he – bending arch-like across the first couple hundred feet of pavement that opened to an expanse of lawn permitting a view of the old-fashioned saltbox house setting in the middle of his thirteen acres. His grandson called the driveway *The tunnel to Granny's house.*

The lawyer didn't mind that his grandchildren did not identify him with such things as the homestead, baking smells and Granny bread. They thought of him in terms of being busy, bad people and paying bills. One granddaughter coined the phrase, "Buy it. Papa will pay." Said with love and humor, it had no sting.

Driving up his drive and watching the house appear had the same effect as a very dry martini. It didn't take the place of one – it just felt like it – leaving Joseph with a relaxed, comfortable feeling at the end of each day.

Pulling into the attached garage, he loosened his tie and greeted Andy, his wolf-like, barn-dog. Joseph felt secure in his home, but wasn't naive. He was comfortable leaving his wife alone in the country knowing Andy was hanging around. He bent over to tousle the dog's furry ruff which Andy accepted with dignity and restraint. He was doing his job and needed no distraction. Joseph looked around satisfied with his world and wondering why he ever did anything to endanger it.

"Mary, I'm home," he called, walking in through the kitchen door, noting the slightly lived-in look of the spotlessly clean room bearing evidence of his wife's hobbies – a knitting needle and ball of yarn on the table – a shopping bag with some new fabric sitting on the floor. It seemed she always had some project going, the finished product always finding its way into another house – a sweater for a grandchild – an afghan for a friend.

Her usual response, "Humph."

"What's for dinner?"

"Nothing."

"Why?"

"Too hot."

"Put the air conditioning on."

"Too expensive."

A conversation repeated thousands of times. Early retirement was the bonus she claimed for the hundred-hour weeks spent raising their kids. She was right.

Reluctantly conceding her victory, he asked, "So, where do you want to go for dinner? What do you feel like eating?"

She knew he would resist going anywhere fancy since he had already pulled off his tie, removed his jacket and was working on getting out of his pants. "Pizza and beer would be nice," she suggested.

Together they did their early evening chores, feeding the animals – three dogs, six cats and two goats. The horses were gone since no one rode anymore. Getting rid of them was traumatic. Anything coming to live at the Joseph household received an *until death do us part* promise. Joseph wanted to raise a couple of pigs along with their other animals, but Mary put her foot down. Hence his collection of glass, ceramic and ornamental pigs housed at the office and in various places at home. His belief that, *He never met a pig that wasn't happy*, was evident in all corners of his life.

Over pizza and beer at a favorite spot, they chatted easily about the day's happenings. Mary didn't have much to report, but the way it was reported took most of the meal and reminded Joseph of life's purpose. "Homely' is a word that's come to be associated with ugliness. It really means "plain' or as Joseph recognized the unpretentious realities of life – a rose or a ragweed.

The evening was so comfortable Joseph was unwilling to put a damper on, but knew he had to. Mary read the papers. "Uh, Mary... You know the murder – the Tucci killing in the paper – the one in Mt. City," he began hesitantly. "Well... I picked it up today."

"What do you mean, picked it up?"

"Uh... Well, Mr. Bellow hired me. He's the husband of the lady that was there and who will probably be charged with the killing."

"No! Not a case that's going to be in the paper. You know I can't stand that. Besides, you haven't handled a criminal case in years. I thought you weren't going to do that anymore. I knew things were too quiet. Why can't you just have clients that don't get into the paper? I won't be able to go to the grocery store..." she groused.

Her reaction was not unexpected. She was serious about his work and truly hated what he did. She was proud of him and his belief in the importance of the legal system, but would never admit it, and Lord help anyone who criticized him in her presence. She would slowly work through her dissatisfaction with his most recent involvement and, sooner or later, forgive him for again screwing up her life. Things would soon return to their usual calm, chaotic, state – conditions not mutually exclusive in the Joseph household.

They returned home and settled into the family room before the television which provided a background murmur to a quiet, peaceful evening. Mary knitted and chattered, a comfortable framework for Joseph to review his notes of the tapes. Slowly becoming aware of a significant peculiarity in his examination of the conversations with both Gay and Arliss, he reached for the telephone. Mary asked, "Now, who are you calling?"

He told her, "I have to talk to Mrs. Bellow." She pointed at the clock. It could wait till morning. They retired and he tried to sleep, but the excitement, and fear, about the case that would live with him for the next several months were already starting to build.

Suggesting Mary might want to stay awake with him resulted in an emphatic "Humph!"

* * * * *

Rising early, he lazily worked his way through the morning chores, not allowing thoughts of the day ahead to interfere with his comfortable feelings. He arrived at the office before anyone else – usually the only time of the day that the office is sanely quiet. The phone was ringing as he walked in – his irritation already starting to build. Phones are a blight. They intrude on a man's peace – a terrible price to pay for a modicum of convenience. Constitutionally incapable of ignoring the ring, he pushed the speaker button and growled, "Joseph!"

"Pat? Mike Redding."

"Yeah Mike, it's me. What do you want this early in the morning? You working nights?"

"Thought you'd like to know. We're going to the Grand Jury today. Probably get a murder indictment against the Bellow woman. Going to ask for something on the daughter, too."

"I've talked to both of them, Mike. Why are you going after the daughter? She's dippy as hell, but I don't know what she could be charged with."

"Accessory. And, I think we'll get it. Cover me on this, Pat. It's my ass if they know I talked to you... " He didn't offer an explanation as to who 'they' were, but continued, "As soon as the indictments are filed, I'll give you a call to surrender your clients – walk them through. That'll save them being arrested and held until a judge can set bond. You know we like to have the night shift serve warrants."

"Thanks, Mike." Joseph was truly grateful for the help. "I'll be around the office all day today. Call me as soon as you hear and I'll have both of them ready to come in. And don't worry, I won't say a word to anyone."

"Okay." Then Redding finished with, "Mrs. Bellow seems like a nice lady. I'd hate to have her spend the weekend in our hotel. She don't look too well. I think her shanty-assed daughter could use a couple of nights with us though."

"Thanks again. Let me know as soon as possible. I suppose I owe you a drink."

"You should pop for a dinner at least."

Joseph punched the phone quiet just as Della walked in followed by the office crew. Joseph sat at his desk thinking and listening to the start-up bustle sounds of the office. He reached for a desk book and began to check the elements of the crimes of murder and an accessory. He could smell the coffee perking. When Della brought him a cup, he asked, "Della, would you get Mrs. Bellow on the phone for me? Redding called and told me an indictment is going to be handed down today and I promised him she and her daughter would be available to walk through booking."

As she turned to leave his office, the lawyer added, "Oh, and get Mr. Bellow on the phone, too. We need to talk to him about money. We have to get our retainer and somehow, guarantee the fees."

* * * * *

As arranged, the Bellows and Conrads arrived promptly. Roger Conrad was tall, slender, and stooped. His elongated head topped with nondescript lanky hair, more gray than expected for his apparent age, was fronted by a hollow cheeked face held upright on a skinny neck. He had nothing to say – literally nothing. When introduced he barely acknowledged the introduction, but extended his hand for a limp handshake. Content with his subservient role, he was a perfect foil for Arliss' petulance. The smallest whine creeping into her voice compelled his attention. It reminded Joseph of how a dog, hearing an unfamiliar command, cocks its head to present a fearful and perplexed countenance to its master. The expression rested familiarly in Conrad's colorless eyes.

On cue Arliss whined, "What's going to happen to me?"

Hiding his impatience at the daughter's self-centered approach to all things, Joseph began to explain, repeating what Redding had told him. "The process isn't difficult, but is time consuming and impersonal. The grand jury has indicted both of you for felonies. Gay, you have been charged with murder and Arliss, complicity. Based on that, a warrant has been issued for your arrest. Rather than have the police serve the warrant, I arranged for both of you to surrender yourselves at the Sheriff's office. A warrant and a copy of the indictment will be served on you there. You will then be in custody and taken to the booking office where they will ask a series of questions not related to the crime, but personal things they need to know about prisoners, health and so on."

The comment caused Arliss to emit a small shriek and Gay to open her mouth as though to ask a question.

Joseph waved them both silent and continued. "Your answers will be typed on a form by a booking officer who doesn't know how to type. All of this time you will be standing in front of a counter getting more and more impatient and upset. They won't ask questions about the crime, but if they do, of course, you won't answer. All other questions, you will answer honestly."

Studying both women to see if they understood, Joseph said, "After this ordeal, your photographs will be taken, a number dangling on your chest – full front and profile. Fingerprints will be collected. A deputy will roll ink on a glass pad and press your fingers in the gooey mess. He will place them on cards. This will be repeated several times – none of which makes any sense. He will provide a piece of gauze to clean your hands. It won't. All of this done in a way that you will find demeaning and demoralizing. The officer does this so often that it, and you, have little significance to him. It is just a job. You will then be placed into a holding cell until it's time to go to court."

He went on to explain what he had learned from Detective Redding. "When someone is charged with a crime and arrested – especially for murder – they are rarely afforded the courtesies that have been extended to you. The warrants are almost always served in the middle of the night. People are usually home then, and when awakened from a sound sleep, are easier to handle – less problem for the police. After being booked, the persons arrested are stripped, searched and given an orange jump suit with the words *Mills County Jail* stenciled across the back and held in jail with other criminals until a court date is set. Under such circumstances people become convinced no one else in the world knows or cares where they are or what is happening. It is truly scary."

The four sat quietly, horror, shock and fear playing across their faces. Gay seemed the calmest of all. Joseph continued. "As a special favor, the deputies are allowing me to be with you during the process. As soon as you're booked, we will walk across the parking lot to the courthouse where you'll be arraigned and bond set. When you make bond, you'll be released."

Joseph decided to take some credit. "All of this has been arranged in advance because you are my clients. Most unfortunates aren't treated so kindly. This is especially so in Cleveland or any other big city. Anyone indicted for a crime is automatically arrested or summoned to court and put through the whole demeaning process by themselves without their lawyer being present. The process usually takes a half-day or more while the individual sits in a cell with a bunch of other people charged with various crimes. Being charged with a crime, is not pleasant. The process is humiliating, embarrassing and frightening."

Having completed the rather lengthy explanation, Joseph stood. "Mr. Bellow... Mr. Conrad... you can either wait here or in the courtroom, whichever you choose. It'll take a couple of hours, but the judge's secretary assured me the courtroom would be empty and the judge would be available for arraignment as soon as the booking is completed. We'll be in Judge Clarke's courtroom – that's courtroom number two in the new courthouse."

He then ushered the four from his office, the men assuring their wives they would be waiting for them. As the lawyer and his clients walked out of the building and across the Square, Joseph noted that everything had a surreal normalcy about it. The sun still shone. It was a beautiful, bright day. The town was alive. Even though it was early in the morning, people were already sitting on the iron benches in the park – children played in the grass and on the canon that memorialized some patriotic historical event. The Gazebo bore remnants of a weekend wedding – the City's service crew tended the lawn and flowers. A beautiful summer day for everyone except the ladies walking on either side of him.

They passed the red brick Victorian structure dubbed the *Old Courthouse* attached to a newer yellow-brick building called the *New Courthouse*, built about twenty-five years ago. Lack of imagination in naming places and things was endemic to Mills County.

The Sheriff's office, the jail and the exercise compound were located to the rear of the courthouses that shared the East side of the Square. Inmates, in bright orange, were working on the narrow strip of lawn in front of the jail, ignoring or smirking at passing pedestrians and vehicles, depending on how close the guard was watching. Several trustees smiled and said, "Hi, Mr. Joseph. How are you? How's it hangin'?" At least some of the miscreants knew him. He hoped Mrs. Bellow and her daughter were impressed.

Joseph returned the smiles and nodded, feeling Mrs. Bellow shudder at his side. She held tightly to his arm. Opening the front door of the jail, they could look up the stairs and see a steel-barred door behind which the sounds of raucous laughter, catcalls and whimpering could be heard. Arliss and Gay crowded close to the plump lawyer.

Downstairs, more bars were visible. A heavy steel door was the only opening into the booking area. The small entry office was manned by a civilian. The lawyer inquired, "Excuse me, is Mr. Redding here? These ladies agreed to surrender to him. He said he'd meet us here."

"He isn't in yet, Mr. Joseph, but he is expecting you," the middle-aged woman at the reception desk responded.

The casual conversation – the air of normalcy increased his companions' horror. They could remember the night spent elsewhere in the same building and wondered how anyone could act so civilly while their lives were being torn apart. He could feel the tenseness growing.

"Can I take Mrs. Bellow and Mrs. Conrad back to booking and get started?" Joseph asked. "Mike can see us when he comes in."

The sympathetic receptionist appreciated what the mother and daughter were going through and, with a smile said, "Sure, why don't you do that? I'll get someone to take you back."

"Thanks," he expressed their appreciation. The women added nothing.

A uniformed prison guard opened the steel entry door with a gigantic, old-fashioned key and escorted the small party into a closet sized area. Another metal door barred the way. Only when the first door was closed and secured, could the second door be unlocked. The solid thud of the steel door had an expected effect. Joseph had been there before but still suffered a claustrophobic, will-I ever-be-able-to-get-out, reaction. He knew what it must be doing to the ladies.

The booking process was accomplished. Redding showed up about halfway through, left again on unexplained business and promised to return in time to walk to the courthouse. Once in custody, the mother and daughter would be allowed to go nowhere unaccompanied by an officer – in fact handcuffs would be used on the short walk across the parking lot – which caused Arliss to break out in hysterical tears and Gay to walk even taller in stony silence after admonishing Arliss to "hush."

Mike kept his word and they arrived promptly at Judge Clarke's courtroom in time for Gay and Arliss to be arraigned.

Nine

Thomas A. Clarke looked like a judge. Well past middle years, he had been on the bench for most of his professional life – a relatively hard working civil servant proud of his office. He made an effort to be fair and dedicated but didn't have the tools. Good trial judges aren't created, they're born. Evidentiary decisions must be made instinctively and immediately while mediating the heat of battle. There is no time to sit and ponder. Judge Clarke was uncomfortable making decisions, at any time, let alone in a courtroom. The failing was masked by an aura of grouchiness and short-temper – a mantle he wore like his robes.

Joseph thought, not for the first time, *He uses words as a device to avoid making decisions.*

When compelled to make a ruling from the bench, Judge Clarke would repeat over and over the facts as he viewed them, rarely the same twice and rarely accurately. The agonized expression on his face articulated clearly his wish that someone – anyone – would relieve him of the ordeal. It was a frustrating experience for a lawyer, to be avoided whenever possible. Fortunately in recent years Joseph rarely suffered through a trial.

Mr. Bellow and his son-in-law, Roger Conrad, as promised, were waiting nervously in the spectators' area of the courtroom. Bellow paled at the sight of handcuffs on Gay's wrists. Conrad, who after glancing at his wife, never raised his eyes from the spot he was studying between his feet and took no notice of her shackles.

Joseph was surprised to see, sitting at the State's trial table, the Prosecutor herself, Jacqueline VanDamm. *She must believe this a very important case. She knows it's a dead-bang winner for her,* he mused.

The lawyer asked Redding to remove the handcuffs and seated Gay and Arliss at the defense table. Walking to the prosecutor, he asked, "Jackie, what are you doing here? I thought one of your assistants would handle such a rather routine arraignment."

Jackie responded, "Oh, I heard you were involved and wondered why. It's pretty cut and dried – what with a confession and all. I wasn't too busy this morning so I thought I would just wander over and see what's happening. Actually Brad," her number one trial assistant, "will be handling the arraignment and bond hearing."

Jacqueline VanDamm had been elected County Prosecutor after a hard-fought, sometimes not-so-nice political battle with the former incumbent. Even though there was a lot of name-calling and thinly veiled allegations of wrongdoing in office, she managed to win without tarnishing her image as a lady. Joseph followed her career in the papers and was rather impressed, even a little awed, despite her youth.

She was quite attractive, with shiny black hair kept short and neat, dark brown expressive eyes, in her early thirties, and with a slender build described by those who make such judgments as being curvaceous. Truly a charmer. Jackie hadn't been in the practice very long when she was sought out by her party to run against the incumbent prosecutor who had become too complacent. Being from an old politically connected family in the community, he was convinced no one could beat him, especially a political neophyte. He misjudged Jackie's willingness to work and, to his dismay, lost a very close race.

Jackie had little trial experience, but talked easily and enjoyed the attention and adulation her office brought. She was willing to, and did, devote a great deal time and energy to the job – a combination that carried her nicely. Thinking of her as *just a young girl* would come back to haunt an unwitting opponent.

Her number one assistant, T. Grant Bradley, had been around longer, having been imported from another county. No one knew what the "T' in his name stood for – certainly not "Timid." He was a capable and competent trial lawyer, but too ready to use any device to gain an advantage, borderline or not. A vicious man, he displayed proudly the white hat of self-righteousness issued with the job as a reason for his behavior. He was not well liked.

He sought convictions, not justice. His attitude exuded a belief that the good people of his state and the criminals were at war and whatever is needed to win, is appropriate. Why be bound by proprieties when the enemy isn't? He kept statistics on his convictions like a ballplayer records his batting average.

The participants took their seats, Scott David the court reporter, at his place in front of the bench. The Bailiff, Art Gruen, intoned the ritual, "All rise... This Honorable Court is now in session pursuant to adjournment... The Honorable Thomas A. Clarke, presiding. All those with business before this Court draw near and ye shall be heard. Please be seated."

Judge Clarke mounted the high bench overlooking the courtroom, nodded "Good morning," and shuffled the papers before him, reciting, "This is case number ... *The State of Ohio vs. Gabriella Bellow.* Present in court is Ms. VanDamm on behalf of the State and the defendant with counsel, Mr. Pat Joseph. Is everyone ready to proceed?"

Jackie VanDamm responded, "We are, Your Honor."

Joseph stood and said, "The defense is also ready, Your Honor."

"Proceed," the judge instructed.

"We have just this morning received a copy of the indictment charging Mrs. Bellow with the crime of murder," Joseph informed the court. "We waive a reading of the indictment, acknowledge receipt and waive the statutory time requirements of service so that we may proceed to arraignment and the setting of bail – if that is all right with the Court?" Joseph had prepared this little speech in advance and was confident that he sounded like he knew what he was talking about.

"Certainly, Mr. Joseph."

"Since we have not had an opportunity to review the charging document, we will not enter a plea for the defendant, advising her to stand mute. I request that the court enter the statutorily mandated plea of *Not Guilty* on her behalf, reserving the right to raise any defects in the indictment."

Judge Clarke nodded his consent, saying, "The Court will enter a *Not Guilty* plea on Mrs. Bellow's behalf," as he made a notation on the papers before him. "Is there anything else, Mr. Joseph?"

"We request that bail be set, and would like to address that issue, your Honor."

"Go on, Mr. Joseph."

"As you know, Your Honor, Mrs. Bellow lives in a neighboring community, is a home owner and her husband owns an old and well-established family business in Cleveland." Joseph hoped this was true.

"She is a parent, grandparent, and as unbelievable as it may seem, a great-grandparent. She has no record – not even a traffic violation – has lived an impeccable life. I request the court set a personal recognizance bond."

Jackie VanDamm shot to her feet. "Judge, Mr. Joseph can't be serious. This lady is charged with murder. She may be entitled to bail – but a P. R. bond is ridiculous."

Joseph flushed but continued doggedly. "Oh, Your Honor, Ms. VanDamm's comment notwithstanding, I don't think I'm ridiculous. I am quite serious.

The only purpose for bail is to guarantee the defendant's presence as required. She has made herself available this morning. In fact, she surrendered herself as soon as she heard there was a warrant for her arrest. She has cooperated in every way possible. To punish her by sending her to jail until bond can be posted would be cruel. Her health is iffy at best and we certainly don't want to add to her burdens. She is more than willing to abide by any conditions of bail that the court might wish to set." Then as an aside, the lawyer needled the prosecutor with, "I thought you said Brad was going to handle this hearing, Jackie."

Jackie VanDamm blushed furiously, but said nothing.

Judge Clarke looked from the lawyer to Mrs. Bellow. A social friend, he believed Joseph would never put him in an embarrassing position and said, almost reluctantly, "Mr. Joseph, I will set a personal recognizance bond on your personal assurance that the defendant will continue to be available as required. She will, however, report weekly to the Adult Probation Department."

Not a minor victory, Joseph was rather proud of himself.

"Accepted your Honor, and Mr. and Mrs. Bellow express their appreciation for your consideration and generosity." A little flattery didn't hurt.

Having completed Gay's arraignment, the process was repeated with Arliss Conrad charged as an accessory. To Ms. VanDamm's dismay, Arliss was also granted a personal recognizance bond. "Joseph," the prosecutor said. "You get away with murder."

"I hope not, Jackie. Fair is fair. I'd like to discuss the matter of discovery with you as soon as possible. Let's get this thing started so my people can get out from under this cloud."

"Don't bullshit me, Pat! You know goddamn well we got a confession! Why don't you just plead her – the Judge won't send her to jail for long – she's an old lady."

Jackie and the lawyer had walked out of Gay's hearing to speak more freely, Jackie adding, "She shot her son-in-law. Maybe he deserved it – I don't know. If you plead her to the charge, we might be willing to dismiss against her daughter. Ask her – see what she says."

"Not yet, Jackie, I need to do some investigating first," the elder lawyer answered secretly pleased. The best he could hope for was a quick plea and a possible reduction to some lesser charge like manslaughter or something similar. He would have to do some quick research.

"Trying to justify your fee, Pat?" The needle was returned. The thought passed fleetingly through the lawyer's mind, *It might be fun to try a case against Jackie. She would make a worthy opponent.*

"Jackie, you're a beautiful girl – sexy as hell – but you got a smart mouth. It really won't do you any good to fuck with me." The obscenity was lost on her – this generation didn't seem to know what's vulgar – she didn't even seem to know he was being insulting. "I'm getting too old to understand you kids," he muttered under his breath – a complaint, he imagined, uttered at least once by every generation.

The lawyer walked his clients back to the office, warmed by the minor victories – warning them that it wasn't necessarily a portent of what was to come. But for now, the sun was shining a little brighter.

"Mr. Bellow," the lawyer said as he shook hands goodbye in front of his office, "Now that this has started, drop off a check as soon as possible. It will, however, be several days before you hear from me."

It would be weeks, or months, before another court appearance – the wheels of justice and so on. There would, nevertheless, be considerable work to do what with investigation, discovery requests and other motions. God he was going to be busy. *Why do I do this to myself?*

Ten

Milltown, being the county seat, housed many law offices. Joseph's was among the busiest. He had several young lawyers who handled routine matters, reserving for himself as little work as possible or that which particularly interested him. He believed he had paid his dues and found it time to reap the benefits. Yet he wanted to know what was happening. In order to stay current with office activity, he scheduled a weekly staff meeting at four o'clock on Fridays. It also acted as an excuse to serve cocktails to Della and himself and break early for the weekend.

Somehow, everyone in the office managed to clear time for the staff meeting. Another tradition born.

After drinks were served, the staff would sit around in the elder lawyer's office, crowding into the client chairs, the couch, and sometimes even sitting on the floor. The relaxed atmosphere encouraged conversation of the week's activities past and plans for the next.

Trent Fillia, recently admitted to the Bar, had clerked for Pat Joseph while a law student. A handsome young man who, with unmanageable black hair and a friendly grin that belied his intelligence and strength of purpose, was unabashedly devoted to the elder lawyer. Though handling it well, he barely tolerated and was often impatient with, the routine work assigned to him, always waiting for the opportunity to show how capable he was. He could hardly wait for "the case" to come into the office.

After clearing his throat to get Mr. Joseph's attention, Trent said, "Uh... I've been looking over the Bellow's file. The B.C.I.'s... you know the State Bureau of Criminal Investigation's report and witness' statements are in it. I've read it all and would kind of like to talk to some of the witnesses if it's all right? You know... go out and see the Tucci home. Kind of get a feel of things."

Joseph had been impressed by the young man's work, and was pleasantly surprised at the way he constantly volunteered time on files not assigned to him. Trent's undergraduate degree was in Criminal Justice. He brought his training, investigative skills and curiosity to each task with such an abundance of youthful exuberance and energy it exhausted others working with him. Joseph was reminded, not without a little envy, of the stamina he used to have.

"I know what B.C.I. means, and, yes, it's all right with me, Trent... " Joseph couldn't be more pleased. He felt somewhat at a loss as to how to begin preparing this particular murder case what with a confession and all. "But, I would like you to listen to the interview tapes of Mrs. Bellow and her daughter. I noticed something odd."

"Be happy to, Mr. Joseph." He could never bring himself to use the lawyer's first name. "What did you hear?" he asked. "I reviewed the transcripts and they seem quite straight forward to me – outside the fact that both women have fantastic recall." He was lost in thought for a minute trying to recreate what he had read, then changed the subject briefly.

"By the way, I put together the usual motions – Discovery – Bill of Particulars – Suppression. Thought you might want to get rid of the statements. They could hurt. The cops have already labeled them *confessions* to the newspapers."

He was talking about the Supreme Court's exclusionary rule that statements or evidence gathered without proper Constitutional safeguards could not be used at trial in an effort to control overzealous police from short cutting their work. The Supreme Court made clear its philosophy about gathering evidence: *Do it right or you don't get to use it.*

"Go ahead and prepare them, but don't file them yet. We might think about it first. Maybe the *confessions* can be used to our advantage." Joseph began to get interested in the conversation despite himself. "I've reviewed the statements several times. Gay never actually said she shot Tucci. In fact she insisted she was unaware Tucci was shot until the police told her. She told Redding she'd been under the impression Tucci had either passed out drunk or was knocked out by the bottle flying off the cupboard. She brought the gun, took it out of her pocket, pointed it at the ceiling and pulled the trigger, but didn't know Tucci was shot until the police told her."

Looking at the file notes supplied by Trent, Joseph observed, "She said she must have shot Tucci, because it happened in response to a question put to her by Redding. Why wouldn't she just say up front, *I shot him?* Especially when she was so willing to admit everything else."

Since they were talking about what Gay said, the lawyer continued. "Getting back to Gay's and Arliss's tapes, I may as well tell you what struck me as being so strange." He was already thinking of the clients on a first name basis – particularly Gay whom he found so appealing.

"I listened to both several times. You're right about one thing, Trent. Both women have almost total recall. Remarkable! When I asked Arliss about her sensory perceptions, she identified everything she saw, heard, and felt. She talked about feeling the guitar pressing against her body, feeling Tucci's hands around her throat. She actually could feel the calluses on his hands. When she started to talk about what she heard, she said she heard the crash of glass breaking – the jingle of dishes in the cupboard. She could see the colors rushing by as she was thrown around the room."

At this point, Joseph paused, hoping Trent would have noticed the same discrepancy as he. He didn't want to look foolish in front of the young man. Trent sat with a blank expression and an expectant smile.

Shrugging, Joseph continued. "It is when Arliss was talking about what she heard that I first noticed a significant gap in the story. I checked it on Gay's tape and found the same gap. Trent, didn't you notice anything unusual about what the women said they heard? Or more important what they had not heard?"

Trent reflected for a moment, shook his head slowly and said, "I'm sorry... but no... I can't think of anything. What'd I miss?"

"Neither woman *heard* the sound of the gun being fired," Joseph said. "It took awhile, but it finally dawned on me. Both women were able to report every detail, even the sound the guitar made as it hit the floor. When neither described the sound of the gunshot, it eventually jumped out at me. I replayed the tapes to find out what both said they saw ... Neither reported seeing the flash of a gunshot."

The room grew silent. "I listened to the tapes two or three times and compared them – same thing! It surprised the hell out of me."

The silence continued, broken only when Trent asked, "Are you sure, Mr. Joseph?" Della tried to shush him with a furtive frown. Not many had the courage to ask Joseph if he was sure of anything.

Joseph's response was immediate and sharp. "Of course, I'm sure. I wouldn't say it if I weren't!" he said, displaying little patience. "I'm just not sure what it means. It seems important enough, however, to warrant a thorough investigation."

Joseph's trepidation at being involved in a murder case was giving way to intellectual curiosity. He began to relax after another sip from his martini glass.

"Trent, why don't you talk to the arms instructor at Akron U? Ask him if he'd mind reviewing B.C.I.'s ballistics reports on the murder weapon. See if there's something about the gun or the bullet we should know. Prepare the motions too, but don't file for Suppression until we have a chance to talk about whether the statements could be useful to us."

Then, to Della he said, "I'm a little worried about our fees. Find out what you can about Bellow's finances." This was her forte.

"Trent, I think you're right about talking to the witnesses. Go ahead do it. Canvas the neighborhood in case somebody might have seen or heard something. We need to know what the gossip is. I think I'll go out to Mt. City and have a drink with *Hey* Smith."

Trent, only a little chastened by his slip, suggested, "We should probably ask Mrs. Bellow and Mrs. Conrad about what you noticed in their tapes – but maybe not at the same time. Like to verify that the lapse in memory wasn't coincidental."

It sounded like a good idea, so the lawyer asked, "Della will you set that up for the middle of next week? Trent, you do it. But not until you've listened to the tapes. In the meantime, I'm going to ask a pathologist I know to take a look at the autopsy report to see what he can tell me about Tucci."

Della took notes of Joseph's instructions. It was good to see him get so involved and begin to get excited about a case. Joseph paused for breath, then said, "I think that's all for now. Have I missed anything?"

No response. He knew Della would type a set of instructions to be placed on each desk Monday morning. The excitement of the case was getting to her too. No one would want to bother with office routine while working on this, the biggest case ever to hit the office.

The mystery filled Joseph's thoughts. He didn't know if the others felt the same exhilaration mingled with trepidation, but it didn't matter. They would respond with a will. It made for a warm feeling.

Joseph settled back to enjoy the rest of his martini.

* * * * *

Just before Monday noon, Joseph made the short trip to Mt. City. Parking in front of *The Bar,* he stepped around the no longer used hitching rail and across the boardwalk, peering into the gloom of Hey's establishment. He called, "Hey, how you doin'? In fact, where the hell are you? I can't see a goddam' thing."

The clear, bright sunshine outside was not invited into the sanctum of *The Bar*. His eyes adjusting to the artificial twilight, Joseph located Smith. There was no need to look far. Hey was at his usual post – generous ass resting lightly on the edge of the high stool, beer spigots in reach.

"Hello Pat. It's been awhile since you been here. Thirsty? Or want somethin' else? You getting too important to drink in my place?"

While bawling out the lawyer with his usual dour good humor, Smith was already drawing a beer from the tap in front of him. He signaled for Joseph to take a stool and placed the chilled mug in front of him. Joseph's vision had adjusted sufficiently to find Hey and the draft. One looked appealing, the other unchanged.

Probably because of the time of day, *The Bar* was virtually empty except for an overall clad farmer, oblivious to all but his world, slumped at the far end of the bar, elbows surrounding a mug over which his chin hovered. Joseph observed silently that the beer wouldn't have to travel far from glass to throat. The only other sign of life was Hey's old yellow cat sitting on the back bar ignoring everyone. Joseph couldn't tell whether a growl or purr occasionally emanated from the shadows – the cat probably didn't know either.

Joseph, satisfied the conversation would not be overheard said, "Just stopped in for a cool one. Going over to Hardrock for a fish sandwich." The Hardrock was an exclusively local restaurant outsiders rarely frequented – to their bad fortune. The owners and clientele wanted it to stay that way. "Thought I'd stop by for a beer first."

"You know Pat, you was always full of shit," Hey said without rancor. "They got beer over at Hardrock. Nothing special about mine. What you after? The Tucci killing?"

Smiling, Joseph said, "Goddam Hey, I'm glad you were never on one of my juries. Can't bullshit you."

He added with a sigh, "You're right, I'm on the Tucci case. Biggest damn thing I've ever done and I'm scared shitless. You know Gay Bellow and her daughter were indicted. I need to know what happened. If anybody around here knows anything, you do."

"Why me?" Hey shrugged. "You know I never leave this place ... you ready?" he asked reaching for the lawyer's glass.

Joseph had consumed little more than half of the beer, but it was such a hot, dusty day, the balance slid down easy. He circled a finger over the glass signing that Smith might pour another. It might make him more garrulous. "All right, one more," he said, adding, "You know goddam' well why I'm asking you. Nothing happens in this town without you knowing. What happened that night?"

Hesitating only long enough to gather his thoughts, Hey began to talk.

"Tucci, the guy what was killed, was here most of the afternoon with his brother-in-law. You know, Jim Black? A couple of other guys was with them – Jerry from over in Grafton, and Chick. They was someone else I didn't know – Chick's brother, I think."

He paused for a minute, hand on the tap, an inquiring look in his eye. Joseph sat with his hand over top of the mug shaking his head. Smith continued, pointing, "They was sitting in that corner over there by that table. At first Tucci was like normal, you know, laughing, noisy, full of piss – but Jim was sitting with his face in his beer, drinking heavy. After a while I heard Tucci say somethin' like, *What the fuck's wrong with you? You look like someone's been banging your old lady?* Then he laughed like it was a joke.

"Jim looked up and said something I couldn't hear – but all five of them got real quiet. I thought to myself, *Oh, shit! Jim's found out about Roper!*"

"Who's Roper? What's there to find out?" the lawyer asked, convinced he'd come to the right source. He would learn more from Smith than anyone else and had already added to his knowledge of the participants. It was getting interesting.

"You know Roper, Pat. He lives out back. He thinks he's quite a lady's man. He's always in some kind of trouble. Nothing big or serious, but the man'll fuck anything that stands still and some things that don't. He and Tucci's sister, Emma, used to get it on back when they was in school. After she married Jim Black, Roper started sniffing' around again. He'd come in here bragging on how he's gonna get some. He's kind of slimy. No one likes him, but that don't shut his mouth. Spreads most of his bullshit here."

Hey paused for breath, not used to talking so much. He drew another beer for the lawyer, this time without asking, and one for himself, paying for both from the change sitting on the bar in front of Joseph. The lawyer didn't protest – not wanting to interrupt.

"Then, about three weeks ago, he comes in here and don't say nothing about Emma. He looks like a man what's got lucky – had a beer and left. He comes in almost every afternoon. Emma had started to come in kinda' regular too – when the kids was asleep – you know, for a quick one. Like I said, they both stopped coming in about the same time. I don't think anyone noticed. At least no one said nothing about it."

He ruminated. "You know Pat, Emma's Mamma used to come in here regular when Emma and Rob was little – like in the afternoons when the salesmen stop by. She started going off with them like she was working the place. I told her I wasn't no pimp and to quit fooling with my clients – sound like I'm a big time lawyer, huh? She finally run off and never come back. Old man Tucci raised the kids by himself and never said nothing about it, except that she'd be back. Maybe the daughter didn't fall far from the tree."

Joseph understood, mixed metaphor notwithstanding.

Hey shook his head to dislodge the reminiscence. "Anyway, I was afraid if Jim found out about Roper somehow, he'd do something bad. Tucci was worse. I remember, when his Mamma disappeared, he sort of curled inside himself – didn't talk to nobody – but got real mean. He took good care of Emma, but if she got out of line, he'd punish her – not like a kid would – like a grown-up. He'd make her stay in her room or sit on the porch watching the other kids – not allowed to play. He'd watch her like a hawk. It was kind of scary."

Again, shifting gears and drawing another beer, searching through the pile of change, he continued. "I don't know what he'd do to her today, if anything, but I could tell he was mad. Not loud mad, but really pissed. He just sat there not saying nothing, sucking down beers and shots with Jim. Didn't do nothing to either of them. Jerry, Chick and the other guy was... like embarrassed... saying they wanted a sandwich or something, and left. Tucci and Jim sat by themselves – must a been an hour. Jerry and the others came back and they all left together out my back door and across the yard to their place. When they passed Roper's, I could see Jim and Tucci looking at the house. I was sure glad I wasn't him, that's for sure."

Joseph looked at the fourth beer, not sure he could finish it without leaving a puddle. He was starting to feel a little lightheaded too, but didn't want to interrupt.

"It was getting dark – maybe eight o'clock. Lots of people were stopping in for a drink before the fireworks, you know, get a beer and go out and sit on the sidewalk to see the fireworks across the street. I was really busy until the fireworks started. At the end, you know, they shoot off all the leftover stuff like a grand finale, so I stepped out to watch. Some folks started to wander back in, and, as I was coming in the door I seen this girl, you know Tucci's stepdaughter, half running toward the corner, carrying a baby. She was crying and swearing at the same time. The guy that had been with Tucci and Chick drove up and said something to her. She stopped and looked at him, real mean like, and said, *Tell that fucker I'm not comin' back!* The guy talked to her for a minute soft-like so I couldn't hear... and she got in the car. They drove away. I didn't think much about it, except maybe Tucci's acting up like he sometimes does."

"What happened next?" Joseph prodded.

"A little later – maybe an hour or so – I hear screaming and someone comes in and says he'd just seen Jim's wife, Emma, running to the corner yelling to Denny the deputy about somebody getting shot. She'd run up to him and says, *Denny! Denny! My brother Robby's been shot!* Then they ran back to her house. I hadn't heard no shooting and didn't know anything'd happened. Later, I heard sirens and looked out the back door. There was like a hundred people in Tucci's yard."

"Hey, you're a gold mine," Joseph smiled. "You damn near destroyed me with the beers, but they're worth every nickel. You sure Emma said her brother'd been shot?"

"Ain't a nickel, it's five bucks, and I ain't sure of nothing. That's what the guy that came in said."

Leaving the change on the counter, Joseph handed Hey a ten-dollar bill, used the john, thanked and waved goodbye to Smith on his way out. He couldn't eat a fish sandwich now with all the beer sloshing around – but he hadn't wanted one anyway. Stepping off the boardwalk in front of his car, an ugly green station wagon skidding around the corner almost clipped him. He jumped back in time to avoid being hit. Looking at the retreating vehicle, he muttered, "What the hell's wrong with her?" Shrugging it off as being of no great consequence, he got into his car and left.

Eleven

The next several days were taken up with routine chores. *The trouble with having to earn a living,* Joseph mused, *is that the work bringing in the money has to be done. Day to day stuff pays the bills. It'd be nice to be so wealthy I could pick and choose only the cases that interest me. Unfortunately, the employees, Mary, Uncle Sam, the Governor and everyone else it seems, wants a piece of me.*

By the following Friday's cocktail/staff meeting, everyone had covered their respective assignments, and more. Joseph reported on the conversation with Hey Smith. Trent had checked and found that Gay and Arliss had no criminal past. Bliss, on the other hand, had an extensive record. She had been in trouble since high school – which she never finished – and did jail time in both Ohio and Pennsylvania. Tucci had nothing major – minor traffic offenses and an assault several years earlier.

Claude Bellow had financial problems. Della was afraid that the fee for representing Gay and Arliss was not protected, so she prepared a note to be secured by a mortgage on the Bellow home. She suggested to Joseph that it be signed before the firm got in any deeper. It was, for all the good it did.

Trent reported on his meeting with the professor from College of Akron criminal justice department. "Dr. Janus said he has some familiarity with the type of gun the State has identified as the murder weapon. It's a .32-caliber Smith & Wesson hammerless revolver manufactured for several years just after the turn of the century. It's small – what they call a pocket model – with a short barrel and a built-in safety that requires the grip be squeezed against the heel of the hand in order to fire it. The cylinder on this gun often becomes loose with age. The tolerances weren't really precise in those days, and it generally sprays gunshot residue on the hands of a shooter when it's fired."

Trent was enjoying being the center of attention as the others listened with interest to what he was saying. He added, "Gunshot residue consists of two chemicals, barium and antimony, chemicals not generally found in combination except when used as a primer charge in bullets. The type of bullet that killed Tucci used barium and antimony in the charge."

Trent consulted his notes and continued. "The test done to determine whether gunshot residue is present on someone's hands is called an *atomic absorption* test. It is done by swabbing the hands of a suspect with a Q-Tip saturated in a diluted solution of nitric acid. The solution is heated, centrifuged and placed in a machine that does an absorption analysis. This detects the most minute particles of barium and antimony, up to 99.5 percent accuracy."

The young lawyer continued pedantically. "As a result of my talks with Dr. Janus, I went to Richfield and talked to the State's ballistics expert. Everything he told me was exactly what I learned from Dr. Janus. But," he smiled pausing to emphasize the importance of the discovery he made, "he provided an additional piece of interesting information."

Trent had everyone's attention. "He explained that the murder weapon was old – which I knew – between fifty and eighty years old. He said it must have sat in a dresser or on a shelf unused for some time because it's in excellent condition. None of the nickel plating's worn off. He said this means that it hadn't been carried in a pocket or purse for any length of time. It had been used, but was well cared for. Very clean. The cylinder is a little loose and would spray the chemicals we talked about. They tested the bullets that were in the weapon when they found it and the casing of the shell that had been fired. Barium and antimony were present in the primer."

Getting to the good part, Trent added casually, "Oh, and one more thing. The trigger and safety are very stiff and it would really be difficult for a lady to shoot the gun. The trigger pull is more than twelve pounds. The criminalist said he repeated the test several times because it was so unusual. There's no question about the stiffness of the trigger pull."

Joseph blurted out, "I don't know how helpful any of this is, but it really aggravates me. None of it's in the police reports or the discovery provided us. They get what they call a confession and the investigation stops. Police refuse to see a goddamn thing but what's right in front of them. Talk about justice! They don't care if they get to the truth or not – just get the case off the books...."

Trent watched with rapt attention. He rarely heard Joseph get excited about anything and was pleased he'd played a part in firing his interest.

Pausing to take a breath and bank his coals, Joseph proceeded more calmly. "When I was a kid, ice was delivered by horse and wagon. The horse wore a device on his head called blinders. Once I asked the iceman what it was. He told me it was so the horse could only see straight ahead – not be distracted by what was going on around him. The police operate the same way."

Trent grinned, thankful the older lawyer was willing to share his feelings about the criminal justice system. It was good to know that some old-timers were able to retain, or maybe renew, the fervor begun in law school. He continued his report. "The autopsy report said Tucci was killed with a .32 slug – a contact wound – with powder burns on his head where the bullet entered just below and to the rear of the right ear. The bullet traveled on a slightly upward course through the brain and most of it came to rest near the left temple. It wasn't like the police described."

Joseph again shook his head. "I'm amazed by what the police leave undone. It's as though they deliberately want to avoid the truth."

Trent said, "I talked to a lot of people in the neighborhood. It's all in my report. There are two witnesses I think you should question, Mr. Joseph. Tom Roper," Joseph's ears perked up at the name, "and Bliss Tucci. She calls herself by that name even though she never married Tucci. She wouldn't talk to me, but I know where she lives. Maybe she'll talk to you."

"Trent, you've covered lots of ground. No more talk – I'll read your report. Now, it's time for another drink. Fix me a martini and put in an extra olive – someone keeps stealing mine."

Della, who had been making notes looked at Trent with a gleam of pride that matched that of the older lawyer. She had not known the boy longer, but saw in him a younger version of her boss. She hoped he wouldn't burn out. She didn't think so.

Twelve

Pat Joseph's eyes opened slowly as he sat up in bed. He'd been dreaming of the station wagon that nearly hit him in Mt. City. He hadn't paid much attention to the incident and wondered why it was on his mind this fine Saturday morning. He had the impression it was driven by a woman, but no one he could recognize – the car had passed so quickly. Putting the thought aside, he reflected, "It must be about seven." His mental clock was accurate.

Even though he lived in fear that someday he would oversleep and be late for something, the lawyer was absolutely incapable of trusting mechanical devices. Alarm clocks had no place in his life. By their nature, they would fail when most needed, just like computers. The screeching of an alarm scared the hell out of him anyway, so he'd rather chance oversleeping – a dilemma he was unable to resolve. Fortunately he had never yet overslept. Nature solved his problem by providing an internal alarm he set before going to sleep. It awakened him within minutes of the desired time. It worked. He didn't know why.

Joseph glanced at the clock on his wife's stand, reaffirming the accuracy of his built-in timepiece. It was 6:58 A.M. Her side of the king-size bed was empty. Usually it contained Mary, a pug dog, and two or three of Mary's cats. She must have awakened earlier than usual and taken the crew with her.

Being Saturday, it was required only that he shower, shave and dress in casual clothing. As he peered out the bathroom window, he admired the golden yellow sun mirrored in his back yard pond. The view brought as much pleasure as his pigs, and drove away the awakening thoughts of the near accident. Sometimes, if the pond was still enough, the White Amur, like small sharks, could be seen feeding on the grasses near the shore. The tranquility of his home and surroundings were all Joseph needed to keep his tanks adequately charged.

Every spring brought to Joseph's pond a middle-aged pair of Canadian Geese who returned to raise their brood of goslings until old enough to send out on their own. They were now half grown and being instructed on how to keep watch while their brothers or sisters ate. Joseph shook his head in wonder as he envied Father Goose's ability to administer discipline without anger – one peck of a parental beak or the smack of a swinging wing and the youngster never repeated the same mistake.

A Great Blue Heron dropped by for breakfast, fishing out back where the cattails grew thick. He'd have to tell Mary about that. Well ... probably not ... she rarely missed the visit.

The smell of coffee assaulted him as he stepped from the bedroom hoping Mary wasn't experimenting with some flavored coffee. She was always mixing or grinding some exotic blend to try on him. She couldn't seem to get it through her head that he liked just plain coffee. For years, she insisted on making blueberry muffins – said he loved them. Each time he'd remind her he disliked blueberry muffins, her response never varied. "You like blueberries don't you?" An affirmative nod would bring, "You like muffins, don't you?" Again a nod.

"There!" she would persist triumphantly. "You like blueberry muffins."

Helpless against such logic, he'd shut up and eat his share. The next time he'd earned a special treat, she'd prepare blueberry muffins.

In the kitchen, he poured a cup of coffee, sipped it – thank God, real coffee – and stepped onto the screened porch. It was the second most used room in the house – the first, being the kitchen which was large and old-fashioned, with adequate space to prepare and serve a meal for the entire family, including grandchildren. When they planned and built their home Mary insisted on a formal dining room and parlor, neither of which had ever been used except to store things.

She was sitting on the porch swing, admiring the antics of the Canadian Geese and the Great Blue. "Why are you up so early?" she asked, gesturing for him to join her.

"Trent is coming to pick me up," he explained. "We have to drive out to Mt. City and talk to a witness." Sitting, he asked, "Do you want your coffee warmed?"

"No. I'll fix some breakfast."

An unusual offer. She often reminded Joseph that she had cooked more than enough meals while the kids were growing up. She was now retired. Well earned by her standards. Most mornings if Joseph wanted breakfast he would fix it himself. It wasn't difficult to figure the reason for her rare generosity – Trent's imminent arrival. Guests were never allowed to go hungry in Mary's house. Joseph was no fool. He had no intention of missing the opportunity for a cooked breakfast – and certainly knew better than to comment on her perfidy.

The honk of Father Goose's instructions, the occasional gurgle and splash in the pond, the frogs' conversations, all mingled with the sounds of the preparatory bustle from the kitchen. Breakfast and Trent arrived at about the same time, served at a round glass topped table on the back porch. The circling animals got their share. After all had eaten their fill, Mary asked, "Why are you here, Trent?" ignoring Joseph's earlier explanation.

"Well, I've been working the Mt. City case for Mr. Joseph and there are some people he needs to talk to. This seems the best time to catch them home. It's such a nice day; I don't want to spend it in the library. I was looking forward to being away from the office. Besides, it gives me a chance to come here and get some of your fantastic cooking." The boy was no dummy.

Mary frowned at the unreasonableness of her husband's demands on this nice young fellow's time. "You mean *he* makes you work on weekends?" she inquired making an obscenity of the pronoun. Not too predictable, his Mary.

"Well, not really," Trent demurred. "It's just that there is so much work to do and I have a hard time getting it done during the week."

"Humph!" Mary responded, making sure Joseph was aware of her displeasure. "Who are these people you have to talk to anyway?" Mary inquired with only mild interest.

Trent explained. "Some witnesses the police know about, and some they haven't found yet. Probably won't. They seem convinced the investigation is done. There's no sign they're doing anything more."

"You know, Mary," Joseph added, "The police quit work on a case when they think it's solved. Can't seem to get it through their heads that the first person they think of just might not be guilty. Either they're too busy, too stupid or just don't give a damn. Oh well, if everyone did what we think they should, no one would need me."

"Yes, Pat, I know how important you are. You're a big-time criminal lawyer now. Don't forget to zip your fly before you leave." He glanced down with a start and saw no adjustment was required. Mary always kept him properly humble. Trent tried to hide his smile at the exchange.

"At least the kids respect me..." he mumbled. "I think."

They left, Trent driving. The trip would take about twenty minutes.

"Mr. Joseph, let's talk to Tom Roper first. I know he's home. He got in about one-thirty this morning and is probably still in bed. It might not hurt to wake him up – be a little easier to talk to. Not in the house, though. His mother will listen in and keep interrupting. She is sooo protective of her baby."

Joseph didn't ask how Trent knew what time Roper got home. It was sometimes best not to know these things.

"Okay, what do I want to ask him? Will he admit to his relationship with Emma Black?"

"Admit it? Hell, he'll brag about it. He's slime." Trent finished his explanation just as they turned off Main Street onto Garden. He pulled into the first gravel driveway, stopping near the side door of an old, neatly cared for, single family house. The back doors of the businesses facing Main Street, including *The Bar*, were on their right. The small front lawn was well trimmed and weed free, as was the vegetable garden they could see out back.

Sounds of activity came from the open windows as the lawyer rapped on the door. "Who's there?" inquired a grand-motherly voice. Without waiting for an answer, Mrs. Roper shoved open the screen door. She looked to be in her mid-sixties, hair gray and bunned, old-fashioned house dress partially covered by an apron. To make the cliché complete, a wooden rolling pin was in her hand and a splash of flour on her cheek.

"I'm Pat Joseph," the lawyer introduced himself. "I'd like to talk to Tom, if I may."

"You're the lawyer from Milltown, aren't you? Tom's not in trouble is he? Come in, he's just finishing breakfast."

Joseph laughed lightly. "Yes, I'm a lawyer, and no, he's not in trouble. I'll wait out here for him. It's such a lovely day, and I'd like to admire your garden."

Without waiting for a response, he started to walk toward the backyard. Trent followed. Tom Roper joined them in a few minutes wearing worn but clean jeans and a sleeveless undershirt, wiping the remainder of his breakfast from his face with a bare forearm. Joseph continued walking, far enough that their conversation couldn't be overheard. Roper sauntered by his side.

"Tom, do you know who I am?" Joseph inquired.

"Yeah, you're the lawyer representing the old broad that killed Robby Tucci, right?"

Joseph ignored the vulgarity of the question, saying, "Yes, I represent Mrs. Bellow. She is charged with Tucci's murder. I'm trying to learn as much as I can about what happened that night. Since you live right next door and know the family better than anyone else, I thought you might be willing to help."

Roper interrupted. "I didn't see nothing – I ain't no witness, and why would I want to help?"

"I understand. I'm trying to learn about the people. We've talked to some of the neighbors. Everyone says you knew these people best. If it's all right, I'd like to ask some questions – I sure could use the help. You can set me straight about some things. Everyone says that if you want to know about anyone, ask Tom Roper." From the expression on the boy's face, the lawyer was not concerned he might be laying it on too thick.

Roper smiled – more a self–satisfied leer – as he responded, "Yeah, I know a lot of people. What you want to know?"

They talked for a while as they strolled around the back yard. After a bit, Joseph suggested they might walk over to *The Bar* and have a drink, "it being such a warm day." They entered through the back door and sat at the same table Tucci and his friends occupied the night he was killed.

* * * * *

Trent removed a small tape recorder from his pocket, without comment, and placed it unobtrusively on the edge of the table. After ordering beer for Tom and coffee for Trent and himself, Joseph said, "Tom, I'm going to have Trent record some of this stuff. My memory isn't so good anymore, and it will be a long time until trial ... " trailing off his request.

"Sure, I got nothing to hide."

"You said you knew Tucci. Did you meet him through his sister? You know, Emma Black?"

"Nah – not really. I knew him when I was little, but we was never friends or nothing. Emma was my age and I knew her better. He was older than us and left home before I finished school. At least he was away from home a lot – he drove a truck or something and was in the service for a while. His sister stayed here. An aunt or something stayed with her until she graduated school. Me and her went to school together. She talked about her brother once in awhile. They didn't see eye to eye about a lot of stuff. When they got married, her and Jim fixed up the old Tucci house pretty good. They made an apartment over the garage for Robby. He moved his stuff there. I got to know him a little better, but we wasn't really good friends or nothing." Roper was at first a little tense, being aware of the tape recorder, but after a bit began to relax and forget his words were being recorded.

Joseph sought no elaboration about the relationship, instead directing Roper to the day Tucci was killed. "Were you there the night Tucci was killed?"

"Not when it happened. I was there during the day. About noon Robby was in the yard and I walked over to talk to him and he offered me a beer. We talked about normal things, everyday stuff. Bliss wasn't home, but I seen Emma. She'd been over to the Street Fair. She cut through our yard to get to her house."

He hesitated, gathered his thoughts, and continued. "That night a friend and me was watching the fireworks. When they was over, we was kind of bored. We was sitting over there," pointing to a couple of bar stools near the back door. "Then we heard this siren and saw an ambulance pull in the yard."

He continued. "So we sort of walked over there and some lady, I think it was the lady from across the street, was trying to talk to Emma. Emma was crying. She kept saying something about Robby's been shot. Then some cop comes up to me and tells me to get lost. I started to tell him I lived here. Then Jim Black jumps in my face. He tries to hit me, but the cop stops him. He grabs Jim and says for us both to knock it off and for me to clear out."

Interested, Joseph asked, "Why'd Jim jump you?" After what Trent had told him, he hadn't believed Roper would so readily admit the confrontation.

"I don't know! He didn't say nothing."

"You mean, he just started swinging – didn't say anything? Nothing at all?" Then, after a short pause, when there was no answer, Joseph asked in a no nonsense voice, "Didn't he say something about you fuckin' his wife?"

Roper looked at the lawyer for the first time since they had begun talking as if wondering, *How much does the old bastard know?*

Cautiously, he answered, "Well, he did say something like that. Right – yeah. A couple of days earlier he mentioned something about shooting me if I ever messed around with Emma. I didn't really take him seriously. I wasn't scared of him," he said, machismo returning to his voice.

"Did he actually threaten to shoot you? Did he have a gun?" Joseph asked.

"I never seen no gun, but I knew he had one. Emma told me he threatened her with one about a week before her brother got himself killed."

Believing that Joseph was aware of the relationship, Roper began to relax and became more animated. "I was over there talking to her. We was on the porch when Jim comes home. He told me to get the fuck out ta' there. He said we was messing around – which we wasn't – just then," he said, with a leer. "After he kicked me off his porch he said something like he was going to kill her."

"Did you actually hear him say it?" Joseph asked.

"Nah. I heard it from Emma. She told me he pulled a gun on her. I don't remember exactly when it was – maybe two, three nights before Robby got killed. Emma said that Jim got his shotgun and wouldn't let her or the kids out the house. She was crying when she was telling me. I know Jim can get crazy – he has a reputation. So I was a little, you know, cautious of him."

Afraid of appearing less than manly, Roper added, "Not really scared, ya' understand, I just avoided him so there wouldn't be no trouble. So when I saw Emma run out the house yelling like *Don't let him get me!* I stayed out of the way. I didn't see Robby and I don't know if he knew about it – but Bliss did. I could hear Jim screaming how he was going to kill Emma. I didn't know what the fuck was gonna' happen – I didn't want to get involved. Someone must of called the cops but by the time they got there, everything was quiet. Anyway, I don't go there no more."

"I don't guess I would, either," Joseph chuckled.

Roper laughed and seemed a little relieved. "Right, but see, Emma and I are still friends. I've known her since we were kids. You might say, we're real good friends. Close, really close... ha... ha," he said, a licentious smirk creeping in.

Trent's right, Joseph thought, *he is slime!*

"By the way, Tom, what are your friends saying about who killed Tucci?"

"Like, you know, they're all saying the old lady did it – that's what I hear."

"What are they saying about the gun?" Joseph pressed.

"Yeah, they found the gun under Emma's porch. The police found it there. It belonged to Bliss' mom."

"Did you talk to Emma about it? Did she say anything about seeing or touching the gun?"

"Uh, yeah. She said she picked the gun up right after it happened," he answered thoughtfully.

"What did she do with the gun?"

"I have no idea, but she said she just dropped it."

"Did she tell you what she did with the gun?"

Roper silently shook his head in a negative response and murmured, "Unh – unh... no."

Joseph repeated most of his questions again, in other ways, to determine the accuracy of Roper's tale. Each time the story was told without significant change. Roper seemed to feel it important to boast that he had no intention of interrupting his friendship with Emma, but did intend to be a little more circumspect. Not that he was afraid of her husband – he just didn't want to make trouble for her. He implied that much of what he told Joseph came from intimate conversations – pillow talk. Roper needed to brag.

Roper ended the conversation with a bit of news the lawyer hadn't otherwise gleaned. "Emma said she was on the landing and heard the shot, so ran upstairs to see what happened."

Joseph was surprised. "Emma said she heard the shot?"

"Yeah, she was on the landing when they came and was turning around to leave – going home when she heard the shot. Her and Robby was having an argument about something and she was walking out when she heard the shot."

"Is this the same fight? Was she arguing with her brother on the same night he got shot?"

"Right," Tom Roper responded.

"What happened?"

"She said she ran up the stairs and saw the old lady standing there. Then she said the old lady picked up the gun and Emma thought she was gonna shoot her – so she ran back downstairs. After they come down, Emma runs back upstairs and they was both – her and Bliss – hugging Tucci and stuff. She got all covered with blood."

"When did she pick up the gun?"

"I guess it must have been after the others left," he said, a quizzical look on his face as though the sequence of events all of a sudden made no sense to him.

Joseph continued the questioning, trying to pinpoint details. Much of what Roper told him was in the police reports but the information about the gun and Emma raised more questions than answers.

"Emma's still a good friend of yours?"

"Yeah," he said, with a smirk Joseph had come to know.

"How many times have you and she talked about that night?"

"Maybe ten, eleven times. We talk a lot."

The lawyer thoughtfully considered for a moment – *had he missed anything?* "How much of this have you told the police?"

"Nothing. They never asked me. They ain't even talked to me."

Joseph was confounded. "You mean to say that, even after the police knew you were there, and broke up a fight between you and Jim, they didn't take a statement from you?"

"Nope, nothing. What they need me for? They already got the bitch that did it."

Joseph ended the conversation. "Thanks again. We'll be in touch." Handing him a card, he added, "If you think of anything that might help, give me a call." He called to *Hey*, asking for and paying the tab. Trent and the lawyer left. Tom Roper sat and nursed another beer the lawyer paid for. It seemed a little early in the day.

Thirteen

"Take me home, Trent, I feel the need to shower after talking to that model citizen." Joseph considered they might get home in time for lunch. Trent with him assured a home fixed meal.

Rural Ohio's rolling hills mixed with flat farmland lends itself to quiet contemplation. Thinking about the interview, Joseph said, "You know, Trent, I think you're right. The police treat these cases as though they have tunnel vision. If the obvious isn't the solution, there is no solution. Even worse, they put each case into a neat little box. If a fact fits, they put it in. If the fact doesn't fit, they throw it away."

He wasn't the first person to consider this phenomenon, but each time it seemed more unbelievable. When would the public's guardians learn? Or would they? Did they want to? Or does the truth get in the way of putting in the time needed for retirement?

Joseph let his mind wander, thinking, *The fertile fields look good. The corn is already tasseling. Soybeans should be abundant this year. Not enough rain for the vining plants, though. Looks like the berries should be plentiful if we beat the birds to them.* The heat, the dry breeze and the hazy sunshine made the lawyer sleepy. He began to doze but was brought back by Trent's comment.

"It's worse than you think, Mr. Joseph," interrupting the lawyer's ruminations.

Joseph asked, "What do you mean?"

"I went to B.C.I. like you said and talked to the criminalist. The one that examined the atomic absorption test swabs. You know, that's the test they use to determine the presence of gunshot residue," Trent began to explain.

Joseph interrupted. "I'm not yet senile. I remember our talk."

"Anyway, they finished the reports on the tests run on Mrs. Bellow and Jim and Emma Black. I got the results here somewhere," he said reaching behind the seat and groping for his briefcase.

Joseph leaned over the seat, found it for him, opened it and extracted a manila folder labeled "B.C.I. Reports." Glancing at the several documents

97

inside, he found the one Trent wanted him to read. It was the standard form used by B.C.I., containing the name of the agency requesting an analysis, the case number, date, type of crime and so on. Joseph skipped to the body of it and read:

Atomic absorption analysis of the hand swab from Emma Black (Item #9) revealed levels of barium and antimony consistent with gunshot residue on the "left palm", "right palm" and "right back" swabs.

"Interesting," Joseph remarked. "It looks like they tested Emma Black's hands the night of the shooting and found the presence of gunshot residue on the palms of both hands and on the back of her right hand."

"Read the rest of it," Trent instructed.

Joseph did as he was told. There were four more paragraphs. The second revealed that B.C.I. discovered the presence of gunshot residue on the left back, left palm, right back and right palm of James Black's hands. Curious....

The third paragraph read:

Atomic absorption analysis of the hand swabs from Gay Bellow (item #11) failed to reveal levels of barium and antimony consistent with gunshot residue.

"Holy shit!" Joseph exclaimed. "According to this, Gay's test was negative. She didn't shoot a gun that night!"

Joseph continued reading in a state of excitement. The same findings were made concerning Bliss, but, oddly enough, there were positive readings on the swabs taken from Arliss.

"Why do you say this is bad, Trent? This is great! ... Especially for Mrs. Bellow. Admittedly, it might create a little problem for Arliss, but that's explainable." Joseph was elated and showed it. "You've done a great job, Trent, especially, getting this information so quick."

"Wait, Mr. Joseph. Like you said, this seems to say Mrs. Bellow didn't shoot a gun so couldn't have shot Tucci. But when the detectives got the report back from B.C.I. they said since she confessed to the murder it couldn't be true. They sent a letter to B.C.I. saying they must have mislabeled the packets. They said Emma Black couldn't have had residue on her hands because she wasn't there, and since Mrs. Bellow signed a confession, they must have mixed up her swabs with Mrs. Black's."

"You're kidding, Trent! They didn't really do that... did they?" Joseph was incredulous.

"They did. Then they asked the criminalist to either change the labels on the tests or say the test results aren't conclusive."

After his initial anger punctuated by appropriate expletives, Joseph calmed enough to say, "When we get to trial, I'm going to have to cross-examine these experts about this stuff. It should be fun." Joseph had automatically begun to think this was a case he was going to try instead of plead, no matter what they offered his client. He stopped, shook his head and, with a queer feeling of butterflies flitting around his stomach, said to himself, *What the hell am I thinking? I can't try this case! I don't know what I'm doing! I was just going to plead her and make a quick fee. Goddamn, this can't be happening.*

Feeling helplessly committed, he said in a more resigned tone, "A jury is going to love this. Such bullshit – it is un-fuckin'-believable."

Trent added, "At least the guy at B.C.I. said he wouldn't do what they wanted when he showed me the note from the Sheriff's office. Anyway, I wanted to be sure what the reports meant so I called a guy I know with the F.B.I. and read him the test results. I asked what we should look for."

"Good thinking. What did he say?"

"He said that barium and antimony are only found together in significant quantities in gunshot primer. We already talked about that."

"The residue," he continued, "is in the form of microscopic particles blown back on a hand when a gun is fired. The F.B.I. doesn't bother to swab palms for residue anymore. They're only interested in the backs of the hands. He said a person could get residue on his palms by just holding a gun that had recently been fired, or even by touching the hands of someone who shot a gun."

Trent went on to explain the significance of his conversation with the F.B.I. specialist. "He said there could be a negative reading even if someone had shot a gun. The chemicals could be washed off, or even wiped off by vigorously rubbing the hands with a clean cloth."

Joseph asked Trent, "Did you explain to your friend the circumstances of the testing on Mrs. Bellow?"

"I did. And he said you would have to find out whether she had the chance to wash her hands before the swab was taken. If she didn't, he said she didn't fire a weapon. If she had shot the gun and was in custody from the time of the shooting until the test was taken, there would be residue present."

Trent thought for a minute and added, "But you know, Mr. Joseph, he was more intrigued with the positive readings on the others. If things are the way the police say they are, the residue should not have been on their hands. He thought you might want to keep that in mind, if we actually have to go to trial."

God forbid! Joseph thought.

"Hell, Trent, we can't worry about that since we only represent two of the people there – Mrs. Bellow and her daughter. But it certainly is food for thought."

Trent snapped his fingers. "Oh yeah, Mr. Joseph. I almost forgot: The concentration on Jim Black's hands was the heaviest, with his wife, Emma, next. He had no idea what that meant but said it certainly should be looked into by somebody."

"Trent, you earned your pay this week, and then some." Joseph laughed and thought, *My pigs are probably smiling – or maybe laughing outright.*

Pleased with the praise, Trent beamed. "I'm glad you think so, Mr. Joseph."

"Now take me home. Mrs. Joseph wants to go to Summit Mall this afternoon. God, that woman can shop seven days a week."

* * * * *

Mary was sitting on the back porch when they returned. Trent walked in with the lawyer to say "Hello." She shushed them so they wouldn't disturb the hummingbirds swarming the feeder, chattering away with mouse-like clicks warning each other off. It amazed Joseph that the tiny birds could secure any sustenance at all, what with being so busy zealously guarding their territory. Somehow, Mary always managed to garner a clan of hummingbirds at her feeder while most folk were thrilled if just one appeared.

Naturally, she asked if Trent wanted lunch. She never asked Joseph. Instead, she expected him to buy her a slice of pizza at the mall on Saturday afternoons. To Joseph's dismay, Trent declined, saying, "I'd love to, but no thanks. I'm still full from breakfast. Besides, I have to study for next week." Mary threw a condemnatory glance in Joseph's direction for his maltreatment of employees, and walked the young man to the door, kissed him on the cheek and waved him out of the driveway.

Trent left and Mary, without a word, slipped on a sweater, said sweet goodbyes to the cats and dogs, and slid into the passenger side of their car – expecting Joseph to follow. He did docilely.

* * * * *

Joseph would never admit how much he enjoyed the excursions he and Mary made to the mall. After eating a slice of pizza at their favorite shop – spinach and ricotta cheese on thick Sicilian crust preferred – Mary would shop and Joseph would visit with the shop owner who considered him a regular and always had a new menu item for the lawyer to try. This day's special – a mixture of pepperoni, mozzarella and other exotic cheeses along with olive oil, all wrapped in a thin, flaky dough baked in the pizza oven – was handed to Joseph for a taste test. Heaven!

Following the culinary experience, Joseph wandered into the Walden book store where he carried a Preferred Customer card, picked up a paperback and settled on a bench at one end of the mall in front of what used to be The May Co. It had a new, fancy name now, having been bought out by some out of state corporation. This was the bench he always occupied while waiting for Mary to complete her inexplicable shopping. He was looking forward to enjoying an uninterrupted afternoon of reading. Uninterrupted, that is, except for the fascinating sights. Young people exhibited themselves in the latest fashions, most of which had repeated at least once as it passed through the several generations comprising Pat's lifetime. Older women, young married or middle-aged, hurried from sale to sale – some well turned out and some dressed as if they didn't give a damn.

Men mostly occupied the benches watching the women – in awe, appreciation or disbelief. Walking for exercise was popular. The movement of flesh, constrained or not, was mesmerizing. Joseph shared his favorite bench with an older gentleman who had a twinkly, youthful eye. Pat was making a real effort to forget the Bellow family and concentrate on the latest J. A. Jance, Detective Beaumont novel – a favorite author even though she was a woman. His neighbor glanced at him and offered a tentative, "Hi."

Joseph glanced up from his reading. The old fellow, Pat thought, looked pleasant enough, so he responded, "Hello, how are you?" opening the floodgates.

"Why, I'm fine thank you. You know, my wife sends me here every day to get exercise. She thinks I walk two or three miles. The doctor said I need the cardiovascular what-cha-ma-stuff after I had my heart attack ten years ago. He said if I'm careful, I could live to be seventy. Hell, I'm seventy-two already and he's been dead seven years. If I ever tried to walk that far, it would kill me."

Joseph couldn't resist asking, "If you aren't here to walk, what do you do?" knowing he'd be sorry.

"Well, I meet some friends and we go over there to the bakery for coffee and donuts. They got some real good stuff. After breakfast we sit here till about noon, eat lunch and leave. My friends ain't here today. I'm holding down the fort by my lonesome. One of my buddies is on vacation, one had to stay home and mow his goddam' lawn. His grandson usually does it but has football practice or some damn thing. Another one died. Been a lot of that going around lately... hee... hee."

He didn't even pause for breath after the little giggle but continued. "Yep, my wife thinks we walk, but I couldn't stand the excitement, so I just sit here. Look at that one!" he exclaimed, pointing at a rather attractive lady walking by in skintight jeans and tank top. It was an interesting sight. "More tits and ass 'round here – couldn't stand it if I were any younger. Sure didn't dress like that in my day."

Joseph wanted to return to his book, but was fascinated by the old gentleman's view of the world. He obviously intended to savor all the visual pleasures life had to offer.

They chatted for about an hour, the old man doing most of the talking, Joseph listening. The gentleman finally stretched, stood, cleared his throat and said, "Well, got t' go now, before the old lady comes looking for me with the rescue squad. She worries that I might exercise too much and have another heart attack right here. Not me though. They only got men on their trucks and I don't want one of them giving me CPR. Anyone gives me mouth to mouth had better have tits. Don't have to be big though. Hee ... hee ... " He left chortling, shaking his head form side to side, completely captivated by his own humor.

Joseph tried to return to his reading, but was no longer in the mood. He stretched his short legs out, crossed his ankles and leaned back on the bench, trying to take some pleasure in his new friend's observations. Instead, he began to think about Tucci. *The investigation is going nicely, but I need to know more about Gay,* he thought. In his mind, he had already begun to distance himself from her daughter.

Joseph allowed his thoughts to wander over what he knew of the case. He considered, *I need to know more about Tucci, too. Who might want him dead? What was he like? Was the killing just a random accident, or did someone take advantage of the opportunity? Good lord, am I really going to have to try this case?* A picture was starting to come together slowly. He mentally ticked off what he didn't know.

The autopsy report had a lot of information, but was missing something. Maybe he should talk to the doctor who reviewed it. The pathologist at Milltown Hospital was a young, good-looking, redheaded Scot. On more than one occasion, he had explained to Joseph that if a man comes from

Scotland, he is a Scotsman. Scotch is something to drink for which he had a particular fondness. Joseph needed to see him. Probably would cost a bottle, but he had a hunch it would be worth it.

Fourteen

Although trying to stay busy with other matters for the next several weeks, Joseph was unable to keep his mind from wandering back to the Bellow's file. Something niggled at the edges of his mind – not about Gabriella – but about the case itself. The file, sitting on the corner of his desk, kept pulling at him.

He arrived at the office early, prepared to get caught up on his paperwork – titles needed to be searched and estate tax returns prepared – that's where the money is. He felt the pull of the Bellow file sitting unopened on his desk, sighed and decided, "The hell with it. I guess I'll give Randy McCallister a call instead... Della!!"

Della placed the call for him and as he picked up the phone he heard, "Dr. McCallister here."

""Randy, Pat Joseph. You free for lunch?"

"Nope. Why?" McCallister answered in his usual laconic manner.

"I'm working a murder case and need to know some things," Joseph explained, getting right to the point. He knew McCallister couldn't tolerate small talk.

"What the hell you doing with a murder case? But, if you need to know something, come on over to the lab now. I have a few free minutes I'll talk to you here."

The lawyer hung up and called, "Della, I'm going over to the hospital. Don't know what time I'll be back."

Without waiting for a response, he grabbed his cap and left through the back door. Taking his truck, he was able to get to the hospital within minutes. He entered through the emergency room and walked directly to the pathology laboratory, waving or nodding to those he recognized. Randy's secretary greeted Joseph with, "Hi, Mr. Joseph, Dr. Mac is expecting you. Said for you to go on in."

Pat walked through Randy's private office into a gleaming laboratory where Dr. McCallister was looking intently at a lump of gray, scored material he held in a gloved hand. "Nice kid," he commented under his breath.

"Motorcycle accident. Nothing wrong with this brain – should have lived to be ninety instead of nineteen." Shaking his head sadly at the things people do to themselves, he placed the brain in a dish on the metal-covered table before him. He wasn't trying to shock or offend Joseph – he was offended at the stupidity of people and the myriad ways they could, and did, end their lives.

With a cheerless shrug he pulled off his rubber gloves, walked to the sink, washed his hands and removed his apron, hanging it on a hook. With a surgical mask dangling from his neck, he nodded for Joseph to follow him back to his office.

"What do you need?" he asked in his doleful manner.

The lawyer produced Tucci's Autopsy Protocol and asked, "Randy, look at this and tell me what it means."

Randy studied the report for a few minutes. "What do you want to know?"

"How did he die? Why did he die? Is there anything unusual or uncharacteristic about the report or the death that might tell me something?"

"The autopsy's signed by Dr. Gerber. He's the coroner in Cuyahoga County. You know what his reputation is – damn good doctor. He's a lawyer too, isn't he?" Joseph nodded, fully familiar with the prestigious Sam Gerber, having met him on several occasions and watched him testify in some of Cleveland's more famous trials.

Reading, Randy commented almost to himself, "His office is more thorough than most. The Anatomic Diagnosis shows, in addition to the gunshot wound, abrasions and contusions on the scalp, face and left upper extremity – arm to you. The rest of the findings aren't remarkable except from a medical standpoint."

Leafing through the document, he looked up and said, "The entrance wound was on the right side of his head. It was excised, that means cut out, during surgery. They tried an emergency operation to see if he could be saved – didn't work. The tissue was studied. After perforating the scalp and underlying soft tissue, the bullet passed through the right lateral aspect of the skull and brain, proceeded upwards and medially through the right to the left lobe, and came to rest there. The bullet was recovered and preserved."

He continued reading silently and then translated, "The gunshot wasn't the only injury he had. There was an abrasion on his forehead at the hairline – a smaller oval shaped bruise in the middle of his forehead."

The lawyer asked, "Could that have been from getting hit by one of those big old-fashioned Coke bottles?"

"It could," Randy agreed after a moment's thought. "There's an irregularly shaped bruise on the left side of his forehead. That makes three bruises on the forehead, one in the scalp line, one in the center and one on the left side. Must have been in a fight. It looks like he had a fairly fresh bruise on the upper portion of the left arm and another on the lower left arm about eight inches long, and a healing bruise on his chest. The last one seems to be remote in time from the injuries suffered at or near the time he died."

Randy studied the rest of the findings, shaking his head. "This boy had lots of years left. It's a goddam' shame."

Randy continued, sounding preoccupied. "The bullet traveled about five-and-a-half inches through and completely destroyed his brain. If it wasn't for that, like I said, he would have lived a long time ... Interesting ... " Randy reflected.

"What?" Joseph asked.

"Remember, I said they kept the tissue from the entrance wound. Well, they did a microscopic section of it and found powder burns, not only on the surface of the wound, but inside the brain itself."

Thinking about Mrs. Bellow's description of the events, Joseph asked with heightened interest, "What does that mean?"

"It means the gun was right up against the deceased's head when it was fired," he explained.

"Do you mean," Joseph asked wanting assurance, "that he wasn't shot from across the room, say from a distance of five to six feet?"

"Like I said," the doctor responded with some exasperation, "the gun was right up against the side of his head. Flush against it or the burned powder wouldn't have entered the brain."

Digesting this, Joseph asked, "Anything else in the report I should know?"

"Not much. The cause of death was a cerebral edema due to a gunshot wound of the head with perforation of skull and brain. Homicide. Pretty obvious, I would think."

"Thanks, Randy. I am really indebted to you," Joseph said as he stood to leave, animated by the scientific support for his burgeoning belief in Gay's innocence. It lent credence to her story.

Almost as an afterthought, as he was leaving, Joseph asked, "Oh, by the way, maybe there is something else. Mrs. Bellow – the lady charged with the shooting – had a serious injury to her arm. She wears a TENS unit for pain. I haven't the slightest idea how it works. When we shook hands, I could tell it hurt from the way she winced, but she didn't say anything. B.C.I. says the murder weapon has a safety feature. It's a lever in the gun's grip that has to be squeezed against the palm of the hand in order to fire. The pistol has a twelve-and-a-half pound trigger pull. I wonder whether she could have fired the murder weapon since she could barely shake my hand. Is there some way a person's strength can be measured?"

Randy thought for a minute, finally suggesting, "Well, I don't know how to do it – but I hear that kind of thing is being done by the sports medicine people at Cleveland Clinic. Our physical therapist trained there and could probably tell you more about it. Want me to call him?"

Joseph marveled that he had gotten more conversation out of this taciturn Scot today than in all the years he'd known him. Something in the case must have piqued his interest. The doctor picked up his phone and dialed. Joseph listened to his end of the conversation. "Sam? Randy. You busy?" He waited for a response and continued, "Can you come to the lab for a minute? Thanks."

He hung up, pulled out a pipe, packed and lit it without saying a word. Joseph sat silently not wanting to interrupt his thoughts. The pathologist had come up with good stuff so far.

A tap on his door was followed by a head covered with tousled blond hair framing a face with an engaging grin. Seeing the two sitting quietly, he walked in. "Hi, Randy, what can I do for you?"

"Sam, this is a friend of mine, Pat Joseph. He's a lawyer. Pat, this is Sam Chester, our P.T."

They exchanged nods and the lawyer stood to shake hands. The younger man's grip was warm and pleasantly firm.

Chester said, without losing his friendly smile, "I know who you are. Read about you in the paper – the Mt. City murder case. Pleasure to meet you."

Thanking him for the recognition, Joseph said, "The pleasure is truly mine, and that's what I wanted to ask you about. I have a problem Randy thought you might help me solve."

Joseph explained in detail, taking some minutes to run through the facts. Chester grinned. "No problem! We have instruments that can measure the strength and output of any muscle group in the body – pretty accurate, too."

The lawyer was curious. "Can you be fooled?"

"Not very easily. We repeat tests using different sequences. The person being tested can't see the gauges so they can't remember how they perform each time. We interrupt the procedure with other tests so that they can't develop any kind of muscle memory through repetition. Every time we measure, we tell them to exert all their strength. If it's the same each time, they aren't faking. We use the tests to tell us how athletes improve in exercise programs or recover from injuries."

"Can you test someone for me?" Joseph asked.

"Nope!" Chester responded positively and promptly.

Taken aback, Joseph asked, "Why not?" He had to know whether or not Gay was capable of pulling the trigger.

"Physical Therapists can't prescribe treatments or tests," the P.T. explained. "Neither can you. We can only do tests on doctors' orders. If you can get some doctor to write a prescription, I can do the test. Without one, I do nothing. I don't take a chance with my license."

Understanding, Joseph smiled. Not only was Sam likeable, his grin and personality were infectious. It is rare to find a man so happy in his work. "No problem Sam," Joseph grinned. "I'll have Mrs. Bellow see a doctor. I'm sure he'll be happy to prescribe the tests you suggest. Just tell me what to ask for."

They talked for a few more minutes with Sam providing the names of the tests and giving instructions as to what would be needed. Randy sat quietly puffing on his pipe. Joseph thanked both of them profusely and left.

Driving back to the office, the lawyer wondered how much to share with the prosecutor. If he shared everything, would it make any difference? *Prosecutors,* he thought, *have a mindset that defies understanding. Even so, I have to know. I think I'll stop at the Deli on the way back to the office for a bite of lunch. Maybe Jackie will be there....*

* * * * *

"Jackie! Wait up!" Crossing the Square toward the Deli, Joseph saw Jackie VanDamm moving in the same direction as he, so called to her. It wasn't exactly a coincidence since he knew she ate there almost daily. In fact, it was where most of the lawyers and businessmen in town met for lunch, making it a mandatory stop for the local politicians.

"Hi, Jackie. Going to lunch?" he asked slightly breathless. Hurrying wasn't his strong point.

"Yes. Why? Want to buy me lunch?" she smiled.

"I wouldn't think of compromising you. But I would like to talk to you for a minute."

"Sure!" They stopped at the counter to place their orders. Joseph admired an Italian submarine sandwich in the refrigerated counter but settled for a cheese on rye. Jackie ordered a salad. No wonder she stayed so slim. On the way to a booth she nodded or said "Hi!" to almost everyone in the place. A good politician. The food arrived at their table the same time they did.

"What can I do for you, Mr. Joseph?" The appellation was probably a concession to his age.

He explained somewhat awkwardly. "I have been preparing the Bellow case for trial and thought we might talk about some of the things I've learned."

"Why? Does your client want to plead? We might be willing to make some small concession because of her age and since she has no record," Jackie said seriously.

"No, Jackie, you don't understand. I have some information that leads me to believe there's a serious question as to whether Gay could have killed Tucci," Joseph began explaining.

Jackie interrupted with a laugh, a pleasant tinkling sound, but not nearly as sincerely as her smile had been. "Sure you have! Look, she confessed. We're going to get a conviction!"

Not being able to hide his frustration completely, Joseph asked, "Do you want to talk about it or not? I don't want to embarrass you or your office. That's why I'm trying to share this information with you. Do you..."

She interrupted again, this time sarcastically. "Please spare me Mr. Joseph. I'm not going to discuss the facts of the case with you except in court. We both know she killed him and confessed to it. I can imagine the headlines if I were to let you talk me into a deal. I don't need that shit. All I want from you is to know whether you're going to advise your client to plead."

Joseph, stung by her remark, could feel his hands beginning to tremble. He said, "Rather smug position for someone with your limited experience isn't it?" Joseph reacted not too judiciously.

"I may be young, but I was elected by this county to be its Prosecutor and intend to be just that! I'll try the case myself. We'll see how much good your experience does you then, old man."

Calming only slightly, Joseph responded, "I deserved that, Jackie. I'm sorry. I didn't mean to be insulting. Look, if you don't want to talk about the case, okay. But I am serious. If you decide you want to discuss what I've learned, let me know. There are some things you might find interesting." He hesitated for a moment. "At least, we can enjoy lunch and talk about more pleasant things. Forgive me?" he asked while thinking, *God damn, I'm really going to have to try the case.* Even though his resolve was strengthening, there was no sense burning all his bridges.

Her color returned, she smiled and said, "Truce." They shook hands and enjoyed lunch. *God damn prosecutorial mindset.*

Fifteen

Pat Joseph wrestled with his conscience for the next several days. He tried, but knew he would be unable to convince himself Gay should plead to a crime he had come to believe she could not have committed, yet he felt hopelessly inadequate – over his head. Maybe he should arrange for someone else to take over and try the case, but was unable to admit his limitations publicly, or privately for that matter. What would Trent, Della and Mary think? Even at his age, ego – no, goddamn pride – got in the way. Hell, he had tried hundreds of cases – maybe none this important – but a trial is a trial. The trial wasn't for several more weeks. No need to make a decision yet. Maybe something would happen. The butterflies were having a field day and the pigs leered evilly at him, even with his eyes closed.

In the meantime, Trent Fillia continued to work the file to the exclusion of almost everything else in the office. He made appointments the older lawyer suggested, interviewed witnesses and prepared memoranda on all of the possible legal and evidentiary issues. The file continued to sit on the corner of Pat's desk getting thicker, drawing his attention while other files needed work he could not bring himself to do.

Go away! he thought staring at it. *You involve stupid acts by dreary people caught up in an effort to give meaning to your life.* Lines from Thomas Kyd's *The Spanish Tragedy* sprang to the lawyer's mind,

> O eyes, no eyes but fountains fraught with tears;
> O life, no life, but lively forms of death;
> O world, no world, but mass of public wrongs;
> Confused and filled with murder and misdeeds.

Staring at his pigs, who stared back malevolently, the lawyer reflected, *In 1594, Kyd wondered why people do the things they do – why they commit crimes great or small. Why the consequences of their acts don't dissuade murder and misdeeds defies belief. History is no argument for the death penalty. It deters no one bent on mischief. All death accomplishes is to eliminate those that don't fit. Stupidity being the prevailing human condition, it must be a constituent element of man's nature. How depressing.*

Joseph suddenly felt the need for fresh air. Striding purposefully past his secretary's desk, he said, "Della, I'm getting out of here for a while. Need to get some air."

"Don't forget, Mrs. Bellow's going to be here right after lunch ... " she called to his retreating back.

He grunted some obscenity in response. Della pretended not to hear as he walked out the front door. The greenness of the Square was exceptional for the time of year. The moisture rich air sparkled with what the Irish call a "soft day." The sky, filled with fluffy clouds, deposited bits of dampness on all available surfaces and made the grass shine and the trees shimmer with crystal droplets. The sun shining through the clouds gave everything a bright, clean look – like Mary's kitchen floor.

Joseph walked through and around the Square, his shoulders beginning to relax with each dew-laden breath. Children were playing, not quietly, on the World War I cannon housed on the Square and around the Gazebo. Their noise was neither grating nor irritating. Twice around the Square and he had regained enough enthusiasm to consider lunch – even felt he might enjoy some company.

Should he eat at Harry's Roundtable or the Deli? The Roundtable produced better conversation. It was where the conservatives gathered. Joseph didn't really fit, but they tolerated him.

The usual group was there – a man that owned much of the real estate in town, a present and a former County Commissioner, two brothers, partners in the construction business who rarely agreed on anything, a politically motivated insurance salesman, and a retired businessman whose wife wanted him out of the house at lunch time. An eclectic group whose lively talk always served to distract Joseph from current problems, if not improve his spirits.

Batteries recharged, he returned to the office smiling. Mrs. Bellow was waiting. "Good afternoon, Gay. It's been awhile since we talked." Joseph leaned over to kiss her cheek, took her arm and guided her to his office. "Would you like some coffee?"

She declined, taking a seat in her usual tentative manner on the edge of one of the client chairs. "Gay, you're looking better than the last time I saw you. Have you been getting some rest?"

She smiled. "A little. But naturally I can't stop worrying about the case. As a matter of fact, it's really all I think about. The shock has worn off some, and I accept the fact I must go to trial," she responded.

There was vitality in her voice and her face looked slightly fuller. It wasn't. The harsh planes were still there, but her spirit had improved – she was ready to fight. Her resolution gave the lawyer pause. He felt a clutch somewhere in his mid-section that generated a quick intake of breath. He hoped her confidence would last, even though it caused him some trepidation.

Keeping the conversation casual, he inquired, "How are things at home?"

She considered, then responded, "Claude is feeling better, I think, but we don't talk much. His business is going so badly for him. He is worried about it and doesn't pay attention to much of anything else. I think it might be a bit of a facade. I know he worries about me, but doesn't want to say so."

"And Arliss?" the lawyer asked.

Gay sighed. "Arliss is a chore. She is so worried that she won't talk about anything else. She constantly wants reassurance from me, and it's difficult. I don't know what's going to happen to me, so I just don't know how to help her. Bliss, on the other hand, won't talk to any of us." She paused as though trying to make up her mind whether or not to say something. "The other day she did what is, even for her, a crazy thing."

"What do you mean?" Joseph asked with only mild curiosity. He needed to talk to Bliss and hoped she would be approachable. At least not overtly antagonistic.

Gay explained. "The other morning, Arliss was coming to my house. Bliss must have seen her drive by because when Arliss started to turn into my drive, Bliss drove right into the back of her car. It was intentional – maybe a spur of the moment thing, but intentional. Arliss jumped out and Bliss began screaming awful things at her, then began punching and kicking her. I was shocked. I just stood and watched."

Gay paused for breath. Her description of the incident brought to Joseph's mind a fleeting memory of the station wagon careening around the corner as he stepped from the curb in Mt. City.

Gay went on. "Bliss had Arliss on the ground and was sitting on her chest, yelling awful things like it was her fault Robby died. I tried, but I couldn't get Bliss to let go. So I called the police. The sheriff came. By the time he got there, the fight was over."

She continued describing the incident with an effort, Joseph again amazed by her accuracy of recall. "Arliss would not be consoled. She sat on the ground rocking, hugging herself. Her dress was torn and she made no effort to cover up. Bliss laughed. One of the deputies put her in his car and asked

Arliss if she wanted to press charges. She did. They all went to the station and I was left standing there like a dummy. That was last week and I still don't know what happened. Bliss made bail – God, I sound like a lawyer – and was charged with assault, I think."

Thinking, *This is one strange family,* Joseph asked, "They won't talk to you about it?"

"No. Arliss just says Bliss is crazy. But it must stem from Robert's death. The girls never liked each other much and Arliss has always been nasty about Robert. Bliss knows this and what with everything else, I guess Bliss just boiled over."

Joseph thought he would have to learn more about this and what effect, if any, it would have on the trial, but not now. Gay had to be brought up to date on his plans. Joseph began explaining.

Gay listened carefully, asking only an occasional perceptive question. Joseph couldn't get over the change in her. She seemed to be, if not enjoying herself, at least involved and interested.

She approved the plan, and her doctor thought the tests Sam Chester suggested appropriate. Della had asked Gay to bring her medical records from Cleveland Metropolitan Hospital. Her doctor ordered the requested tests and the necessary prescription forms were signed. Della had made an appointment with Chester for that afternoon. Gay was amused that the plans were complete before she was consulted. It was a good sign she offered no argument.

Gay and the lawyer drove to the hospital and walked the endless corridors until locating Sam's tiny office. Knocking and walking in, Joseph began to make introductions. "Dr. Chester, this is Gabriella Bellow ... "

"Not doctor," Chester interrupted. "I'm a physical therapist, not a physician. Hi, Ms. Bellow. Please call me Sam."

Gay, like everyone else, was taken by his charm and glowed like a schoolgirl. As he bowed over her hand, the lawyer expected Chester might kiss it. He didn't. Instead, taking her hand in his, he put his other arm around her shoulder and, ignoring Joseph, led Gay to a small cubicle surrounded by white curtains.

"Please sit on the cot. I'm going to sit on this stool in front of you. Before we start, I have to ask a few questions. Then I will explain exactly what we're going to do."

Chester opened the metal clipboard he was holding and removed some forms. Filling in the information he secured from Gay about identity, age, medical history and the usual things medical people ask, he explained. "Mr. Joseph said he needs to know about the strength in your hands – particularly in the index or trigger finger of your right hand. To do that, I am going to use a couple different instruments."

Showing them to her, he explained. "This one is called a grip strength hand diometer and the other a pinch grip diometer. I'll make several checks in different sequences so you won't know which test is coming. The gauges will be facing away from you so you can't see them."

Grinning at her as though sharing the knowledge that she would never try to fool him, he added, "If you try to fake a response, I'll know right away, not only from the gauges, but from other physical reactions. When a person exerts all her strength, a small tremor appears in other parts of the body that I can see. There are other things I look for as well. If you think you can fool me, try, and I'll let you know when you are."

Responding to his charm, Gay said with an almost girlish grin, "No. Frankly, I am as anxious as Mr. Joseph to know what the tests will reveal."

"Another thing, Mrs. Bellow I notice you are wearing a TENS Unit. I am going to run the tests first with the unit in place. Later we'll do them again without it. That is, if you think you can tolerate the pain."

"That's fine. I can do without it for short periods of time ... Please call me Gay."

He ran through the series, first her left index finger, then her right, then her left hand, and lastly the right. He did it several times, but in different sequences with pauses of varying duration in between – stopping and chatting with her as if they were old friends. They had a pleasant visit.

Despite the air of cordiality, it was obvious to Joseph that Chester was all business. Sam studied Mrs. Bellow's face carefully while administering the tests and never allowed the chart from his side. He made notes the lawyer could not decipher. It was fascinating to watch him work. Neither seemed aware of Joseph's presence.

During one of the breaks, Sam asked to see Gay's medical records. He clucked over them, verifying some of the findings with her. "My God, you were really mauled by that dog. Was it almost two years ago?"

"Yes, that's right." She showed him the scar on her arm.

Sam continued. "It looks like they debrided quite a bit of the muscle tissue from the biceps clear down into the triceps, is that right?" He traced with his finger the path of the injury as he spoke.

Gay nodded in agreement.

Grimacing as though feeling the pain, he commented, "It says here they removed most of the muscle tissue," pointing to the chart. "There was a full muscle avulsion down to the anterior phase of the humerus bone. That means there was a ripping or tearing of the muscle clear down to the bone. The doctors cut away most of the dead tissue. That must have been horrible!"

Gay shuddered. "I really don't like to remember it."

"No wonder you have to wear the TENS unit. I'm sure it was explained to you that it is designed to stimulate the nerves electrically through the surface of the skin to persuade the brain to manufacture an opiate that deadens the pain in your arm. Does it help?"

"Without it the pain is intolerable unless I'm so doped up I can't stay awake. Even with it working, I'm in fairly constant pain. The doctor's call it discomfort – but to me its pain!"

After this conversation, the testing procedures were repeated without the TENS unit in place.

Sam turned to the lawyer. "Do you want the findings now or can you wait for me to send the report to the orthopedic surgeon?"

"I know you have to send him a report, but I'm too curious to wait. What are the results?" Joseph inquired.

"On the pinch-grip test – that is the one simulating a trigger pull – the tests are consistent, showing a range, depending on whether or not the TENS unit is in place and allowing for fatigue, from 3.2 pounds to 4.2 pounds in her right index finger. In her left index finger, she tested at 11.1 pounds. That one didn't vary at all."

He continued reading from his cryptic notes. "Although her left hand had a grip strength of forty-two pounds, her right hand was incapable of producing more than ten pounds at any time. Not unexpected with the kind of injury she suffered."

Joseph was elated. "If I understand what you are saying, it would be impossible for her to fire a gun that has a trigger pull of twelve-and-a-half pounds, is that right?"

Sam thought through his answer before replying, "If you mean fire a revolver the way we usually think of a gun being fired, yes, that's true – with either hand. Of course, my opinion is based on her condition today. Although, candidly, I have to believe she is stronger today than when the shooting occurred last August. There is some evidence of healing, and there should be some improvement."

"Are you prepared to express that opinion in court?" Joseph asked.

"Of course – if I'm subpoenaed," he responded with a grin.

"Please send us your report – and your bill," Joseph said with an answering smile.

Sixteen

"Mr. Joseph, the Bellow's trial is scheduled to start in about two weeks," Trent Fillia steeled himself to comment at Friday afternoon's staff/cocktail meeting, "and all the pre-trial work, motions and stuff is done. The witness folders and exhibit lists are ready, but," he added, "you still haven't talked to Mrs. Bellow's daughter, Bliss Tucci – that's not her real last name."

Knowing he had been avoiding the interview, not only because he didn't know what to ask, but by way of wishful thinking that the need for trial would disappear, the lawyer ignored the mild reprimand. "That's true, Trent. Why do I need to interview her? I've read your reports. You seem to have a pretty good handle on what she told the police and plans to say at trial."

"Well," Trent explained, "she was there when Tucci was killed and might give you a little different slant on the facts. You know, something different from the official version. Besides, she is living with some new *friend*, and it's only a few months since Tucci died. I wonder how broken up she really is over his death. She might give you some helpful insight about the others."

Joseph knew the young man was right, but with the press of business he was using as an excuse, he just had not had time to see her and wanted to rely on Fillia's reports. Nevertheless, he was embarrassed. Sighing and agreeing it was something that must be done, he would devote another Saturday morning to the case. He hated to work on Saturdays so suggested, only half joking, "You are available for breakfast tomorrow morning, aren't you? Stop by the house about eight." Damn kid accepted with alacrity.

Drink in hand and now curious as to how Trent had located Bliss, since both the prosecutor and police claim not to have her present address, the elder lawyer asked for an explanation.

"Like I said, she's living on a small farm in Grafton. I remembered Mrs. Bellow telling us about the fight Bliss had with Arliss and the Lorain County Sheriff's office involvement, so I checked their records. Bliss was charged with assault and is on probation. The probation department has her address and phone number listed in some man's name. No big deal," Trent finished modestly, glowing from the compliments elicited.

Trent continued. "I drove by the house. It's really a beat-up old farm. Two cars were in the yard. One belonged to Bliss and the other one is registered in the name of her daughter, Elaine."

"I'm impressed, Trent. You've done a lot of work on this case. When the hell do you get time to get our office work done?"

"Aw, shucks!" he shrugged, a finger to chin, with a grin of feigned humility. "This is more fun."

The rest of the hour degenerated into silly-time and giggles. Della and Joseph decided there was no good reason for keeping the office open or going home to cook, so called their respective spouses and agreed to meet at a favorite restaurant, *The Spruce Tree*, for drinks and dinner. Mary thought it a good idea. The evening was fun, marred only by Joseph's glimpse of a green station wagon that brought to mind the incident in Mt. City. It dampened the evening for him but no one seemed to notice.

Before retiring, he mentioned to Mary that Trent was picking him up in the morning. Naturally, breakfast was hot and on the table when Trent arrived. *Any time I want a cooked meal, just invite one of the kids over,* he thought. *Would that be too manipulative?* he wondered. *Nah!*

Trent driving, the rotund lawyer feeling full and content, they arrived at their destination in short order. Even though Grafton was a small village in Lorain County with a decidedly rural flavor, many factory workers from Lorain and Elyria lived there.

It had two claims to fame. First, as the home of the Grafton Honor Farm, a minimum security prison without walls or fences. A penal experiment for a self-sufficient facility that trusted the inmates. To everyone's surprise, it worked. Rarely did anyone walk away and the production from the farm fed the residents, with more than enough left over to sell and pay some of the operating costs.

Its second claim to fame was a fine authentic Irish public house. The pub, in the center of town, was identified by an emerald green sign bearing the Irish legend *Cead Mile Failte,* granting one hundred thousand welcomes to its guests. The sincerity of the welcome might be questioned but the beer and food was great. As they drove past the restaurant, Joseph thought, *No wonder I'm so fat – I have favorite eating-places in most towns east of the Mississippi. I identify places by restaurants.*

Trent took a road, the name of which Joseph didn't catch, and pointed out the house they sought. His description of it as "an old, beat-up, half-assed farm," was accurate. The house was close to the road and the driveway mere ruts worn into the yard without benefit of gravel or design. The night's light rain had spotted the drive with puddles of mud and water. At the end of the lane, just past the house, barely stood a dilapidated barn, its doors sagging open and looking as though they had for some time. The farmhouse itself had no front door, its only entry, not counting a covered cellar door, from a side porch that consisted mostly of missing and broken boards under a drooping roof. The door, visible behind a sagging screen, was closed against the dreary weather.

There being no way to tell how deep or mushy the ruts were, Trent pulled cautiously into the drive, parking as near the road as possible. Rhythmic, chopping noises were coming from back of the barn. Joseph and Trent picked their way through the uncut grasses along the edge of the lane and walked around the barn where there seemed to be a path of sorts.

A small area behind the barn was cleared of scrub and brush that dominated the abandoned fields beyond. A man of substantial size, wearing faded bib overalls, a baseball cap and rubber boots was using a double-edged axe to split wood into stove length pieces.

Peering around the corner of the disintegrating structure, the lawyer ventured, "Hi ... my name is Pat Joseph and I'm looking for Bliss Tucci. Does she live here?"

The man paused in his efforts, drove the axe into the stump he was using for a splitting block, spat and asked, "Who wants to know?"

Up close, he looked younger than Joseph had been led to expect by Trent's comments, his full black beard and dark curly hair hanging to his shoulders, flowing from beneath the grimy cap sitting squarely on his head.

"I've already told you my name. I'm a lawyer from Milltown. I represent Bliss's mom and need to talk to her about it – if it's all right with you." Joseph felt intimidated by the man's size and presence – didn't want to anger him.

He slowly looked the lawyer over, finally saying with a shrug, "Sure, you can talk to her. She lives with me and Elaine. I don't want you bothering Elaine though."

Ah! It was the young man and Elaine who were living together. Bliss was just a part of their extended family. Under normal circumstances, he would have been Bliss's son-in-law. Joseph wondered, *Why do I keep expecting the world to be as it was in my youth?*

Remembering that Elaine was also at the house the night Tucci was killed and it was her fight with him that put things into motion, Joseph suggested,

"I certainly won't bother Elaine, but I would like to ask her one or two questions. Okay?"

Picking up his axe as though dismissing the pair, the worker returned to his task, responding between grunts, "Since she ain't my wife, I can't tell her what to do. I don't mind you asking her questions – If the baby's up ... but, don't pester her. The baby's been sick and Elaine hasn't had much sleep. If she's asleep, leave her be."

"Sure, no problem," Joseph assured him. "By the way, I didn't get your name."

"No need. I don't know nothing except what I been told," he responded without putting down the axe.

"Did you know Tucci?"

"Some," he paused, swiping at a pesky fly. "We ain't friends or nothing. He lived with Elaine's old lady. I didn't like him much. He was always griping and moaning about drugs and women. He said women was no good and neither was drugs. Weird! Real weird!"

He turned back to his attack on the cordwood, muscles parading up and down his back with each swing of the axe. Joseph shuddered, thinking, *No way in hell I want him mad at me.*

Trent followed the puffing lawyer back to the house looking sheepish. "All right, I screwed up about who was living with whom. But I found her," he muttered as they slogged through the mud and weeds of the overgrown yard. Joseph hesitated in order to catch his breath and studied the porch, wondering whether it would hold their weight. It did.

The door was cracked open in response to his knock. The face of the woman peeking through the spotted screen Joseph recognized immediately to be Gay's daughter even though he had never met her before. She was a triplicate to Gay and Arliss, with the same drawn triangular face, lifeless brown hair with half-hearted curls from an aborted home permanent. Bliss had the same angular, shapeless, almost skeletal body which was covered by shabby black stretch stirrup pants and a loose-fitting sweatshirt with a faded legend of an unrecognized rock group emblazoned on the front.

"Hello, Mrs. Tucci?" Joseph inquired. "Or perhaps, Ms. Bellow? I'm not sure how you call yourself these days."

She ignored the greeting and demanded, "Who are you?" her voice slightly hoarse, throaty.

The lawyer began to introduce himself when she interrupted, "Wait, I know you. I seen your picture in the paper. You're the lawyer what's representing my mother for killing my husband?" Although framed as a statement, the sentence ended in a question mark.

"Well, yes, I do represent your mother and she is charged with Mr. Tucci's murder. That's why I need to talk to you. I asked the man out back if it was all right."

Her eyes shifted back and forth between the obviously harmless old lawyer and the younger Trent. Reluctantly she opened the door a little wider, saying, "Come on in. I was just fixin' some coffee. Want a cup?" An abundance of hospitality.

"Sure," Joseph responded congenially as he moved aside the squeaky screen door and stepped over the threshold. Inside, the house matched the decrepitude of the outside. Cracked plaster walls that had sometime in the not too distant past received a coat of pinkish paint – probably an unwanted clearance color – furniture old, shabby, cigarette scarred, uncared for. The portal led into a dining area furnished with a chipped enamel kitchen table, the leaves of which were pulled out and drooping perilously, surrounded by mismatched chairs, all sitting on a bare, dirty splintered wooden floor.

Bliss walked through the dining area into what was apparently the kitchen, leaving the pair to fend for themselves. The pop of a gas stove was followed shortly by the smell of boiling coffee. An archway on the opposite side of the room led into a parlor where there sat a younger version of Bliss holding a baby clothed in diaper and undershirt, both of which could use changing. The baby was awake but lethargic, sniffling, nose runny, face crusty. Clearly it wasn't feeling well but not crying. "Hi, are you Elaine?" Joseph inquired.

The young women acknowledged her identity without interest and affirmed the relationship to Bliss – she would have had a hard time denying it. In response to Joseph's question, she said, "The baby's been sick. We took her to the hospital for a shot, but she still don't feel too good."

The lawyer began to ask about Tucci's behavior on the night he was killed when Bliss returned bearing three mugs of coffee on a battered tin tray. "Got canned milk if you want some. Sugar's on the table." It was – in a cracked, flyspecked, jelly jar.

"No thanks. We both drink it black," Joseph responded with a smile.

Bliss sat at the table, lit a cigarette and pulled an already overflowing ashtray to her. She began. "First of all, no one says who I can or can't talk to – so it don't mean shit what the guy out back said. Second, why should I help you defend my fuckin' mother? She killed my husband."

"I understand how you feel, "Joseph commiserated, not wanting to alienate her." But I got a job to do. To do it I need to know what happened. Your mother said some things to the police. I have to find out whether they're true or not and whether I should be trying to make a deal for her. I thought you'd probably have more information that anybody."

"Who's the kid?" Bliss changed the subject, nodding toward Trent, a tendril of smoke trailing from her nostrils and rising in front of her face, eyes squinting.

Joseph smiled as Trent bristled. "His name is Trent Fillia and he's my assistant – been doing some leg work for me. If it bothers you to have him here, he can wait in the car." It angered the young lawyer, but he held his tongue.

"I got nothing to hide," Bliss said, lighting a second cigarette from the one now smoldering in her hand. "He can stay. What do you want to know?"

"Just tell me what happened the night your husband was killed – in your own words."

Bliss shrugged and said, "My old lady shot him."

Joseph waited silently. Bliss then began to talk hesitantly. As she got into her story, the words flowed more freely. Occasionally the lawyer nodded or clucked sympathetically. Bliss lit one cigarette after the other, smoking almost constantly.

Her telling continued without interruption except for an occasional visit to the kitchen to replenish the coffee cups or the scratch of a match to light another cigarette.

"Around midnight my sister and mother got there." The word "sister' sounding like a curse. "The bitch lorded it over me for years – better than anyone else – had everything I never did – she was always lying to Ma about me and Robby – made life miserable for me whenever she could."

Joseph interrupted her litany briefly to inquire, "Is there a particular reason you were mad at your sister that night?"

She shrugged. "I was always mad at her about something. She did things to make me mad. She told Robby about me getting some Valium at Ma's house. Ma had a prescription for them and I needed something to relax me. Robby didn't believe in pills. When he found out he beat the shit out of me – said he'd kick me out. It was Arliss' fault, and she did it just to get me in trouble. But I got even with the bitch. Cost me a hundred buck and a couple days in jail, but it was worth it!" She said this with the casual manner of one for whom jail holds little fear.

Bliss continued. "When they got to our place, they come storming up the stairs – just pushed past Robby and his sister Emma. Robby and Emma was *duking* it out on the landing. Ma and the bitch shoved past and just busted into my house. That fuckin' high and mighty Arliss picked up Jake's guitar and yelled for them to get their stuff 'cause they was going home. She didn't ask or nothing, goddam' bitch. Robby was, like, stunned for a minute, then come chargin' in after them yelling who the fuck she thought she was giving orders like that in his house. He was already pretty steamed anyway – what with Emma and all."

This was a new twist. Joseph didn't want Bliss to know he was unaware of the argument between Tucci and his sister. "I heard Robby and his sister were mad about something," he said. "But, I don't know what they were fighting about. Tell me what were they saying to each other."

"Robby and his sister?" Bliss answered, "Well, Emma was... well... they was arguing pretty good about some family thing."

"They were? I knew that, I just don't know the details," Joseph said, pulling closer in a conspiratorial manner. He asked, "Tell me about it, please?"

"Well, you know, Emma was doing things she should'na with that Tom Roper next door. Jim got suspicious about it – caught Emma in a lie. The day Robby was killed, he and Jim was drinking and Jim told him something – I don't know exactly what – that made Emma come roaring over just a couple of minutes before Ma got there. She was standing down at the bottom of the steps screaming up at Robby. He goes to the door and starts yelling back something about like she was just like their mother and no goddamn good. They both end up in each other's face. I thought she was gonna take a swing at him she was so pissed. If she had, he'd a knocked her on her ass."

When she paused for breath, Joseph asked, "Can you remember what they were saying to each other? The exact words, if you can?"

"Well she started by yelling, *You motherfucker! What the fuck'd you tell Jim? He says he's going to kick me out and take my babies from me! And you're going to help him!* I couldn't hear or understand everything she said, but it was like that.

"Robby shot right back at her with, *Fuckin' A! Jim is going to divorce you and get the kids. You're no good! A slut just like Mamma. I hope he busts your ass before he kicks you out!* There was more like that, Robby getting hotter and hotter. They was going at it for a few minutes when my old lady showed. They came past them like they wasn't even there – didn't hear nothing they was saying. Robby and his sister stopped yellin' and just stood there looking..."

She stopped. Remembering what followed, the gossip was no longer fun. Bliss began talking again, almost in a whisper. "Then Robby come in the kitchen... and all hell broke loose...."

Matching her mood, the lawyer asked quietly, "What do you mean?"

Bliss described the confrontation pretty much the same as had Arliss and Gay, adding an occasional detail that filled some gaps. Gay was in front of the washer, leaning against it trying to stay clear of the fray. Bliss was in the arch between the kitchen and living room. Arliss and Robby were struggling near the glass-fronted corner cupboard – she was worried they were going to break it. "I yelled at them to quit... please quit... Robby, leave her be...." she said as though in a trance.

She gestured toward a piece of furniture in the corner. "That's the cupboard they was banging into." A cheap, pseudo oak piece designed to fit into a corner, it had a single glass door through which shelves could be seen on which sat a mixed bag of plates, cups and saucers along with a small collection of cheap gewgaws. Three empty old style heavy glass Coca Cola bottles occupied the top.

"I kept my Coke bottle collection there. Those," she said, gesturing, "are the only one's I got left. I had a couple more big ones that got broke in the fight. Arliss was trying to hit Robby with the guitar and he fell against the cupboard." She walked over and pointed to a gouge. "This is where they banged into it. One of the Coke bottles fell off the top and hit Robby on the head so hard it busted."

She returned back to her seat and listlessly lit another cigarette, forgetting the one already burning in the overflowing ashtray. She continued her narration. "At first, I thought that was how he got hurt, 'cause when it hit him he fell right on his face. He didn't move. I could see he was unconscious so I ran to the window yelling for help. I ran back to Robby – tried to turn him over – see if he'd wake up. He was so heavy – I pulled him on my lap – he wouldn't wake up – there was blood all over his face. My mother," she said distastefully, "Arliss and them just walked right out the house like there was nothing wrong."

Reliving the moment, she explained. "Emma and I was both kneeling by Robby trying to wake him up – calling his name, but... nothing." Her eyes glazed over, looking inward. "I ran back to the window and yelled for help again. No one came. Emma was by Robby. I screamed at her to go and get help. She left – I held Robby's head in my lap for a long time then some men came to take him away. He never woke up."

124

Sitting there silently digesting her story for a few minutes, the lawyer finally asked her to repeat the part about going to the window and calling for help. She did. "When Robby fell down, I could see he was knocked out. I knelt down and called his name. He didn't answer, so I ran to the window to see if someone would get help. It was hot so there was a lot of people outside. I just yelled as loud as I could for someone to help me 'cause Robby got hit on the head and was hurt."

The events were forming into a clear picture. Something could have happened after Gay left the room and while Bliss was at the window. "Bliss, how long were you at the window calling for help?"

"I don't know – maybe a minute – maybe less."

"When you talked to the police, did you tell them everything, just like you told me?"

"Pretty much," she nodded, immersed in the telling. "'Cause that's the way it happened."

"How many times have they talked to you since?"

"Only once, when I called and asked the detective if it was okay for me to take Robby's car and put it in my name. He said I could. No one's talked to me since ... except the prosecutor. She called and said I was gonna have to testify at the trial – which is all right with me – SHE killed my husband!" A look of loathing accompanied the words.

A good time to end the interview, Joseph thought. He stood and said, "We appreciate your help. I'm sure we'll see you again."

She was still sitting at the table, a lit cigarette in her lips, a cup of cooling coffee in her hand as they walked out. Her daughter hadn't moved from the couch, slackly holding her limp baby and staring at a flickering television screen. Even though not asking the questions of Elaine he intended, there was not much she could add and the lawyer wanted to think about what her mother had told him. He did wonder about the world to which her child had been assigned.

Seventeen

Sunday morning Joseph was awakened by a small, black wriggly body – a wet, pink tongue protruding from a concave muzzle licked his face, ear and as much of his head as could be reached. His Pug dog, Squeezer, decided it was time the lawyer arise. Spoiled, the dog refused to jump out of the bed – it's too high – so she woke Joseph to be lifted down. Wriggling, squirming, grunting, as only Pugs can, she was all over. Pretending he believed it to be his wife, Joseph reached over and patted a round bottom, saying, "Quit it, Mary. It's too early in the morning for such behavior. Besides, I have a headache."

A grumbled response that sounded vaguely like, "Not very funny ... mumph," came from beneath covers pulled over her head. Her cats watched from various vantage points, trying to decide if the warm bed was going to interfere with their breakfast.

The lawyer got up, put Squeezer on the floor and, disdaining his robe and slippers for a pair of jeans and tie-less tennis shoes, led the dog and several cats downstairs. Stopping only long enough to put the coffee on and open a can of cat food, *How can they eat that shit?* he thought as he walked outside. Squeezer wouldn't perform her daily toilet without being watched and praised. Together they walked to the barn, fed the goats and let out the barn dog. He not only looked like a timber wolf, the only weather he could tolerate was the arctic variety.

The dogs and lawyer trekked down to the mailbox to pick up the morning papers – his morning constitutional and the sum total of exercise he wanted for a Sunday. The *Cleveland Plain Dealer* waited in its blue plastic box, the *Akron Beacon Journal* in one colored green. The local newspaper, The *Milltown Reporter* was delivered in a yellow container – each provided by the respective newspapers. Joseph wasn't sure who chose the colors for the home delivery boxes or what their significance.

By the time he got back to the house the coffee was ready. Joseph retired to the porch to sip and read. Mary was in the shower, getting ready for church. She complained they never got to Mass on time and it was, somehow, always

Joseph's fault. It didn't matter he was usually dressed, ready and sitting in the car with motor running.

The morning serene, the view from the porch fantastic, the geese grown and gone and the barn swallows readying their kids for the long flight to somewhere for the cold months ahead. Joseph enjoyed none of it.

Coffee finished and papers read, the lawyer wandered in to shave, shower and dress. Mary, in her dressing room applying make-up or combing something, said, "You'll have to hurry or we'll be late."

The lawyer finished his toilet and left the bathroom, Mary was still staring into the mirror. He could never figure out what there was to look at for so long. He adjusted the seat in her car and backed out of the garage. She wouldn't ride to church in his pick-up – something about God not approving of truckers. She ran through the litany of her cats as she settled into the car. "Are Tony, Abner, Puff, Tabatha and Pappy in the house?"

Joseph nodded affirmatively while backing into the turnaround.

"I know Arnold is in," she said. "I saw him. Did you lock Andy in the pen? Is Squeezer in her cage?"

Joseph continued nodding, moving down the drive.

Mass, as always, was beautiful and fulfilling. One of the parish priests had a special style of delivering a homily that made participants of all in attendance. The congregation loved it, and him. This morning, none of it reached the lawyer.

After Mass, as was their practice, they went to breakfast with several friends. Eggs may be bad for the lawyer, but he reasoned God wouldn't permit cholesterol to be augmented on Sunday morning – especially after attending Mass. The usual group was there.

Knowing and enjoying each other, they spoke of many things – the cabbages and kings' variety. Mary, impatient with her husband's morose spirit, said, "What's bothering you? You're usually a grump, but ... " She didn't finish.

"I know you don't like to hear about my work, but the Bellow's case is on my mind. I keep thinking of the talk Trent and I had with Gay's daughter. I'm convinced Gay didn't kill Tucci. Bliss seems convinced she did. Everything I know tells me Gay shouldn't have to go to trial. I don't know how to persuade Jackie."

Mary smiled. "Don't worry about it. Try the case, win it and then tell Jackie you told her so." Nothing was ever complicated for Mary. "Now, cheer up."

127

Joseph learned early in their marriage never to say "You don't understand," even with the words on the tip of his tongue. But she didn't – no one did. The prosecution is supposed to be as much a part of the system as the defense and should want to search for the truth, whatever the hell that is.

He tried to explain. "Mary, everyone blames today's breakdown in morals, crime and drugs on lawyers and judges. If we didn't let criminals off, there would be no problems. Clichés like *criminals belong in jail* and *judges are too soft* may have a seed of truth in them, but aren't the only answers. Prosecutors have to get elected. The only way they think they can is by playing a numbers game. Make a record of convictions and do it publicly."

Warming up to the subject, he continued. "Everyone loses sight of the people involved – the victims and the defendants. Sometimes the defendant is as much a victim as the injured party. There must be a way of removing someone from the system without a trial, in a case like this. It bothers the hell out of me and it's the frustration of not being able to do a damn thing about it that has created my shitty mood on this otherwise beautiful morning."

The table grew silent. Joseph looked at his friends. They didn't know what he was talking about. He tried to stop but couldn't. "I suppose the nature of my work creates conflict. But it seems to me, those in the business shouldn't add fuel by doing things that make lawyer bashing acceptable. *The first thing we do, let's kill all the lawyers,* said Shakespeare tongue in cheek, knowing the lawyer's voice is the only one raised against a tyrannical government. The public today is unwilling to recognize the truth of that."

The lawyer sighed, realizing he was putting a damper on what was supposed to be a fun morning. "Mary," he groaned. "This is just my way of saying I don't believe Gay killed Tucci. She shouldn't have to go to trial."

She leaned over toward her husband and whispered, "Well, why don't you just tell Jackie?" She really believed it was that simple. God love her. The others remained silent.

The diatribe hadn't lightened his load but convinced him he should leave the gathering. He and Mary returned home where he changed clothes, went down to the barn and fastened a leash to his goat, laid it across the goat's back – he liked to carry his own lead – whistled for the dogs and took off walking through the back pasture. The woods are beautiful – especially in spring when hidden in a clearing, a field of trillium would glisten white surrounded by impenetrable woods. Why God hides beauty where so few can see, escaped, but pleasured, the lawyer. Unfortunately the growing season was rapidly drawing to a close, but there were still some unnamed blooms and wild flowers left to enjoy, fallen logs to jump over or sit on, and scurrying critters to chase.

Joseph carried his stick. Billy the goat stayed close. Andy roved the woods, never quite out of sight. They were great company and didn't seem to mind his degenerate attitude. They enjoyed the outing. If he didn't, it was his problem.

Their unquestioned acceptance of him at his worst always did wonders. He returned from the walk convinced Mary was right. All he had to do was tell Jackie. "Hi," Mary said. "Feeling better?"

* * * * *

Holding onto the unrealistic optimism, Joseph looked for a break in his Monday schedule to call Jackie VanDamm's office and ask when he might stop over. Her secretary, after a short wait, said, "Mrs. VanDamm says she is available now if you need to see her, Mr. Joseph."

Any excuse to get away from the office and the ever-present paper work was acceptable. He thanked her kindly and asked that she tell Jackie he'd be right there. On the way out Joseph told Della, "I'm going to the prosecutor's office. I'll probably stop at the deli on the way back. Want to meet me for a sandwich?"

Fall had arrived, but the promise of an Indian summer made the days pleasant. The leaves were edged with varying hues, promising that the Square would soon be a riot of color. The fluffy clouds were scudding across the sky. Joseph liked the picturesque word, "scudding." It tripped off the tongue as descriptively as the moving clouds.

At the corner the lawyer nodded to the crossing guard. He once represented her boyfriend for some minor infraction or other. Wonder why she stayed with him? He would beat the hell out of her on occasion, get drunk and steal beer from a convenience store. Dumb bastard! Must be some good in him if she's still with him. "Hi, Becky. How's Howie?"

"Fine, Mr. Joseph. He's been sober since he got out. We really appreciate what you did."

It was no more than a five-minute walk to Jackie's, past the library and a couple of shops. Her office was in what had once been a funeral home. Mills County bought it about the same time the New Courthouse was built and converted it into an office for the prosecutor. Access to the lower level was through a garage door where the bodies used to be delivered. Joseph wondered if the stainless steel table was still in use in the little room behind the garage door. Entering, he wondered *How can justice live in a house of the dead?* His optimism was fading.

"Hi, Mr. Joseph," the receptionist greeted. "Mrs. VanDamm is expecting you. Go right up."

He did, passing parlors where bodies had once been displayed, now housing the secretarial pool and private offices. Narrow stairs led to Jackie's office.

Sitting behind her desk, she smiled a greeting. "You wanted to see me, Mr. Joseph?"

He detected some residual formality – must still be a little put out. Joseph was again taken by the dark beauty she bore so well. "Yes, I do, Jackie. Please call me Pat. We need to talk about the Bellow's case."

"Why? Is she ready to plead?" Jackie asked coolly. "I wouldn't mind working something out – save the State the expense of a trial," she said, still refusing cordiality.

"God damn it, Jackie! Will you relax and talk to me like a human being? I'm trying to save all of us money, embarrassment and a lot of needless work. If you'd listen to me, maybe you would understand why Mrs. B. couldn't have killed Tucci. She shouldn't go to trial. In fact, you might want to suggest to the Sheriff's office some avenues of investigation they ignored. You could be a hero and get some good press." The lawyer was trying hard to restrain his impatience.

"Mr. Joseph, I'm not hard-nosed. But, goddamn it, we have a confession. The Sheriff's department is satisfied your client killed Tucci. So am I. I work with them everyday and will not second-guess them, especially on **just** your word! I've been warned about you."

She continued in a more reasonable tone trying to be patient with a senile old bastard. "I have to run for election. This case will give me a lot of publicity. I intend to try it. The voters are going to know they did the right thing in electing me. They got their money's worth." She warmed to her subject. "I will not back off simply because you are in this case. If that's what you're trying to do, forget it... If the defense is as good as you say it is, try the fuckin' case and get an acquittal – if you can....

"In fact," she added, "If your case is so damn good, why are you trying so hard to convince me? Maybe you're not so sure."

"I think you know better than that, Jackie. Then again, maybe you don't. I've never backed off from a fight in your lifetime. Mrs. Bellow has been through enough and no one – especially you – gives a shit! She's just a number to you... Oh, fuck it... see you in court!"

Walking out, Joseph said to himself, *Well, aren't you proud? You blew it again, you dumb shit – sexist bastard!*

Joseph, no longer hungry but seeing Della walking across the Square, remembered his promise. Catching up to her near one of the park benches scattered around the park, he called, "Della ... I need somebody to gripe at and I don't feel like sitting inside."

"Why don't I just get some sandwiches and bring them here?" she suggested.

"Good idea. I'll wait." As she started on her way, he called, "Get a couple of those cookies I like – you know, the honey-nut-raisin ones?"

She waved that she heard while he walked to and sat on the park bench. It was a warm day and lunch outside might soothe his ruffles. He knew he hadn't handled Jackie well, but didn't know what he could have done differently. With any trial, there's a risk. The final decision would be Gay's. A bad deal was sometimes better than no deal at all. Besides, it was her freedom if they lost. The lawyer's job was simple. Inform her of the options.

Della arrived with lunch. "You look pensive. Worrying about Mrs. Bellow?"

"Let's forget about the office and enjoy the sunshine. It isn't going to be with us much longer," he suggested. "Pretty soon the ladies are going to be wearing those winter coats that cover up the short skirts and long legs. I don't like winter. Did you get my cookies?"

Eighteen

It was just two weeks before Christmas and Gay's trial was to start the next morning. The hesitant lawyer was as ready as could be but a final client conference was necessary. The trauma of a trial cannot be understood until experienced.

Gay sat regally straight on the edge of one of the client chairs. Claude slouched unobtrusively on the couch, obviously wishing he was somewhere else.

"Gay – Claude, thanks for coming in," Joseph began. "We need to go over some things before trial. I want to be satisfied you understand what you face." No smile – serious talk was all that was on the agenda. "Some hard decisions have to be made. Yours will be the most difficult."

"I understand ... please go on," Gay instructed as though she were chairing the meeting. She appeared comfortable despite her rigid posture. Joseph was getting used to it. It was as though she feared flexibility in posture would reflect in her attitude. She was more comfortable in her rigidity than her husband in his slouch.

Speaking to both of them but addressing his remarks to Gay, the lawyer said, "As you know, the charge is murder. In Ohio, murder is the purposeful taking of the life of another with prior calculation and design. Each element must be proved beyond a reasonable doubt before you can be convicted. If the State can't prove any one of the elements, you must be acquitted.

"In other words," Joseph continued. "If the State is unable to prove the element of *purposefully*, you cannot be convicted. The jury may be able to find you guilty of some lesser crime, such as negligent homicide, but not murder. Do you understand?"

Gay nodded she did. Claude didn't move. It was as if he heard nothing yet shuddered each time the word "convicted" was uttered.

"A crime is a crime only because the State says so. It is an act that is prohibited like murder, or mandated like wearing a seat belt. In addition to the act, the legislature must also specify a penalty. In other words, if there is no punishment, there is no crime."

Joseph paused long enough to be sure Gay was still with him. She was, and even appeared intellectually interested.

"The punishment for murder is an indefinite sentence from fifteen years to life. Yours is not a capital case since the prosecution is not seeking the death penalty."

Since Jackie VanDamm had said she might consider a plea to *voluntary manslaughter*, Joseph explained the elements.

"Voluntary manslaughter is knowingly causing the death of another while under the influence of sudden passion, or in a sudden fit of rage caused by an act of the victim sufficient to incite the use of deadly force. It is punishable by a sentence of from five to twenty-five years – but it is also probational."

"Why are you telling me these things?" Gay asked with a quizzical look.

"Mrs. VanDamm told me she would consider a plea to voluntary manslaughter so I have to tell you about it. I feel confident that due to your age and circumstance she might be willing to deal some more and, with some creative argument, we might get her to make a recommendation of probation. She doesn't necessarily want you to go to jail. She just wants a conviction." Joseph could feel the nervous sweat trickling down his armpits. Without saying so, he hoped Gay would be tempted to accept this last minute reprieve.

"Mr. Joseph," Gay began formally, still sitting perfectly straight on the edge of her chair. "If I go to jail for fifteen years or fifteen minutes it would make no difference. I will die there." She said this with no change of inflection – neither emotional nor theatrical – but with such conviction that it never occurred to the lawyer to doubt her sincerity. "I have thought of little else for the past several months. I cannot live in jail – under any circumstances. Claude and I have talked about it and he knows exactly how I feel."

Visualizing Claude entering into any kind of meaningful conversation with Gay was beyond the lawyer's ability, but he could see Bellow listening to her and attending her every wish.

"We have decided to go to trial and take our chances." Her use of the plural pronoun was obviously for Claude's benefit. The decision was hers. "There is really no need for any more talk, Mr. Joseph. It is distressing to me and upsetting to Claude."

The lawyer felt a chill. Her certainty unnerved him. "Please call me Pat," he stammered. "Uh... let's get on to other matters then. As you know, we filed a motion to suppress your so-called confession. It was denied as expected, but we had to do it to preserve an appeal in case you are convicted. I know you're not interested in these details but I'm telling you about them to assure you we are waiving none of your rights. I like to tell clients we waive nothing but the American flag."

The mini-lecture continued. "The strength of the State's case is your confession. There is a series of cases decided by the U.S. Supreme Court and the Ohio Supreme Court that establish when, and under what circumstances, a confession can be used. In 1897, a case called *Bram vs. United States* held that a confession can only be used if it is free and voluntary and not extracted by threats or violence, or obtained by any direct or implied promises, however slight, or by the exertion of improper influence. Quite strong language. It's still the law today."

Gay was listening with rapt attention. Again, she seemed intrigued as much from an academic standpoint as anything else.

"A series of cases followed over the years – *Miranda, Wilson, Lynumn, Edwards* – all names that mean little to the layman, but a great deal to lawyers and defendants. These are the cases that define the Constitutional rights of a criminal defendant. The impact on your case is important only from a technical standpoint, but necessary to protect your rights."

The lawyer gestured toward Trent Fillia and said, "He has done most of that work and will be in and out during trial. He will not, however, be sitting at the trial table with us."

Trent looked crestfallen. "Aw, Mr. J.," but made no argument beyond that.

Talking to Gay, but for the boy's benefit, Joseph continued. "I don't want the jury to see anyone but you and me at the trial table. Jackie VanDamm is going to have her chief trial assistant, Grant Bradley, with her as well as Mike Redding, the detective. I want it to look like they're ganging up on us. It might evoke some sympathy and we need every advantage possible."

For the first time, Joseph addressed Mr. Bellow directly. "Claude." His eyes shifted slightly, but he made no move to look at the lawyer. "You won't be able to sit with us, but will be in the front row of the spectator seats directly behind us. At every break, talk to Gay. Let her know you're supporting her. The jury will be aware of that. Put your heads together – talk – touch – as you usually do. The jury will learn how close you are to one another and will see that you are real, flesh and blood, human beings."

Claude needed no instructions about expressing his feelings for Gay. His devotion would be illuminated – his forlorn fear of losing her evident on his face and figure far better than anyone could ever orchestrate it.

"Gay, you always dress beautifully so you don't need any special instructions on how to dress for your trial. Neat, clean, and conservative is the key. Hair neat, not radical. Juries don't like modern or unusual. If you're too perfect, they will resent you. If you are not well turned out, they will look down on you. If you try to fool them, their anger will be aroused. We walk a tightrope."

Joseph explained exactly how he wanted Gay to dress on the day she would be taking the stand in order to provide the greatest impact when she demonstrated her mangled arm and the TENS Unit she wore. "Your injury, the constant pain, the terrible weakness in your hand, are vital to our case. We don't want its presentation to appear contrived, but the impact is of the utmost importance. The jurors must have a vivid recollection of it during deliberations."

Joseph tried to explain the reasoning behind what appeared to be an artificially concocted scenario. "Gay, the people that are going to decide your guilt or innocence are strangers. We are asking these strangers to decide the most important thing in your life – whether you live in freedom or die in jail. To guarantee fair treatment, they must not only know you, but like you. We can't allow them to be indifferent. If the members of the jury can identify with you, feel sympathy and understanding for you, they are much less likely to vote for conviction. If they don't care, it's easy to say *Guilty*! I cannot stress this enough."

He paused, studying Gay's face intently. "Do you understand everything I'm saying?"

A tentative nod, followed by, "Not completely, but I trust you know what you are about." Joseph wasn't so sure.

The lawyer added, "Gay, you have to be what you appear to be. If you come across the least bit artificial, the jury will think you're trying to fool them – not sincere. They won't tolerate that. I will be with you – but it is your life. You have to convince the jury to save that life..." thinking, *At least one of the jurors....*

* * * * *

The end of the business day was near. Joseph wanted Gay to see the courtroom where they would spend the week of trial. "Gay, you already saw Judge Clarke's courtroom during your arraignment but I want to explain some of the things that will be happening there. The Judge isn't there now. I asked his secretary to let us in. Do you mind walking over to the courthouse with me?"

They walked into the courtroom that would be their home for the next few days. It overlooked the Square – a fantastic view from the west windows, rarely appreciated by those there. They had hurried to avoid the threatening rain. Like the novelist said, *It is going to be a dark and stormy night* – one not conducive to pleasant thoughts for the Bellows.

Joseph wanted Gay to experience the impact of the courtroom with no one else present – not to walk in cold on the morning of trial to a roomful of prospective jurors. They might see the look of fear and horror that flashes across the face of a defendant when first realizing, *This is the room where my future will be decided!*

He took Gay's arm as they entered. A small involuntary gasp escaped her and she stumbled slightly over a nonexistent sill. She gathered herself, quickly, and shook off his hand. Her resolve strengthened perceptively. She patted her hair in place and checked her skirt for lint. "Which will be my seat?" she inquired in a steady voice. She would do fine.

Joseph showed her and Claude where they would sit – she next to him at the trial table – he immediately behind her in the spectator's section. Joseph always chose the same table nearest the jury box. He wanted to be right next to the jury – wanted the jurors to pay attention to them – the first thing they'd see as they took their seat each morning and the last when filing out each evening. He wanted the jurors to be so familiar with them that, if they choose to cast a ballot against Gay, it would be like voting against one of the family. Joseph's proprietary interest in that table was never challenged by any member of the local bar or the prosecutor's office. Even Judge Clarke expected Joseph to occupy it when in his court.

Walking around the room, Joseph ran his hand over each piece of furniture with lost intimacy, familiarity returning as he touched each. Although frequently in this room, it had been a long time since trying a case of this magnitude – and never one in which he believed so strongly in his client's innocence.

"This is the jury box. Each chair will be filled. The same juror will occupy the same chair each day. You will get to know them. Be comfortable with them. Smile when it seems appropriate. Nod good morning. Let them know you are aware of their importance – be serious about the case but don't lose your warmth or humor."

The room was impressive, dominated by a bench large enough to accommodate three judges behind which sat three high-backed, well-upholstered leather chairs. The room was sometimes used for oral argument by the three member Court of Appeals. Immediately before the bench is a small desk for the court reporter – the witness box to the right. The bailiff's desk occupied a position behind and to the side of the witness box, permitting an unobstructed view of the room.

The gallery, behind a heavy walnut rail, consisted of long church-like pews sans kneeler. The room itself was painted a soft cool blue, like a sunlit sky just before dark, trimmed in highly polished, dark woods.

Joseph tried to look at his workshop through Gay's eyes. She walked with him, touching the jury rail – the bar that separated the participants from the observers – the witness box – the Judge's bench. She ran her hand gently over both trial tables, creating tactile impressions of their future occupants. She looked out of the windows – outside was important – with quiet intelligence and intense interest. Claude followed behind, looking at nothing but Gay as she moved about the room.

Joseph pulled a chair from the trial table and sat with them, explaining how Gay would help make decisions. Her involvement was important.

The elderly lawyer had recently visited England where he observed a murder trial at the Old Bailey – a particularly vicious stabbing death of a young girl. The courtroom was not at all like this. The Judge, robed in scarlet and wearing a powdered wig, sat at a high bench overlooking the contestants. The jury box was slightly below the judge, but also elevated. The defendant, on the same level as the jury, did not accompany his lawyer, but sat in a dock at the rear of the courtroom. The gallery looked down at the participants from on high, much as the Romans must have watched combatants in The Coliseum. The barristers – their weapons books, papers, pens and half-glasses – were also properly wigged and robed occupying desks in the center of the room, on the floor at the lowest level of the chambers.

At first glance, the robes, the wigs, the stylized atmosphere appeared stilted – ludicrous – a caricature. But as the trial progressed, it became obvious who the participants truly were. The battle was joined on the floor of the chamber – the war waged by mercenaries hired for that purpose.

The jury may decide the victor – the judge may demand the war be fought fairly within the rules – the defendant's future may be the spoils – but there was no question who was doing the fighting or where the war was taking place.

Such civilized combat may fit in England's proper society, but Joseph wanted no part of it. He wanted the jury to know and love Gay as a participant – *she has to join the fight,* Joseph thought. *There may be much to say about the British system that fathered ours – the dignity and formality are appealing. The Marquis of Queensberry philosophy may do much to prevent surprises or dirty tricks by either side, but in this country prosecutors need to be elected. Politics do not provide incentive for a fair fight.*

In the morning the courtroom would begin to fill.

Nineteen

At precisely nine-fifteen, the paneled door opened and Judge Clarke entered his courtroom with a flourish, mounting the bench without looking around. Not for the first time, Joseph thought, *What a ham. He enjoys parading in his robes – being looked at and playing at being a judge. It would be nice if he weren't playing.*

Art Gruen, the Court's bailiff, intoned the formula, "Hear Ye! Hear Ye! Hear Ye! This Honorable Court is now in session pursuant to adjournment. All having business before this Honorable Court draw near, and ye shall be heard. The Honorable Thomas V. Clarke presiding!" Art always looked embarrassed while reciting the proscribed speech.

Now, for the first time, Judge Clarke looked at the assembly with a slightly surprised expression as though not expecting anyone to be there. "Please be seated..." he suggested.

While the crowd settled in, Judge Clarke arranged himself behind his high bench shuffling and stacking the papers before him. Looking through his reading glasses perched on the end of his nose, he read, "We are here in the case of the *State of Ohio vs. Gabriella Bellow.* Mrs. Bellow has been indicted for the crime of Murder in violation of Section 2903.02 of Ohio's Revised Code. She is in court this morning represented by counsel, Mr. Patrick Joseph. The State is present and represented by Mills County Prosecutor Jacqueline VanDamm and Assistant County Prosecutor T. Grant Bradley."

Having satisfied the recording requirements, Judge Clarke looked up from his papers and addressed the roomful of prospective jurors, twelve of whom were already sitting in the jury box, to impress upon the jurors the gravity of the occasion.

"You are the array drawn by chance from the jury wheel. A jury will be picked from among you to try the issues in this case. You will be questioned by the Court and counsel for the purpose of determining your qualifications to serve. Each side has the right to challenge any number of you for cause. In addition, each side has six peremptory challenges. That means each side has the right to excuse up to six members of this panel for any reason or no reason at all. If this right is exercised, you are not to consider it an insult, nor shall you take the challenge personally. Each lawyer here has had a great deal of trial experience. It is their duty to choose a jury they believe will best serve their client.

"The reasons for challenges for cause are set forth in Ohio's Revised Code and include such things as age, bias, and so on. You need not concern yourself about it unless it applies to you. If the question comes up, it will be explained."

He paused and looked over his half-glasses around the room and gestured toward the people occupying the trial tables before him, "Now, I will introduce the parties."

Joseph had heard the canned speech before.

The judge introduced each participant separately, starting with those occupying the State's table and giving the prospective jurors a brief biographical sketch. This included Detective Mike Redding. As the officer in charge of the investigation, he had a right to sit at the prosecution table. After each introduction, the judge inquired if any of the prospective jurors knew, had any business with, or was represented by those named.

Joseph always found it humbling to realize how few people on the venire had done business with his office. *Maybe it's not so surprising,* he speculated, *considering my practice. Jurors are drawn from the polls, and most criminals, petty or otherwise, are not inclined to vote.*

The judge introduced Gay last, saying, "The defendant is Mrs. Gabriella Bellow, charged with the crime of murder." This brought everyone's attention to Gay, who stood with the introduction. Joseph tried to read their faces. How could anyone believe this gentle lady could commit murder?

Clarke continued. "It is enough for you to know the Grand Jury indicted her. You may draw no inference from that fact. An indictment is merely a piece of paper that informs a defendant of the charges and tells her she is to be here. Our system says she is innocent until proven guilty beyond a reasonable doubt. That mantel of innocence remains with her throughout the trial."

Judge Clarke had been reading the boilerplate opening to the prospective jurors in a casual, relaxed manner from papers sitting before him. He now adopted a serious expression, peering at the group and intoned. "Those phrases are not clichés. They have real meaning in this courtroom. If you do not believe me, or do not accept it, you do not belong here and may be excused right now."

He paused, looking around the room sternly, daring a challenge. No one moved. He was at his best with an audience. "Now, I am going to ask the bailiff, Mr. Gruen, to swear you in. That means you'll take an oath to answer all questions put to you, whether by me or counsel, honestly, truthfully and fully. Do you understand?"

Heads nodded soundlessly. He was not trying to frighten the venire so much as to impress upon them the seriousness of the task at hand.

Art stood before the group, instructed them to stand and raise their right hands and administered the oath. He handed each lawyer a list of the names and personal data about each prospective juror. As he handed the papers to the defense lawyer, he slipped him a couple of mentholated cough drops.

Joseph smiled. He had lived through many trials with Art, who was aware of most of the older lawyer's habits, including that of holding a cough drop in his cheek to keep his throat moist. He also knew Joseph usually forgot to bring them to court and so kept a supply handy. A fresh pot of coffee was always ready in his office as well. He truly liked lawyers and did his best to serve without taking sides.

While the judge ran through a series of questions to those in the jury box, Joseph looked at Gay. He was thinking about the session held in the Judge's chambers earlier that morning. Jackie had renewed her offered plea bargain. Joseph delivered the message to Gay standing at the trial table alongside her husband.

"Gay, the prosecutor has again offered the plea we talked about earlier. Do you want me to accept or reject it?"

It's not unusual for defendants, faced with the immediate reality of trial, to insist on changing their plea at the last minute. Fearful of the possibilities, they sometimes prefer dealing with the known rather than the unknown.

Before Gay could answer, Claude spoke. "Gay, I need you. I don't want you to spend the rest of your life in jail. I can wait for a few years, and will. Probation is even a possibility, isn't it?" he asked, as he glanced at Joseph. "Whatever happens, I want you with me. Please, don't take any chances." His eyes were edged with tears.

It dawned on Joseph this was the first time he heard Claude's voice since their meeting months earlier. Though frequently in the office with Gay, she did all the talking. He was now speaking from the heart, his eyes large and moist, his face an unhealthy color.

Gay looked at him. This was also a first. Joseph had never seen her look directly at her husband. Her expression – the novel softness around her mouth

– spoke volumes. She loved him as much as he loved her – but she made the tough decisions he couldn't.

"As I said before, we are going forward with this trial. It doesn't matter whether I'm convicted or plead guilty to something. If I go to jail, I will die there. When I die, I want it to be in bed, next to you. I am not going to plead to anything." Her eyes, also moist, held a smile for him alone.

After a silence, long enough for a lump to grow in the lawyer's throat, Gay brought him back into the conversation. "Please tell them we are ready to proceed."

Without a word, Joseph returned to Judge Clarke's chambers and said, "No sense wasting any more time. Let's get it on."

The Judge reached for his robes and shooed them from his office. Although Gay had paled slightly when she realized the trial was actually starting, she did not falter. At least her resolve was firm.

Listening to the questioning by the court and prosecutor he had heard so many times before, Joseph tried not to allow his mind to wander, no matter how tempting. Each significant response was noted. He began to develop a feeling about each juror. It would soon be his turn.

* * * * *

Judge Clarke addressed the defense table. "Ms. VanDamm has passed for cause, Mr. Joseph..." meaning that she had found no legal challenge to any of the twelve jurors presently sitting in the box. "You may proceed to inquire if you wish."

They had been sitting at the trial table for several hours, even with occasional breaks ordered by the court. Joseph could feel his throat dry, the butterflies battering the walls of his stomach trying to get out with the realization he was actually going to have to talk to the jurors about this case. He arose slowly, smiled at Gay, touched her cheek gently and walked to the jury rail. Resting his hands on it, he took several seconds to look at each prospective juror. He held no notes, but did have, within easy view, their names and personal history.

"Ladies and gentlemen," he embarked tentatively with a slight quaver, beginning the rote recitation of a presentation thoroughly prepared. "This is my first chance to talk to you. If you are chosen as a juror, there will be two more opportunities called opening statement and final argument. On those occasions, I will be doing the talking. This is the only chance you have to talk to me. We can talk about the case and about other things as well, things about which you are interested."

Changing directions slightly, he continued easily. "I used to thank jurors for coming here, for taking time from their lives to serve. I quit doing that when I realized how well paid you are for jury service."

This drew a small laugh, knowing that each would be paid the munificent sum of twelve dollars a day. "Okay, maybe not in money, but with the knowledge that you are perpetuating the criminal justice system which protects each of us – you too. If you ever find yourself in the same boat as Gay," he said, gesturing in her direction, "there will be others like you to sit in judgment. The knowledge of that is damn good pay! The jury system is all that stands between us and a potentially tyrannical government."

They were beginning to listen and think.

Joseph tried to remind the prospective jurors of the things they learned in school, things quickly put aside when bombarded by media hype about how criminals have taken over our streets. It is unfortunate, but true, that jurors have to be re-indoctrinated in the way of life conceived by the Constitution. Everyone should be required to read the Bill of Rights at least once a year.

"What we are doing is called *voir dire*. The judge told you that it, loosely translated, means to tell the truth. I hate to disagree with the judge so early in the trial," he said, smiling to remove the sting, "but literally those words in French mean *to see, to speak*. We get to look at each other, speak to each other, and decide collectively whether we can work together to guarantee Gay a fair trial."

By now they were listening attentively. "We tell you things like we do not intend to pry or get personal." This was a shot at the prosecutor who assured the jury she did not intend to pry into their affairs. "Not true! We have no more than several hours to get to know each other – to pick a jury that will decide the most important thing in Gay's life – her entire future. We would be fools to allow someone to make a life or death decision about us without knowing everything we can about that person. If you are embarrassed in the process, I'm not going to apologize. I need to know what embarrasses you – what makes you mad – what pleases you. We need to be intimately acquainted with one another before we can allow you to make this most important decision about Gay."

The preliminaries out of the way, Joseph began questioning each juror separately, occasionally repeating questions already put to them by the Judge or Mrs. VanDamm – asking about their jobs, their families, their background. He asked them about their beliefs, church, reading material, television habits – questions designed to get them to talk and tell something about their bent.

In the everyday world, friendships take a long time to develop – they don't just happen. People meet and talk. It is talk that breaks down, or creates barriers. It is in dialogue that mutual interests and opinions held are discovered. All of this takes time – time that is not available in the microcosm of a trial.

People are usually reluctant to talk about themselves in front of strangers. Joseph had to overcome that normal reticence and persuade each prospective juror to talk about his job and family, things about which he or she is proud. Ask with interest, step back and listen – really listen. It is the only way to break down the constraint that exists between strangers.

* * * * *

Within two days, the jury was picked – seven men and five women. The original panel of sixty-five now reduced to twelve, ranging in age from early twenties to a retired sixty-eight year old. The group of seven men and five women were all honorable, working people – a farmer, teacher, postman, nurse, retired engineer, housewife, secretary, student, school counselor, two factory workers from the Ford plant in Brook Park and a self-employed sales representative – plus two alternates who would have to sit, listen and be ready to step in and take the place of any juror who was unable to complete the trial – usually a thankless task.

During the process, several had been removed for cause and each side exercised peremptory challenges. Each time Joseph would consult with Gay before announcing his decision. He wanted the jurors to know Gay was actively participating. When the judge advised Joseph he had his last challenge, he leaned toward Gay, lips close to her ear. "Gay, look at each juror – in the face – one at a time. Take your time. If you are satisfied with the one you are looking at, smile and nod. Start with number one and go all the way through."

She whispered back, "You decide. If you're satisfied, just tell the Judge."

"Look, Gay, it's your life, not mine. I want the jury to know you picked them! Do what I ask."

The lawyer leaned back in his chair as Gay allowed her gaze to settle on juror number one. She studied his face tentatively, then smiled and nodded. Turning to the lawyer she began, "Is th...?"

He cut her off with a gesture, directing her to continue. She did, looking into each face in turn, studying it, smiling and nodding as though pleased that juror was willing to participate in her trial. She did it beautifully – better than Joseph had hoped.

Finished, she leaned toward Joseph and whispered, "Did I do it right?"

He responded, "Yes, beautiful. Are you satisfied?"

"I have no way of knowing. I guess so."

Joseph turned to the bench, stood and said in a voice loud enough for all to hear, "Your Honor, Mrs. Bellow and I are pleased with the make up of this jury," as he smiled and bowed to them.

Two alternates were then chosen without incident, then Judge Clarke relaxed in his chair and said, "Ladies and Gentlemen, we have a jury. Art, please swear them in." It had taken a little less than two days.

Judge Clarke, glancing out the window and commenting on the inclement possibilities of the weather, announced his decision to adjourn for the day with his usual admonition not to discuss the case, read newspapers, watch television, form any opinions and instructing everyone to be in the courtroom promptly by nine the following morning.

Twenty

Judge Clarke's observations about the weather were prophetic. The sky had darkened and the Victorian lights surrounding the Square shone with a soft yellow glow making liquid amber of the puddled streets. The temperature was falling. The town would almost certainly be snow-covered by morning. Pat Joseph observed, *The unexpected is the norm for December in Northern Ohio. We can anticipate playing golf or skiing this month and be right at least half the time.*

The clouds held their content while the group walked toward the lawyer's office. He suggested, "Gay, why don't you and Claude go home? Try to get some rest. There is nothing we need to talk about now and I have some things to review before morning."

Acquiescing to his request, they left without comment while Trent and Joseph entered the office together. "Did you review the witness files, Mr. Joseph?"

"Yes. Nicely put together. We're ready. There is nothing we really need to do. I just didn't want to talk with the Bellows any more today. I'll sit and visit with my pigs for a bit. You go home."

"Good idea, Mr. Joseph," Trent said without entering the lawyer's sanctuary. "See you in the morning."

Sitting at his desk, feet propped comfortably, Joseph gazed at his pigs thinking nothing. The building was quiet. After a while, knowing the battle would be joined in the morning, he drew a deep breath, sighed, left his chair and office. Reaching for the light switch, he glanced back and whispered "Good night," to the pigs. Their smiles were provisional at best, not knowing what tomorrow would bring.

* * * * *

The morning began as gloomily as the preceding day had ended. The clock was the only clue that it had arrived. Joseph prepared by getting to the courthouse before the appointed hour. So had, it seems, everyone else. Nothing about the weather made anyone want to be outside.

Court was convened and Joseph smiled a surreptitious "Hello," to the jurors. Looking toward the rear of the courtroom, he noted each seat filled. Murder, a rarity in Mills County, commanded a great deal of attention, not only from the media and the usual court loungers, but also from members of the local bar, several of whom had joined the eager observers. This created within Joseph a not so small tremor of fear. The discomfort was increased with Tucci's family fixing their stare on the back of the lawyer's head. Claude was in his seat directly behind the defense table accompanied by a young lady Joseph did not know – he thought she might be a family member he had not met.

"Good morning ladies and gentlemen," Judge Clarke said. "I hope you are well rested and ready to work."

Then he addressed the jurors directly, in his best pedantic form. "You have been sworn in and should be prepared to fairly and truly decide all the issues presented to you. Your job is much the same as mine – certainly equal in importance to it. I decide all issues of law, and will instruct you accordingly. You can't assume that you know what the law is and must – I repeat, must – follow my instructions. You decide the facts in the case – I can't do your job just as you can't do mine. Your decisions on the facts are final. We each have our roles to play to guarantee both the State and Mrs. Bellow a fair trial."

He continued reading his preliminary instructions to the jurors. "From time to time, I will have to make decisions outside of your hearing. These concern things about which you need not be informed. It is not to offend you or try to hide something from you, but your decision can only be made on the basis of evidence properly before you – anything else would merely be a distraction."

Sounding like a teacher, he continued. "From time to time, the lawyers will make objections. I know they will – I have yet to try a case in which it doesn't happen, and frequently. There are rules controlling a trial. If one of the lawyers thinks a question is improper or is outside those rules, it is his duty to call it to my attention by objecting. I may ask them to come to the sidebar to discuss it; however, when I rule on an objection you are not to question why, nor may you speculate what the answer to a disallowed question might have been. You consider only the evidence I permit to come before you.

"You may not take notes during the trial. If you are writing, you might miss something of importance. You must rely on your collective memory as to what is said here. The trial will last several days, I am sure. Of utmost importance, you are not to talk about this case with anyone before you have rendered a verdict – that includes husbands, wives, family, anyone – or allow anyone to discuss it in your presence. What is more difficult to understand is that you are not to talk about it among yourselves until I have given it to you for deliberation. The reason is simple – you are not to be influenced by outside sources or each other until all – I repeat all – of the evidence is before you. To do otherwise would not be fair to the defendant.

"There will be articles in the papers and possibly reports on television or radio. You may not watch or read anything about the case. If anyone attempts to talk to you about it, report it to Mr. Gruen or me at once. I will repeat these instructions whenever there is a recess, but if I forget they still apply. Don't you forget!

"Mrs. VanDamm, are you ready to proceed with your opening?"

Jacqueline VanDamm, dressed conservatively in a cream-colored winter weight wool suit, looked lovely and harmless. She made Joseph think of a Panda bear – its perfect markings make it look lovable – belying its ferocious capabilities. She stood slowly, gracefully, reaching for a pad Brad quickly handed her. She glanced at it and replaced it on the table.

Walking past the bench, she acknowledged Judge Clarke with a nod. "Your Honor." She glanced in the direction of the defense table and murmured, "Mr. Joseph," proceeding without pause to the jury box where she stopped, smiling. "Ladies and Gentlemen of the jury..." she began with an easy elegance.

Her presence was relaxed, her raiment impeccable. Up close, her suit glistened with hidden silver threads, a blouse of raw silk that Joseph thought probably cost more than the suit he wore, could be glimpsed over the collar of the form-fitting suit jacket. Her jewelry, a simple wedding band protected by a solitaire and a diamond pendent that nestled happily between her lush breasts glimmered with her movements. A red, Chinese silk scarf peeked from a pocket of the suit jacket lending a splash of casual color. Her jet-black hair was cut in a fashion Joseph's generation called a "bob." It swung pertly with her head, marking emphasis to her words. Joseph thought, *God, she looks sexy. We got problems.*

"Robert Tucci awoke on the morning of August 24," she began slowly, thoughtfully, "intending to spend the day with his family and friends. A simple gathering to enjoy the Street Fair was planned and he looked forward to it with enthusiasm. He spent the day with his wife, family and friends not knowing it was to be the last day of his life."

She could work an audience – at her best talking to a group. No notes cluttered her hands and she spoke to each juror as though chatting in their living room. Her expression became more serious as she turned slightly to look at Gay.

"The defendant, Gabriella Bellow, also awoke on the morning of August 24, not knowing that this day would be different from any other day in her life. But this day would be different, and she..." she said, pointing at Gay, "caused it to be different. She purposefully ended the life of Robert Tucci."

Pausing, as though sorrowing over the forces that dictated Gay's action, Jackie moved her head from side to side, saying, "She became angry with Robert – her victim – for things she believed he had done. Listening to the ravings of her daughter, she took a gun from her home – a gun that had sat for years in her closet – and went to her son-in-law's home. Yes, Robert Tucci was her son-in-law. She confronted him... in his own home... When he failed to meet her demands, she took out that gun, aimed it at Robert's head and pulled the trigger, sending a bullet crashing into his brain killing him...!"

Jackie allowed her upraised hand to drop to her side. She deliberately turned away from the jury and took a step toward the defense table, looking directly at Gay. "She..." Jackie said scornfully, "meant to – and did – take the life of Robert Tucci..."

Jackie turned back to the jury and stood quietly before them for several moments, took a deep calming breath, unintentionally causing her breasts to move beneath the silk in a way that made Joseph and the other men in the room think of things other than what she was saying, and continued. "Mrs. Bellow is charged with the crime of murder. It is the State's duty to prove beyond a reasonable doubt each and every element of that crime as Judge Clarke will instruct you. To meet that burden, we will present a number of witnesses."

She identified the witness she would call and briefly outlined what would be elicited from each. She then closed with, "We will have each of those witnesses tell you their story so that at the end of this trial you will be satisfied, beyond a reasonable doubt, that the defendant, Gabriella Bellow, did purposefully take the life of Robby Tucci. He is the only witness we will be unable to produce..." A nice touch, using the victim's nickname. "Since he can't be heard, you must speak for him." Dropping her voice to a husky whisper, "Do not forget him..." her voice trailed off.

She stood pensively for a moment. Satisfied she had forgotten nothing, she bowed slightly to the jury with no smile on her face now, turned to the elder lawyer and said, "Mr. Joseph..." as she walked back to her seat.

Joseph smiled at her thinking, *Damn, she is good.*

He remained seated, ignoring her implicit permission to speak. After several seconds of silence Judge Clarke looked up and asked, "Are you prepared to proceed with your opening, Mr. Joseph?"

"Of course, Your Honor," he smiled.

Taking no notes with him, the lawyer stood, saying over his shoulder as he approached the jury, "Ms. VanDamm, Mr. Bradley ... " Passing behind Gay's chair, he touched her shoulder lightly – a brief caress – and strode casually toward the jury box. Gay smiled up at him, placing her trust in the bald, chubby lawyer dressed in a rumpled gray suit as surely as he placed his hands on the jury rail. Tense as he had ever been in his life, Joseph nonetheless *appeared* relaxed as he slouched casually before the jury, pausing momentarily to gather his thoughts and allowing his gaze to touch each juror in turn.

"Ladies and gentlemen of the jury," he began slowly. "I have been using that phrase for more than thirty years. Each time I utter those words a little catch forms in my throat. I'm afraid that words, frequently repeated, often lose meaning. But this is still one of the few countries in the world where we trust our neighbors enough to let them sit in judgment of us. The jury system must be preserved in order for our country to continue – it must never be taken for granted. That is why I welcome the little catch every time I utter the words *Ladies and gentlemen of the jury* at the beginning of a trial.

"The purpose of an opening statement," he explained, "is, as Judge Clarke told you, to tell you what the trial is about – to let you know what to expect. A road map if you please, to make it easier to follow what comes from the witnesses."

Moving slightly along the jury rail to talk to all – he looked at each face in turn saying, "As you listen to the witnesses, Gay and I would like you to keep in mind the things we talked about during *voir dire* – the principles by which the criminal justice system works that each of you said you understood and accepted.

"Gay," he said, "isn't hiding behind those principles. She is demanding she be tried in accordance with them. Candidly, that is the only thing standing between us and excessive intrusion into our lives by the government and the potentially unchecked or unfettered police power of the State." Joseph wanted to plant a seed so the jury would be amenable to the idea that the State failed to investigate the case adequately – how the police had leaped to an erroneous conclusion the prosecutor made no effort to correct.

"In this case, the State didn't study the facts to reach its conclusion – it arrived at its conclusion first, then tried to make the facts fit."

Joseph paused, stood straight and snapped, as though with a sudden realization. "You know, less than five hours after Tucci was shot, the police quit their investigation. Since that time, they have bent all of their efforts in the direction of trying to secure a conviction. No effort has been made to solve the crime!"

Gathering speed, the lawyer said, "We have little disagreement with most of the facts so dramatically outlined for you by Ms. VanDamm. The decedent did arise on the last day of his life not thinking about dying. I'm not sure what he thought about, but I know what he did. What he did was spend that day drinking, arguing and being vicious. He kicked and abused a harmless dog. He fought with his live-in girlfriend's daughter. He kicked and dented the car of a friend who dared to intercede between he and his victim. He fought ferociously with his sister. Attacked, beat and strangled his live-in's sister, throwing her against a cabinet and putting into motion the actions that resulted in his injuries and death."

Joseph slowed to catch his breath. "Now, the confusion begins. Confusion that the police are unwilling, or unable, to clarify. Some time after Tucci was knocked unconscious, a gun was placed against his head and fired. A bullet tore into his brain, killing him. It is the why and when that bullet was fired you will **not** hear from the State. Nor will you hear from them **who** fired that shot!"

Watching the individual jury members closely, Joseph waited long enough to give them time to think about what he had said. As understanding began to dawn in several faces, he continued, "Listen to the evidence carefully ... listen to, and observe each witness as they speak. Satisfy yourself why Tucci was shot. Once you do, you will know who shot him. It was not Gabriella Bellows!"

Joseph turned and bowed to the Judge that his comments were complete and took his seat. Judge Clarke looked toward the rear wall of the courtroom dominated by an unexpectedly modern clock and said, "It is close to the noon hour. We will recess for lunch before hearing the first witness. Return to the jury room promptly at one-thirty. Again, remember not to talk to each other or anyone else about the case. Do not form or express an opinion until the matter is finally submitted to you. If anyone tries to talk to you about it, inform me or the bailiff at once. See you after lunch."

Rising, robes flapping, the judge said, looking at no one, "I will see counsel in chambers." The lawyers waited quietly for the jury to file out. Now what the hell was going on?

Twenty-One

By the time the lawyers reached the Judge's office he was already in his inner sanctum, door closed. Joseph said to the judge's secretary, "He sounds pissed, Candy. Is he mad about something?"

"I don't know," she responded with a cute shrug. "Go on in and see."

Jackie, Brad and Joseph entered, Art following. The judge sat frowning behind his desk puffing, on a small odorous cigar. Pointing the cigar, "You are not going to turn my courtroom into a zoo! It is so goddamned crowded with the media, observers and everyone else just wandering in from the cold, we'll be lucky to get anything done. The fuckin' photographers have demanded they be given permission to take pictures. I don't want cameras snapping all over the place and I won't allow pictures of witnesses who don't want it. Unfortunately, I can't deny the media *reasonable access* – goddamn First Amendment. I'll ask each witness if they object to their picture being taken. If they do, I'll enforce their wishes. Understand?"

"Hey, Tom, it's all right with me," Joseph said. He was not going to cross the Judge while he was in this mood, even though Clarke usually worked himself into just such a lather at least once during every trial to show the participants who is boss.

Jackie said, not too wisely, "I'm not sure you can do that. If the papers want pictures, I think they have that right."

Good, Joseph thought. *Get him mad at you.*

The local paper, *The Reporter*, had been represented since the first day of jury selection. The Akron and Cleveland papers and two television stations were there with their own camera crews. Milltown didn't usually get this kind of attention.

Headlines in the morning papers read, "MURDER TRIAL STARTS TODAY!" and "TRIAL OPENS IN MT. CITY SHOOTING!" The publicity guaranteed a full gallery and more chaos than Judge Clarke wanted to handle.

"Bullshit!" he stormed. "It's my courtroom and I will control it! If I say no pictures, that's the way it will be. I told you what I intend to do. Do I hear any objections?"

"No sir," said Jackie, meekly.

"None from me," Joseph added wisely.

"Okay, let's get this fucking show started. I want at least one witness finished today, understand? Eat and get your asses back here promptly by one-fifteen," Judge Clarke said gruffly as they exited his chambers.

* * * * *

Judge Clarke began the afternoon session by asking, "Are you ready with a witness, Madam Prosecutor?" At Jackie's nod, the Judge commanded, "Call your first witness."

Jackie spoke loudly enough for the bailiff to hear. "The State will call Officer Dennis Baker."

The witnesses having been separated were not permitted in the courtroom until called to testify. Art went into the corridor to call Deputy Baker. The deputy entered in full uniform, including his service revolver. *A man with a gun in a courtroom always makes me nervous,* Joseph thought. *I hate to ask an armed man embarrassing questions.*

The officer walked directly to the witness stand, stopped, turned toward Art and raised his right hand, waiting for the oath. He'd been there before. "Do you swear, or affirm, the testimony you are about to give in this case will be to truth, the whole truth and nothing but the truth as you shall answer unto God?"

Baker responded, "I do," and calmly took his seat, looking expectantly toward the prosecutor's table.

"Good afternoon, Deputy," Jackie began. "Would you please state your name – spelling your last name for the record?"

And so the testimony began.

Baker explained that he was a deputy in the employ of the Mills County Sheriff's Department, that he had special training to prepare him for the job, was certified by the State of Ohio as a peace officer and was on special duty the evening of August 24. After explaining why he was in Mt. City during the Street Fair, he admitted he knew Emma Black, the victim's sister. During the fireworks he was standing near the corner of Main Street when Emma came running, screaming, hysterically, *"Denny ... Denny ... My brother's been shot!"*

He told how he followed her back to the house where he left her in the front yard while continuing on to Tucci's apartment. Since he was the first officer on the scene, it was his duty to secure the area and make sure no one left. He went upstairs to examine the victim.

"Before going into the apartment," he said, "I spoke to the suspect, Mrs. Bellow, and her daughter, Arliss Conrad, instructing them to remain in the yard with the boys. I searched their purses for weapons and talked to them until a second officer arrived. Leaving them with him, I entered the apartment."

"You did go into the apartment?" Jackie asked.

Baker replied, "Yes ma'am."

"Who was in the apartment when you entered?"

"The victim and a woman I took to be his wife."

"Anyone else?"

"That's all."

The witness was then given a number of photographs that had been prepared and marked as exhibits by the prosecutor's office showing the apartment, blood spatters and locations of people and things in the room at the time of his arrival, all of which he identified.

In response to questioning, he told how he checked the victim and noted his injuries, saying, "I had several people tell me he had been hit with a bottle and one individual told me he was shot."

The deputy closed his direct testimony with, "Glass from a broken Coke bottle was all over the floor and on his clothes ... The china cabinet with plates and cups appeared undisturbed."

Jackie, stating, "I have no further questions," turned Baker over to Joseph for cross-examination.

The lawyer walked slowly over and stood next to the jury rail, resting one hand lightly on it while studying the witness. Clearing his throat to cover the slight quaver, he began asking the questions he had prepared. He didn't expect much from the witness, wanting only to emphasize that Emma Black was the first and only person to state her brother "was shot."

For that reason, when the witness was asked to identify who was in the upstairs room when he first arrived, Joseph was amazed by an unexpected response.

"When I got upstairs and seen the victim and the woman I believed to be his wife before the medics got there, an unknown male subject entered the room. I asked him to leave."

Joseph glanced over at Jackie, angry. She had not revealed this in discovery. The bland expression on her face revealed that it was not news to her although she tried to feign surprise. The lawyer continued cautiously, "Have you determined the identity of the unknown male on the scene?"

"No sir."

"Can you describe him? How was he dressed?"

"He was a white male, about my age, dressed in a black T-shirt and Levi's, you know, like jeans. He had dark hair."

"Do you know whether or not he was ever alone with the deceased?"

"No sir, I don't."

"Did you report the presence of this unknown male to your superior officer, or whoever was in charge of the investigation?"

"I don't believe I did."

"At some point, you learned that Mr. Tucci had been shot, didn't you?" Joseph asked, a little sarcasm creeping into his voice.

"Yes, sir."

"And you didn't think it important to report there was an unknown male subject at the scene – before Tucci was taken to the hospital?"

"No sir," Baker said sheepishly.

"Is today the very first time you told anyone about the unknown person?"

"No, sir."

"Whom did you tell?"

"I think I may have mentioned it to the prosecutor, Mrs. VanDamm."

Interesting – why hadn't Jackie revealed it in discovery as required of her? In fact, why had she tried to act surprised by the news a few minutes ago? Joseph quickly finished his cross-examination of Baker – his thoughts staying on the unidentified white male in the black T-shirt – fuming over the prosecutor's perfidy.

Before the second witness could be called, Joseph gestured to Trent. He came to the rail and leaned over to hear the lawyer's whispered instruction. "Why the hell didn't you find out about this? I want to know who the man in the black T-shirt is. Jackie is playing some kind of bullshit game with us. I want it to bite her on the ass!"

"Do you want me to go now or when we finish for the day, Mr. Joseph?" Trent whispered, face flushed.

"Now!" Joseph hissed.

During the whispered conversation, the next witness had been called. He was the second police officer to arrive at the scene and the one who had found the gun determined to be the murder weapon. In response to an inquiry, he identified a photograph showing the weapon lying on the ground beneath Emma and Jim Black's back porch.

"Can you identify the photograph for us?"

"That is the back porch of the Black residence, Mrs. VanDamm."

"Where did you find the gun?"

"Just like it shows in the picture – just under the back porch – sort of in the crawl space."

The deputy didn't add much to what had already been said. His role was inconsequential – important only because it was he who found the murder weapon and kept the defendant under observation until his superior arrived. Jackie quickly turned him over for cross-examination.

Thanking her and securing the permission of the court, Joseph began. "Officer, you stated you found the gun?"

"Yes sir."

"And took a picture of it?"

"Yes sir."

"Did you touch the gun before you photographed it?"

"Yes sir."

"In fact, officer, the pictures you identified in court today were actually re-created the day after you found the gun so they could be used in this trial, isn't that so?"

"Well, yes sir," the witness admitted reluctantly.

"Did the prosecutor instruct you not to mention that fact?"

"Yes sir," he said, his voice hardly above a whisper.

"Officer you have to speak up so the jury can hear you. You just told us that the prosecutor instructed you not to mention the fact that the photograph of the gun was not taken when you found it, but at some later date. The picture was actually manufactured – I mean created – for this trial, isn't that true?"

"Objection!" Jackie yelled, her face red.

Good! Joseph thought. *She deserves to be embarrassed – manufacturing evidence.*

He was aware of what the witness had done because Gay had seen the officer take the gun from the scene before any pictures were taken. The only way the picture could have been made was if the gun were returned to the site for that purpose.

"Well Judge," Joseph said politely. "It looks like we don't really need an answer to that question. I'll withdraw it."

Joseph had read the witness' report and knew he had been the one to break up the fight between Roper and Black, so he asked about it – another subject Ms. VanDamm neglected to mention on direct.

The witness responded, "When I arrived, Mrs. Bellow and another lady were in the back yard. Jim Black came out of the front house about the same time as Tom Roper walked over from next door. I started to tell Roper to stay out of the way when Black, who was standing behind me, threw a punch at him over my shoulder. He was yelling at Roper, telling him he would shoot him if he stepped in his yard or if he ever saw him with his wife again. He wasn't talking too clearly, but it was that kind of stuff. I separated them and sent Roper home. I assumed the gun I was told to look for had something to do with that threat. I didn't know then that Tucci was shot. When I found the gun, I gave it to the detective in charge without asking any questions."

The officer testified he had remained at the crime scene for the balance of the night, keeping Mrs. Bellow and the others under observation during all the time he was there.

In response to a question put to him by Joseph, the witness said, "She didn't go nowhere except to stand in the backyard with her daughter where I could see them. Detective Redding asked Mrs. Bellow to sit down at the picnic table and write out a statement. She did and then he put her in the back of his car. She didn't even go to the john." The last comment produced a titter from the crowded room, quickly quieted by Judge Clarke's scowl.

Joseph persisted. "Did Mrs. Bellow at any time leave your presence before she was taken away in the back of Detective Redding's car?"

"No sir!" he responded positively.

It was early the next morning, the witness explained, that Detective Redding instructed him to return to the scene with the gun. "He told me to put it back exactly where I found it and take pictures of it."

"For what purpose?" Joseph inquired gently.

"So we could show where I found it."

"Can you be sure you replaced it in precisely the exact same spot where you found it?"

"Well," he said with a shrug. "It would be close." He was completely oblivious to the fact that he helped manufacture evidence.

"Just a couple of more questions, Deputy." He seemed immune to sarcasm. "You found a gun? It was taken away? You got it back? You placed it where you *thought* you found it to take pictures of it to use in this murder trial? As evidence?"

"Yes, sir."

"Did Ms. VanDamm tell you not to mention this either?"

Again Jackie was on her feet screaming. "Objection!"

"Overruled!" snapped Judge Clarke. Then to the witness, "Answer the question!"

Joseph commented, "Well Your Honor. The prosecutor's interruption has given this witness ample opportunity to think up an explanation. It makes me wonder how factual his answer will be."

"Mr. Joseph, please just ask questions. Editorial comments are neither necessary nor appropriate," Judge Clarke scolded, but not very convincingly. Then to the witness, "Go ahead ... "

"Well ... when I looked at the pictures with Mrs. VanDamm and told her about them, she said I didn't have to mention anything about when they were taken unless you asked. If you did, I wasn't supposed to lie about it. But I wasn't to mention it unless you asked."

The lawyer studied him thoughtfully for a long minute. "Is there anything else she told you not to tell us about?"

Jackie, red-faced and still standing, uttered, "Objection!" sounding like an expletive.

"Never mind, Judge, I will withdraw the question," Joseph said walking back to his seat. There was more he would have liked to ask of this witness but thought it better to end on this note. It was late enough that Judge Clarke would not permit another witness to be called and Joseph wanted the jury to be able to think about the prosecutor's tactics over night.

The judge ordered the witness to step down without giving Jackie a chance to ask any questions on redirect. She was too agitated to object even though Bradley tried desperately to get her attention.

The judge continued without pause. "All right, ladies and gentlemen, that's it for today. My usual admonitions apply – don't talk about the case – don't read about it – don't form or express opinions – see you at nine-thirty tomorrow morning."

As the judge and the jury filed out, Joseph called to the court reporter. "Scott, hold on a second. I want to call something to the court's attention. On the record..."

Sighing, Scott sat back down before his stenotype machine. He was tired. It was his job to hear and record every word uttered in the courtroom. Sometimes in the heat of battle more than one person speak at the same time, each trying to be heard over the other. He had to make order of it and get it all. He somehow did.

Judge Clarke, hand on the doorknob to his chamber, said, "Now what, Pat? For Christ's sake, I'm tired."

"I know Judge, but this is important and it'll only take a minute. It's the first chance we've had to talk outside of the hearing of the jury since these things came up." Jackie and Brad, stuffing papers into their brief cases, stopped and looked at Joseph distrustfully.

"I know your minutes, Pat," the judge said, resigned.

Joseph was on his feet and began. "Your Honor, I am making a formal motion for a mistrial – for two reasons," ticking them off on his fingers. "First, based on the testimony of Deputy Baker about an unreported stranger being present in the room at the time of the killing, and second, because the State manufactured evidence which Ms. VanDamm attempted to hide."

Jackie's face went from red to white. Both she and Brad began to talk at once. Joseph ignored them, speaking loud enough to be heard over their protests. "Deputy Baker testified there was an unknown white male in a black T-shirt at the scene. It was not in his report, nor was it provided in discovery – but," pausing for emphasis, "he said he told Mrs. VanDamm. Clearly someone on the scene who had an opportunity to shoot the decedent is exculpatory evidence and," he continued, pointing at Jackie, "she did not provide that information to me!"

Joseph continued looking directly at the prosecutor. "Mrs. VanDamm has not denied knowing it. The record reflects I made the appropriate Rule Sixteen Motions. If the Court would like I would be happy to provide citations."

Judge Clarke waived the offer aside asking, "Mrs. VanDamm, What do you have to say about this? Did you know about it? Do you have an explanation?" He no longer looked tired.

"Quite frankly, Your Honor," Jackie began, reasonably. "I did not feel the unidentified person was pertinent to the case. After all, the victim had already been shot when he arrived. I don't know who he is."

Scott was about to earn his pay. "You what?" Joseph shouted. "Mrs. Bellow is on trial for murder and YOU decide the presence of an unidentified person at the murder scene is unimportant! I have never heard such bullshit in my life! You have no way of knowing when Tucci was shot, before or after this stranger arrived, and you say it's not exculpatory! You're as bad as the cops who didn't bother to investigate. No wonder we'll never know what really happened!"

The reporters from all three newspapers and the television stations were eating it up, writing as rapidly as Scott while cameras clicked and whirred.

"Not only is it relevant, it's vital," Joseph yelled. "An unidentified person was there when Tucci was killed and you don't think it important. I demand a mistrial and that the charges against Mrs. Bellow be dismissed!"

He turned his back on the prosecutor, ignoring her spluttering attempts at explanation. "No question about it Judge, we're entitled."

Judge Clarke had not returned to his seat during the diatribe, but was leaning against his door. He paused thoughtfully and walked to a position behind his chair. Leaning his crossed arms on back of it, he signaled for quiet.

"Mr. Joseph, you know all comments are to be addressed to the bench and not counsel." He didn't seem particularly upset by the lawyer's failing, or his rancor, but continued without pause. "The court doesn't feel at this time you are entitled to a mistrial. However, I must say Ms. VanDamm, your behavior leaves a great deal to be desired. If there is any further indication you have not provided prompt and complete discovery – if there is any further evidence of efforts to manipulate evidence – I will declare a mistrial and consider sanctions against you. Let's see what develops, but I am warning you..." His voice trailed off without verbalizing the warning.

"As for you Mr. Joseph, I didn't expect so much excitement this early in trial. Quit playing to the press. As I said, all of your comments will be directed to the bench. If either of you has anything to say, say it to me. It looks like this is going to be a long trial. Please, no more... " his eyes sliding upward with the prayer.

As Joseph began to defend himself, the judge raised a hand cutting off further comment. "Do you both understand?"

Joseph nodded. He didn't think the judge particularly angry with him, but didn't want to take any more chances than he already had. It was clear Judge Clarke intended to control his court, so the lawyer responded meekly, "Yes, Your Honor." He was satisfied and didn't want to press his luck.

He turned to Gay and said, for her ears alone, "Not too bad for the first day. We'll keep her," indicating the prosecutor, "on edge if we can. You and Claude go home now and try to get a good night's sleep. You're doing beautifully. Good night."

They exited the courthouse together. The rain that had fallen most of the day had stopped. The air smelled crisp – clean – especially after being locked inside all day. It was getting colder. Snow would probably be abundantly evident by morning. It would be good to go home and relax with a before dinner martini.

Trent was waiting at the foot of the courthouse steps. "Mr. Joseph we have to go to Cleveland."

Twenty-Two

Trent's compact car was parked at the curb, motor running. The day's rain left puddles which mirrored the soft golden street lights surrounding the Square, the buildings outlined in miniature white lights – dressed for Christmas. On the north side, volunteers from the Junior Chamber of Commerce were busy erecting a brightly colored child-sized shed with an elaborate roofline where Santa Claus dressed in the traditional red suit and white beard would soon be distributing candy canes to children making their annual strident demands loud enough for parents to hear. No sense taking chances – Mom and Dad had to believe they still believed.

At the end of this first day of trial, all Joseph wanted to do was go home, have a drink and eat dinner. Resigned, he handed his briefcase to Trent and climbed clumsily into the car, allowing himself to fall limply into the passenger seat. "What's up?"

"I found the *unidentified white male in the black T-shirt*," Trent replied with a smug, self-satisfied grin.

The lawyer paused in his efforts to close the door. "You're kidding!" as Trent rushed around the car and jumped into the driver's seat. "How the hell did you do that?"

The boy explained. "Mr. Joseph," he still couldn't bring himself to call the older lawyer by his first name – a courtesy practiced by few in this enlightened age. "You told me Hey Smith knows everything that goes on in Mt. City. I figured the quickest way to get the information you wanted would be to see Mr. Smith. So I went to *The Bar* and had a drink – a cup of coffee actually – Hey wouldn't sell me a beer. Anyway, I explained what happened in court. He told me a family by the name of Gordon lives catty-corner across the street from the Blacks and was having a cookout that night. Mr. Gordon is in the Navy Reserves. Some of his friends from his Reserve unit were there. Mr. Smith didn't say how he knew about it. I walked over to their house and Mrs. Gordon was home. She said she thought the man we were looking for was her husband's recruiter. He works at the Federal Building in Cleveland. I called him. He's our man. That's where we're going now."

"It's late," Joseph interjected. "By the time we get there the office will be closed."

"True," Trent said. "But I called him and he said he'd wait for us. I told him we're in the middle of a murder trial and it's really important we talk to him. Seems like a nice guy."

Marveling at how quickly Trent did what the police didn't do at all, Joseph called Mary to tell her he might be late and settled back to enjoy the thirty-five minute ride. Surprising how comfortable some compact cars are. He would like to see the expression on his pigs' faces now. He listened to the enthusiastic explanation several times – how Trent discovered the witness and what he might offer.

As they traveled north on I-71, they passed a rest area Joseph learned enjoys a certain celebrity in the Fillia family. Trent explained how, on his twenty-first birthday, his brother took him to The Flats to celebrate. Visiting several bars and receiving more than a few complimentary birthday drinks, Trent was feeling quite good. On the way home the enjoyable feeling evaporated with an overpowering urge to rid himself of the drink's by-product. His brother stopped at the rest area just passed. Trent made hurried use of the facility and when returning to the car, became convinced a large green refuse can lurking on the curb insulted him or, at least, failed to pay the respect due a twenty-one-year-old. The possessor of a black belt in karate, Trent warned the can of his expertise, demanding proper deference. When not forthcoming, Trent attacked with a perfectly executed drop kick, missed, landed on the pavement and suffered a small bloody gash on his forehead. His brother bundled him into the car, deciding Trent needed home more than medical attention. Trent held his head in a blanket to avoid bleeding all over his brother's car the rest of the way home, he explained sheepishly. Dumping him at his father's door, the sibling rang the bell and waited only long enough to be sure someone was coming. The beleaguered elder Fillia spent the rest of the night assuring Trent he wasn't an unworthy son and would one day feel better.

Trent had the grace to blush as they drove past the offending rest area while Joseph smiled, remembering embarrassing experiences of his own.

The journey didn't take near as long as expected. At this time in the evening, most of the traffic was traveling South, away from the City. They were on the Inner-belt before Joseph knew it, exiting onto East 9th Street. As always, he admired the beautifully designed stone arch and wrought iron entry gates of the Erie Street – East 9th St.'s name in an earlier life – Cemetery.

"Have I ever told you how many times this cemetery has been involved in litigation?"

"Yes!" Trent interrupted. They laughed. It was often said the elderly lawyer wouldn't be remembered so much for the stories he tells, but for the frequency with which he tells them.

North on East 9th, they crossed Euclid, Chester and Short Vincent – probably the shortest street in the world – at least the shortest in Cleveland – known for housing some of Cleveland's finest eating and drinking places – one in particular frequented by the defense bar – The Theatrical Grill. The second floor lunchroom served the world's finest rye bread, salt sticks and onion rolls.

Their destination came into view. It was across from Erieview Tower and The Galleria still busy with the going home crowd of shoppers. Although generally called the *Federal Building*, its true name is *The Anthony G. Celebrezze Federal Office Building*, for one of Cleveland's true, but mostly unsung, heroes. A giant of a man at just under five feet five who, although diminutive, could captivate an audience by the power of his presence. An Italian immigrant who entered the State Senate following World War II, elected six times as Cleveland's Mayor and tapped by Presidents John F. Kennedy and Lyndon B. Johnson to serve in their cabinets as Secretary of Health, Education and Welfare until appointed by President Johnson to the Federal Appellate bench, where he served well into his eighties.

Judge Celebrezze and I have much in common, Joseph thought. *We're both short, sport full mustaches, and married women who adore us – hah!*

Parking in the Auditorium Hotel Garage, they walked to the East 6th St. building entrance, fighting the cutting wind usually whipping across any open area in downtown Cleveland. Chicago may bear the name "Windy City," but Cleveland deserves it. Signing in at the security desk, the lawyer asked for the Naval recruiting office.

The guard looked him up and down, saying soberly, "A little old, ain't you, Pops?"

"Never mind smart-ass. Where is it?"

Without changing expression, the uniformed guard pointed to a bank of elevators. "Take those to the fourteenth floor."

Following directions, Trent and Joseph found waiting for them as they exited the elevator a tall handsome young man in the uniform of the United States Navy. The guard must have called ahead.

"Hi, Mr. Joseph? I'm Les Stiles," the young man said, offering his hand without waiting for the elderly lawyer to introduce himself. "Someone in your office called saying you needed to talk to me."

Joseph was impressed by the firm handshake and cordial smile. Trent acknowledged he had placed the call.

Not knowing Stiles correct title, Joseph used none, inviting him to join them for a drink at the Auditorium Bar or Pat Joyce's. Very military – ramrod straight – the young man replied, "Not necessary sir."

They followed Stiles to his office which was furnished with a slightly battered standard military green metal desk and chairs made of the same stuff with vinyl padded seats and backs, painted walls decorated with recruiting posters showing beautiful young men and women in places few had ever seen. The officer offered seats.

Confirming the essentials of Hey Smith's information, Stiles explained, "About midnight, on twenty-four August, after the Fair fireworks, we were relaxing in Gordon's back yard. The party was about ready to break up. All of a sudden someone across the street began screaming. There was a lot of commotion. We ran out of the yard and there was a lady crying. All I could make was, *Help him! He's been shot!*

"I tried to calm her and ask some questions. She settled down long enough to tell me it was her brother who was shot and pointed at a garage in back of the house. I ran to where she pointed and there were people standing around looking toward the garage. I went in and found the stairs to an apartment.

"Upstairs," he said, "I saw a man laying on the floor with his head in a woman's lap. Her hands were covering her face and she was sort of rocking – crying. There was blood on his face and her hands and all over the floor. His eyes were open but he didn't seem conscious. I had trained in CPR and First Aid. I felt a pulse at his neck, so was going to start CPR just as an ambulance pulled into the drive and a medic ran up stairs. I told him what I found. Almost immediately a police officer showed up and told me to leave. So, I did."

"Did the police talk to you anytime that night?" Joseph asked.

"No, not that night or anytime since. I waited for a bit, but had to leave because I was taking an early flight the next morning to go to Washington for a brief tour. When I got back no one had called or left a message for me so I forgot about it. I read in the papers the guy was dead. I'd have called, but guessed they didn't need me," Stiles explained.

Joseph sat quietly for a moment wondering how best to use the information. Trent had no suggestions. They thanked the Naval officer for his help and again offered a drink. Stiles declined. Leaving together, Trent suggested, "If you're really anxious to buy a drink, I'll join you."

Joseph smiled as they quit the building, signing out at the same station where the same guard inquired, "Y'all enlist?" a grin on his face. Still a smart-ass, but without relief, the boredom of his job would drive anyone crazy.

On the way to Pat Joyce's, they walked past the Auditorium. For the thousandth time, Joseph wondered why the builder inscribed the letter "V" where a "U" belonged in the words carved into the parapet.

At Pat Joyce's, relaxing with drinks in hand they could see few people in the gathering dark on Superior Avenue. "You know, Mr. Joseph," Trent observed, "It looks like Mrs. VanDamm's right. There is nothing sinister or significant about Stiles' being at the Tucci house. He verified some of the things we already knew, but really added nothing."

"What do you think we should do about it?" Joseph asked. "Do you think we should share this information with the State? Or keep it to ourselves?"

"Hell no!" Trent exploded, not unexpectedly. "We found him in less than an hour and without the resources they have. Fuck 'em," he said, blushing at the obscenity. "If they want him they can look, just like we did."

Sounding surprisingly like Mary, the lawyer said, "Don't swear."

"Sorry," Trent continued. "You know, Mr. Joseph, maybe you can say something about an unidentified man at the scene – maybe he knows something about the killing – reasonable doubt and so on, in final argument. The cops can't find anything unless it's handed to them."

Joseph sighed. "You're right, Trent. I don't like it but you're right. You know, you're going to make a fine trial lawyer some day – better than me – you have good instincts."

"Trent," the lawyer added as he ordered his second martini. "Why don't you give Mrs. Joseph a call? Let her know we'll be a little late for dinner."

Trent returned to the table saying, "She said not to worry – you're eating out."

Ever suffering, Joseph signed, finished his martini and said, "Let's go."

Trent was grinning.

Twenty-Three

As expected, the rain changed to snow during the night leaving a light dusting on the grass and trees. Dick Goddard, a local weatherman with a national reputation, was right, as usual. Even without significant accumulation, Joseph appreciated the beauty of the drive into town, the ice crystals shimmering on the tree branches, the weight pulling them low over his driveway.

Gay and Claude were already waiting – he brooding – she inquisitive. "What's

going to happen today?"

The lawyer smiled at her, briefly explaining what to expect, and then telling of the previous evening's adventure.

"Is it helpful?" she wanted to know. "Is it good we know who that man is?"

"Maybe a little," Joseph suggested. "Of course, it's good we were able to locate Stiles and a goddam' shame the police didn't. Unfortunately, he didn't add anything to what we already know."

"But," he said, explaining their strategy session, "Trent and I talked about how the information might be used for your benefit. We won't bring him into the trial but will take advantage of his absence and the police's failure to locate him when we make our final argument. Another peg for the jury to hang reasonable doubt on – if you will pardon my improper grammar."

"That's for the end of the trial. For now," he added, "let's get over to the courthouse."

As they crossed the Square, it was filled with kids on their way to school. The giggles of the girls and boastful yells of the boys lent an air of party to the crisp morning. Joseph, as always, enjoyed their presence and was thankful he was not too preoccupied to notice. Claude was, and Gay held tightly to his arm.

As they walked, Trent suggested, "The State will probably call the pathologist first. I didn't see a Cuyahoga County license plate parked behind the courthouse, so we'll probably get a late start. There shouldn't be any particular problem with her, but I have a copy of Dr. Mac's report in case you need it for your cross-examination."

As they entered the courtroom, Joseph noticed Jackie VanDamm leaning over Scott at his stenotype machine, talking earnestly. She straightened with a guilty start when she saw Joseph watching. He grinned, knowing what she was up to.

Any trial lawyer knows how easy it is to lose sight of the forest while advocating. Those with the best handle on what is happening are the observers with no stake in the outcome – the court reporter, the bailiff, an experienced watcher. Unburdened by involvement, they formulate and express objective opinions. Both Art and Scott are capable of making accurate educated guesses as to what's going on in their courtroom, predict the outcome and be right more often than not – a valuable resource. Neither was reluctant to help. Joseph thought, *I'll have to talk to Scott later.*

Judge Clarke made his usual theatrical entrance. "We ready to proceed?" he asked, settling into his chair and adjusting his robes without waiting for a response. He shuffled the papers in front of him and instructed, "Bring the jury in."

Joseph smiled a pleasant good-morning to the jurors, receiving some tentative smiles in return. By this time the jurors had developed a degree of familiarity with each other and were no longer hesitant or uncomfortable in their role.

Jackie announced in a clear voice after everyone quieted, "The State will call Dr. Karin Khandelraj."

Art left, returning with an attractive lady who appeared much too young to be a full-fledged pathologist – who looked more like a medical student. Standing next to the witness box, she waited to be sworn. She was not as young as she looked and this was not her first trip to court.

Saying, "Yes I do," in the peculiarly pleasant singsong voice of those native to India, in response to the oath administered by Art, she took the stand, seated herself comfortably and placed a small leather folder on the shelf before her.

Jackie began. "Good morning, Doctor."

Doctor Khandelraj responded, "Good morning," smiling at the judge, the prosecutor and finally inclining her head toward the jury, including them in her salutation. Her slender body encased in tasteful western clothing obviously as a concession to her job and the world in which she did business. Nevertheless, the straight part in her shiny black hair was tinged with traditional carmine marking her marital status and origin. An ancestral beauty spot was affixed above her brows. *An exotic creature*, Joseph thought. *She would be gorgeous in a sari.*

"Please state your full name and where you work," Jackie asked.

"My name is Karin E. Khandelraj. I am a physician in the employ of the Cuyahoga County Coroner's office. I work for Dr. Samuel Gerber as a pathologist and deputy coroner." Mentioning the name of the nationally known Dr. Gerber would lend credibility to her testimony.

"My responsibilities," she added, looking directly at the jurors, "include assisting the Coroner in cases of deaths due to violence – or suspected violence – trying to determine the cause of death, as well as make other pertinent findings." She appeared too delicate for violence to touch her life.

In response to a series of questions, she told the jury of her background, education and experience. Dr. Khandelraj's reputation was well-known, but Joseph had never seen her testify. Her credentials and her ability to communicate were impressive. *Thank God we need her testimony and it isn't going to hurt us,* Joseph thought. *In fact, the autopsy protocol shows it should help. Jackie seems unaware of this ...*

Dr. Khandelraj, explaining medical terms in common, everyday language told of articles she had written, the many times she had been published and her frequent lectures on forensic pathology, then finally got to her reason for being in court.

"Did you conduct an autopsy on Robert Tucci?"

"Yes, I did."

"What were your findings?"

"Mr. Tucci was a normal well developed, well-nourished white male, sixty-eight inches in height and weighing about 158 pounds who appeared to be his stated age of thirty-one years. When first examined at our laboratory, he had a surgical dressing on his head, a nasal-gastric tube into his stomach, intravenous catheters in his right forearm and an airway placed ... "

She went on to detail her findings, painting a vivid picture. When Tucci was received at Milltown Hospital, it was apparent he needed extraordinary care – care that Milltown Hospital could not deliver. He was stabilized as much as possible and a life-flight helicopter summoned to fly him to Metro Hospital where a team of surgeons waited. He died during surgery. "But," Dr. Khandelraj added, "he had been brain dead long before his body ceased to function."

The doctor's words, so precise, so soft, brought the jury into the operating theater. The crowded courtroom was silent. Joseph was every bit as enthralled as they and pleased the witness was able to make a real person of Tucci. He thought how important it was to Gay that the jury thinks of all the participants as real – including the victim. They had to know what kind of person he was in life and why he died in order to assure themselves Gay had no part in it.

Judge Clarke noted a news photographer walking through the back door of the courtroom. Reluctant to interrupt, he said, "Excuse me, Dr. Khandelraj, there is a photographer coming into court. We have to allow it, but if you do not want your picture taken, you may refuse." She flashed a beautiful smile at the judge and indicated, with a tiny shrug, it didn't matter to her. There was no question in Joseph's mind whose picture would be gracing the front page of *The Reporter's* next edition.

"Proceed," the judge bid Jackie, the camera clicking.

Smiling her thanks, Jackie handed several glossy photographs to the court reporter, asking they be marked for identification. Scott did so and returned them to Jackie, making notes on his pad. The prosecutor passed them to Joseph for review. Looking at them quickly – he had seen each before – he handed them back. Jackie had Dr. Khandelraj identify the series of photographs of Robert Tucci's body taken during the autopsy showing the wound, its secondary effects and the other bruises and marks earlier mentioned. Those were the marks Joseph was anxious for the jury to see.

The prosecutor next handed Dr. Khandelraj a small plastic bag saying, "Handing you what has been marked as State's Exhibit 18, Doctor, can you identify this?"

Looking for her mark, Dr. Khandelraj declared, "Exhibit 18 is a bag containing the bullet I recovered from Mr. Tucci's brain. I inscribed it with my initials after removing it and placed it in here," gesturing. "I marked the case number on the envelope in my handwriting and submitted it to your officer for deposit in your property room."

Leaving Dr. Khandelraj and returning the exhibits to the evidence table, VanDamm walked back to her seat as though finished. She then turned back to the Doctor and asked in a carrying voice, "Doctor, can you tell us, based upon reasonable medical certainty, whether or not you have an opinion as to the cause and manner of death suffered by Mr. Robert Tucci?"

Recognizing the proscribed formula required for securing an expert's opinion into evidence, Joseph was nonetheless amused by Jackie's dramatics.

Dr. Khandelraj responded with the appropriate, "Yes, I do have an opinion."

"What is that opinion, Doctor?"

"Mr. Robert Tucci came to his death as the result of a cerebral edema. That is the swelling of the encephalon, causing permanent irreversible damage to the brain cells due to a gunshot wound perforating the skull and brain."

"And Doctor, your opinion please, based on reasonable medical certainty, as to the manner of death?"

"The manner of death is homicide."

"Thanks for your time and assistance Doctor," Jackie smiled and sat down.

Judge Clarke looked from Jackie to the defense lawyer and inquired. "Mr. Joseph, do you have any questions of this witness?"

"Yes I do, Your Honor – one or two."

"I've heard that before," the judge observed dryly. "Try to keep it brief."

"Of course," the lawyer nodded pleasantly. Then walking to his usual spot near the jurors, he tried to clear the nervousness from his throat and said, "Dr. Khandelraj, My name is Pat Joseph and Mrs. Bellow is my client. I have never had the pleasure of meeting you but am familiar with your work and impressed by what you have accomplished, especially so young. It is truly a pleasure meeting you."

Although he had approached the witness with his knees quaking and hands shaking, Joseph was a little surprised he really meant what he said and looked forward to a pleasant few minutes with her.

She smiled her appreciation at the compliment and waited for a question. "Doctor, can you explain to the jury what the word 'bruising' means?" Because of the lawyer's position in back of the jury, it was easy for the witness to maintain eye contact with both the lawyer and jurors.

"Simply put, bruising, or contusions, result when any blow is delivered with sufficient force to cause hemorrhaging beneath skin that is still intact."

"Are contusions and bruises the same thing?"

"Basically yes."

"Is a laceration different?" Simplistic, but important for the jury to understand the terms and remember them when the marks on Tucci's head was discussed.

"A laceration," the doctor explained, "means there is some interruption in the integrity of the skin surface. A tear or a cut."

"Doctor, what causes bruising?"

"Bruising is caused when blood and fluids accumulate at the portion of the body that has received the blow or trauma. It is nature's way of protecting the body."

"Does that mean, Doctor, that in order for a bruise to appear on a persons body, a blow must be struck while that person is still alive? In other words Doctor, if someone were to strike a dead body, would a bruise appear?"

Obviously amused at the thought, she answered, "You are right, Mr. Joseph. A dead body does not bruise."

Walking toward the evidence table and picking up the sheaf of photographs, Joseph asked if he might approach the witness. Judge Clarke nodded permission. Joseph walked to the doctor and handed her certain of the photographs he picked from the packet, asking, "I take it Doctor Khandelraj, that the bruises in these photographs on the forehead, face and arm of Mr. Tucci were made while he was still alive?"

"Yes, that is true."

Asking the doctor to examine one of the photographs showing a large bruise on Tucci's forehead, Joseph asked, "Do you agree that by the size and shape of this bruise it is consistent with what is commonly referred to as a blunt object trauma... say if a large Coca Cola bottle were to fall from the top of a cabinet and strike the deceased's head with sufficient force to shatter the bottle, would such a bruise be present? Of course, assuming he is alive when this happens?"

She agreed, "It is." Joseph let out a silent sigh of relief – solid physical evidence was corroborating and giving credence to the story Gay told the police and would be telling this jury.

Now one more significant detail remained to discuss. "Doctor, you indicated a microscopic examination of the tissue preserved by the surgical team at Cleveland Metropolitan Hospital when they operated on Mr. Tucci's brain was done by you. Is that correct?"

"Yes, I did."

As he returned to his position behind the jury, Joseph could feel the witness's eyes following him. "Tell us, please, the findings revealed by the examination."

"There were large amounts of gunpowder residue imbedded in the soft tissue immediately beneath the entrance wound, and, in fact, deep within the wound itself." Bingo!

"As a forensic pathologist, does that have significance to you?"

"Yes, it does. It means that the shot that killed Mr. Tucci was fired at contact range. By that, I mean the gun was held up against – touching – his head when it was fired."

Now for the icing. "Doctor, with your experience as a deputy coroner who has investigated hundreds of gunshot cases, would you please consider all of your findings in this case – the entry wound – the depth the bullet penetrated – the gunpowder residue – the path taken by the bullet – the amount of brain tissue damage – everything about which you have testified. Consider all of those facts, Doctor," Joseph paused in the delivery of his hypothetical question long enough for the doctor to get straight the details. "Are they consistent with the following scenario? A man lying on the floor unconscious – on his left side. A gun placed flush against his head behind his right ear discharges and sent a bullet crashing into his brain with the resultant destruction you found. Is that scenario consistent with your findings?"

The doctor paused to consider, a small frown of concentration on her lovely face as she thought about the complex question, then responded deliberately, "Yes, it would be consistent with that scenario."

There were many more questions the autopsy protocol suggested, but Joseph didn't want to lessen the impact of the testimony just given. "Thank you very much, Doctor. It's truly been a pleasure meeting and talking to you." Turning to the bench he said, "I have no more questions, Your Honor."

Without asking Jackie if she had any redirect, Judge Clarke said, "We have reached the hour for the morning recess," intoning his usual admonitions then added, "Counsel, I would like to see you in chambers ... " leaving his bench without looking to see if they had heard or would obey.

The lawyers waited for the jurors to clear the courtroom, and entered the Judge's outer-office where his secretary was busy typing. "Hi, Candy," Joseph grinned. "Tom wants to see us. Is he in a good mood?"

She grinned back. She was petite, attractive, always happy and friendly – except to those she believed may misuse her boss. "Grab a cup of coffee, Pat," she said. "We're working on the jury charge. I imagine he wants to go over it with you. Go on in."

They did, Joseph saying, "Morning, Tom," to Judge Clarke.

"Hi, Pat. I'm working on the instructions. Candy has typed a draft. I want to review it with counsel so we won't waste a lot of time when we get to the end of the trial."

"A little premature aren't you, Judge?" Joseph suggested. "We still don't know but what the State might want to dismiss or maybe you'll grant my Rule 29 Motion, or charge on a lesser included."

Rule 29 of Ohio's Rules of Criminal Procedure permit, when the defense lawyer makes such a motion, a judge to take a case from the jury when he believes there is insufficient evidence to convict.

172

Jackie emitted an unladylike snort and Judge Clarke said, dryly, "I'll take my chances." Turning to the prosecutor, he asked, "How soon will you be finished?"

"I'm not exactly sure Judge, but I don't think before the end of the week. Of course that depends on Mr. Joseph's cross-examinations. He does tend to go on. We think the only charge needed is straight murder."

Ever suffering, the judge said, "Okay, take your break. Be back in the courtroom in ten minutes."

Leaving as the judge was firing up one of his foul-smelling cigars, Joseph asked VanDamm, "Who's your next witness Jackie?"

She snapped, "You'll know when we're back in session!" She was still pretty steamed. Joseph didn't ask why.

Twenty-Four

The firearm examiner from the Bureau of Criminal Investigation and Identification at Richfield was called next. Joseph hadn't expected him to be called this early in the trial and didn't have with him the notes he thought he might need. The criminalist's testimony was important to the defense, so much so that Joseph planned to call him if the State hadn't.

While the witness was being sworn, Joseph signaled to Trent. "Trent, go get my file on this witness. It has some questions suggested by your professor friend at Akron. I'll need them for cross."

"Now?" Trent asked. "Or, do you want me to wait for a break? I've been taking notes on the witnesses to help prepare your final argument."

"Now! I'll delay things until you get back. You'll hear most of his testimony."

The judge looked at the lawyer impatiently. "May we proceed, Mr. Joseph?"

"Of course Your Honor," he replied politely. "But, with your permission, may we approach?"

Resigned, Judge Clarke said, "Come on," waving counsel to sidebar, turning a pained smile toward the jury. "Excuse us. I am going to wear a hole in the floor if we have many more of these conferences..." his voice trailing off as he rolled his chair to the far side of the bench. "What is it now, Pat? Can't we just get on with it?"

While the judge was talking, the lawyer signaled Scott to bring his stenotype machine. He wanted a record.

Scott placed his machine on the corner of the judge's bench – Joseph answering the judge's questions. "We could, Judge, if Jackie would call her witnesses in proper sequence..."

Without waiting for the defense lawyer to finish, Jackie blurted, "Bullshit, Joseph! I'll present my case and my witnesses any way I goddam' please! It's my case..."

He interrupted her in turn, coldly, "Don't bullshit me, Ms. VanDamm. This isn't your first trial and you know you can't present witnesses out of order without first asking the court's permission and having a damn good reason. I didn't hear you ask." Turning his back on her, Joseph addressed the judge.

"This witness, Your Honor, is a firearm expert. There has been no testimony linking the gun to Mrs. Bellow nor has a proper chain of evidence been established. Without that this witness has nothing to talk about. Anything he might say isn't relevant without the proper foundation."

To VanDamm he added a little dig, "God, I hate to educate everyone in your office on how to try a case ... " rubbing in the last bit of salt with a polite smile for the benefit of the jurors intently watching. They couldn't help but notice the flush of red creeping up the prosecutor's face.

The judge, in a stage whisper, silenced both.

"Just a minute both of you. If there is any educating to do around here, I'll do it."

Then lowering his voice even more, he asked, "Pat, what the hell is this all about? You know damn well I decide who will testify and when. If you have an objection, make it and I'll rule on it." Then without waiting for an objection, he added, "Or are you trying to delay things?" Answering his own question, "I saw you send Trent scurrying out of here."

With a sheepish grin Joseph said, "I can never fool you, Judge. But I do object to the State calling this witness out of order without first asking – and I do want that on the record. It is another in a long line of dirty tricks. She's trying to catch us unprepared. I want that on the record, too. The Court has already had to admonish her for not abiding by the rules regarding discovery."

Judge Clarke looked to make sure Scott was taking the conversation down and then at Jackie who was still flushed. "Well, Ms. VanDamm, do you have anything to say?"

"I'm sorry, Judge. I should have asked, but, HE..." delivered as an invective, "knew I would be calling this witness. His name is on the witness list and his scientific report has been provided. Mr. Joseph is aware we can, and will, tie it all up. He's just being pricky!"

Hearing her out, Joseph turned to the bench, saying graciously, "With that assurance, Your Honor, I will withdraw the objection."

"For the record, Ms. VanDamm, since Mr. Joseph has withdrawn his objection, you will be permitted to proceed with the witness at this time, out of order..." then, waving Scott back to his usual base of operations, he added, "and off the record I am not pleased, Jackie. And you, Joseph, don't play games with me! I'll not tolerate any of that in my courtroom – if you need time – ask, don't ... " He didn't verbalize the undelivered threat as he rolled back to his accustomed spot.

The prosecutor walked to her table where she shuffled through a stack of files, looking for the right one. Mike Redding handed one to her with a barely restrained grin. "Here, Jackie, is this what you're looking for?" Both Bradley and Jackie glared, first at Redding, then Joseph. She handed the file to Bradley so that he might examine the witness. She needed the time to collect herself.

As Bradley walked toward the podium, Jackie turned toward the witness sitting silently throughout, trying to regain her composure.

"Please state your name, spell your last name for the record, and tell us your employment." Bradley asked.

The witness intoned his response. "My name is Ronald Bey, spelled B-E-Y, and I work for the State of Ohio, Attorney General's office, as a Criminalist with a specialty in firearms. I'm with the Bureau of Criminal Investigation Laboratory in Richfield."

"Will you tell us how long you have been employed in that capacity and about your education, training and experience that qualify you as a firearm expert?"

Settling in his seat, the experienced witness turned toward the jury and said easily, "I have been with B.C.I. for about six-and-a-half years. I received my B.S. Degree from Akron University and am a Member of the Midwest Association of Forensic Scientists. My job is to examine firearms or projectiles to determine whether a specific bullet was fired from a particular gun and occasionally whether a shell casing has been fired in a certain weapon. We test fire guns and do chemical evaluations to establish whether there is gunpowder residue on skin or clothing. I have done all those things in this case.

"To prepare myself for this work, in addition to my college degree, I have attended numerous seminars and classes, including several at the F.B.I. Academy, as well as on the job training."

Bradley quickly lead him through his testimony, showing him the bullet removed from Tucci's brain and the weapon said to have been found beneath Black's back porch. He identified both items from marks he had placed on them. He had him establish the chain of custody on each piece of evidence from where it was collected, to B.C.I. and back to the Courtroom.

The witness had test-fired the gun and described to the jury exactly how. "I received the weapon, sealed in a plastic bag, along with five rounds of .38 caliber Smith & Wesson ammunition. Four were unfired. Also in the bag was a shell casing from a round that had been fired. In our laboratory, we have a large barrel filled with a material similar to cotton. We can fire a weapon into it without damaging the projectile. This gives us the projectile and shell casing to study and compare against known examples of the fired bullet and the shell casing recovered from a murder scene. This also tells us whether the weapon can be fired – that is if it's operable in the condition it is when we receive it."

He explained. "Each weapon is unique. It makes separate and distinct marks on a bullet as well as on a shell casing. An indentation is caused by the firing pin of a weapon on the casing when the weapon is fired. It is the depth and location of that mark from which an identification can be made. Striations on a projectile are made as it passes through the barrel of the weapon. Both can be used in determining what weapon either the projection or shell casing came from."

The jurors watched the criminalist with great interest. He had their undivided attention and was making a favorable impression. In his early thirties, he had prematurely graying hair that defied a comb. He looked both studious and professorial with the underdeveloped body and permanent stoop of a scientist who spends most of his life hunched over a microscope. He spoke easily using understandable language. Joseph smiled, pleased the witness was creating an impression the defense wanted undisturbed.

The assistant prosecutor asked, "Have you been able to form an opinion, based upon reasonable scientific certainty, whether this bullet was fired from this gun?" He held up the gun and bullet already identified.

"Why, yes I have ... and it was ... " he answered, going into detail about test bullets, milling defects, lands, groves and microscopic comparisons.

Having elicited all of the information desired, the assistant prosecutor turned to the defense table and said with frosty politeness, "Your witness, Mr. Joseph."

"Why thank you Mr. Bradley," the lawyer responded, equally polite. Trent handed him the folder he had gone to fetch. Joseph walked slowly to his usual spot, smiling at the witness, "Good afternoon, Mr. Bey. We've talked before, have we not?"

"Yes we have Mr. Joseph."

"You're being a bit modest about your credentials, aren't you?"

Bey responded with a self-deprecating smile.

"Please may I tell the jury how you have been accepted in, and have completed all but your thesis for a doctorate in the specialty about which you are testifying today?"

The witness continued to smile modestly and nodded agreement.

"And that you are recognized, at least in Ohio, as one of the foremost experts on ballistics and firearms?" Without waiting for a response Joseph continued. "And you are frequently called upon by state and national police agencies for opinions in firearm identification matters? "

Again the witness nodded, appearing embarrassed.

"Now then Mr. Bey, I would like to talk a little about the weapon in front of you – the gun that has been identified as the murder weapon."

Joseph began with very specific questions about single and double action revolvers and the safety mechanism on this particular weapon. The jury had to be familiar with these features of the murder weapon, handle it and dry-fire it, to understand the defense theory of the case.

"Mr. Bey," the lawyer asked, "Can this weapon be accidentally fired?"

Bey wasn't sure what Joseph was asking, so looked at him quizzically. Joseph continued smoothly, "In other words, if one were to hold this weapon, say by the trigger," demonstrating, "could the weight of the weapon alone cause the trigger to be depressed sufficiently to fire the gun?"

Now understanding, the witness responded, "Oh, no, that's not possible. You see, this revolver has a built-in safety feature." He pointed to a mechanism in the butt of the gun, saying, "This lever must be depressed in order for the gun to fire. The weapon must be held so that the grip is squeezed, depressing the safety and pulling the trigger at the same time..." again demonstrating. "This weapon cannot be fired accidentally."

Wanting this point emphasized, Joseph requested the court's permission to approach the witness. Without waiting for approval, he strode to the witness stand and held out his hand. As the witness began to hand the weapon to him, Joseph withdrew slightly and asked, "You're sure it isn't loaded?"

Nervous giggles from the jury box and gallery.

Smiling, Bey said, "Of course it isn't loaded. I never pick up a weapon without checking." Nevertheless, he broke it open to demonstrate there were no bullets in the cylinder.

Closing the weapon, he again handed it to the lawyer. Joseph took it, pointed it at the ceiling and, snuggling the grip tightly against his palm, pulled the trigger producing a loud click in the suddenly quiet room.

"It seems to take quite a bit of strength to do that, doesn't it?" Joseph suggested. "Can you measure the force it takes to pull the trigger?"

"I can and did. It takes exactly twelve-and-one-half pounds of what is called *trigger-pull*. That is the amount of energy needed to pull the trigger and fire this weapon," Bey responded.

"Is that a lot Dr. Bey?" Joseph promoted him.

"The average pistol has a trigger-pull of from seven to eight pounds. The topside, or maximum, is around fourteen pounds. For a modern weapon, this would be considered high – what we would call a stiff or heavy trigger-pull. I measured it because it felt a bit stiff to me when I test-fired it."

Holding the weapon in his hand and gazing at it wonderingly, Joseph wandered back to his spot behind the jury, the jurors eyes following. Shaking his head from side to side and clucking his tongue, Joseph murmured, "Imagine that..."

As though returning from a distant place, the lawyer looked at the witness and said, "Oh... no more questions... thank you very much."

Slightly theatrical, but it gave the jury time to think about the witnesses' explanations before Bradley could try to rehabilitate his witness or downplay his testimony.

Surprisingly he did neither. "No redirect," Bradley said nonchalantly. Joseph couldn't believe he didn't know where the defense was going.

Prosecutor VanDamm next called a Detective Bireley to tie the gun into the investigation as promised. She asked about the discovery of the weapon, its placement into the Sheriff's evidence lockers and transportation to B.C.I. He was questioned in great detail about the photographs taken at the scene of blood spatters and patterns. Finishing, she turned him over for cross-examination.

For some reason she seemed quite anxious to be through with this witness. Either he knew something she didn't want revealed or she wanted to get to her next witness before the day's end. Joseph wasn't sure which, but he wasn't going to play.

"Detective Bireley, can we talk about each item of physical evidence gathered and the route it took?"

Bireley was one of the few thorough and meticulous police officers in the County and filed copious reports. The defense had all of those filed in this case and Joseph used them in his cross-examination. Jackie objected frequently, adding to the witness' time on the stand, defeating her intended purpose.

Just before the afternoon adjournment, the lawyer indicated to the court he had no further questions. Ms. VanDamm said, "I have just one on redirect, Your Honor."

With Judge Clarke's tired nod, Jackie asked, "In the course of your investigation, Detective Bireley, do you find that some of the items you retrieve are irrelevant to the investigation?"

"That sometimes occurs Ma'am," Bireley responded.

Judge Clarke looked at the defense table, "Anything further, Mr. Joseph?"

"Just one question, Judge."

The witness began to rise, but now waited for the lawyer's question. Neither the question asked by the prosecutor nor the one to be asked by Joseph meant anything but the elderly lawyer was not going to let Jackie have the last word. He had enough of her.

"Tell me, is the converse also true, Detective? Are there times when you find things that do not appear to be relevant, but later become essential to the investigation?"

"That happens too – sometimes – sir."

Twenty-Five

A less harried Judge Clarke swirled into the courtroom the following morning in a manner slightly reminiscent of Loretta Young. He looked over his half-glasses to make certain all was as it ought to be in his domain. Satisfied, he directed, "Be seated..." with a flip of his wrist. "Bring the jury in, Art. We're ready to proceed, aren't we?"

He settled into his throne-like chair leafing through the ever-present yellow legal pad to find his place. The jurors entered in correct sequence, not having to climb over one another to reach their assigned seats. They were getting used to being a jury. Joseph smiled at them expecting to and receiving a good-morning grin, much less tentative than at the beginning of trial.

"Call your next witness, Ms. VanDamm."

She responded, "Good morning, Your Honor," as she flashed a smile at the jury. "The State will call Emma Black."

Art left the courtroom and returned with Tucci's sister. She wore a loose fitting, multicolored wool sweater and knee length denim skirt. Dressed conservatively, she could still not hide the lush figure freely advertised on less solemn occasions. Fat was not many years away, but for now she was able to maintain a look of provocative seduction. Glossy brown hair hung to her shoulders unbound with a hint of a smooth wave. Some would consider her mighty attractive.

Judge Clarke addressed her. "There are news photographers in the courtroom. You have the right to refuse to have your picture taken."

"It doesn't matter," She responded with seeming modesty – but sitting a little straighter thrusting her plump breasts against the confines of her sweater and brushing back a stray strand of hair.

The prosecutor approached the witness with, "Hi!"

The witness responded with a "Hi!" accompanied by a smile. They obviously knew and were sufficiently familiar with one another so that the witness did not feel intimidated by Jackie, even though the setting made her a bit uncomfortable.

Backing away from the witness so their conversation would not appear too intimate, Jackie began. "Make sure that you speak up so we can all hear you. Please tell us your full name and spell your last name for the record."

"My name is Emma Tucci Black. B-L-A-C-K."

The prosecutor elicited from Mrs. Black that she was the sister of the deceased and still lived in Mt. City on Garden Street in the house she and her deceased brother had owned and grew up in. She now lived there with her husband and three children, two of whom were in school. Her brother – accompanied by a little sob – and his "wife" had lived in the apartment over the three-car garage behind the house. That was where he was murdered.

Her story was told without interruption. She explained to the jury how her brother some fourteen months earlier had brought home with him a "friend, Bliss Bellow." Although Mrs. Black didn't think they were married, Bliss used his name and called herself his wife. She liked Bliss right away. They were still good friends.

After leading the witness smoothly through the preliminaries and asking her to identify photographs and exhibits, VanDamm asked, in a more somber tone, "Now, Mrs. Black. I would like to direct your attention to the day last August when your brother was killed – do you remember that day?"

With a shudder the pleasant look again left Black's face replaced by one of studied sadness. She responded softly, "Yes."

"Was the Mt. City Street Fair in progress?"

"Yes it was."

"Starting with the morning, please tell the jury what you did that day?" the prosecutor asked, moving toward the back of the jury rail to the spot usually occupied by Joseph – nothing's sacred.

Emma Black began – a little hesitantly at first and then more fluidly – with her rising, feeding the kids, cleaning the house, waiting for her husband to get home from work. "He is a carpenter, you know," she said, describing a very normal day in the life of very normal people. "Bliss came over for coffee and talk. Later her sister visited and we sat around for a while and then went over to the Street Fair."

"About what time was that?"

"By this time it was close to ten o'clock in the evening."

As she talked about the rapidly ending day, Black began to appear more nervous as though the coming portion of her story was the part she most dreaded telling.

She and Bliss walked over to the front house before midnight and chatted for a minute or two on the porch. When she left, Emma went into the house where her husband was watching television – the kids were in bed. "I told Jim I wasn't tired yet, and since the lights were on in Robby's apartment, maybe he and Bliss might come over for a cup of coffee. Jim said okay. So, I went to see if they would."

She described how she walked to the garage and up the steps to the apartment. "I called my brother from the landing." She was getting more tense – sweat beginning to bead on her fine brow. Joseph watched her closely and thought, *Now come the lies!*

"Jim comes down to where I was standing. We talked a couple of minutes. He was in a good mood, laughing about something. I asked him and Bliss to come over for coffee. I didn't want to leave the kids alone. Just then a car pulled in and stopped in front of the garage. Robby said something about it looking like he was getting company. All of a sudden Arliss comes storming in with her mother. They pushed up the stairs past us, not saying nothing. Robby looked at me and kind a' shrugged."

Jackie didn't interrupt her. The jury, and everybody else in the room, listened attentively. "Robby followed Bliss and Arliss up the stairs into the kitchen. I stayed on the landing. I could hear them talking, but not the words. No one seemed mad. They was talking in normal voices."

She took a deep calming breath and added, "I seen Robby starting to walk across the kitchen away from the dishwasher. Then I heard a real loud noise – like a bunch of light bulbs busting all at once – and I seen a flash – like an electrical flash..." expelling the words in a rush with the air she had sucked in.

"I ran up the stairs... Robby was laying on the floor... On his side... I didn't see no blood – but I seen the gun laying there on the kitchen floor."

She paused to take another deep breath, seemingly unaware of how it made her breasts quiver. The room remained silent. This was the first time the jury heard from a witness a description of what happened that night. In a quaking voice, she told how Arliss and Gay walked toward her while "I stood there yelling at them 'Y... You... shot my brother...'"

A hint of anger entered her voice and she reported, "Arliss kept on walking toward me and told me I was *full of shit*. She just picked up the gun and walked right outside with her mother behind her."

Jackie interrupted, "When you say her mother, do you mean the defendant, Gay Bellow?"

"Yes I do!" she said pointing a quivering finger at Gay. "Her ... She is the one shot my brother!" Her voice rose in an accusatory crescendo.

Jackie apologized. "I'm sorry for the interruption. Please continue with what you were saying."

After pausing long enough to recall where she was in her tale, Emma Black related, "I ran to Robby and knelt down by him. I felt to see if there was a heartbeat. His eyes was fluttering. I ran to the living room window and yelled for someone to help, but no one was out there except," pointing again, "her and her daughter! So I ran down the stairs and over to the Street Fair to get someone to help me."

She paused for breath and to sip from a glass of water Art provided. Jackie asked in a soothing voice, "At this time, where were Arliss, Gay, your husband and the boys?"

Emma described where each was in the back yard between the house and the garage as she ran past. "I feel for certain they all was on the patio, but I was crying so hard, I couldn't tell for sure.

"After I got Denny, I was too upset to go back into the house. I waited in front for the ambulance. After they took Robby away, Jim – my husband – drove me to the hospital to be with him. At the hospital one of the Deputies asked me to make a statement, so I wrote one for him. They took Robbie away in the helicopter. I had to talk to the detectives and make a recorded statement – at the police station. We got there around two or two-thirty in the morning."

No smile now, Jackie stood before the jury box so that every eye was on her. She held the gun in her right hand and in a soft voice easily heard in the silence asked, "Emma did you touch this gun at all that evening?"

Shaking her head from side to side, answering in a practiced sincere voice, Black responded, "No, Ma'am. I've never touched that gun," ending with a shudder.

Jackie allowed the gun to fall to her side. In a clear voice she asked, "Emma, did you shoot and kill your brother?"

"No!"

Joseph expected the next series of questions from Jackie would be an effort to clear up the business about the gunshot residue the B.C.I. expert reported being on the witness' hands. He was sure the prosecutor had talked to Scott about providing that information for the jury as part of her case. She had to know defense counsel would make sure the jury heard about it. The only way to handle adverse evidence is to downplay its importance. If she let Joseph introduce it, it would look like she was trying to hide something.

Stunned, Joseph heard Jackie say, "I have no further questions."

Joseph frowned, thinking, *What the hell is wrong with Scott? Either he gave her bad advice or she didn't follow his suggestions. I can't believe she's trying to hide this stuff. Or does she think I forgot it? Am I missing something? Shit! What the hell's going on?*

Joseph's mind raced until Judge Clarke interrupted his musings with, "Mr. Joseph, do you intend to conduct a cross-examination?"

"Yes, I do Your Honor," he said, heart fluttering. "May I have just a moment please?"

Leaning toward Gay, he asked almost without moving his lips, "She is lying... isn't she, Gay?"

Gay hissed uncharacteristically, "Yes! Get the bitch!"

Picking up a piece of blank paper, Joseph walked toward Scott. Taking it, Scott looked at the blank surface then at Joseph. The lawyer said for the court reporter's ears alone, "Didn't follow your advice, did she?"

Scott, smiling and making sure no one but Joseph could see, mouthed, "Dumb broad," made a mark on the paper and handed it back.

Joseph said aloud, "Thank you, Scott," and returned to his table for Emma Black's folder.

Walking toward his usual spot behind the jury box so recently usurped by Jackie, Joseph didn't realize the usual feelings of anxiety were absent – in fact he was relishing the forthcoming cross-examination of this witness.

"Mrs. Black. You know who I am." A statement – not a question – continuing smoothly, "The last question asked by Mrs. VanDamm about whether or not you killed your brother – do you remember it?"

She acknowledged the memory with a tentative nod and a look that indicated she trusted the lawyer not at all.

"Was there a reason you wanted your brother dead?"

"No, of course not!" she said emphatically.

"Was your relationship with him good?"

"It certainly was!"

Switching gears for the moment, Joseph began asking about the physical characteristics of the apartment and how maybe it wasn't exactly as she described it. He wanted the jury to know she had been embellishing the truth enough to lead them gently into her camp.

Being caught in a few discrepancies, she was more careful with her answers – but she was also getting used to Joseph's questions. No peril yet – she felt safe. She hadn't yet been brought into a danger zone.

Joseph began to build the pressure by returning to the subject of an argument between her and her brother that night – she denied it vehemently – denied arguing with her husband – denied the affair with Roper. She was good, but her body language disclosed she was being evasive.

Joseph again changed his line of questioning to inquire about the "loud noise' and the "flash' she had testified to, jumping from subject to subject, keeping her a little off balance but allowing her to become complacent with the thought he would never get to questions she was unable to answer.

She insisted the noise and flash were true, then the lawyer asked mildly, "Did you tell the police about the flash that night?"

"I'm pretty sure I did..." she said, a little plaintively.

"Did you include it in your written statement?"

"I... I'm not sure."

"How about in the recorded statement?" Joseph knew it didn't appear in any of the three.

"I... I don't think so."

On it went – reviewing each bit of story just told from the witness stand – parading each discrepancy before the jury. It was essential the jury see the inconsistencies, but it was equally important it be done gently so she not appear sympathetic. The jury had to believe her a liar, not confused. She was squirming in her seat – Joseph was solicitous.

Finally getting back to the portion of her story about "seeing the gun on the floor not touched by her," Joseph politely asked Judge Clarke, "May I approach the witness, Your Honor?"

"Certainly," Judge Clarke agreed. Black looked on warily.

Walking to the evidence table and picking up the gun already admitted into evidence, the lawyer lumbered toward the witness box, stopping directly in front of the witness. He was only slightly more disheveled than usual, appearing completely harmless. The witness wasn't sure.

"Mrs. Black," he asked holding the revolver out to her, "Is this the gun you saw on the kitchen floor the night your brother was killed?"

"Yes..." she nodded hesitantly.

Handing the weapon to her, Joseph instructed, "Here, take it, please..."

Her hand reached for it reluctantly. She didn't know how to refuse. She looked helplessly to the judge and then toward Jackie VanDamm. Neither offered any help. Bradley was whispering at a furious pace into Jackie's ear, but she shushed him. Before an objection could be offered, the gun was in Black's hand.

Joseph asked in his most sincere voice, "Is this the very first time you ever touched that gun?"

"Yesss..." she answered sibilantly, staring at her hand, looking neither at the lawyer nor the jury. She couldn't draw her eyes from the gun lying on her palm.

"Please pull the trigger," Joseph suggested mildly.

She still couldn't remove her gaze from the weapon. She and the lawyer were alone in the courtroom. Making an obvious effort, she looked up slowly and said, directly to Joseph, "I ... can't."

"I know it's difficult, but please try," Joseph importuned, standing in front of her so she would see no one else.

A light mist of sweat appeared on her upper lip, brow creased, the room was still – so still her small grunt of effort could be heard just before the suddenly loud click of the internal hammer striking the firing pin, followed by a gasp from the observers.

Joseph gently removed the gun from her hand and returned it to the evidence table. Taking longer than necessary, he walked back to his usual spot behind the jury. No eyes followed him; the jurors looking for several uninterrupted minutes at the witness who sat unmoving, betraying hands folded in her lap, seeing nothing from downcast expressionless eyes.

The judge cleared his throat warning of his impatience with the time Joseph was taking. Before he could suggest the lawyer continue, Joseph asked, "Mrs. Black, did there come a time when the police swabbed some chemical on your hands?"

Nodding affirmatively, still looking at her traitorous hands, she responded, "It was after we left the hospital and went to the Sheriff's department."

"Did they explain to you – or do you know why they did that?"

"Yes, they said it was like a paraffin test, but more modern. It was to see if there was anything on my hands to show whether I shot a gun."

"Had you shot a gun that day?" Joseph asked.

"No sir!" she responded positively. She was beginning to awaken from her daze.

"Did they tell you what the result of the test was?" The lawyer was firing his questions rapidly to get responses before Jackie could interrupt with objections.

"Yes sir."

"And?"

"They said the test was positive – but I must have gotten the powder or whatever on my hands when I touched my brother – I didn't shoot a gun that day!" she protested.

Joseph stared at Black for several moments, saying nothing.

Judge Clarke broke into the silence. "Mr. Joseph, it's near the end of the day. I would like to recess. We've been working pretty hard and everyone could use an early break. Would you like to complete your cross- examination tomorrow or are you about done?"

"I have no objection to continuing my examination tomorrow Judge, even though I only have a few more questions to ask." Actually, the judge's suggestion thrilled Joseph. He would love for the jury to spend the night thinking about this witness' perfidy, but he added, reluctantly, "There are a couple of things I need to take up with the court if I might at a side bar before we adjourn."

Turning to the jury, Judge Clarke said, "I don't like to interrupt a witness but we only have about twenty minutes left until the usual hour of adjournment. Why don't you stand and stretch while I see what Mr. Joseph wants? Maybe we will be able to finish this witness today." Waving counsel forward, the judge invited, "Please join me."

As soon as the prosecutor, her assistant and Joseph gathered at the end of the Judge's bench away from the jury, Joseph wasted no time.

"Judge, this witness is lying through her teeth. Her testimony today is completely different from all of the statements given by her earlier. I'd like you to read them and allow me to cross-examine on the statements. The jury has to know what a liar she is."

"Relax Pat," the judge cautioned. "Well, Jackie what do you have to say?"

"Oh, hell, Judge, there might be one or two discrepancies, but nothing significant. No reason to do what Mr. Joseph asks. I object to the use of the statements. Joseph is just grasping."

Joseph turned to Jackie and said in a harsh whisper, "I'm not grasping – you know goddam' well she is a liar and are trying to cover it up. Just give the report and statements to the judge. Let him decide."

"Easy Pat," Judge Clarke warned again. "Talk to me – not each other – do you understand?"

Joseph nodded sheepishly while Judge Clarke looked at Jackie. "You don't have to give me the statements and reports. I've read them and Mr. Joseph is right. There are numerous discrepancies. I haven't decided whether she is outright lying or just has a poor memory. Some time has gone by since the incident. At any rate I'm going to let Pat cross-examine on the statements and let the chips fall where they may." The Judge always had a unique way of turning a phrase – he not only looked a cliché, he sounded like one.

"And," he said for the benefit of both lawyers, "I don't want any more shit from either side. Jackie you can ask a question or two to try and set her straight. Then, I am going to let Pat have at her. You will," he said with emphasis, "both be finished within the next fifteen or twenty minutes."

Joseph walked from the bench to his seat with a light step and winked at Gay who was still sitting ramrod straight. He was no longer feeling the exhaustion that usually sets in near the end of a trial day.

Claude had come from the gallery and was holding Gay's hand, oblivious to whatever else was going on. Joseph asked him to return to his seat as the jury was reseating itself. Then he glanced at Emma Black, gratified to notice her discomfort. Maybe she hadn't heard what was being said, but had seen her statements being waved around in front of the Judge.

"We are going to finish with this witness after all," Judge Clarke informed the jury. "Mrs. VanDamm will ask a few questions and then Mr. Joseph will finish. We may run over a few minutes – but not much. Proceed, Mrs. VanDamm."

"Emma, have you seen any of your statements since giving them to the police?"

"No."

"Did you ever get copies?"

"No, I did not."

"Has anyone ever sat down with you and gone through each statement page by page, and point out to you...?"

"Your Honor!" Joseph was on his feet. "That question is certainly not proper. I can understand Mrs. VanDamm wanting to rehabilitate her witness but she can't testify for her. It isn't our fault the prosecution failed to prepare its witness properly. Anyone just out of law school should know to have their witnesses review prior statements. I think Ms. VanDamm not only knows it, but also probably did it. It's obvious this witness just doesn't want the true story revealed. Probably because it will..."

The judge interrupted dryly. "Mr. Joseph, if that's an objection, it's sustained. If you want to make a speech, do it at a side bar or in final argument. You're more than a year out of law school yourself and know better. Your objection is appropriate, but no more editorial comments. Do you understand?"

Ignoring Joseph, Jackie asked the witness, "Emma, I will ask you one more time, did anyone ever review with you, in detail, your prior statements?"

"No!"

"Have you ever, in your life, shot a handgun?"

"No! Never!"

"Thank you," Jackie said as she sat.

"Are you finished Mrs. VanDamm?" the judge inquired.

"Yes, Your Honor."

"Proceed Mr. Joseph."

Standing, Joseph walked toward the witness without requesting permission, rather than to his usual spot. He wanted the jury to watch him. He looked directly at Emma Black. She tried to avoid his gaze, but as the silence built, she finally had to glance up. The lawyer studied her face, her eyes – haunted – feral. No longer sure of herself, she had to look away.

"Mrs. Black," he began. "We have been talking about things you may or may not have said to the police. Judge Clarke has reviewed your statements and wants to give you an opportunity to correct any inconsistencies between what you said to them and what you are telling us today. With that in mind, do you want a chance to look at your handwritten statement?"

"Sure!" she responded, an unsuccessful effort at bravado. She took several minutes to read her handwritten statement, lips moving. She returned it. Without a word, Joseph handed her a transcript of her recorded statement, which she also read quickly.

"You have now read your two-page handwritten statement." With her nod of affirmation he continued, "And a five-page transcript of the recorded statement you gave the police as well as a summary prepared by them. Have you had enough time to read them?"

"Uh huh ... " she nodded in response.

Joseph was not going to let her get away with that. "You have to answer in words Ms. Black. Scott David has to get them on his stenotype machine. If you don't answer out loud, he won't be able to."

"Yes sir!" she snapped.

"Do they appear to be accurate copies of what you said and wrote that night?"

Again a barbed, "Yes, sir!"

"You made the handwritten statement at the hospital before you knew your brother was dead. Is that true?"

"Yes." She was going to give no more than she had to.

"Earlier today, you said Arliss and Gay pushed past you and your brother on the steps saying nothing. Your brother shrugged his shoulders and was in his usual good mood. Is that what you told this jury?"

Again a bit off "Yes!" But looking around nervously, her lips suddenly needing moisture not adequately provided by the tip of her tongue.

Holding up the sheaf of papers, Joseph declared, "But that isn't what really happened that night, is it? At least, that isn't what you told the police."

"Uh ... not exactly."

Reading from the statement he said, "Is it more accurate to say that Arliss and Gay rushed up the stairs and that Arliss said something to him about acting like a S.O.B., and he responded by telling her to shut up and who the fuck she thought she was bustin' into his house so high and mighty?"

"He did say something like that but it was mostly mumbling and I couldn't really tell..." her voice trailed off.

"Again, now that you have had a chance to read through all the reports, do you remember testifying earlier about a flash of light and a loud bang?" Again she nodded. "Look through them again and point out to me where you said anything about either a loud bang or a flash."

Without looking at the papers or taking them she whispered, "They don't..."

Joseph didn't have to ask her to speak louder. The room was so quiet her voice carried easily to the furthermost corner. He looked toward the jury to assure himself they were following the testimony. Each was studying her intently. The lawyer had feared his questioning might engender sympathy for Emma Black. None was apparent on the faces of the jurors.

"Earlier, you testified there was no blood on Robby's face when you first saw him lying on the kitchen floor, do you remember?" She nodded.

"But, in your statement you say that you *seen blood all over his forehead,* isn't that true?"

"Let me see that!" she demanded. When Joseph showed it to her, she continued, "Uh... I guess that's right... I forgot."

There was more. It was well past the twenty minutes allotted by the Judge. No one seemed to notice.

"This afternoon you said everything was nice and quiet all day and there was no problem, no argument. Do you remember saying that?"

"What time was that?" she evaded.

"Anytime that day or evening you want to talk about," Joseph responded patiently.

"I didn't say no arguments were going on." She continued her evasion.

"Let's take a look at your statement and see what it says." Pointing to it in her hand, he suggested, "Please read along with me at the bottom of page five. *They was fussing – they was just familying it out.* Are those your words?"

"I guess I must have said that."

"Do those words mean that Robby and some of his guests were arguing about something? Were upset with one another? Were they having a family quarrel? Or perhaps, you were having a family quarrel with your brother?"

"I... uh... I... " she stammered for a few moments, finally closing her lips firmly. She had nothing to say. Joseph didn't press.

Studying her closely, the lawyer could see only the top of her head as she slumped in the witness chair, the picture of dejection. She wasn't the fetching creature that had taken the stand several hours earlier. He was unable to see the expression in her downcast eyes or the emotions racing across her face. Joseph suddenly felt old and as the tenseness left him allowed his shoulders to droop, finishing with a sigh. "Just one more question Mrs. Black. When you denied these statements earlier," gesturing with the papers he held in his hand, "you were not telling the truth to this jury, were you?" he asked in a quiet, gentle voice – an adult disillusioned by a disingenuous child.

She made no answer as she raised her eyes to his face with such a malevolent stare that a sudden chill tripped down Joseph's spine.

"Thank you, Your Honor, I have no further questions."

"Anything from you, Ms. VanDamm?"

"Nothing, Your Honor."

"It is well past the hour for recess," the judge said, rising to leave the bench. "Remember my usual admonitions. See you in the morning."

Twenty-Six

The chubby lawyer slouched at his breakfast table looking out the window at the cold silence of morning, missing the honking of the Canadian Geese and the fussing of the Mallards. The *Milltown Reporter* was spread in front of him. He knew the trial would be the subject of much local gossip since it was the biggest thing to hit town in years, but couldn't help but wonder at the ease and swiftness with which the newspaper changed its views. His glance dropped from the crisp, crystalline lawn to the page one headline:

WITNESS PRESSED IN MURDER TRIAL

The newspapers' daily coverage of the trial, until this morning, had conveyed a not too subtle belief in Gay's guilt. This article evidenced an editorial bias intimating its opinion was no longer so firm.

While Mary placed a single slice of buttered toast before the slumping, tired looking middle-aged lawyer – she had no idea the replacement energy required for a murder trial – he read to her:

> Following intense questioning by the defense attorney, the sister of a Mt. City man who was shot and killed last August testified she did not shoot him.

Accurate punctuation is not a journalistic requirement.

"Well, did she?" Mary asked, bringing two cups of coffee to the table. Her nature required she get right to the heart of an issue, and not bother with frills.

"I don't know..." Joseph answered slowly and thoughtfully, scraping his hand across a scratchy cheek. "And, I guess it isn't too important... It seems to be a toss-up between her and Bliss – I just don't believe Gay did it."

After taking a bite of toast he added, "What really matters though is what the jury believes."

Feeling the need to persuade his wife of so many years, Joseph climbed slowly back onto his soapbox, "You know, we give lip service to the *innocent until proven guilty* crap... but it isn't true. When someone is charged with a crime, most people automatically assume he wouldn't be in court unless he did something wrong. Hang the bastard! It's virtually impossible for the public to believe police make mistakes. If they did, it would make a lie of everything they're taught from childhood – the policeman is your friend – he's here to help you – our parents and teachers repeat over and over. A jury may come to believe a defendant is innocent, but only if it is proven. Our Constitution doesn't say that – in fact it says just the opposite. But believe me any poor son-of-a-bitch on trial has to prove he's innocent."

"Don't be vulgar. Is she innocent?" Just plain speaking.

"I believe so." Somehow he did not appear so prepossessing sitting there in his tatty bathrobe, legs bare, few remaining hairs undirected, gray whiskers peeping out from wrinkled cheeks. But he believed and verbalized his posture with the same conviction as though robed in his courtroom attire.

"Well, then she'll be acquitted." Absolute faith. Joseph never knew whether her faith was in him or the system. He didn't have the courage to ask.

* * * * *

The next several witnesses produced by the State with the prosecutor and Bradley taking turns examining them, testified concerning the technical requirements needed for the presentation of any criminal case – necessary but not particularly interesting. As expected there was nothing of great public interest. Bradley's opportunity to share in the chore appeared to mollify him somewhat at having to sit second chair in the highly publicized trial. Going through the several witnesses quickly, the prosecution called the victim's *friend* Bliss, just after the midmorning break.

"Would you please state your full name and spell your last name?" Jackie intoned.

"Bliss Bellow Tucci. T-U-C-C-I."

Responding to questions from the prosecutor, the woman who called herself Bliss Tucci described her living arrangement with the deceased stating, "I was the wife of Robby Tucci."

Jackie asked, "May I call you Bliss?" It was easier and less odious to use the first name. Jackie was uncomfortable with the inappropriate surname.

"Certainly," she replied, with a gracious smile.

A smile didn't sit easily on the gaunt face surrounded by straggly, curling hair. She looked like a bad painting of a pioneer woman wasted by a covered wagon journey across untamed wilderness.

"Bliss, do you know Gabriella Bellow?"

"Yes, I do."

"Who is she?"

After a brief but noticeable pause she answered, "She is my birth mother..." glancing in Gay's direction.

An unusual choice of words, Joseph mused. *Maybe the jury will be interested in the apparent animosity – is it of long standing? Or as a result of the present circumstances? Should be able to play on that theme for a while.*

Jackie VanDamm had learned a lesson from the Emma Black fiasco and knew that defense counsel would capitalize on Bliss's checkered past – children fathered by different men – a criminal record – jail time – a son taken from her and adopted by her parents – so paraded it out for all to see in an attempt to minimize the potential damage. She wasn't going to chance a repeat of what happened to her other star witness.

VanDamm drew from Bliss her view of the events occurring on August 24 – the last Saturday of the Mt. City Fair. "I planned a visit with my children and granddaughter for that day. Robby, you know, my husband was going to have a couple of friends over."

Good, clean family fun. Every time Bliss referred to her "husband" there was a strangled sob in her voice – a sympathy provoking mannerism. This was added since Joseph had interviewed her. He wondered if she practiced.

She described the evening. "We opened the garage and brought some chairs outside in the yard. We live so close to Main Street we can see the fireworks from there. It was nice and warm. We had the radio on and had a few beers. A couple of times the men walked over to the Fair to check it out and get some Italian sausage sandwiches. When the fireworks started, we was going to watch from in front of our place..." another little choking sound, "and... we... we... were all talking and just having a good time..." her voice subsiding plaintively.

No mention of the fight between Tucci and her daughter – no mention of the dog – of her daughter taking her baby and running for safety – just a restful fun day with family and friends.

Jackie continued, "Did there come a time when things pretty much settled down for the evening?"

"Yes, everyone sort of left and Robby and I were there with the boys. We were getting ready to settle in for the night."

"Was your daughter planning to stay the night?" That was not the right question to ask.

"Well, she was ... but decided to leave with her baby." Bliss at least had the grace to appear slightly embarrassed. "Her and Robby had a small argument about nothing much ... She had a little too much to drink and didn't like something Robby said so decided to leave."

Having heard this piece of fiction, Joseph was curious as to how, if at all, Bliss was going to describe the violent quarrel between Tucci and his sister that preceded the shooting.

"About midnight, Emma came over to talk and ask us to her place for a cup 'a coffee. Her and Robby was on the landing – I mean she was on the landing and Robby and I was at the top of the stairs by the kitchen door."

"Did it appear they were arguing?"

"Yes ma'am. They was having a small argument. Not serious like – they was just arguing – family stuff. Emma yelled at Robby a little and he just laughed at her. He said something like she was his sister and he loved her – wasn't much of an argument. It was while Robby and Emma were talking – she'd just been there a couple of minutes – that my sister and mother come busting in. My sister Arliss," the name sounding like something obscene, "was in a real foul mood."

Bliss described her version of the incident that lead to "her Robby's' death.

"Arliss come storming in like she owned the place and yelled at the kids to get their stuff 'cause they was leaving. Jake was playing with his guitar. She grabbed it right from his hands and told him and Con to get their things together. She stood there holding the guitar in front of her, telling everybody what to do. Robby was just kind of leaning against the door – shocked the way she was acting. He wasn't saying nothing. She was screaming real foul words at him. Finally, Robby couldn't take it anymore and headed for her, telling her to get out of his house. He put his hands out like he was going to..." she paused trying to find the right word, "sho... push... her toward the stairs – but he didn't really grab her or touch her. She backed away from him in front of the china cupboard holding the guitar in both hands and screaming. She swung it at Robby, but hit the cupboard and knocked a bottle off the top – one of my antique Coke bottles. I had several up there. It hit Robby on the head, then fell to the floor and broke."

"You actually saw the bottle hit Robby's head?" It seemed the prosecutor was surprised by this answer.

"Yes, ma'am."

"Then what happened?"

"My mother moved away from the sink – got right between them and... "
She paused taking a deep breath and started speaking quietly, "Then there
was a loud noise and glassware rattling... and Robby just went... my mother
went behind him... he was going to shove Arliss but he never made contact...
then he turned toward me and I could see blood an' a blank look ... I grabbed
him – we sort of slid down together to the floor... " Her words came faster –
disjointed phrases that made little sense. Jackie made no effort to interrupt
or clarify what Bliss was saying.

"Then Emma come running up the stairs and I saw this silver .38 fall on
the floor and I saw my mother pick up the gun and put it in her right-hand
pocket. Arliss said something like *that isn't a gun,* and *Emma is full of shit*
and then screamed at the boys to get their stuff 'cause they was leaving ... "
Bliss' voice rising in pitch and volume. She suddenly stopped, took a breath
and said in an almost normal tone, "Then they all left and they didn't care we
didn't have no help."

"Objection, Your Honor," Joseph interposed mildly wanting to mark the
moment so the jury would be aware of the incongruity in Bliss' speech pattern.

The judge addressed the witness. "Just answer the questions. You need
make no comment about what they were thinking. You have no way of
knowing what was in their minds."

Ignoring the byplay, Jackie VanDamm ended her examination by showing
Bliss a photograph and asking her to identify it. "That's my Robby," she said
with a sob, "when he was alive. He was playing with our family cat!" she
wailed.

Nice touch.

Without waiting for Jackie to take her seat, Joseph addressed Judge Clarke,
"Your Honor, I think my cross-examination might be rather lengthy."

Taking the hint, the judge ordered an early lunch break as a courtesy to
avoid interrupting the interrogation. It seemed he was looking forward to it
himself.

* * * * *

The lawyer was seated at the trial table when Bliss walked back into the
courtroom after lunch. She had to walk past Joseph and her mother to reach
the witness stand, looking at neither, concentrating with the effort to ignore
their existence. Joseph watched her for a few minutes and realized she didn't
have much of a fuse left. He would have to handle her carefully since he
didn't want her to appear sympathetic.

The jury was brought in and Judge Clarke began the afternoon session

197

with his standard ritual. Joseph noted incongruously that for some reason the butterflies failed to make an appearance, causing him to wonder if he was now accustomed to being a trial lawyer or just getting old. Taking his position behind the jury box, he quietly contemplated the witness for a few moments. He was again struck by the similarities between her, her mother and sister. So remarkably alike, yet the impact of each was different. It gave meaning to Shakespeare's words:

God gives you one face, you make yourself another.

Gay's mouth was pinched from suffering – Bliss' from meanness and self-pity. Gay's eyes deep set, sad, having seen much unhappiness – Bliss' were bright and vicious, always looking for an advantage. *Maybe,* Joseph thought, *What I'm seeing isn't really there. We'll soon know.*

He addressed the witness, "I am not sure what to call you. Do you prefer Mrs. Tucci or Mrs. Kovacic or Mrs. Pringle or Ms. Bellow?" These were all of the names she'd called herself at various times in her short life.

"It is **Mrs.** Tucci," she replied stiffly.

"I know, but all of the names I've mentioned are names you've used, isn't that so?"

"Yes sir!" Her reply was clipped and sarcastic. She was becoming convinced she had no reason to like the lawyer.

"You and Mr. Tucci were never married, were you?"

"Not formally, but he was my husband, sir!"

Joseph again ran through the series of names she'd used and established her relationship, marriage or lack, with each of the men whose names she'd accumulated. Having adequately exposed her moral standards to the jury, he now wanted them to learn about her relationship with her mother.

"When Mrs. VanDamm asked you to identify the people in your apartment on the night in question, you referred to Mrs. Bellow as your *birth mother,* isn't that true?"

"Yes sir." Her replies were still clipped with restrained fury. She would answer questions but give nothing.

"Does that description indicate you are not on friendly terms with your mother?"

"No sir." Jackie must have talked to her. "It's just that so many people have stepmothers. I wanted to clarify that she is my natural mother. I like my mother – I love my mother and I want to help her." Joseph's thoughts turned back to Shakespeare and the line about *protesting too much.* Her tone and demeanor made a lie of her words. The lawyer turned to other areas.

Despite careful questioning, Bliss continued to downplay Tucci's arguments on the day he died. She even denied his heavy drinking or that his behavior had been in any way disruptive. The questions became more and more pointed. Jackie's objections became more frequent.

Finally Judge Clarke became exasperated with the constant interruptions by the prosecutor and the defense lawyer's dogged efforts to get the truth from Bliss. "Ladies and gentlemen, we are going to take a short recess while I talk to counsel. Go back to the jury room while I straighten this out."

Turning to the lawyers before the door to the jury room had closed, he demanded, "What in the name of hell is going on? Both of you knock it off. What's the matter with you? We'll never get this goddamn trial finished! Now, let's get back to work. Call the jury..."

Before he could finish, Joseph interjected, "Judge, it's the same old stuff our good friend, the prosecutor, has been pulling throughout the trial. This witness made several statements, verbal, written and recorded, early on in the investigation. They differ completely from the testimony she is giving today. In fact, I talked to this witness and recorded our conversation. What she is saying today is different from what she told me. I intend to cross-examine her about the statements and the discrepancies, but Ms. Prosecutor here keeps butting in and making me the heavy. She doesn't want the jury to hear what a liar her *poor widowed victim* is. She should know that won't stop me – won't even slow me down – just delay the trial."

Turning to Jackie with a sigh, Judge Clarke said, "Come on, Jackie. You know what he's doing is proper and the old bastard is stubborn enough and he is going to get it out one way or the other. Your interruptions are going to make the jury think maybe you have something to hide."

Good advice Joseph hoped she wouldn't take. Why was the Judge trying to help her? Might be some reflexive chauvinistic paternal instincts.

"I'm sorry, Judge. I just get the feeling he's picking on her – and he is. He should be instructed to get off her back!"

"Your Honor, I'm not he. I have a name?"

"We're all getting tired. Let's cool down. Art, call back the jury and let's proceed with fewer interruptions – okay?" The judge glared at the lawyers.

The jury reseated, Judge Clarke explained. "Again, I am sure you have guessed the questioning involves prior statements given by this witness not consistent with her testimony today. Counsel is permitted to examine her about those inconsistencies in order that you may evaluate her credibility or truthfulness. Proceed, Mr. Joseph."

Bliss Bellow Tucci had sat through the exchange and knew that everything she said outside the courtroom, as well as in, would be heard by this jury. She didn't like it and was not going down without a fight. The truth would be spent grudgingly – each admission dragged from her.

Joseph phrased his questions carefully so the witness knew he wouldn't permit her to vary one iota from what she had said in the past. He wanted that thought fixed firmly in Bliss' mind when he asked about the fight between Tucci and his sister.

"It was about midnight when Emma Black came over, is that correct?" The lawyer was looking at a paper the witness knew to be her handwritten statement.

"Yes sir."

"And she and Robby were having a conversation on the stairs?"

"Yes sir."

Joseph drew another sheet of paper from his file. Bliss had seen it earlier and she knew it was a transcript of her recorded talk with one of the investigators. Looking at it he asked, "Were they having an argument?"

"A small one... "

"What was it about?"

"Personal!" she snapped.

"What was the argument about?" Joseph insisted placidly. Before she could respond, both Jackie and her assistant were on their feet yelling, "Objection!" *Excellent*, Joseph thought. *Their reaction put exclamation points on both sides of the question.*

"Overruled!" Judge Clarke ordered. "Answer the question."

"All I heard was Emma yelling at Robby," she replied, still being evasive.

"What words did you hear her yell?" Joseph asked, walking toward her with the transcript outstretched.

Her shoulders slumped. "She was saying, *'Why did you tell Jim?'* "

"Tell Jim what?" he continued, moving toward her.

Jackie was on her feet. "Clearly irrelevant! Objection..."

Judge Clarke glared at her. "Sit down!" Then, to the witness, "Mr. Joseph is asking you about the argument between Mr. Tucci and his sister. Tell us what you heard. Do you understand?"

"Yes sir..." she responded to the Judge in a voice much more meekly than anything Joseph had gotten from her.

During the exchange Joseph had returned to his spot behind the jury. He wanted the witness looking directly toward the jury as she answered so they could see her flushed, angry face – defiant glare – a trap she didn't like but could not avoid.

"Go on," he suggested quietly. "Please tell the jury what you heard." He sounded like an amiable, harmless old man asking questions.

"All I heard was Emma asking Robby why he told Jim those things about her, like, *"Why did you tell him those things? What did you bring that up for? It happened a long time ago. There is no sense bringing it up now'."*

"Was she angry while she was asking those questions?"

"Yes... " She wasn't calling the lawyer sir now.

"She called him names didn't she? Very vulgar names?"

"Yes... " she said in a whisper.

"The argument had to do with an affair Emma was having, isn't that true?" Jackie stood to offer an objection, then sat without saying anything.

The lawyer continued when Bliss nodded. "Robby told her she was just like their mother and he would see to it that Jim got the children from her, didn't he?" Again she nodded without looking at her tormentor or the jury, speaking into fists clenched tightly in front of her mouth, muffled response almost inaudible.

"Robby told her he would stand by Jim, whatever he wanted to do?" She would rather have bitten out her tongue than give that answer.

"That is what Robert Tucci and Emma Black were arguing about at your apartment on the night he was killed?" Joseph asked with mild persistence.

"Yes sir ... " she said in a resigned monotone. The sir was back.

Allowing the silence to build, the lawyer walked slowly to his seat and sorted through several file folders. The jurors looked at him expectantly. Joseph was giving them a chance to think about what had been said. Finally picking up a folder, he returned to the questioning.

"Earlier today you told us that your sister Arliss was the aggressor in the confrontation between her and Robert – that she picked up the guitar and attacked him with it, is that correct?"

"Yes sir," she said a little more positively. She felt this a safer subject.

"I would like you to review this statement," he said, handing her a copy of a hand written document prepared by her, "that you gave to the police... May I approach again, Your Honor?" Joseph asked as he walked toward Bliss without waiting permission. "Look, right here," he pointed. "Please read with me... *Robby said what are you on your high horse about? And my sister said, You sent Elaine home walking over a stupid fight about a dog, and they were fighting and swearing, and then Robbie lunged for my sister...*

Is that what you said in your recorded statement to the police the morning Robert Tucci died?"

She sat, saying nothing, fists again clenched, long bony fingers intertwined tightly, her mouth a grim line, for so long Judge Clarke ordered, "Please answer the question."

"I don't think she has to, Your Honor. She already has." A great stopping point – but not yet – Joseph needed to continue.

Over the next forty to forty-five minutes he kept returning to her several statements until he established, using her words, that Robert Tucci had not only been the aggressor in the argument with Arliss, but that he had been choking and throwing her slight body about while Bliss tried to hold on to Robby's arm and pull him away. He was too strong in his rage, finally throwing Arliss against the china cupboard causing the coke bottle to fall, hitting Tucci on the head with enough force to shatter the bottle. She saw him drop to the floor.

"You told the police that night you did not hear a gunshot, didn't you?"

"Yes... " she said with her head down, barely heard.

"You are familiar with guns, aren't you?" Without waiting for her to answer, Joseph continued, "In fact you regularly carry a hand gun, don't you?"

"Not recently," she said in a monotone, finally recognizing the only way she would leave the witness stand was to answer the old man's questions completely and truthfully.

But she hadn't given up the fight. Suddenly she straightened from the slouch she had assumed and pointed at her mother with a shaking, scrawny finger. "Then, she... she came into my house, pulled out a gun and shot my husband...! My Robby...!"

Ignoring her tears Joseph, no longer fearing she would appear sympathetic before the jury, shouted over her voice, "You want the jury to believe that, don't you? You are going to get even with your mother, aren't you? You have hated her for years because she doesn't approve of your lifestyle?"

"Objection! Objection!" This came from the prosecutor's table.

Judge Clarke pounded his gavel, screaming, "Order!"

"I don't care what they believe. That is honest to God what happened!" Bliss yelled.

In the sudden silence that followed Joseph felt faint with insight – felt the blood leaving his head. *Maybe this woman didn't kill her lover even though the evidence seems to point that way.* Another picture was beginning to form.

Shaking his head to clear the thought, the lawyer asked quietly, "Are you telling this jury you saw your mother shoot Robert Tucci?"

"I didn't see her with the gun, shooting, but I seen her pick the gun up off the floor and put it in her pocket."

Joseph secured the murder weapon from the exhibit table and walking purposefully toward the witness, held it out to her. "Is this the gun you saw?"

She drew back as though the gun were alive – a snake. "Take it," Joseph commanded. "You've carried a gun – you're familiar with them – take it!"

"No... I don't want to touch it... " she wailed, shaking her head from side to side, pushing with her hands against the front rail of the witness box, shoving herself back as far as she could in the seat, ready to leap from the chair and run from the room.

"Do you need a moment to compose yourself?" Joseph asked not unkindly, returning the gun to the evidence table. He too, needed to slow his heartbeat. *Maybe ...*

She took several deep, sobbing breaths once the gun was no longer in view, visibly gathering herself, hiccuping in a shaky voice, "No... I'm okay."

"Just once more Mrs. Tucci," the title a minor concession, "Let's return to your statement. Please read along with me, to yourself..." as he pointed out the place. She did, lips trembling.

"Now, then," he asked. "Didn't you tell the police on the day following the shooting, that you had not seen any gun that night?"

"Yes sir..." she said in a whisper.

Joseph felt fortunate he had already removed the gun from in front of her. He walked to his seat, standing pensively before it. He began to lower himself into it. The prosecutor stood to start her redirect examination. She had to try and rehabilitate this witness. Joseph waved her off and said without rising, "Oh, just one more question Mrs. Tucci. I forgot. Have you ever been convicted of a felony in this or any other State?"

"Yes I have." She looked as though she would not need the gun to eliminate her tormentor.

"Armed robbery, wasn't it? You've served time in both Ohio and Pennsylvania haven't you?"

Jackie banged on her table and yelled, "Objection!" Furious, but the witness had already answered, "Yes sir."

There was no way Jackie would be able to rehabilitate this witness and she knew it. Still standing, she whispered, "I have no further questions, Your Honor."

The court helped by calling a recess. "Do not form or express an opinion... Oh, hell, you know the rest... " he trailed off as he left the bench. The timing couldn't have been better.

Twenty-Seven

While waiting for the judge to finish doing whatever it is judges do in chambers, Pat Joseph sat in the bailiff's office with Art and Scott, sucking on black coffee from a foam cup that makes all coffee taste the same – bad. He was, nevertheless, grateful that Candy always kept a pot going in Art's office. She knew what kept lawyers quiet.

"Scott," Joseph quipped, "You kind of blew that one."

"What are you talking about?" the court reporter asked with a puzzled look.

"You know," the lawyer laughed. "Telling Jackie not to ask about the gunshot residue tests on her direct," knowing full well Scott would have told the prosecutor the importance of minimizing the weaknesses in a case by calling it to the attention of the jury yourself. He had a better grasp on trial strategy than practically all lawyers appearing in his court.

"You know goddam' well what I told her, Pat. She didn't listen – dumb broad. Or maybe she forgot – damn air head." Scott was serious. He couldn't believe Joseph thought him capable of such a rudimentary error.

"Oh..." Joseph grinned like a jolly elf. "Now I have to try cases against you and the prosecutor. Why aren't you helping me instead of her?"

Scott grinned, finally recognizing the needle. Art laughed aloud. "Yeah, you really need a lot of help in this one Pat."

A major trial is, at best, traumatic – extremely stressful to all participants no matter what their role. Sometimes a sense of humor is all that enables those involved to maintain any semblance of sanity. All the court personnel were vividly aware of this and made an effort to keep the atmosphere light. They knew that most lawyers truly appreciated help. Sometimes the humor got pretty rank and the litigants would be hard pressed to accept it, but it was needed – sort of like M.A.S.H.

Candy stuck her head around the corner. "The boss is ready to start."

Joseph chugged the rest of his coffee, wondering why, and walked into the courtroom to gather his little coterie and see what Jackie intended next. It didn't take long.

205

* * * * *

"The State calls detective Mike Redding."

Joseph smiled at Mike as he took the stand – an old friend – an old adversary. Redding returned the smile with little warmth. It was a mask for underlying hostility, not necessarily directed at Joseph, but at all those not on the same side of the legal fence he perceived to be his. He was one of the good guys – everyone else the enemy. Mike literally couldn't understand how anyone with moral integrity could align with criminals. He was able to accept it in the abstract but not in his gut where it counted. What made it worse from his standpoint; he really liked Pat Joseph, liked to socialize with him and helped when he could. He just couldn't fathom his thought process at all.

If Redding ever reflected on the country's founders, he thought of them as patriotic freedom fighters. That they were rebels fighting against an established government never occurred to him. The revolutionaries weren't seeking individual freedoms. They were creating a new government with the police on the side of God. Criminals don't have rights.

Too concrete to verbalize such thoughts, Mike believed the Constitution a piece of paper, interpreted by old men to create problems for him. It didn't apply – what did these fancy Supreme Court Justices know about life on the streets. Their decisions got in the way of good people trying to do their jobs – an impediment smart-ass lawyers used to make things tough.

Unfortunately he was sincere. Not devious enough to make this kind of analysis, his thoughts followed a *pattern. I investigated the crime. I'm an honest man. A good cop. I **know** what happened. Why don't the judge and jury get on with it? This trial is a waste of time and taxpayer's money. The bitch is guilty. Why the fuck don't she just plead and let's get to the sentencing?*

Mike was briefly startled when Jackie VanDamm broke into his contemplation, "Detective Redding, would you please tell the jury your name, spell your last name and tell us how you are employed?"

Mike turned toward the jury smiling, telling them of his background, training and experience. Having been a witness hundreds of times, he was aware of how juries needed to be handled. None of his anger showed.

He answered questions easily without being glib. His voice rumbled, a counterpoint to the roll of thunder outside. The day had darkened and warmed enough for the snow to change back to rain. Lightning could be seen in the distance. Unusual for this time of year. *But, why not?* Joseph pondered. *We've had everything but the expected happen inside this room, why not outside too?*

206

Mike told the jury how he was called to the crime scene in the early morning hours. A crowd had already gathered. Initially there was some confusion as to whether a shooting had occurred – the incident had been reported as a domestic dispute. Uniformed officers had things under control by the time he arrived. As the senior officer on the scene, he took charge of the investigation and ordered the "suspects' separated from one another and kept under observation so they could not share information or dispose of anything. He talked to each separately, first the defendant.

"She said," he explained to the jury, "that she and Arliss Conrad, her daughter, had come to the Robert Tucci residence for the purpose of picking up two teenage children. The victim was drunk and argumentative. They entered the apartment and a fight ensued between Arliss Conrad and Robert Tucci."

He stated that he was the one that performed the atomic absorption tests to determine if there were gunshot residue on the suspect's hands. Detective Wolfe assisted him in conducting the interviews. All of the witnesses were then transported to the police station. He corrected himself, saying, "That is, all except Bliss Tucci and Emma Black. We allowed them to go to the hospital with the victim. But they were with police officers and kept under observation at all times. They were transported to the station after Tucci was life-flighted to Cleveland Metro.

"At headquarters," Redding explained, "I obtained a tape-recorded statement from Gabriella Bellow, the defendant."

The lawyer glanced at Gay who was staring intently at Redding reliving the interrogation the jury would soon hear, but could never imagine. She was now convinced Redding made her believe she killed Tucci and that he did it during the interview conducted in the early morning hours at police headquarters. She held no good feelings toward him.

"At what time was the statement taken?" Jackie prompted.

"The taped statement was begun at 5:41 A.M.," Redding responded, neglecting to mention that he and Detective Wolfe had been taking turns questioning Gay for some four hours before starting the tape recorder. *The jury will soon learn about that,* Joseph thought.

The prosecutor handed a document to the witness to identify.

"This is the rights form used by our office. It contains the Miranda warnings. I hand it to a subject, read and have them initial it at each separate right, and then sign it in the presence of witnesses."

The constant reference to Gay as "the subject" annoyed Joseph. *If they're so goddamn sure of their case, why is it necessary to depersonalize her?* he thought. *She has a name and Mike is going to use it before I get finished with him!*

"Who signed the rights form?"

Turning toward the jury, Mike responded, "The form was signed voluntarily by the defendant, one Gabriella Bellow."

Several more questions were asked, designed to convince the jury that everything was done to protect Gay's constitutional rights and that there was absolutely no pressure applied.

Jackie, with a flourish, produced the tape – her big moment – the climax to which she had been building. This was *THE CONFESSION* upon which her entire case and mind-set rested. The perception of guilt. The reality is, that it was also the point in time when, for all practical purposes, the investigation stopped.

Holding the tape to her bosom like a precious stone tablet brought down from the mountain, Jackie strode back and forth before the jury and asked questions of Detective Redding to satisfy the technical evidentiary requirements. The tape had been properly stored and secured so it could not be adulterated. Joseph allowed her to have the moment without interruption.

Still holding her cherished gem, Jackie asked, "What did you do when you completed the recorded statement of the defendant?" She also refused to use Gay's name.

"I notified our Chief and informed him we had obtained a statement of admission from the subject."

Enough is enough. "Objection, your Honor! Mr. Redding," intentionally demoting the witness to civilian status, Joseph stood and said, "knows better than to characterize the evidence. He has a great deal of experience in court and knows that conclusions are for the jury to draw. As a matter of fact, this statement is an admission of nothing." If the witness wanted to play, Joseph could too.

"Sustained," Judge Clarke ruled. "The jury will disregard the witness' conclusions."

Jackie still tried to elicit from Redding his interpretation of what was on the tape. "Judge," Joseph interrupted patiently, "if Mrs. VanDamm is so anxious for the jury to know what is on the tape, why doesn't she just play it for them? They look intelligent enough to be able to figure out what it says. We don't need Mr. Redding or Ms. VanDamm to interpret it." He added gratuitously, "It is their failure to interpret it accurately that brings us here today."

Jackie reddened. She wanted to build to the moment she would present the tape to the jury. The lawyer's suggestion that it be played stole the dramatic presentation. The only thunder left to be heard was rumbling outside. Hers had been stolen.

Judge Clarke, again impatient with both, said, "That's enough, Mr. Joseph. Ms. VanDamm, if you want to play the tape, do so. But please get on with it. If the tape requires explanation, you will have an opportunity to do that in final argument. Now move along, please ... "

Jackie was furious, but could do nothing. She had to play the recording without the planned preamble. A typist had transcribed the tape and a copy was passed out for each juror to follow while listening to the tape. Joseph could have argued successfully that the procedure was improper since the transcription was merely someone's interpretation of what was on the tape, that is, hearsay. But he chose not to. Joseph was equally anxious for the jury to hear not only what and how each word was uttered, but to know the exact wording, and he wanted to be able to make use of the transcript during the cross-examination of Redding.

Jackie handed the tape to the detective, who took it and left the witness stand to insert it in a portable player with remote speakers strategically placed along the jury rail. After making sure the machine was working properly, he turned it on.

This would be the first time Gay's voice would be heard by the jury. They sat quietly leaning toward the speakers. The media and gallery strained forward. The room was still. The speakers buzzed and crackled until the voices began. Mike's gravelly voice was easily recognized even with the slight electronic distortion.

"The time is 0541 A.M. The location is Mills County Sheriff Department's Detective Bureau. Being interviewed is Gabriella E. Bellow, spelled B-E-L-L-O-W. Conducting this interview are Mike Redding and Jerome Wolfe of the Mills County Sheriff's Department. First of all, Mrs. Bellow what is your date of birth?"

Gay's answering voice sounded dull and lifeless. The jury couldn't know how she normally sounded, but they could tell the voice emanating from the speakers seemed almost somnolent – without will. Having been with her all these months, Joseph knew what she must have gone through to reach that state. "November 15, 1925."

"Do you understand that you are not under arrest?"

"Yes... " It was a sigh, almost a whisper.

"We have made that clear to you several times? In fact, when we left the room, the doors were left open. You haven't been locked in here, have you?" Mike was a pro. He would make sure the Miranda requirements were satisfied.

"No..." The voice was listless.

"Have you been held against your will?"

"No..." There was no volition.

The recording went on. The jurors turning page after page of a transcript, reading the questions and answers while listening to the words. Each detail of the preceding evening was explored. Gay, explaining as best she could what she did and her intentions in doing so.

Finally after many minutes, Redding began asking about the fight that ended in Tucci's death. Probing and picking over each bit of the altercation, he asked, "Then what happened?"

Her voice unchanged, Gay responded, *"Then, I guess I must have shot him."*

This was the *confession* – the admission upon which the police and the prosecutor relied – the State's entire case!

Mike's voice continued without interruption asking questions designed to include information not covered in the recording. It was obvious the detectives had been talking with Gay long before the tape had been turned on and were now recreating details for the benefit of those who would later listen to it.

"Do you recall where you were standing when you shot him?"

A little of the hypnotic quality left Gay's voice and some confusion appeared – some hesitancy as though trying to visualize what had happened. "Um... Robert was facing Arliss and I was... ah... standing next to Arliss – and I used my right hand, so I don't know where I hit him – or – I don't know..." she said, her voice trailing off.

"Okay, don't worry. Let's try to break it down a little."

After the point was exhausted, Mike left the subject to return several minutes later. Good interrogation technique. Joseph was impressed. "Okay, what kind of gun was it you took to the Tucci apartment?"

"I just reached up on the closet shelf. There were two guns there and I think I took the bigger one."

"Which one would that be?"

"I think it was a .32."

"Revolver or automatic?"

"It's like a revolver. It has a cylinder."

"Okay. When Robert was struggling with Arliss were you in front of him or behind him?"

There were several moments of silence as though she were trying to return to the moment to report it accurately.

"He was sort of facing me, like that," apparently gesturing, "um ... um ... Well, he still had a hold of her. But it seems to me that he was turning his head to look at me or at Bliss – I'm not sure. Then I lifted up the gun so he could see it – I hoped he would get scared and quit – but he didn't. That's all I remember about how he was."

"You said that he was pushing Arliss around while he was choking her and bouncing her off the walls and cabinets and so forth?"

"Yes sir, he was."

"So things were happening pretty fast? Do you remember at what point you reached in your pocket and pulled out the gun?"

"Not remember, remember..." This was the important phrase – this was what Joseph wanted the jury to hear and absorb. She had no actual memory of what the police persuaded her had happened. "But, I must have reached in and done it."

"Why do you say that you must have reached in and done it?"

"Because it was done..." she said, as though the answer was obvious.

"Did anyone else in that room have a gun?" he asked, directing her thought process, knowing she was the only one in the room with a gun and so the only one who could have shot Tucci.

"I don't know – I honestly don't know – I know I had one."

"You know you did, and you remember pulling that gun out of your pocket. We talked about that," he said, reminding her of their prior conversations.

She would not be led. "I think I did."

The interrogators were now taking turns asking questions. First Redding's and then Wolfe's voice could be heard. Wolfe seemed to get more of a rise out of Gay – his questions were framed more as statements rather than questions. He wasn't as good as Mike.

"You told me you remembered pulling that gun out and pointing it at Robert?"

"Yes, sir. I did take the gun out and pointed it up in the air like this," again apparently accompanied by a gesture. "I wanted Robert to quit and I thought if he saw the gun he would."

"Did he see the gun?"

"I don't know."

"Did Arliss see the gun?"

"I don't know what Arliss saw."

"Did Bliss see the gun?"

Impatience crept into her voice. "I don't know what anyone saw – all I know is what I did."

"Okay, after you shot Robert and dropped the gun, did anybody see the gun after that?"

"Emma and Bliss were standing by Robert. Arliss and I were staring down at them. But, I can't honestly say what anybody saw."

On it went, each officer taking turns with her. Half an hour passed and the jury continued to listen attentively, neither bored nor distracted, glancing frequently at Redding, perhaps somewhat provoked at the pressure he brought to bear on a woman almost twice his age.

Again the inquisitors returned to their theory. "After you shot Robert and the rescue squad was called, I understand most of the people there didn't know exactly what had happened to Robert. Did you tell anyone you shot him?"

"No, because I didn't actually know that I had at that time. I didn't know I had shot him..." her voice trailed off into a smothered sob.

"Did you think it was pure coincidence that you pointed the gun at him, the gun went off, and he fell to the floor?" he sounded like a sarcastic bastard – without pity.

"No... He was so drunk. I... I... thought maybe he lost his balance. I didn't know until I saw the blood he had been injured."

"When did you know that you shot Robert?"

"I didn't know I had really shot Robert. But when the police came and sat me in their car, I thought there must be something more wrong with Robert than him falling, or they wouldn't be making us wait like this. Then when the officer asked if he could do that test on my hand, I figured they knew something then."

"Where did he do the test?"

"In the back seat of his car."

"Did you submit to the test voluntarily?"

"Of course I did."

"Did you think the test would show that you had fired a gun?"

"That's what those tests are for."

"Who did the test?" Redding's voice asked.

"Why, you did," Gay answered slightly perplexed. *Didn't he remember?*

After a brief pause, Redding's voice continued, "Is there anything else you would like to add to this statement?"

"No... It has been a very confusing, nightmarish night."

"Has your statement been truthful?"

"As truthful as I can remember."

"Have we made any promises or threats to get you to make this statement?"

"No, sir."

"At this point we have no further questions and are concluding this interview at 08:08 A.M."

The speakers buzzed – no other sound in the room. Judge Clarke broke into the silence, clearing his throat. Everyone had listened for so long it seemed unnatural to interrupt the silence. "If there are no further questions, Ms. VanDamm, we will recess for the day and allow Mr. Joseph to begin his cross-examination tomorrow morning." Then looking toward the jury, he said, "We are in recess for the day – usual admonitions."

Twenty-Eight

Grumbling and rumpled, Joseph woke to the sound of his wife feeding and talking to the cats. He quickly showered, shaved and descended to where breakfast was spread on the round oak table, Mary standing at the sink, her place at the table not set.

"Looks like you're a little upset with me this morning," the lawyer suggested, no great concern apparent in his voice.

The rain had stopped, the snow not renewed. Frost crinkled on the grass and veiled the pond. Mary grumped. "Well, you should be satisfied. I can't go to the grocery store anymore. I want my name taken off the mailbox."

Not a new demand, but one not recently voiced. "Now, what?" Joseph asked with resignation.

"You did it again – the newspaper. Why can't you handle cases like other lawyers? Why do you have to be in the paper? My friends have been following this case and say they have breakfast with you every morning."

Patiently he asked, "Mary, what the hell are you talking about?"

"Don't you swear at me! You know! Your Bellow's case is in the paper again. Look at the headline. I may have to stay in the house 'till I die," she said, handing him the *Milltown Reporter*.

BELLOWS: SHOOTING UNCLEAR!

was spread across the front page, headlining the article reporting Redding's testimony of yesterday. The article was a surprisingly accurate description of the proceedings, making the point that the tape was not as clear an indication of guilt as the State had been saying. At least the local newspaper was questioning the quality of the investigation. Joseph hoped the jury was too.

He tried to explain this to his beleaguered wife, but she continued to bemoan her shopping problems.

* * * * *

Pat Joseph's spirits improved as the result of both the breakfast and the newspaper article.

Back in court, the elderly lawyer felt mild amazement that he was beginning to feel less a stranger to the courtroom and more at home asking questions. He began his cross-examination of Redding by asking the detective to explain again how he had been aroused from sleep and arrived at the scene at about 2:15 A.M. By the time he got there Gay had already, in a sense, been taken into custody. She was isolated in the back of a patrol car and there kept under observation by the first police officer to arrive on the scene.

Redding explained it was standard procedure for suspects to be restrained in this manner, isolated from one another and kept under observation until an arrest made or the suspect released.

"First of all, Mr. Redding," Joseph stated firmly but without heat, "Mrs. Bellow is not a *suspect* or *subject*. She is a person and has a name. Would you mind using it when referring to her?"

Redding did not answer but lowered his eyes, the color of his face slightly heightened. Friend or no, the lines were drawn.

"Now then," Joseph asked not pressing the point but sure it had not slipped past the court or jury, "Is that what was done here?"

"Yes, she – Mrs. Bellows – was kept segregated and under observation." He was a quick study.

"Did you learn that as soon as you arrived on the scene?"

"That is true. That's what the first officer there said."

"As the results of that conversation, did you perform any test on Mrs. Bellow?"

"Yes I did. An atomic absorption test to determine whether there was the presence of gunshot residue on Mrs. Bellow's hands."

The defense lawyer encouraged the detective to describe how the test works and exactly what he did. With his explanation, it became clear Gay had no opportunity to wash her hands or otherwise interfere with the test results.

When asked about the results, Redding reluctantly admitted, "Her hands were clean, the test result was negative – but they aren't always accurate."

Joseph ignored the editorial comment for the time being, knowing the judge would have caused it to be stricken if asked. Instead, the lawyer asked about the recorded statement, suggesting the detective had given Gay as much information as he had received from her.

"Are you telling this jury, officer, that you did not talk to her for several hours while she was in your custody before you made a recording of her statement?"

"I don't know what you mean. Are you asking me if we talked to her before taking her taped statement?" He was seeking time to gather his thoughts.

"Yes, that is exactly what I am asking!"

"Well, she was being interviewed..." Redding evaded.

Joseph would not be denied. "Officer Redding, the taped interview began at approximately a quarter to six in the morning. Mrs. Bellow had been in custody from two-fifteen A.M., some four hours earlier, isn't that correct?"

"Yes."

"Was a cot or couch made available to her?"

"She didn't ask for one."

"Was she sitting in a straight, wooden chair?"

"Yes..."

"And both you and Detective Wolfe took turns asking her questions?"

"We both asked questions, yes."

The jury was beginning to get a picture of what Gay had endured. An elderly woman – distressed – confined in intimidating surroundings – deprived of comfort – badgered by men devoid of sympathy or understanding. It is little wonder her voice sounded tired, resigned – a monotone Redding had described as "calm."

"Officer," Joseph asked stridently, "It was you who informed Mrs. Bellow that Tucci had been shot, wasn't it?"

Before realizing what he was admitting, Redding responded, "Yes."

Allowing a moment for the concession to sink in, the lawyer continued more quietly. "Mr. Redding, is there anywhere in that taped interview that Mrs. Bellow admitted she shot Tucci?"

As if thinking back through what the jury had heard, he answered, "Well, not in the taped statement directly."

Having laid the foundation, Joseph wanted to establish how the police ended the investigation once Mrs. Bellow was interviewed. It had to be driven home.

"Did you make any effort to verify the allegation made by Arliss Conrad that she had been beaten and choked?"

When Redding silently denied the failure, Joseph continued. "Didn't you think it important to determine if Arliss Conrad had been choked by Tucci?"

"If she had sustained any serious physical harm, it would have been noted."

Back and forth for an hour or more. Mini-wars, skirmishes and interruptions flowed between Jackie VanDamm and Pat Joseph, accompanied by frequent rebukes from the court. Finally, Judge Clarke suggested, "We have been proceeding jerkily, for quite a while. Let's take a short recess."

During the recess, Jackie VanDamm conferred with Redding and her assistant. The exchange became heated, but never loud enough to carry to the defense table. As soon as the judge reconvened court, Jackie stood and said, "Your Honor, since there are no more questions of this witness, we will now move for the introduction of our exhibits and rest. But we received a message from our office just now that may bear on the case. Would you adjourn for lunch so we can attend to this problem?"

Judge Clarke studied the prosecutor for a moment. "Jackie, can you tell me what this is all about?"

"I can't yet, Your Honor. It is probably nothing, but we have to check."

"Other than this, you intend to rest?" Judge Clarke asked.

"Yes we do!" VanDamm answered, Brad in obvious disagreement.

Joseph looked incredulous. This was unexpected. He was sure the State had not proved its case. *Why were they relying on the so-called confession alone? What the hell was the message about?* He thought the State had at least another day or two to go. He wasn't ready to start.

The court must have been taken aback as well. Judge Clarke called for an early, and long, noon recess. "All right, Jackie. We will adjourn now until two o'clock. Be ready to proceed or rest at that time. I'm sure there will be motions, so Art, tell the jurors they can go to lunch and don't have to be back until about two-thirty. We are recessed."

Joseph gathered his crew. "Let's get back to the office. We have a hell of a lot of ground to cover in the next two hours."

* * * * *

Leaving the courthouse, Joseph could see Jackie VanDamm and Mike Redding hurrying across the parking lot. The bailiff had handed her a note saying, "Call office before you do anything else – about case." The note was signed, "L."

"What is it, Linda?" Jackie asked her secretary as she rushed into her office. Linda reported, "Mrs. VanDamm, I got a call from a lady named Diane Heath. She sounded excited and said something about the wrong lady being on trial. I didn't know what to do so I thought I'd better call and tell you about it. She left a number."

Ignoring the apologetic tone, VanDamm said, "Don't worry, you did the right thing."

Jackie said to the detective, who had followed her into the office, "What the hell is this all about?" Then to Linda she said, "Get her on the phone. We'd better talk to her right now!"

Redding left while Jackie picked up the phone. A pleasant but slightly tense female voice answered before the second ring, "Hello."

"This is Prosecutor VanDamm returning a call from Mrs. Heath. Is she there, please?"

"This is Mrs. Heath. I called about the case being tried – you know – the Bellow case."

"I understand," Jackie broke in, lying smoothly. "I'm in my office with Detective Mike Redding, the investigator in charge. He said he didn't recognize your name. Has he ever met or talked with you?"

"No. I've been away on vacation and was just reading the *Reporters* we saved while we were gone. The picture of the lady on the front page... "is not the one..."

Before she could finish, Jackie suggested, "You're right. It's important we talk. I'd rather it be in person. Detective Redding will send a car for you. Could you come to the office right away? The judge gave us a long lunch hour. What is your address please?"

"Uh ... 328 Garden St., Mt. City. It's right across the street from where the killing was. I was there that night and overheard a conversation ... "

Listening, Jackie wrote down the address and handed it to Bradley, mouthing, "Get it to Redding." Bradley rushed to another phone and called the dispatcher to patch him through to Redding or any cruiser in the Mt. City area. Redding answered and Bradley told him what Jackie wanted. A police car was dispatched to the Heath home.

In the meantime Jackie kept talking. "Why did you wait so long to call?" She wanted Mrs. Heath on the phone until the cruiser arrived, if possible.

"Like I said, we were on vacation and didn't get home until about a week ago. The newspapers accumulated and I didn't get a chance to read them until last night. You know, what with the laundry and setting things right after vacation. We took the kids to Disney World. Anyway, when I read the papers – I started with the earlier dates – I saw the case was being tried. Since I live across the street, I was interested. It wasn't until the second or third day *The Reporter* printed a picture of Mrs. Bellow. It didn't look right to me. You know, she looked older than I thought, after what I heard that night. Anyway, I thought I'd better call and let you know. I thought someone would come talk to us, but no one did except for the young man from the lawyer's office – you know, Mr. Joseph. Nice young man... Oh, excuse me, there's someone at the door..."

Jackie said, "That's okay, I'll hang on."

Mrs. Heath returned after a short wait and said, "It's a policeman – he wants me to go with him."

"Yes I know." Jackie said. "He is one of our officers and we asked him to stop by to pick you up so we could talk in my office. Is that all right with you?"

"Sure, but I have to be back here no later than three-thirty. That's when the kids get home from school. I have to be here."

"No problem. You'll be home in plenty of time. I'll wait for you."

Redding walked in with Bradley as Jackie was hanging up the phone. "God damn it, Mike. What is going on? Didn't your men canvas the neighborhood?"

Mike stood red faced and began to stammer. "Never mind!" Jackie interrupted, "Just go and get pictures of the original suspects. Get back before this Heath lady shows up. Son-of-a-bitch! Nothing ever goes right!"

Embarrassed, Redding hurried back across the parking lot to pick up the fairly voluminous investigatory file and returned to Jackie's office at a run, arriving just as a cruiser pulled up. The deputy politely opened the rear door of the cruiser. A fairly attractive woman in her mid-thirties dressed in slacks and a sweater covered by a puffy nylon jacket exited. She appeared unperturbed – neither intimidated nor frightened. Redding didn't recognize her. A quick perusal of the witness list did not reveal her name. None of his men had apparently talked to her either. Jackie was going to be pissed.

"Mrs. Heath?" Redding inquired politely.

"Yes. You're the detective that was there the night of the killing, aren't you? I saw you," she responded with a pleasant smile.

The detective nodded and introduced himself as they entered the prosecutor's offices.

At the receptionist's signal, Mike ushered Mrs. Heath up the stairs to Jackie's room overlooking the street. Jackie was staring out the window.

She turned with a smile and walked toward Mrs. Heath, hand outstretched. "Hi, I'm Jackie VanDamm. Are you Mrs. Heath? Please be seated," she said, offering a comfortable chair in front of her desk. A consummate politician.

Jackie had none of the standard government issue furnishings in her office. Her trappings were feminine and comfortable. Seating herself in one of a set of matching chairs before her maple desk, leaving vacant the tapestried chair behind it, she ignored Mike leaning against the doorframe.

219

Jackie studied Mrs. Heath and saw a slightly plump, youngish, motherly type. She began. "Please tell me what this is all about."

"Well, I began to tell you on the phone. On the last night of the Street Fair – it was a Saturday – my husband – he's in the Navy Reserves – was home. We had a cookout for some of our friends. We were sitting around afterwards having a nice visit. It was warm and we'd played volleyball and some other games earlier and were a little tired – kind of relaxing. We heard a commotion across the street – a lady screaming and crying – and then we saw someone running with a policeman from the corner – Mrs. Black – I don't remember her first name – we aren't good friends, you know."

Jackie offered, "Emma?" in a flat voice.

"Yeah that's it, Emma. Anyway she was standing in the front yard crying – kind of sobbing. My husband and his friend know CPR. They thought someone might have had a heart attack or something so ran across the street to help. I followed behind."

She paused for a second to collect her thoughts and catch her breath. Jackie sat silently waiting.

"I said something to Mrs. Black but she acted like she didn't see me so I went out back. People were standing around – a young man – a teenager maybe – holding onto a big mean-looking dog – and another young man standing next to him by the garage door. Between the house and the garage there is like a cement patio. Two ladies were standing there – they looked alike but one was a lot older than the other – like mother and daughter. A woman was leaning out the upstairs garage window yelling. I didn't know them. We don't neighbor much."

Mrs. Heath continued telling her story much like back-fence gossip – enjoying herself. "Anyway, my husband went over to talk to the boys while our friend ran upstairs to the apartment. I asked the ladies standing on the patio if they knew what happened and if I could help. When I tapped the young one on the shoulder, she turned on me with the strangest look I ever seen and said, *"Is he dead?"* I didn't know what she was talking about and she looked..." Mrs. Heath stopped speaking as though searching for a word to adequately describe the look.

"Go on," Jackie instructed. "She looked how?"

Speaking slowly, seeking just the right words, she said, "Well, she was kind of wringing her hands together – they was up in front of her mouth. Her face was wet but she wasn't crying right then. Her eyes were wild and kind of crazy. She's taller than me, so I had to look up to see her face – it was like she didn't see me or even know I was there – like she was looking through me... "

"She said – like to no one – her voice was hoarse and raspy, "*He tried to kill me... I hope the son-of-a-bitch is killed...! I hope he is dead...! I hope I killed him...!*" Those are the exact words she said. I'll never forget them as long as I live... or the sound of her voice."

Mrs. Heath shuddered, and after a moment continued. "The older woman – she had curly hair and, like a heavy sweater on – I noticed because it was warm and couldn't understand why she had a sweater on – she put her arms around the younger one, you know, like to make her feel better and kind of crooned at her, "*It's okay... now hush... be quiet... everything is going to be all right now...*" and like that. She looked at me and snapped, "*Leave her alone!*" I did! Believe me, I did! Then my husband called me to leave because the police and rescue people were there."

While Mrs. Heath was talking, Redding searched through his folders and pulled out several photographs. He spread them on Jackie's desk with a conciliatory glance at the prosecutor and asked, "Mrs. Heath would you look at these pictures and see if you can identify any of the people you are telling us about?"

He had quickly assembled a line-up. Two rows of photographs with five pictures in each. One row contained a picture of Gay Bellow and the other one of Arliss Conrad.

He turned the pictures face up one at a time while Mrs. Heath looked over his shoulder. Without hesitation she pointed to Gay's picture and said, "That is the older lady – the one whose picture I saw in *The Reporter* – the one on trial. She's the wrong one. It was the younger one that said she hoped she killed the – and then said a swear word."

"You're absolutely sure?" Mike asked.

"Why yes. I was as close to her as I am to you right now."

Mike continued turning over the pictures. When he came to Arliss Conrad, Mrs. Heath stopped him. She pointed to it and said, "She's the younger one. She doesn't look so wild and crazy in that picture but she's the one that said he tried to kill her and hoped he was dead."

"What did she sound like?" Jackie asked.

"I'm not sure what you mean. I told you her voice was raspy like she had a sore throat, and she kept putting her hands to her neck like it hurt. There were red marks on it and her face, but I could understand her. As I think about it, I'm not even sure she knew I was there – her eyes were so wild and crazy – like she wasn't aware of anything."

Jackie slouched in her chair, hands tented before her as in prayer. She thought silently for a few moments, then reaching a decision sat up and dismissed Mrs. Heath with, "Thank you very much for talking to us Mrs. Heath. You did the right thing. The deputy is waiting for you. He will take you home now. Thanks for being a good citizen. I don't think we'll be needing you but please keep yourself available in case."

"Bu..." Diane Heath began to ask a question. Jackie didn't let her finish, taking her elbow and escorting her to the door, closing it firmly behind her.

She turned to Redding, furious. "Doesn't your department know how to investigate a murder? Now I got to call Joseph and tell him about this. I'd rather take a stick in the eye. God damn it to hell. He'll probably ask for a mistrial."

"Why tell him, Jackie? I sure as hell won't, and no one else knows. My deputy doesn't know why she was here and wouldn't say anything anyway. Bellow fuckin' confessed! This other stuff is all bullshit!"

"Didn't you hear anything she said? She talked to someone she thought was Pat's son. Probably Trent. Joseph knows already and is laying for me. I got to call," she said reaching for the phone.

* * * * *

Joseph was in his office with Claude and Gay when Della walked in and said, "Mrs. VanDamm is on the line, Mr. Joseph."

"Yes Jackie?" the lawyer asked into the phone.

She gave a condensed version of her conversation with Diane Heath. Joseph recognized the name as belonging to the lady that told Trent about the black T-shirted male. Trent missed this, but Joseph wanted to say nothing about it in front of the clients. Another lesson – ask the right questions. It suddenly dawned on the older lawyer that he too had missed the boat. Roper had mentioned the *lady across the street* when Joseph had interviewed him.

Though surprised, Joseph pretended to know all about Mrs. Heath. "Are you ready to ask for a dismissal Jackie?"

"Hell no!" she replied. "Nothing's changed. Your client confessed! She's going to be convicted!" Joseph wondered who the prosecutor was trying to convince.

The lawyer retained his composure, adding sarcastically, "See you in court," and hung up.

He sat back, feet propped on the desk, contemplating his pigs and sorting through the possibilities provided by the information. After several minutes of silence, he reported the conversation to Gay. "Look Gay, this changes things with Arliss – a conflict we can't ignore. I have to tell Arliss she needs another lawyer. I'll get one for her if she can't. Now we have to get back to court." Before leaving, Joseph paused long enough to instruct Della and Claude to arrange for the attendance of those he wanted at a meeting in his office after court adjourned for the day.

Claude raised his eyes from his lap long enough to nod.

Twenty-Nine

For the first time since the trial began Gay and Pat walked to the courthouse unaccompanied by Claude – time for the defense to begin.

Joseph's mind wandered. The older lawyer had been anxiously awaiting the opportunity to present his first defense witness. But the events of the morning somehow made it anticlimactic. The witness, carefully chosen by Trent and Joseph to begin their case, was the criminalist from the Bureau of Criminal Investigation – an expert on atomic absorption tests. Since he was a State employee and had assisted in the investigation, the prosecutor's failure to call him made him that much more attractive to the defense lawyer, and perhaps, Gay's story more credible.

Joseph began asking the prepared questions, feeling he was just going through the motions, but quickly warmed to the task. They could afford to take no chances at this stage. They had to proceed with the planned defense.

After qualifying the scientist as an expert, Joseph asked him about the atomic absorption tests the Mills County police had used as part of their probe. The witness described the procedures, the nature of the chemicals involved and how they were related to the firing of a gun, concluding, "Mrs. Bellow, the defendant, had no gunshot residue on her hands. They were clean. But both Bliss Tucci and Emma Black had antimony and barium on their hands in amounts sufficient to qualify as gunshot residue."

Bradley, in his usual aggressive manner, cross-examined the witness, trying to discredit his testimony, but the chemist persisted. "The results of the test administered to Mrs. Bellow showed no gunshot residue on her hands. As to both Emma Black and Bliss Tucci, the findings were consistent with the presence of gunshot residue."

He would not be led into expressing an opinion that either had fired a weapon, only that his findings were consistent with that conclusion.

Brad closed his cross-examination with, "Could the tests have been mixed up? That is, one confused with the other?"

The expert answered testily, "Certainly not in our lab. I would hope your police aren't that sloppy. Proper police procedure would not allow it to happen."

Joseph felt a little sorry for the expert. As an employee of the State, his court appearances were all previously on behalf of the prosecution. Instead, a prosecutor was now tormenting him. He was having difficulty with the role reversal and his confusion was obvious during the vigorous cross-examination. It didn't matter. His findings were based on solid scientific principles. Very professional – he would not be budged from the truth.

On redirect Joseph concluded his questioning. "The State of Ohio accepts this test – the atomic absorption test – as a scientifically satisfactory, investigatory tool to determine if a person has fired a gun or not, is that true?"

"Yes, sir. It is an investigatory tool based upon reasonable scientific certainty."

"And the same test is relied on by the several state and city police departments, as well as the Federal Bureau of Investigation, isn't that true?"

"Yes sir."

Thanking the scientist for taking the time to testify and for his unswerving candor, Joseph excused him and called as his next witness the first emergency medical technicians to arrive at the Tucci home the night of the killing. After identifying himself and the role he played, he was asked about the unidentified male at the apartment when the EMS arrived – the man in the black T-shirt. The witness acknowledged the presence of a man fitting the description, but had not included him in any of his reports. "I didn't record his presence. That isn't my job. I expected the police to do it."

The lawyer couldn't have wanted a better response. The door was open for Joseph to argue how the police failed to investigate the case adequately – a solid basis for reasonable doubt. Jackie VanDamm, only slightly flustered, made no effort to cross-examine the witness.

As the EMS technician left the courtroom, Joseph looked at the clock. It was just past three and, he was sure, Judge Clarke could not be persuaded to adjourn this early no matter how anxious the lawyer was for the day to end. So Joseph decided to produce Gay's grandchildren, more for delay than the expectation of substantive testimony on their part.

Waiting in the witness room, the boys were anxious to help. Gay had reluctantly given permission for them to be called – Claude insisted if the lawyer thought it important they would testify. First Jake Bellow, then Jason Conrad. Gay was upset. She didn't want them put through the ordeal but, along with their grandfather, they insisted. They were hardheaded kids reared in her likeness. Joseph was glad.

The boys were typical teenagers – slender, blue jeaned and tennis shod – hair longer than the rotund lawyer's generation found acceptable – one boy's slightly spiked. *How the hell do they do that?* Joseph thought. *And why?* Pimply faced and shy – they had all the attributes of an age best forgotten by adults.

Despite their appearance and lack of volume, they spoke knowledgeably of Robert Tucci's drunkenness – his anger – the argument with Jake's sister over the dog – his sending her away – Tucci's argument with his own sister on the stairs, neither knew what the argument was about – and the fight with Arliss. Their testimony was not only substantially consistent with each another, but consistent with the story told by Gay from her very first meeting with the authorities. Some discrepancies, but only those expected when the same act is viewed by different people from differing perspectives – the differences that lend a ring of truth.

They both withstood the test of rigorous cross-examinations, one by Bradley, the other by Jackie VanDamm. Joseph glanced at the jurors and was pleased to see what looked like admiration on several faces for the way the young people handled themselves.

Finally, when Joseph was convinced the day would never end, Judge Clarke called for adjournment. Collecting Gay and Claude, who had returned in time to hear his grandchildren testify, the lawyer bustled them from the courtroom. In their rush they failed to note or appreciate the Christmas decorations illuminating the Square.

Arriving quickly at his office, Joseph checked to make sure everyone he wanted was present. Joseph asked Della to arrange coffee for everyone – his cup kept perpetually filled.

Paul Gaines, already there when the group arrived, was asked to wait with Arliss and her husband. Della introduced them to one another. Gaines, a relatively young criminal defense lawyer from a nearby town, chatted pleasantly with them.

Getting everyone organized, Joseph invited Arliss and her husband into his office with the others while he talked briefly to Paul in the hall. They entered together, Joseph taking a seat behind his desk, Gaines sitting on the leather couch by the Conrads.

* * * * *

"Thanks for coming Paul. I wanted a lawyer here to talk to the Conrads in case they couldn't find one on such short notice. They are going to need

226

someone with enough criminal experience to make sure Mrs. Conrad's rights are protected. At the family's insistence she has been my client – until now. A conflict has developed I cannot ignore. Her mother and I are in trial in Judge Clarke's room." Gesturing toward Arliss, he said, "So, I need someone to look after Mrs. Conrad." He did not have to explain the nature of the trial to the younger lawyer – the publicity kept everyone in town sufficiently advised. The entire Mills County bar followed the trial with interest.

Arliss, who had been sitting on the leather couch next to her husband, clutched his arm with bony fingers. A squeal escaped her throat before she could get her voice into a more normal register, and hiccuped, "Wh-wh-what do you mean?"

"Arliss," Joseph began patiently. "I've explained to you more than once why I cannot represent you if there's a conflict between you and your mother, haven't I? There's been one all along that we've tried to overlook. Now it's much too serious to ignore. A Mrs. Diane Heath lives on Garden Street across from the Blacks. She called the prosecutor today and told her she believed the wrong lady was on trial. Jackie, not surprisingly, is refusing to call her as a witness. Her testimony's important so I intend to call her. When she takes the stand she's going to say you are the one she thought was on trial. That is going to make you appear to be the guilty party. Some of the jurors just might think you killed Tucci."

Trying to overlook Arliss' near hysteria, Joseph related the conversation Jackie VanDamm had with Mrs. Heath. Arliss, shaking her head from side to side in denial, slid deeper into the couch as though trying to disappear – her usually sallow complexion paling – ashen. Her fingers worked nervously, clutching at her husband, making little grasping motions. She sucked air, trying to speak, but nothing came. Arliss had been indicted for obstruction of justice, a felony not nearly so serious as the charges against her mother. Joseph had hoped, not very realistically, that she would willingly join in the strategy he was proposing. Wishful thinking. Arliss, from birth, was incapable of considering anything beyond her own well-being. Gay left her chair to kneel in front of her daughter, trying to console her. It reminded Joseph of Diane Heath's depiction of the incident in the Tucci back yard.

He interrupted harshly. "Sit down Gay! You, not Arliss, are on trial. If you're acquitted, the charges against your daughter will probably disappear." Exasperated, he said, "God damn it, can't you get it through your heads? We must win this case convincingly enough so you'll all be left alone."

Their attention secured, he continued more calmly. "Mrs. Heath and her story gives us the opportunity to do two things. First, show how inadequate the investigation was – although there seems ample evidence of that – and, of more importance, give the jury another suspect."

Once Arliss fully understood what the lawyer was suggesting, she uncoiled, leaping to her feet reaching for Joseph, fingers splayed, nails pointing like talons, eyes wild, spraying spittle. "No! No! No!" she screamed while other unintelligible guttural sounds originated somewhere in her body. Her husband desperately tried to hold Arliss back while Joseph observed her dispassionately for several seconds thinking, *"It seems, Mrs. Heath's description is really quite good'.* He could visualize Arliss as she must have appeared that hot August night. No wonder the scene was burned into Diane Heath's memory.

There were several moments of confusion as Arliss's husband tried to enfold her in his arms and Gay tried to comfort her. Mr. Bellow sat unmoving without lifting his eyes. Paul Gaines making no effort to interfere, observed everyone with mild amusement.

Joseph, finally losing patience with the display, said loud enough to be heard over the commotion, "Mr. Gaines is a lawyer with quite a bit of criminal defense experience," ignoring Arliss's tears and rejection. "He may seem young, but he's been at it for some time. Personally, I have a great deal of faith in him. He's here at my request, so you can talk to him if you want. If you don't, I am sure he will leave quietly."

Speaking to the Conrads, he said, "You don't need to consult with him – you certainly don't have to retain him – you can talk to any lawyer you want. But aside from me," modesty notwithstanding, "he is the best around. Take advantage of it.

"Arliss, you are no longer my client. Is that plain enough? With the obvious conflict between you and your mother, I cannot represent both of you, and I choose to represent your mother. Do you understand?"

Sobbing aloud, she nodded her head. The lawyer doubted she understood anything save the fact she was being abandoned.

"Paul," Joseph explained, "Arliss will be called as a witness tomorrow morning. I intend to tell the court she is not my client. I will ask her about the scene described by Mrs. Heath and then, if she killed Tucci."

This produced another string of words, tears and hysterics. "You ca-ca-can't. Nooo!" She was becoming uncontrollable and, Joseph thought, tiresome.

Still talking to the younger lawyer, Joseph calmly said, "I'm certain you'll advise Mrs. Conrad that she has the right to refuse to testify – that she need not answer my questions and invoke the Fifth Amendment," referring to her Constitutional right against self-incrimination.

Paul smiled and said, "I always thought you a sly old bastard. You know goddamn well I can't let her testify. You don't want her to. You just want her on the stand so the jury can see, and hear, her refuse to testify."

Turning his back on Joseph, Paul spoke directly to Arliss and her husband. "Mr. and Mrs. Conrad, please call me Paul. If you want, I will be happy to confer with you on this matter. You don't have to hire me, but based on what I'm hearing, it's important you get legal advice as soon as possible. If you want it from me, I'm available."

Conrad, arm draped protectively around his sobbing wife, nodded and said, "Please."

Paul said, "Pat, is there a room where I can have a private conversation with my clients?" emphasizing the last word.

Della ushered the three from the office, unbearable tension leaving with them, replaced by Gay's anger. "Mr. Joseph, you are terrible! That is an unspeakably dirty trick! I cannot and will not tolerate you using my daughter this way! I ..."

Joseph jumped at the sound of Claude's voice interrupting his wife. "Gay! Shut up! Sit down! We hired Mr. Joseph to represent you. You will not interfere – Do you understand?"

Claude was sitting almost straight, shoulders back, and, for the first time in Joseph's experience, looking directly at Gay. As surprised as the lawyer, Gay saw something in her husband's posture that reminded her of their youth – before the weight and pressure of time, family and business had rounded him.

"Yes, Claude," she responded meekly. Good God! Something about the worm and turning flitted through Joseph's mind.

Needing no further argument, Joseph added, "Gay, you don't seem to appreciate what's going on. If you're convicted, you'll be a long time in jail – like you said – probably die there. If that's what you want, plead guilty. Don't waste my time and energy – lord knows I have little enough left – or your money with a trial. If you want to go free, listen to your husband."

She settled back, acknowledging with some admiration their little victory. "You win. I'll behave." Claude's physique relaxed back into its hangdog posture.

The next half hour was spent examining the plan and discussing possible problems. Would it backfire? They finally agreed – Gay reluctantly – it made sense. Trent's pleasure was blemished by the knowledge he should have known much earlier of Mrs. Heath and the information she held.

When Paul Gaines and the Conrads reappeared, the group in Joseph's office was discussing Gay's testimony – preparing her for the ordeal. The more arduous the preparation, the easier the real thing would be.

Joseph stopped long enough to ask, "Okay, Paul, what have you decided?"

"I'm representing Mrs. Conrad. What we've decided is none of your business except we are not going to play your game. She will not appear to testify in her mother's case. So, if you will excuse us, we're leaving. Good night."

Joseph grinned and said, "Trent," nodding toward Arliss.

Trent pulled a subpoena from a folder before him which commanded Arliss Conrad's presence in court the next day and handed it to her. She took it automatically with shaky hands, looked at it and, with a gasp, dropped it. Paul picked it up and placed it in his pocket without a word.

"You're right, Paul," Joseph said. "We have nothing to talk about. I assume you will appear with Mrs. Conrad in the morning." Disregarding his instinctive inclination toward courtesy, the older lawyer failed to escort the Conrads to the door.

When the small party left, Joseph sighed and said to those remaining, "I'm tired and want to go home. You know how Mary gets when I'm late. She's going to kill me. I assume everything's ready for morning, Trent. You have a subpoena to serve on Mrs. Heath this afternoon, I trust?"

When Trent nodded, the older man yawned, scratched his pate, washed his hand over his face and glanced at his pigs, their smiles not quite so irritating.

Trent accompanied Joseph to the door, saying, "I'll finish with Mrs. Bellow and check the witness files before I leave, okay?"

"Not too late, Trent..." Joseph responded paternally, thinking, *Have sons to plow the field while the old man sleeps....*

Thirty

"All rise!" Art Gruen called as the jury was brought in to begin what everyone hoped would be the last day of trial.

"Mr. Joseph call your next witness," Judge Clarke directed, after smiling a welcome at the jury and spectators. He knew who voted.

"Thank you, Your Honor," Joseph said. "We would like to call Sam Chester."

The lawyer expected Sam to be a key witness of great impact. He would establish Gay could not have pulled the trigger of the murder weapon – would describe the horrid injury she suffered leading to the physical limitations that made it impossible for her to fire the gun. Though his importance could not be understated, Joseph was impatient. Only three witnesses remained.

As expected, Sam Chester won over the jurors with his warm, friendly grin and his engaging personality. Legs crossed comfortably, he settled back in the witness chair and gave the impression he was talking to each juror individually, with eye contact accompanied by boyish grimaces.

He told them of recent advances in sports medicine that made it possible to measure the strength and power of individual sets of muscles permitting him to conclude, "It is impossible for Mrs. Bellow to have mustered the strength necessary to fire the murder weapon. It is my professional opinion, based upon reasonable scientific certainty, that Mrs. Bellow, on the night Tucci was killed, did not fire this gun," as he held the pistol in his hand.

He continued explaining why the tests were foolproof. The jurors listened attentively. First he had studied her hospital chart, learning from it the terrible damage she had suffered – the constant pain bearable only with the use of what is commonly called a TENS Unit – a Trans cutaneous Electrical Nerve Stimulation device.

Bradley did his best to discredit the physical therapist with a barbed cross-examination. He tried to anger him – confuse him – to no avail. He answered all questions patiently, simply, and truthfully, accompanied by his infectious grin. The assistant prosecutor was experienced enough to know when to sit down and shut up and was soon shrugging and saying, "I have no further questions ... " acting as though the testimony were of little import.

When Joseph had no questions on redirect, the judge excused Sam Chester, who left smiling at everyone and nodding his thanks to the judge. Judge Clarke, glancing at the clock, decided not to take the morning break yet, ordering instead another witness be called.

"Before doing so, Your Honor, may we approach the bench?" the defense lawyer asked, moving forward. "Judge, we've been going for about an hour-and-a-half. I need a break"

"Okay, Pat. We'll call a recess, but I don't see you crossing your legs," he said, smiling. "Is it all right with you, Jackie?" he asked without giving her an opportunity to object. "But, let me warn you both, I intend to finish today."

Jackie responded, "Sure. Who's your next witness, Pat?"

"I'm not sure. I think what you told me when I asked the same question, was something like, *"It's none of your damned business."* Anyway, I have to see who's here." Damned if he was going to give anything away now, or give the prosecutor a chance to prepare.

With court recessed, Joseph glanced to the back of the room. Trent was there. He nodded. Everything was ready. Jackie, face red and angry, ignored the byplay. Joseph said loud enough for VanDamm to hear, "Trent, walk with me?" As they left, Trent assured the older lawyer everything was set.

Returning to the courtroom, Joseph whispered to Gay, "Our next witness is Mrs. Heath. We'll call Arliss as soon as she is finished. The two of them won't use up the balance of the morning. You'll take the stand immediately after Arliss. I don't want any interruptions. I know you're ready, but if there is anything you need to take care of, do it now. I don't want you distracted by anything when you're on the stand. The case will go to the jury today. Do you have any questions?"

She shook her head "no' tentatively. Joseph knew no matter how well or thoroughly a witness is prepared, there is no way to know how she'll do until actually on the stand, facing the jury and her interrogator.

As soon as everyone took their places, Joseph spoke into the quiet. "The defense will call Diane Heath." He heard a resigned sigh from Jackie accompanied by a mild expletive.

Trent, standing by the door waiting for Joseph's announcement, opened it to allow Mrs. Heath's entry. Jackie stood and began to offer an objection, but stopped in mid-word, dropping dejectedly into her seat. The jury looked on with mild interest, not knowing what to expect.

Bringing Mrs. Heath through her story took less than twenty minutes. She told it just as she had to Jackie, in an honest, homey way. Jackie didn't even try. "No questions, Your Honor."

In the stony silence following her account of the death night, Mrs. Heath found her way out of the courtroom, followed by several reporters. Joseph turned to Gay, saying in a low voice, "I'm going to call Arliss now. After she's finished, it's your turn. Ready?"

She whispered, "Yes," and placed her fingers lightly on the lawyer's arm – an expression of trust.

Joseph spoke over the buzz that replaced the hush in the courtroom following Mrs. Heath's testimony. "The defense calls Arliss Conrad."

Jackie had enough. "Your Honor!" She walked directly to sidebar without seeking permission. As soon as Clarke and Joseph arrived, the prosecutor whispered with some heat, "What's the old bastard up to now? He knows she is under indictment and he represents her. He can't let her testify."

"I don't know Jackie," the judge responded without guile. "Why don't we wait and see?" He rolled back to his usual spot, leaving the prosecutor with her mouth open and no one listening to what she had to say. She stared at his back for a moment, then walked to her seat.

Trailed by Paul Gaines, Arliss entered the courtroom, hurrying to the witness stand on stilted legs, hands reaching out to each side looking for something to grasp – fearful she might fall. Shaky legs had trouble carrying her slight weight. When Art Gruen administered the oath, she mumbled a response and took the seat as directed, perching on the very edge, hands clasped tightly in her lap. A frightened bird without the power of flight.

When Art positioned the microphone in front of her, amplified ragged breathing could be heard throughout the room. Paul Gaines placed himself between her and the jury box, slightly behind her but close enough so she could touch him if she felt the need.

Judge Clarke observed the activity quietly. When everything was still, he looked at Paul quizzically and asked, "Mr. Gaines is there something we can do for you?"

"I represent Mrs. Conrad, Your Honor. She is here in response to a subpoena and asked me to accompany her. I trust the court has no objection."

"Of course not. Proceed, Mr. Joseph," the judge instructed, a puzzled frown on his face.

As the lawyer walked toward his usual spot behind the jury box, every eye followed. The jurors' glances traveled from the witness to the defendant. They could not help but notice the resemblance. Joseph said, "Would you please tell us your full name? Please spell your last name for the record."

Arliss looked at the lawyer stonily – for the first time since he had known her, she was absolutely still. Her expression face sent cross messages – fear – hatred – *How dare you put me through this.* Joseph shot a silent prayer skyward that she would hold together for the few minutes needed. His concentration was intense. Even so, he felt no little dismay at her attitude. She didn't care at all that what was being done was designed to help her mother. It never crossed her mind. *Fuck her!*

Biting off her words, she responded, after clearing her throat several times to make it start working, "My name is Arliss Bellow Conrad. C-O-N-R-A-D."

"You are here in response to a subpoena, is that correct?"

"Yes."

"Are you related to the defendant, Gay Bellow?" She didn't need to answer – the relationship couldn't be denied.

Paul Gaines stepped forward as the witness began her response and said, "Excuse me Your Honor, if I may interrupt. I would like to identify myself for the record. My name is Paul Gaines. As I said earlier, Mrs. Conrad is my client. At my advice, she intends to exercise her right to refuse to testify in this case."

Judge Clarke looked only mildly irritated. "Does your client intend to respond to any questions?"

"Your Honor, she will answer no further questions."

"All right," he said. With a smile of understanding playing on his lips, Judge Clarke turned to the jury and explained, "Everyone has an absolute right to refuse to testify if their testimony may tend to incriminate them in any way. That is a right guaranteed by the Fifth Amendment to the Constitution. Mrs. Conrad's attorney says she chooses to exercise that right. She cannot be forced to testify in this case."

Judge Clarke flashed a knowing look at Joseph. "Mrs. Conrad, you are excused."

Joseph was pleased with the result and remained standing as the tap of Arliss's heels marked her unsteady gait from the room. She looked neither at him nor her mother, passing within inches of the rumpled lawyer.

Knowing it is a rare case in which a defendant should be called to testify in their own behalf, knowing they could and generally did more damage than good for themselves, Joseph knew this defendant must tell her story. In the silence following the closing of the door Joseph said, "We call Gabriella Bellow, Your Honor."

Gay stood, every eye immediately drawn to her.

Thirty-One

As always, Gay was dressed conservatively, in a two-piece linen suit of muted colors that set off her best features. She appeared exactly what she was – a lovely lady whose life had been filled with obstacles. Differences between her and her daughters were emphasized by the similarities. Triplets born at different times exposed to different environments. In contrast to Arliss' jerky, unsteady steps leaving the stand, Gay approached in a gliding, steady stride – not eager, but aware of the need to tell her story. Responding "I will" to the oath, she looked at the jurors – not smiling, but pleasant – confident they would recognize the truth.

Pat Joseph watched closely, evaluating her impression. He was amazed that this lady who possessed no individually attractive features created such a handsome appearance. Her hair was combed smooth over her ears not quite to her shoulders with just a hint of curl, naturally pale skin with a trace of heightened color at the cheeks that didn't come from make up. The lines around her mouth spoke of the years of suffering that were unable to destroy her humor or cloud her perception of the goodness of life.

The rumpled lawyer waited quietly as Mrs. Bellow settled into the witness chair and Art Gruen adjusted the microphone. All eyes in the room studied her carefully. Joseph, ignoring the attention focused on Gay, asked in a mild conversational tone, "Mrs. Bellow please tell the jury your name and spell your last name for the record."

No false starts – she answered in a low pleasant voice. "My name is Gabriella Bellow. That is spelled B-E-L-L-O-W," looking directly at Joseph while answering – her eyes did not waver.

"You are the defendant in this case, are you not?"

"Yes sir, I am." No break in her voice.

"How old are you Mrs. Bellow?"

With a little smile at the indelicate question, but without a hint of the coquet, she said, "I am sixty years old."

The lawyer asked about her background, marriage, her family successes and failures. She responded fully and truthfully in the same pleasant, unruffled manner. Joseph held loosely all of the notes painstakingly prepared – the list of questions readied in such detail. He didn't once look at them. Everyone faded from the room – the judge – the jurors – the spectators. Gay and Joseph were sitting in his office – no – his living room, getting to know one another, talking of every day pleasant things. Two people fond of one another visiting and speaking of things they would never think to talk about in public.

She told how she raised her daughters – the eldest headstrong and promiscuous, in trouble at a very young age. Gay and Claude had to raise her children, both legitimate and illegitimate. Not that they complained about it – it was the thing to do. Gay loved her daughters dearly. They joined the Girl Scouts, 4-H and all of the other similar organizations available to young girls. "We were very close. We had a good time when they were little."

She spoke about her husband and his inherited family business. "He worked there his whole life. He really didn't care for it but thought it would make us happy and it was expected of him. I know he isn't really a good businessman, but he is a wonderful husband. I'm so proud of his efforts."

Claude's perpetual slump straightened a bit as he heard the words, but he continued to study his shoes. A gleam of wetness shone on his cheek – no one noticed.

She detailed some of the problems of raising daughters in this permissive age, the willfulness of Bliss, her pregnancy at fifteen by a man several years her senior with whom she had run away. Gay didn't spare herself accepting responsibility for her daughter's behavior even though she didn't understand it – nor would she be critical of Bliss. Her daughter's actions were what they were and Gay must assume a portion of the blame. It was her job to try to make matters right. No self-pity or martyrdom – she didn't think that way.

She reported in the same accepting way her health problems – reluctantly. She answered questions because they were asked but health was neither important nor appropriate to public discourse. She was too polite to suggest it was none of the lawyer's business.

"Gay, were you injured in the past couple years?"

"Yes," she responded thoughtfully. "It was two years ago this month – December. Just before Christmas. Claude, my husband," her glance proceeding gently in his direction, "was giving a Christmas luncheon for his employees. He asked me to come to the plant during the noon hour because he was expecting a delivery from the UPS man. He had a dog at the plant for security. Claude said he'd feel better about me being there with the dog handy," she said, smiling at him to show she understood, appreciated his concern and

236

bore him no ill will because of what happened. "The dog was kind of a pet. I was comfortable with her. She's one of those pit bulls but was always gentle as a lamb with us. Anyway, the UPS man came and walked in like he usually does, without announcing himself. He startled me and I made a little sound the dog misunderstood. She went after the UPS man. I tried to pull her off but she's so strong. By mistake, she bit down on my arm and wouldn't let go."

Joseph interrupted long enough to ask, "Was that the part of your body that was injured?"

The prosecutor objected, "Your Honor, this is interesting but certainly not relevant – an obvious effort to elicit sympathy from the jury."

"Not at all Your Honor," Joseph explained. "It is a vital aspect of our defense. I've said before, and Ms. VanDamm knows full well, the injury suffered by Mrs. Bellow rendered her right arm all but useless. She is physically incapable of firing the death gun. This was explained to the jury by Sam Chester. I *thought* Ms. VanDamm was in the courtroom at the time," the lawyer continued, adding gratuitously, "Maybe if the State had explored this at the time, the real killer might be on trial."

"Speeches aren't necessary Mr. Joseph. Go ahead and answer the question Mrs. Bellow. Objection overruled Ms. VanDamm ... " the judge ruled wryly.

Having watched the byplay between the lawyers and the court, Gay returned her attention back to Joseph. "It was my right arm, just above the elbow. The dog had it in her mouth. She sort of worried it, like grinding her teeth. When the doctors examined me, they explained that the muscle and artery in the upper arm were pulled loose. The dog had to be knocked out before they could get my arm out of her mouth. I felt bad for her. She didn't know she was doing wrong. I was taken to the hospital and had surgery. In fact, I had several operations over the next six months before I regained any use of my arm. It is still weak and causes fairly constant pain." The last words said in a deprecating manner as though of little import.

"Are you scarred?"

"Yes sir." Gay began to remove her suit jacket as Joseph had instructed her to do when the question was asked.

Caught napping, Gay had her jacket almost off before VanDamm could yell, "Objection! Objection! Play for sympathy..."

At the intrusion Gay paused, leaning back, suit jacket half on and half off, looking to the judge for instruction.

Judge Clarke, leaning over the bench for an unobstructed view of Gay's arm, snapped at Jackie, "Overruled."

"May we approach Your Honor?" Jackie implored.

"No! Continue Mr. Joseph. If you want Mrs. Bellow to show her arm to the jury, she may." Then to the jury, "You are to consider the appearance of it only insofar as it may assist you in consideration of her testimony and that of Mr. Chester."

Gay continued to remove her jacket, exposing a yellow silk blouse with a high neck and long, loose fitting sleeves – ruffles at the neck and cuffs. Unbuttoning the cuff of her right sleeve, she pushed it slowly up her arm, almost to the shoulder. As her arm came into view, small sounds of anguish could be heard from the audience. Her right arm from wrist to where it disappeared in the folds of the sleeve was a mass of puckered, scarred flesh – sickly white valleys and jagged red peaks – a relief map of a dermic mountain range.

Attached to her arm were electrodes with wires trailing under her blouse to a small black box hooked to the waistband of her skirt. Gay pointed to it and said, "This is the TENS Unit Mr. Chester was talking about. I haven't the faintest idea how it works. The doctors told me it somehow interrupts the pain signal to the nerves. I do know that without it the pain is intolerable."

At Joseph's suggestion, Gay turned toward the jurors, holding her arm in such a manner that they could easily see it. Having done as directed, she turned back to answer any more questions the lawyer might ask. Her jacket lay folded neatly across her lap – the horribly disfigured arm diminishing not one whit her dignity.

Joseph began talking with Gay about the last day of Tucci's life. Again the spectators magically disappeared – they were alone. She described how Arliss came to her home in the middle of the night and the nearly hysterical way she told about Robert. As the story unfolded, Gay told how she felt a growing concern, almost a panic. The two of them rushed to prevent further problems. At the last minute, as though preordained, she ran back into the house to take a gun from her bedroom closet shelf. She could offer no explanation.

"Are you in the habit of carrying a gun?"

"Why, no sir," she said, a little surprised at such a question.

"Do you know if it was loaded?"

"I believe it was."

In response to more questions, she described the late night ride to pick up the children, the fight between Arliss and Robert, her futile attempts to intercede, the crash of glass accompanied by Robert falling. The play of emotions fleeting across her face as she relived the events, painted a vivid backdrop to the tale.

She told how afterwards Arliss became frantic and how "I tried to comfort her..." the depiction matching in almost every detail the story told by Mrs. Heath. "Oddly enough," she said with a slightly perplexed frown, "I don't remember Mrs. Heath being there, but what she said was accurate."

Gay and Arliss didn't move from where they were standing until the police came. When they arrived, she was placed in the back seat of a police car. She sat there alone, worrying about the children and Arliss.

It began to dawn on her something terrible must have happened – more than Robert falling and hurting himself. The jury trembled with Gay as they felt the emotions building in her as they had that night. Each juror sat with her in the back of the police car – watched the officer approach – held out their hands as ordered while an unsympathetic detective swabbed some kind of chemical on them, saying,

"I don't know anything, Ma'am. This is routine. If you know what's good for you, you'll cooperate."

Gay wasn't put out by his attitude. She had no reason to be uncooperative. She was concerned for her daughter, and even for Robert.

As she described that August night, the jurors rode with her to the station in the police car, entered through a rolling steel gate in a chain link fence with curls of razor edged wire coiled across the top, walked across the compound through a locked steel door down a poorly lit corridor into a concrete block room where a heavy metal door slammed behind them. They suffered through the endless questions asked by two men, strangers, taking turns. They felt the exhaustion and, finally, after being told over and over again what she had done, they were with her when she agreed it "must' have happened.

Her quiet dignity, her honesty and simplicity in answering questions – never searching for words to describe the permanently implanted memories – conveyed more than argument or oratory.

Joseph closed the examination with, "Mrs. Bellow, what is your belief? Did you shoot and kill Robert Tucci?"

Answering quietly, confident she would be understood, "I do not believe I shot him."

"Did you, at any time, intend to shoot and kill Robert Tucci?"

"No sir, I did not."

"Did you shoot and kill Robert Tucci?"

She sat quietly for a moment. "No sir, I did not."

"Thank you Mrs. Bellow. I have no further questions. I'm sure Mrs. VanDamm will want to ask you some." Joseph smiled at her serenely and walked to his seat.

The prosecutor requested a short break before beginning her cross-examination. When granted by a nod from Judge Clarke, she used it to gather a number of notes she had made while Gay was testifying. She and Brad held a short whispered conference. Judge Clarke hadn't left the bench, waiting patiently for Jackie to begin. When she indicated she was ready to proceed, he called for all to take their places. Joseph had used the time to talk quietly with Gay, offering her assurance she didn't need.

Jackie began her questioning by delving into Gay's reasons for returning to the house and getting the gun. She tried to establish motive – implying Gay hated Tucci because of his relationship with her daughter. Gay's answers changed not at all from what she had already told the jury. The spirited cross-examination only served to impress the jury with Gay's candor.

After an hour or more of relentless questioning, Jackie VanDamm ended with, "Mrs. Bellow, you testified that you went to Mr. Tucci's house with a gun in your pocket. You then said you pulled the gun out of your pocket, pointed it at Robert Tucci and pulled the trigger, isn't that correct?"

"Yes, Ma'am, only I pointed the gun more toward the ceiling than toward Robert"

"Then Mrs. Bellow," Jackie said in a sarcastic tone, "You said in your statement to the police that you *GUESS* you shot him! Isn't that correct?"

"Why, yes Ma'am, I did say that. But, I know now that I couldn't have."

Jackie, appearing disgusted at what she considered Gay's dissembling, walked briskly toward her seat, "I have no more questions!"

Judge Clarke looked toward Joseph who gave a negative shake of his head, saying quietly, "We rest Your Honor."

Joseph had feared it would be a mistake to allow Mrs. Bellow to testify. Defense lawyers are universal in their belief that a defendant can only harm himself by testifying. Rarely are they able to help themselves. Joseph was thrilled that it was not always the case. He believed Gay had done a wonderful job and had won over the jury.

Immediately Jackie interjected, "We have no rebuttal, Your Honor."

The Judge looked at the clock. "Ladies and gentlemen, we will break for lunch now. Since the defense has rested and the State has no rebuttal, final arguments will begin this afternoon. You will probably begin deliberations before the dinner hour.

As the jury filed out, Judge Clarke ordered, "In chambers!"

With the lawyers gathered, he inquired, "Any objections to the jury charge?" Copies had been provided earlier and Joseph had Trent review it. He was pleased and told Joseph so. Neither lawyer offered any objection. "Very well, how much time will you need for final argument? Jackie?"

"I'll need at least an hour."

"Pat?"

"Seems about right, Judge."

"Very well. Jackie, you may divide your time as you wish, but do it fairly. Be back no later than one-thirty. This case will be finished today," he said, dismissing everyone from his chambers.

Thirty-Two

Trent breezed into the older lawyer's office, "Mr. Joseph, do you want t... Oh, I'm sorry. I didn't mean to interrupt. I thought maybe you wanted to grab a bite."

Joseph acknowledged, but wasn't truly aware of the young man's presence, thinking instead how his morning began. He woke early, knowing it was the last day of trial, intending to dress carefully – make a good impression on the jury. No matter how expensive or well tailored his attire, within minutes of dressing he appeared to have slept a full night in his clothing. *At least, I'll be fairly well color coordinated,* he thought since Mary had laid out suit, shirt, tie and socks neatly on her empty side of the bed. Left to his own devices, he and Mary both knew, his choices would make no sense.

The vestiges of a none too pleasant dream fleeting from his conscious mind, Joseph sat on the edge of the bed, his morning toilet completed. Pulling on his socks, he stood and felt a little light-headed, attributing it to standing up too fast. For some reason, his knees buckled, sitting him back unceremoniously on the edge of the bed. Clammy moisture collected on his brow and he felt warm and cold at the same time – it was difficult to breathe. His chest felt heavy – not painful but weighty. *I wonder*, he thought, *if this is what a heart attack feels like?*

The aging lawyer continued to sit unmoving on the edge of the bed until he heard Mary call, "Pat, for heaven's sake, what are you doing? Your breakfast has been ready for ten minutes."

Taking a deep breath and appreciating the concerned note of impatience in her question, it brought back a feeling of normalcy. He wasn't sure what was bothering him, but believed it wasn't physical. *If this is what being a criminal defense lawyer is like, I don't think I care for it.*

* * * * *

"It's all right, son. Come in," Joseph instructed Trent. He had slid down in his oversize desk chair, head leaning against the hand woven rug decorating the chair back, feet propped, gazing at his pigs. *Goddam pigs...* he thought. *What're they so smug about? They know something I don't?*

242

"What's the matter, Mr. J.? It looks like the trial's going great. I watched Mrs. Bellow's testify. She held up beautifully. No one on the jury could take their eyes off her." Trent rattled encouragement.

"Trent," the older lawyer sighed, scrubbing his hands across his remaining ruff of hair, making himself look more unkempt than usual. "It seems to me that a lawyer's worst fears are that one day he will have to represent a truly innocent client. The fear, as far as I am concerned, has been realized. Gay shouldn't be put through this. It's wrong! Goddamn it – it's wrong!"

Joseph's feet dropped to the floor, hands spread on the desk's surface. "The founders of our country were men of genius. They knew what they were doing when they wrote the Constitution and the Bill of Rights. The documents are so simple they'll last forever – if we let them. But today people are so damned anxious to give up their liberties – let the police take care of them. They can't get it through their silly heads – there is no security from creeping government bureaucracy. The government is invading every part of our life..."

"Hey, easy Mr. Joseph," Trent said with a tentative smile. "Are you warming up for your final argument or preparing a civics class?" Trent asked, backing through the door.

"Oh, sit down!" Joseph apologized, accompanying the words by flopping back into his chair. "You're right." He continued in a more moderate tone. "I've been sitting here asking my pigs how to convince the jury what their responsibility is – to Gay – to the system. Shit, most lawyers don't know what I'm talking about. How can I expect laymen to? They think lawyers are some aberrant life form that should be trotted out twice a year – on the Fourth of July and maybe Law Day. Come one! Come all! See the dinosaurs! Here are the lawyers that protect our liberties. During the rest of the year we're slime. We make our money getting criminals off and keeping drunks on the road. Maybe they're right.

"Trent my boy, we are dinosaurs – a throw back to when men paid more than lip service to words like *freedom* and *liberty*. The *don't burn my flag* philosophy doesn't mean a thing if we allow the tyranny of government to piss in our faces. If the average persons would only once read the Declaration..."

He could feel his heart beginning to pound and knew he was getting worked up again, so stopped, sighed and added, "Pay no attention to me, Trent. Our job is just to keep the pendulum from swinging too far. Sometimes we push too hard in the opposite direction to accomplish it. We do what we do because we have to – but it takes its toll. I'm tired."

Trent looked at the suddenly old man. Joseph could read understanding, concern, sympathy in the young man's eyes – he felt the pain with Joseph – something else too – maybe pride. "Mr. Joseph, I know what you mean, but forget it for now. You have to argue for Mrs. Bellow in just a few minutes. I'll run next door and get you a sandwich, okay?"

"No – but thanks – just get me a cup of coffee. I'll put something together. Didn't mean to lecture." Putting his feet back on the desk, he glanced toward the pigs – smiles still offensive.

* * * * *

"Ladies and gentlemen of the jury," Jackie VanDamm began her summation. She stood before the jurors still and straight, clad in the armor of her charcoal gray suit, skirt marked with unobtrusive red threads and double-breasted form fitting jacket, mannish white shirt and red silk cravat. Her only concessions to fashion were patent leather high heeled pumps and a bit of lace peeking from the cuffs of her jacket. The simple costume was enchanting and emphasized her femininity.

After the salutation, she paused without smiling and looked deliberately into the face of each juror. Satisfied with what she saw, she visibly relaxed and said, "Before I begin, I would like to say on behalf of the people of the State of Ohio we appreciate your presence here and the attention you have given this very important case. Your job will be ended soon, yet the most difficult part is before you. You heard all the evidence – everything you need to reach a decision." Smiling warmly she continued, "The State is confident you will reach the proper decision and render a verdict of guilty.

"Before reviewing the evidence I'd like to express my personal appreciation to Judge Clarke and his aides for helping us through a trying – no pun intended – time. With such competitive lawyers as in this case, he was still able to maintain order." She threw a cute little smile in Joseph's direction. He thought, *Bitch!*

"I would also like to thank Mr. Joseph for being, as always, a gentleman. He has many years of experience as a trial lawyer," *Neat way of telling them I'm an old fart,* Joseph thought, "and I have learned much from him."

She knew how to work an audience and was doing it beautifully. Not only was she buttering up the old man, she was asking the jury for a little help since she hadn't been around nearly so long as he – poor thing.

Turning her back to Joseph, she continued. "We have only one thing to think about in this courtroom. Did the defendant," the accent on the last syllable to depersonalize Gay, "Gabriella Bellow, with purpose to do so, take the life of Robert Tucci?" She paused. "Did she murder him?

"The answer to that question is simple. Consider ... " Jackie went on reciting at length the facts elicited from her witnesses and her interpretation of those facts. She recited in vivid detail how each witness placed the murder weapon in Gay's hand, how Emma Black described hearing a gunshot *like a hundred light bulbs breaking*, the flash of light, Tucci falling to the floor. She epitomized compassion as she depicted Bliss turning over the still body of her *husband*, the stark red of the blood on his face and her hands – each picture painted in graphic detail. Everyone listened and was engrossed.

Jackie VanDamm became more animated as she spoke. If she didn't truly believe what she was saying, she was the only one in the courtroom to know it.

She spoke for more than the allotted time, its passage not apparent. Finally she paused, standing in the same spot where she began, took a deep breath and turning slightly toward Gay, raised a condemning hand and pointed, "And, to this crime, **she** confessed!"

The posturing and gestures were pure theater, but seemed so natural they could not have been contrived.

Raising her voice, still looking full faced at Gay, still pointing, "**She confessed!** She knows exactly what happened. **She** took her gun – the murder weapon – from the shelf in her closet where it lay waiting to take the life of Robert – she took that gun and placed it in her pocket where she could feel the weight of it as she drove to Robert's home. I wonder if it gave her comfort. She intruded into the victim's home, argued with him, took the gun from her pocket, pointed it at him and pulled the trigger!"

Her voice increasing in volume and intensity, body straining forward, "SHE PULLED THE TRIGGER AND... SHOT HIM..."

She paused to collect herself, and turning back to the jury, continued in a quieter tone, sarcasm building. "Oh, we have heard some theory that she didn't have the strength to pull the trigger. But if you believe any part of her story, believe it when she told you of her concern for her daughter. We hear tales all the time of mothers doing miraculous things when their children are in danger – lifting cars – subduing crazed beasts. Pulling a trigger certainly is not as difficult."

The prosecutor shook a finger at the jury, admonishing them like children. "Let's think about her words when she was talking to the police... *I must have done it, because it was done...* she said."

Looking once more at Gay, Jackie said in a quiet voice that managed to carry to the furthest corner of the room, "She knows she killed him. She knows she wanted him dead."

Turning back to the jury, with an emotional quaver in her voice, she said, "Your task is difficult. We all feel sorry for this old lady. But you swore an oath at the beginning of this trial, you would render a true decision, on the evidence alone, unswayed by sympathy or pity. Yes, she is to be pitied... but... she took a life – intentionally. That cannot be tolerated. A crime such as this must not go unpunished."

Gathering her waning strength, Jackie rose to her full height. "The State expects you to do your duty whether you want to or not. We have done ours. We have proved beyond a reasonable doubt that Gabriella Bellow on August 24, in Mills County, Ohio, did shoot and kill Robert Tucci intentionally. You must return a verdict of GUILTY!"

Jackie paused. She stood before the jury of seven men and five women as though searching for something else to say. When nothing came, she said simply, "Thank you," turned and looking neither right nor left walked back to her seat. The room was quiet.

* * * * *

As Pat Joseph arose to address the jury, he was unable to concentrate on what he intended to say. Instead his thoughts returned to that morning and how he, too, had dressed carefully in combinations selected by Mary, knowing the trial was drawing to a close. She didn't want the jury to see her husband in his usual dishabille – she had some pride even if he didn't. He recalled, while performing his morning tasks, looking from the bathroom window, missing the Canadian Geese, the Mallard Ducks and barn swallows summer provided. Other varieties of birds gathered at the feeders so diligently tended by Mary. The finches, bright yellows and purples, faded into winter's drab colors, and were hanging around because the pickings were good. Cardinals, jays, doves and juncos kept summer's promise alive – thank God. He wondered why?

Contemplating these miracles and recovering from his feeling of lightheadedness, he had slipped into the dark brown suit, polished cordovan shoes, oxford cloth white shirt and soft silk maroon tie with a muted stripe. Mary chose well, the selections lost on the lawyer. He looked into the mirror, arranging the tie to place the knot precisely in the middle of the short, pointed, button-down collars – not that it would stay there. His remaining fringe of hair was brushed back, moustaches trimmed so no loose hairs would dangle in front of his mouth. Everything just so – the jury had to hear his words and think only of Gay – no distractions.

Judge Clarke looking at the clock, noted the time and nodded for Joseph to begin. The lawyer returned from the reverie, tapped his sheaf of notes into a neat pile and placed them carefully on the podium. Standing slowly, having difficulty concentrating, he could feel his knees quiver. His heart began to flutter again. He had to say the right things. Nothing came to mind. As he turned to Gay to place his hand reassuringly on her shoulder, he was surprised to see a slight tremble in his fingers. It disappeared when his touch prompted her to look up and smile. Looking into Gay's eyes, he returned the smile, confidence reappearing.

"Your Honor," the lawyer began, ignoring the podium and walking slowly toward the jury box, stopping a scant foot from the rail – hands placed solidly on it. "Ladies and gentlemen of the jury," looking in the face of each juror in turn. "Do you remember when first we talked how I explained that every time I say those words I get a little catch in my throat, butterflies... I have said them many times – but never without the same reverence I felt the very first time I uttered them.

"Our jury system is unique to all the world – begun by our founding fathers with their concept of freedom. Not the kind of freedom to choose what clothes to wear, what color to paint the bathroom or what hair style to wear ..." touching his bald pate and smiling, "even though it's important we are able to make those choices. They were talking about the kind of freedom born out of opposition to a tyrannical government dictating to us – controlling our lives – without us having any say. Our forefathers found themselves charged with crimes merely because the King's police said so. They broke into homes without leave or warrants – jailing us without benefit of trial.

"We finally said *enough!* The basic freedoms we take for granted today had been denied too long. Once our founders broke from those terrible controls they determined we would never again be subjected to those mischiefs. How did they guarantee that?

"Our Constitution – Our Bill of Rights was born. The genius of those men created the guarantees of which you today are so much a part. This jury is the culmination of the dream that preserves for us – you – me – Gay – the promise we will never be convicted of a crime without a public trial conducted by a jury of our peers. Our neighbors – not politicians – not government bureaucrats or lackeys – will decide our fate. The people that walk the street with me will be my judges."

Joseph had begun speaking with a familiar unsettled feeling – his mind felt clouded – he wasn't sure what he was going to say and feared no words would come – a familiar concern. He felt lightheaded, thinking, *not unusual when one's head is empty*. He tried to recall what he'd prepared, tried to recapture the essence of the week long trial, reaching in several directions at once.

"Before talking about the facts of this case, I would like to express our..." he began, walking towards and thanking the alternate jurors for so attentively listening when they would never be allowed to deliberate on the case or participate in reaching a decision.

Then returning to the center of the jury rail he continued, "As for the rest of you, as I said when the trial started, I used to express my appreciation to juries for doing their duty. I quit doing that a long time ago when it dawned on me how well paid, I reminded you, you are for your services." This time there was no laughter knowing that the elderly lawyer was reminding them how the jury system protected them.

"You need not be told how important is the decision you are about to make," Joseph said, walking to the defendant and placing his hands tenderly on her shoulders. Looking down at the back of her head, he asked, "Did Gay, as the prosecution claims, murder Robert Tucci?"

Without moving he continued, "Judge Clarke has given me one hour to talk to you about Gay's innocence – a mere sixty minutes. Speeches are mere combinations of words, the greatest we've known being the shortest – The Gettysburg Address delivered in less than five minutes – The Lord's Prayer in twenty-two seconds. Even though my heart is as deeply committed to Gay as Lincoln's was to the preservation of our Union and Christ to his Father, I do not possess the oratorical skills to say what needs to be said in such a short time."

Leaving Gay, he strolled back toward the jury, talking. "When I was a child, I used to argue with my brother. My father, a gentle, wise man, would suggest, *"To really argue well, you have to know about what you agree. When you have done that, you will know about what you don't agree. You may be surprised how little you have to argue about.*

"Today we can agree with the prosecutor that Robert Tucci is dead and dead because he was shot in the head with a bullet from this gun..." the lawyer said, picking up the murder weapon from the evidence table and holding it casually in his hand. "Gay had this gun in her hand. She brought it from her home to the place where Tucci was killed. We can agree it was an unwise thing to do – an unhappy memory Gay will carry with her the rest of her life. These being the things about which we agree, we need not speak of them again. It is about the other things the State wants you to believe which we must talk.

"You heard Gay say she is truly sorry Robert is dead. She can't change that, but did Gay murder him? The State says she did. Ms. VanDamm tells you Gay is guilty of murder. This case is called the State of Ohio against Gabriella Bellow – State vs. Gay. It is not called the State of Ohio attempting to seek the truth about Gabriella Bellow. No, the entire State is aligned against Gay.

"The trial began with the judge telling you about the mantle of innocence draped across Gay's shoulders which cannot be removed until the State has proven beyond a reasonable doubt Gay is guilty. We say we believe those words, but I am an old man and a realist to boot. It is simply not true!

"Even though each of you promised you believed in the concept and would judge this case accordingly, you were simply not telling the truth. Be completely honest with yourself now – examine your hearts. Ask yourself if you didn't enter this courtroom believing that, since Mrs. Bellow was indicted for this crime, she must have done something wrong. Didn't you believe her innocence to be in question? Isn't it fair to say that your thoughts went something like, *Why Mrs. VanDamm seems convinced Gay is guilty, and she seems to be a reasonable young lady, maybe there is some truth in what she believes? The police are hard working, dedicated, honest men, and they believe her guilty, there must be some truth to it.*"

The jurors looked a bit sheepish but, not hardened at least. They were willing to hear more.

"No matter how hard you try to be fair, there is in your background that which causes you to want to believe in the police, in your government. That is a terrible burden for Gay – for any person charged with a crime. No matter what our laws tells us, a defendant must **prove** she did not commit a crime ... Thank God, Gay has done just that!"

Joseph was, by this time, standing almost motionless before the jury, finger tips resting lightly on the rail, looking from face to face as he spoke. When he began talking, each of the jurors had no difficulty returning his gaze. Now some were troubled, eyes cast down, not quite able to face him. Good! He wanted them to recognize their bias. If they intended to find Gay guilty, it was not going to be made easy for them.

"Again, thank God Gay has been able to prove her innocence. I tremble at the thought of an innocent person being unable to bring to a jury what Gay has brought to you."

Like the prosecutor, he reviewed the testimony, emphasizing the negative aspects of the State's case. He spoke of the facts the police overlooked or ignored.

"The police try to do a good job, and there is no question they are overworked. They gather evidence and want things to fit neatly into a package. Unfortunately, human frailty suggests when a pattern begins to emerge, quit looking. In this case, the only things they looked at were things that pointed to guilt. If it fit, they put it in the box. If it didn't, they threw it away. For whatever reason, they were unwilling or unable to find another box, or change the shape of the one they had, to seek the truth – Gay's innocence.

""I keep harkening back to my childhood – a sure sign of age I'm told. But I remember when milk was delivered by horse drawn wagons. The horse wore a device that permitted him to see only to the front – never to the side. The contraption was called *blinders,* used so the horse would think about nothing but his job. The police, in this case, wore blinders."

Joseph reminded them of the "unidentified white male in the black T-shirt." He reminded them, "Gay is physically incapable of pulling the trigger. The police, with their unlimited resources, either failed to discover that fact or ignored it. Gay **could not** fire the weapon that killed Tucci. The police should have known that. They could have easily discovered it. She spent more than six hours with them the night Tucci died, wires dangling from her arm, hooked up to a TENS unit, scars on her arm painfully obvious. None of the investigators even asked *Why?*"

He underscored the failure of the State to explain the lack of gunshot residue on Gay's hands, the presence of it on the hands of others – others who had opportunity and motive to kill Tucci. "Atomic Absorption tests were performed on everyone there and **no** gunshot residue was found on Gay's hands. But ... there was on the hands of at least two others – Bliss What's-Her-Name and on Tucci's sister, Emma Black ... At least one of them wanted to see Tucci dead."

His voice grew strident. "The State offers no explanation. It isn't important – let's throw it out! It doesn't fit in the box. What's even worse," a scathing glance at Jackie, "they tried to hide it from you. It wouldn't have been mentioned – you would never have known about it if Gay hadn't brought it to you," he said with sarcasm heavy in his voice. "The lack of gunshot residue on Gay's hands doesn't point to guilt – doesn't fit their theory of the case –

doesn't fit in the pretty box the State wants to build – let's throw it out – forget it – pretend it doesn't exist!"

Indignation raged. He had begun by speaking softly, slowly, with a little hesitation, but as he continued his voice rose and fell in peaks and valleys. Because he was talking faster and faster, he was forced to pause for breath. He looked away from the jurors to hide the rush of emotion to his face.

Gay was sitting as she had throughout the trial, ankles crossed in a ladylike manner, hands folded quietly in her lap. As Joseph glanced at her, her lips curved gently into a half smile, approbation in her eyes and concern for the depth of feeling she caused him. He detected a hint of moisture on her cheek. A single tear escaped her tight control. This moved Joseph and calmed him at the same time. He again walked around the trial table to stand behind her, facing the jury, hands once more on her shoulders. He could feel her tenseness, touched her cheek and gathered the tear on the back of his hand oblivious to the watchers.

Standing with hands resting gently on her shoulders, he said in a more moderate tone, "I apologize for allowing my emotions to show. It probably has something to do with my ethnic origins."

Returning to the far side of the trial table, leaning his backside against it, he spoke from a half sitting position. "Judge Clarke will instruct you in the law about circumstantial and direct evidence. Circumstantial evidence is a fact that may be inferred from direct evidence.

"For example, if, before you go to bed at night, you look out the window and see your driveway clean and dry, but when you wake in the morning it's covered with snow. You didn't see it snow and it isn't snowing now, but it's reasonable to infer it snowed during the night. That is circumstantial evidence.

"The judge will tell you that if the inferences drawn from the evidence are consistent with either guilt or innocence, you cannot convict. You must adopt any reasonable theory that points to innocence. Simple enough. Listen to the instructions and apply them to the evidence you've heard."

He had begun this academic discussion to calm himself. It worked and he did relax, breathing a little easier. He could continue his argument rationally and pointed out how the prosecution's case was built on circumstances the police concluded pointed to guilt. He then suggested several theories where the same circumstances pointed to innocence. The jurors were paying attention.

The lawyer walked slowly from one end of the jury box to the other, taking the time to look into the face of each. Their heads turned in unison to follow him. He wanted them to face Gay so he walked to her side.

"Ladies and gentlemen," he said, his voice barely above a whisper. "I am about to conclude my remarks. I don't want to. As always, I fear I have missed saying something important – something that would make you understand. But my time is drawing to a close. We ask only that you think about everything that has happened in this courtroom. Consider your role. Gabriella Bellow appeared before this court publicly saying *I have not committed murder!*" Gay looked at him gently.

"When she said that, the whole system kicked in to bring her to trial. The State of Ohio sent the prosecutor and her entire staff into this courtroom with all the police and scientific help Ms. VanDamm might need to prove guilt – the unlimited resources of the people of this great state. Spend what you need to prove her guilty."

Striding back to the center of the rail, his voice growing in volume, he said, "Gay was given nothing to prove her innocence except the promise of a fair trial. Her resources are not unlimited like the State's. But that's all right, we are told. After all the State has the greater burden. She doesn't have to do anything. The State must prove her guilt beyond a reasonable doubt."

He was getting worked up again and this time didn't care. "Imagine, if you would, Gay chose to do nothing – relied on your promise to presume her innocent. We would not have heard of her injuries – of the fight between Tucci and his sister – of the lack of gunpowder residue on her hands – of the powder burns deep in Tucci's brain because the murder weapon was tight against his head when fired – not across the room as the prosecutor suggests. Imagine if you would Gay's reliance on the State's help – Imagine if you would the placement of the hangman's noose by those who just don't give a damn.

"But Gay didn't just say *Not Guilty*. She talked to you. She told you what happened, good and bad. She told you how she was persuaded, and believed, she must have killed Tucci. She even told you she went there with a gun. She hid nothing from you. She didn't say someone else killed him – you saw her – no one could have told the truth in a more straightforward manner. "*I don't know what happened,* she said, *'I only know I didn't kill him'.*"

Joseph gathered himself, tensing slightly, positioning himself to the left of the jury box so he could see both the jurors and the gallery. The room was full – every seat taken – police and media standing ready to react. No one moved – all attention drawn to the arena.

Tucci's family sat in the front row – his sister and brother-in-law Emma and Jim Black – others, strangers to the lawyer. Next to Emma sat Bliss. All watching him – the room still. Joseph could feel their eyes on him and knew the jurors were anxiously awaiting a reason – an explanation – something to allow them to reach the same resolution as did the elderly lawyer.

Now was the time for Pat Joseph to provide that explanation. Building to the planned opportunity of providing the jury with a perfect example of different conclusions drawn from the same circumstantial evidence, Joseph strode toward the gallery appearing rejuvenated. He said loudly, voice hoarse, "Gay may not know what happened but the facts speak loud and clear. Gay doesn't know what happened because she wasn't there when Tucci was killed. Who had gunshot residue on her hands? Who had a motive to kill? Who had the opportunity? Who wanted Robert Tucci dead? Who had reason to fear, if Tucci lived, he would cause her to lose her children? Tucci was a threat to someone there that night – not Gay."

As he said the words, he stood directly in front of and fixed his gaze on Emma Black, startled by the sudden vision of a green station wagon parked in front of the courthouse as he entered that afternoon. Shaking the image from his head, he stopped. Emma Black neither looked away nor lowered her eyes, but returned his stare venomously. Her body tensed, half rising in her seat to meet his challenge – she seemed to levitate from her seat – the lawyer braced for an attack. He thought she would be happy to use once more the gun sitting on the evidence table. Her husband put a restraining hand on her. She didn't notice.

Joseph interrupted the contest, turning back to the jury and saying in a voice so low they had to strain to hear, "That is a theory that fits the circumstances. It is consistent with Gay's innocence."

He stood quietly for several seconds, then said, "Gabriella Bellow has a family. A family destroyed by this trial. We ask that you find her *Not Guilty* and send her back to what is left of her life."

He had more to say, but could not. Nothing could pass the constriction in his throat, so he returned slowly to his seat. Gay hadn't changed her position – tears now flowing freely. Tears were burning behind Joseph's eyes as well. He turned back to the jury, somehow muttering "Thank you..." then slumped in his chair. Like a long distance runner, he'd spent the last of his energy crossing the finish line.

It was four seconds short of the allotted time. The stack of notes placed so meticulously on the corner of the podium waited, untouched. For the life of him, he couldn't remember what was in them.

Jackie had a last shot at the jury, but it didn't matter. Joseph hardly heard what she said. When she sat, the judge began his charge. The lawyer didn't hear much of that either, but must have made all the right responses. The next thing he knew, the jury was being lead out by Art with the verdict forms and exhibits.

The Judge left the bench – cameras clicking – people trying to talk to the lawyer. He paid no attention. Gay took his arm and they walked untouched through the crowd – Claude followed. As they walked across the Square in the waning afternoon sun, Joseph noted the snow was still holding off. They would wait in the lawyer's office – pigs watching. Art would call when the jury reached its verdict or had a question. There are always questions.

The jury began its deliberations a little after five, broke for dinner at seven-thirty and resumed deliberations just before nine. At midnight the Judge sent a message that, if they wished, they could discontinue deliberations and resume in the morning.

The jury sent a message back, "We need a few more minutes," offering no explanation. They were close to a decision.

The waiting groups were notified at 12:32 A.M. the jury had reached its verdict. Joseph's heart lurched – the familiar hollow feeling invading his chest. Neither Gay nor he had eaten, even though urged to do so. What the lawyer wanted more than anything was a quiet drink away from the leering pigs. Instead, they all gathered themselves once more for the short walk across the Square. One room, on the second floor of the Courthouse, had a light shining from its window. The snow had begun to fall in earnest.

The jury had asked no questions.

Thirty-Three

Headlines in the morning *Reporter* screamed:

BELLOW FOUND INNOCENT
JURY REJECTS MURDER CLAIM!

Pat Joseph sat at his breakfast table, newspaper propped against the sugar bowl, wearing a beat-up corduroy bathrobe and needing a shave, fringes of hair yet uncombed. Although exhausted, his heart was light with the euphoria that follows victory – the battle always succeeded by a great high or terrible low.

The view from the kitchen window revealed a skin of ice on the pond and drifts of snow across the yard. The chill of the morning did nothing to reduce his warm feeling.

Mary brought coffee and toast, enough for both, to table. "You shouldn't read at breakfast."

Paying no attention, the lawyer began reading aloud, voice slightly hoarse from his week's work:

> Milltown – A jury on Thursday found Gabriella Bellow not guilty of shooting and killing her daughter's common-law husband after a domestic dispute in Mt. City last August.
>
> Bellow, who appeared calm and stoic through most of the trial, mouthed the words "thank you" to the jury after Common Pleas Judge Thomas V. Clarke read the not guilty verdict.
>
> The five women, seven men jury deliberated five hours and fifteen minutes before reaching a decision...
>
> The 60-year-old Bellow held her husband Claude's hand while the verdict was being read. Afterward, she stood up, hugged her attorney, Patrick Joseph, and her husband and said, "Let's get out of here!"

Joseph paused to sip his coffee while Mary broke in, "I told you so."
Puzzled, Joseph asked, "You told me what?"

"You were so worried about the trial and I told you if she was innocent the jury would say so."

"Mary, for God's sake. Do you know how hard we worked to get that *Not guilty* verdict? We busted our asses! There was a hell of a lot of evidence to overcome – including **the confession**. At least that VanDamm bitch won't be able to gloat," Joseph griped, face turning red.

"Don't swear. I told you the jury would see the truth." Life was simple for Mary.

She shooed her watching cats from the breakfast table, not too strenuously, and straightened the tablecloth after them, cleared the dishes and refilled the coffee cups all the while chatting quietly about her anticipations for the day. It was a bit of a treat having her husband home this late on a Friday morning.

While she talked and the lawyer's coffee cooled, his mind wandered back to the early morning hours when the call came that the verdict was in. They hurried across the Square to the lit and waiting courthouse – unusual for that time of night – anxious to hear the jury's pronouncement, but fearing the worst, reluctant to face the verdict. Gay walked between Claude and Joseph, clutching both their arms. They could feel her tremble and knew it was only partly due to the cold. She felt the need to touch someone that cared. As they exited the elevator, the halls were filled with familiar faces of strangers, reporters and cameramen the past week had burned into their memories. They shoved through without comment and came face to face with Tucci's family. Bliss, now publicly aligned with them, glared at her mother with undisguised animosity. Strangely absent were Arliss and her husband. Maybe not so strange. None of Gay's family, except her husband, was there.

The increased pressure on Joseph's arm told him of the depth of Gay's distress at the size of the waiting crowd. He could see her gather herself, feel her resolve stiffen, as she prepared to run the gauntlet. Claude and he stayed at her side – Trent following close behind. As they entered the courtroom, Claude turned toward his usual seat in the first spectator's row. Gay couldn't, or wouldn't, let go of his arm. Joseph suggested he join them at the trial table. No one objected.

Jackie VanDamm, Bradley and Redding were already at their table, complacent smiles in place. The lingering crowd followed, buzzing until Judge Clarke, obviously fatigued, cranky and otherwise disheveled, entered and ordered, "Quiet!" He looked to see all were there and called for the jury.

Standing as they entered the box, Joseph looked intently at the jurors' faces for some clue as to their decision – some eye contact. Nothing. It is said jurors usually refuse to look at a defendant they have convicted. The jurors were exhausted, looking only to find their seats. Once seated, they glanced around the courtroom, eyes un-focused. They seemed surprised at the number of people there. Joseph willed them to look at him – none did.

"Ladies and gentlemen of the jury, have you reached a verdict?" Judge Clarke queried.

The foreman, one of the teachers, clutching the verdict forms in his hand, responded, "We have, Your Honor."

"Very well, please pass the verdict forms to the bailiff."

Art approached the foreman, reached across the rail and gently took the slips. He didn't look at them but carried the folded forms to the Judge. *Would that I could read them,* Joseph thought – heart thumping – finding no blood to pump. He could feel the beads of sweat dripping, and glancing at Gay wondered how she could sit there looking so calm. Her fingernails digging into his palm told him otherwise.

He looked again at the jury waiting for the verdict to be read. Several of the jurors were looking at Gay. Judge Clarke took his time, quietly reading the jury forms as one of the Sheriff's Deputies moved unobtrusively between the defense table and the crowd. Others guarded each door to the courtroom.

Joseph, eyes fixed on the Judge, could tell nothing from his expressionless face. Finally selecting the form signed by all twelve jurors, Judge Clarke intoned, "In the Case of the State of Ohio versus Gabriella Bellow," repeating the case number and the required interminable formalities, "We the jury, do find the defendant Gabriella Bellow *Not Guilty* of murder as she stands charged in the indictment ... " It took a moment for the verdict to register. The courtroom erupted in sound. Joseph stood to thank the jurors – to hug Gay. She had not released his hand but lifted it to her lips holding it there until their eyes met. He could see the flash of a camera. Gay turned to her husband, hugging him close while tears mingled on their faces – impossible to tell the source.

Gay turned to the jury mouthing, "Thank you – thank you," but no words could be heard.

Joseph looked at the prosecutor's table. Jackie and Bradley were exchanging what appeared to be heated words with Mike Redding. He shrugged.

Joseph motioned to Trent. "Trent, grab that photographer and tell him to squelch the picture. Gay was kissing my hand when that camera flashed. She doesn't need to see that in the paper. She's had enough embarrassment ... "

Trent scurried from the room without comment. The older and very tired lawyer, buoyed by the verdict, walked over to the jury box, shaking each hand he could reach, wanting them to understand his and Gay's appreciation. Most of them, men and women alike, had tears in their eyes. One of the ladies said, "All I want to do is go home and cry."

Claude, still holding Gay in his arms, said, "Let's get the hell out of here." Then to the lawyer, "Can we leave?"

Judge Clarke was standing, pounding for order. Finally, he gave up, banged his gavel once and recited the necessary formula to the court reporter for the benefit of the record. "Scott, the court accepts the verdict of the jury and the defendant is released." He dragged off his robes while leaving the bench.

Joseph turned to Claude. "Go home, both of you," feeling sure that, for the first time in six months, they would rest – or if not rest, find some peace.

The memory of those moments passed through the lawyer's mind as he waited for his coffee to reach drinking temperature, still holding the newspaper. He read the rest of the article. It recapped the happenings of the early morning hours and the trial, but at least Trent had been able to stop the printing of the picture. The media had enough others from which to choose, using one of Gay and Claude containing expressions of unbelievable joy. It seemed appropriate for this time of year. Joseph was glad.

The article quoted interviews with conflicting opinions. Tucci's family was "mad as hell!" Mike Redding said, "We had the right person, the jury just didn't see it." Poor loser – not unexpected. The prosecutor refused comment except, "The defendant got a fair trial."

Joseph sighed deeply, leaned back in his chair watching one of the cats scratching at the glass trying to get at the birds feeding outside the window. Dumb cat. He wondered if the birds were amused at its frustration.

He was nicely tired with the exhaustion that follows a hard-fought trial. The older one gets, the more meaning the phrase "bone tired." Probably getting too old for this work – felt like he could sleep for a week – at least he would take the day off and have a long weekend to relax.

Looking at the paper he thought, *What's said and written has little meaning now. We accomplished what we set out to do. Should have stopped back at the office this morning after the verdict was read. Bet this changed the expressions on those damn pigs.*

He refolded the paper so Mary could read it later. She liked to look at the ads. As he did, he noticed another headline on the lower half of the front page:

MILLTOWN MAN ARRESTED FOR MULTIPLE STABBING DEATH OF LOCAL WOMAN – DRUGS SUSPECTED!

He read the article that followed, stood and stretched. "Mary, I think maybe I'll stop by the office to check the mail – probably grab lunch at the Roundtable but I'll be home early. We can have dinner at the mall. Maybe you can get some shopping done, okay?" he said, adding to himself, *Should see what those pigs are up to, anyway.*

Mary's response, "Humph."

Epilogue

"Mr. Joseph, can I come in for a minute?" Trent tapped on the doorframe and walked in without waiting for permission. The lawyer was at his desk, feet up, contemplating the ever-changing smiles of his pigs – flipping through a scrapbook given him by his twelve-year-old granddaughter. She had read, clipped and pasted all of the newspaper articles from the Bellow's case now six months past, as only young girls can. The daughter of his eldest daughter – the only one of his children not to follow in his line of work – she was probably the most sensible. Unlucky for her, her daughter developed a taste for law and followed Papa's cases whenever she could. Those capturing her interest were memorialized in scrapbook form.

"Sure, come on in. What do you want?"

"Well," Trent said, a little worried, "we haven't gotten all our money from Mr. Bellows. It's been six months and I thought I'd best say something. Do you remember the case I'm talking about?"

"Of course I remember. Do you think I'm senile? What's wrong? I thought we were secured – you got a note and mortgage on their house, or something, to guarantee payment, didn't you?"

"We did, but they still owe us around fourteen thousand. It's not quite as bad as it sounds because it's office time. All the expenses, experts and investigators have been paid, but we've only received about half our fee."

Joseph started to fume but Trent went on, "We did have the debt secured... but Mr. Bellow had some reverses. He didn't pay attention to his business from the time Tucci was killed until after the trial. He had been having problems, but it really went bad and last month they were forced into bankruptcy. Their home was exempt, so I was going to suggest foreclosure. But when I heard about their most recent problem, I sort of backed off..."

"You what?" Joseph snapped — then Trent's comment struck him, "What most recent problem?" he asked instead.

"Bliss is dead... "

* * * * *

It was mid-April, the wettest spring on record in Northern Ohio. The rain, along with the warm temperatures, had encouraged the grass to green, trees to bud and bulbs to explode in a colorful array of hyacinth, crocus and tulips. The days were cloudless, sunny and warm, creating all of the promises that spring brings.

Bliss, by whatever name, from the age of fifteen was incapable of existing without a man. Even though she grieved for Tucci, in her way, it wasn't long after his death she secured an arrangement with a man some ten years her junior. They began living together even before Gay's trial.

Bliss and her new friend, Ted, wintered in a cheap two-family house on the near west side of Cleveland subsisting on general relief and whatever they could pick up. Neither worked. By April they were months behind in rent. With eviction threatened, they moved.

Ted had many friends. He was fun, his popularity enhanced by a ready source of recreational drugs. One such friend lived in a western suburb of Cleveland – a neat little home owned by his grandparents. Bliss and Ted invited themselves to *visit until they could find a place of their own.*

Bliss was excited about living in the suburbs. The three-bedroom ranch house sat on a corner lot surrounded by lawn. They moved in. Bliss had to tell someone the good news, and so called Emma Black. They hadn't visited for a while.

"Hi Emma? It's Bliss."

"Bliss? My God, how are you? I haven't talked to you since... the trial." The line was silent for several seconds before Emma continued, her voice growing a little colder, "Where are you? Where you calling from?"

Bliss told of her good fortune and all about the house they "just today' moved to. They talked for over an hour – it didn't matter it was a long distance call – it wasn't Bliss' phone. When they finally hung up, Bliss was looking forward to seeing Emma again.

The next morning, Sunday, Bliss woke up next to Ted in the new bedroom they shared. It was at the rear of the house and she could see the side street from the bedroom window. Children were already up and out, riding bikes. She marveled at that – it was hardly eight o'clock. She looked at Ted still sleeping. Basking in the afterglow of their first night of lovemaking in a real bed since leaving West 43rd St., she thought, *He is so beautiful and he loves me. I'll fix him breakfast before he wakes up.*

She puttered around in the kitchen brewing coffee, fixing bacon and eggs, making toast – enough for Ted and their hosts. They were late sleepers too. She hummed as she worked, with a giggle at her memories of the night just past and the shared passions. *What do those books say?* she mused, thinking about the romance novels to which she was addicted. *His erect throbbing member showed the depths of his desire for her. Her juices flowed as they came together in a pulsating embrace, he buried in her.* A line she had memorized. *Oh... just thinking about it gives me a chill and makes me hot all over!* She thought, shivering with the recollection.

The table set, she walked into the bedroom. "Ted... Ted... breakfast is ready." She kissed him lightly. "Get up. Come on and eat. I made enough for Matt and Terri too."

Ted grumbled about being awakened so early, but they hadn't been together long enough for him to get really irritated, and the night's lovemaking had left him in a pleasant mood. He knocked on their hosts' door. "Matt – Terri – get up – Bliss made breakfast for us."

Satisfied with the sounds of movement, he went to the kitchen and sat at the breakfast table, hair mussed, dressed in jeans and a white T-shirt he'd pulled over his nakedness.

Bliss poured a cup of coffee and stood at the sink, smoking a cigarette while Ted drank. As soon as the others came to table, Bliss began serving. She only set three places – she never ate breakfast – coffee and cigarettes satisfied her morning needs.

Matt complained, with a smile, "Hope you don't expect us to get up this early every morning. Sundays are for sleeping." They groused in good humor, Terri adding, "It's really nice having help around the house."

After breakfast, they talked, visited and smoked. When the stores were open, Ted left to get some beer, snacks and a copy of the Sunday *Plain Dealer*. The day was good for sitting around, watching television and reading the funnies. Ted and Matt wanted to watch an afternoon Indians ball game on television. Ah – peace and tranquility.

While the game was on, Terri, not used to getting up so early, went in to take a nap. Bliss didn't like baseball much, so went to her room to maybe call Emma, or lay down for a while herself. Ted, engrossed in the game, gave her a kiss and a distracted pat on the ass, "See you later, Hon."

The Indians were doing poorly and by the ninth inning were behind a couple runs. Terri came out of her bedroom yawning. "I'm hungry. You guys want me to make some sandwiches?"

"Sure... " they said in unison, laughing.

Heading to the kitchen, Terri heard a popping sound, looked around and didn't see anything out of order, so called to Matt. "Hey, Matt. Did y' hear that?"

"What?" Matt asked, still looking at the TV screen.

"That noise. It sounded like a balloon busting or something."

Ted said, "I heard it. I thought you dropped something. Maybe it's outside." He started to walk into the bedroom he shared with Bliss to wake her for a late lunch.

As he opened the door he could feel the late afternoon spring breeze blowing through the open window next to the bed. *Bliss must have opened it for a little air,* he thought. She was sleeping, sprawled across the bed, her lank hair stirring slightly in the breeze.

"Bliss, did you hear that noise?" Ted began, snapping on the light and walking toward the bed. No answer. He put his hand on her shoulder to jiggle it. *It's my turn to wake her up,* passing through his mind.

"Come on, wake up! Oh, my God!" he shouted as Bliss's head lolled back on the pillow, eyes wide and staring. "Matt! – Matt! – Get help! Something's wrong with Bliss!"

Matt came running, in almost stumbling over an object just inside the bedroom door. He looked down and saw a small gun he had never seen before. He didn't touch it, running to call 911.

Bliss lay on her back, arms askew, wearing a dark brown robe. When Ted touched her shoulder, the bathrobe fell open revealing her only clothing, a very feminine lace bra and, incongruously enough, practical cotton briefs, a hole smaller than a dime just above her navel. From the wound, a narrow trail of blood ran across the mound of her belly, pooling between her slightly spread legs. The bed wasn't mussed.

Ted stood helplessly at the foot of the bed until he heard the sound of sirens screaming, the squeal of brakes, a horn blowing and a vehicle screeching to a stop.

The ambulance, careening down the residential street, lights and siren working, neared the intersection its driver was searching for. As it slowed to make the turn, the driver yelled, "Jesus Christ! That crazy broad pulled right in front of us! Damn near hit us! She's got to be the dumbest..."

"Yeah," responded his assistant. "Look what she's driving. It's got to be the ugliest station wagon ever built. Never saw one painted that color green. She ain't bad looking though."

"Good looking or not, I damn near creamed her! Here's the address we want!"

Slamming to a stop, both medics rushed into the house carrying their equipment, pushing past Ted still standing at the foot of the bed staring at Bliss. After a quick examination of the body, the EMT said, "Get on the phone! She's been shot. We need the police."

The assistant pushed Ted from the room, asking him to make the call. "We'll see if we can do anything for her."

They were still working when the police arrived – the house suddenly full of people. The police asked some questions, but were soon satisfied. They concluded there was no evidence of wrongdoing by anyone in the household and learned of no motive for murder. Bliss's brief troubled life was probably too much for her. Their report concluded:

Bliss Tucci, 38-year-old white female, died of a single gunshot wound to the abdomen delivered by a .25 caliber automatic pistol. She was found by her friend lying on a bed in the bedroom of their home. The covers were pulled back and there were no signs of a struggle. No powder burns at the entry wound.

The weapon found was a Raven Model MP 25, automatic, chrome plated with ivory handles, no clip in the gun. One .25 caliber empty shell casing 100, was found by the entrance door to the bedroom, standing on end. These items were placed in an evidence bag.

A further check of the room revealed the following: A purse was found under the bed. In the purse was another purse, black clutch type. In the second purse were six more .25 caliber rounds and numerous prescriptions. These items were taken into evidence.

This officer, with assistance of a second officer on the scene, lifted the mattress from the bed and discovered an ammo clip between the mattress and the box spring on the east side of the bed, near the middle. The ammo. clip was to a .25 caliber gun and had four .25 caliber rounds in it, also taken as evidence.

A check along the east side of the bed revealed a plastic bag containing liquid fluid, possibly vomit from the victim. Under the east side of the bed, a bottle of liquor, less than half full, was also found. This item was taken into evidence.

Resuscitation efforts by the EMT's produced no response. Even though satisfied she was dead, they continued life support while loading her in the ambulance. Siren wailing, they sped from the drive, racing toward the nearest hospital.

The death certificate said Bliss Tucci was DOA – Dead on Arrival at Hospital. The police report proclaimed:

Probable suicide – cardiac arrest following self-inflicted gunshot wound to abdomen.

Finis